Praise for Lucy Dillon's

*About the author*

Lucy Dillon was born in Cumbria. She now divides her time between London and the Wye Valley, where she enjoys walking in the Malvern Hills with her Basset hounds, Violet and Bonham.

LUCY DILLON

# lost dogs and lonely hearts

HODDER

First published in Great Britain in 2009 by Hodder & Stoughton
An Hachette UK company

First published in paperback in 2009

14

Copyright © Lucy Dillon 2009

The right of Lucy Dillon to be identified as the Author of the Work has been asserted
by her in accordance with the Copyright, Designs and Patents Act 1988.

All characters in this publication are ficticious and any resemblance
to real persons, living or dead is purely coincidental.

A CIP catalogue record for this title is available from the British Library

B-format paperback ISBN 978 0 340 91920 0

Typeset in Plantin Light by Hewer Text UK Ltd, Edinburgh
Printed and bound by CPI Group (UK) Ltd, Croydon, CR0 4YY

Hodder & Stoughton policy is to use papers that are natural, renewable
and recyclable products and made from wood grown in sustainable forests.
The logging and manufacturing processes are expected to conform
to the environmental regulations of the country of origin.

Hodder & Stoughton Ltd
338 Euston Road
London NW1 3BH

www.hodder.co.uk

For the volunteers who work so hard to make second chances happen for lost and lonely dogs everywhere

# I

When February started, Rachel Fielding had a middling-to-glamorous career doing PR for internet companies, a boyfriend who regularly bought her flowers and dressed better than she did, a cleaner, and a skin-age three years younger than her actual age, which was thirty-nine.

By the second week, however, she had, in one simple manoeuvre, managed to lose the love of her life, her Chiswick flat and her job. Rachel also discovered, that same morning, her first grey streak, which stood out a mile in her thick dark hair, and got a text from her sister Amelia, accusing her of forgetting her niece's fifth birthday 'because not having children doesn't mean you can be so bloody selfish'.

The sacking, or the dumping, or the grey hair was depressing enough on its own. But all three together was more punishment than even someone skilled in spinning bad news could take. Rachel longed – *yearned* – to be lying face down in a puddle of Bailey's ice cream, listening to Joy Division, but instead she was sitting on a plastic chair in a solicitor's office in Longhampton, a country town where the arrival of Waitrose was still something of a talking point, listening to a lecture on inheritance tax from a middle-aged man who kept referring to her as 'Ms Fielding', and to himself as 'myself'.

Rachel had just inherited what Gerald Flint was 'pleased to call a substantial holding', but all she could really focus on right now was the fact that she, like her late Auntie Dot before her, was headed for a dwindling twilight of dog hair and ready meals for one. Every time she tried to concentrate on her new capacity as executor and pretty much sole beneficiary of Dot's estate, comprising family house, kennels, dogs, more dogs, and some dogs, Oliver's dark-eyed wickedness slid across her mind like a masochistic screensaver: his face caught in the moment she confronted him with the receipts – shock, then fear, then, horribly, a flicker of something she now realised was smugness.

'Have we lost you there, Ms Fielding?'

Rachel shuddered hard, and snapped her attention back to the meeting. *Get a grip*, she told herself. *He's gone. You're here. This is important.*

'I'm with you, Mr Flint,' she said and tapped her pen against her notebook. 'Well, actually, no. Can you just run through what exactly I'm supposed to do, as executor?'

Gerald was sitting at his desk underneath a large photo-to-canvas portrait of his four owlish grandchildren. On his right was a blonde woman in her twenties, who was apparently the manager of Dot's kennels. Next to her was a miserable black and white Border collie.

Rachel couldn't remember what the dog was doing there. But then Dot had been legendary in the family for her bonkers attitude to dogs ('bonkers' being Rachel's mother's terse diagnosis; Rachel herself thought it wasn't so weird, compared with Val's own passion for hygienic storage). It was entirely possible that the dog was actually a co-executor.

Gerald mistook her Oliver-induced vacancy for bereavement distress. 'It's a lot to take in but we're here to handle most of it for yourself. I'll recap, shall I?'

Rachel turned to a fresh page in her notebook. It fell open at the angry to-do list she'd made the previous day – *pack stuff, phone storage company, change locks, book holiday* – and she hastily turned to a new page.

As Gerald spoke, she jotted down notes. Before she could inherit Dot's house, and the boarding kennels, and the rescue centre that was part of it, she'd have to arrange a valuation for probate, then the solicitors would send off the various forms, the Revenue would calculate the inheritance tax to pay, nothing would be hers until some of that was paid, blah blah blah – but, even as her pen moved dutifully across the page, Rachel's entire chest ached from intensive regret.

Ten years of her life, gone just like that. The best, ripest, decade of her life. She was never, ever going to touch Oliver's black hair again, pushed back off his forehead in a style that shouldn't work, but somehow did. The smell of him after work, that musty, masculine odour around his white shirt as he threw his jacket with the gold lining over her chair . . .

'. . . and Gem, of course?' added the blonde girl, breaking Rachel's train of thought. She was Australian, so it sounded more like a question than a statement. The huge sunny grin she was directing at Rachel suggested she thought it was the best bequest of the lot.

Rachel squinted at the gold necklace hanging above her t-shirt. Megan.

'Sorry, I don't remember anything about a dog in the will,' she said, glancing over at Gerald for confirmation. 'Was it mentioned? Sorry, the last week or so's been a bit of a nightmare for me . . .'

'Dot left me instructions to tell you about Gem once you got here.' Megan pointed at the dog who'd been sitting at her feet since the meeting started, obedient but somehow morose, his tail and ears drooping sadly.

It looks more grief-stricken than me, thought Rachel, with a flash of guilt.

'Gem's seven, and he's a Border collie. Dot wanted you to have him. She was very specific about that, wasn't she, Gem? Only a special new home for you.' She gave the dog's feathery black ears an affectionate caress and it leaned into her side.

'But I'm not a dog person,' Rachel protested, and as she spoke the dog looked up and she recoiled at the spooky ice-blue eyes that searched her face as if it was trying to recognise her. Were dogs meant to have eyes like that, she wondered? It seemed to be looking into her head and seeing a woman who couldn't even be trusted with house plants.

'Dot wouldn't have left you Gem if she didn't think you were the right person for him. She had this knack for matching up people with the right dog,' Megan explained, very seriously. 'She could tell, soon as they walked into the room. Wouldn't let one of her rescues go home with the wrong person, not even if they begged and begged.'

Rachel glanced at the solicitor, expecting a faint shake of the head at this sub-Disney madness, but Gerald only smiled indulgently. 'She certainly matched me up with two little smashers. The dog matchmaker, we used to call her.'

Oh God, thought Rachel. This *must* be a dream.

'Does it run in the family?' Megan enquired. 'Dog whispering?'

'Not as far as I know,' said Rachel politely, then changed her mind. 'Actually, no. No, it definitely doesn't. We weren't even allowed goldfish, growing up. I don't know where Dot's dog thing came from.'

But then Dot wasn't a typical Mossop in all sorts of ways. She hadn't got married at twenty-four, never had kids, and refused to turn up with clockwork regularity to the fruit-cake-and-sherry gatherings thrown by Rachel's mother, Valerie. Though neither did Rachel. It was a good job Val had made Dot Rachel's godmother before her mysterious midlife relocation to Longhampton; as it was, Rachel was starting to get the impression Val thought Dot had passed on spinsterdom to her niece like some kind of hereditary affliction.

'Pardon me for saying but you're very alike, you and Dorothy,' said Gerald, in a tone that made it clear he meant it as a compliment. 'In looks, I mean. Something about the . . .'

Rachel knew what he was going to say; it was what everyone said. That they both looked like eccentric Edwardian suffragette-gardeners. Or pre-Raphaelite avenging angels, with their long noses and dark, round eyes, so unlike Val and her other daughter Amelia's English rose blondeness. Rachel had longed to be pretty like Amelia for years; it was only Oliver who'd convinced her that 'striking' would see her through to her eighties.

'The nose?' she suggested.

'. . . something about the nose,' Gerald finished, more nervously than he'd begun. Rachel knew her resting expression was fiercer than she meant it to be. He tried to rescue the situation. 'Dorothy was a fine figure of a woman, striding around the common with her dogs. We always wondered if she'd been in the secret service or some other . . .' He floundered. 'Something about her confidence, perhaps.'

'I know,' said Rachel, unhappily.

Oliver had always loved Rachel's confidence too. Her breezy, polished manner in client meetings, that she'd almost convinced herself was natural and not a side-effect of a liver-clenching coffee habit or her burning need to impress him.

'Well, we have *some* things in common,' Rachel conceded, because her heart had given another lurch. 'But not dogs, sorry. I'm serious, Megan,' she added, spotting an indulgent smile from the other side of the desk. 'I don't have anywhere to put a dog. I travel a lot, I work full time.' She raised her hands.

OK, so she wasn't working full time or living in a flat in Chiswick right now, but she definitely didn't want a Border collie. She worked in PR, not on *Blue Peter*.

'Ah, Gem's not a *dog*. Gem's like, an old pal? Aren't you? And if Dot thought you and Gem were meant to be together, then you're definitely a match made in heaven.' Megan's cheerful smile faltered, and a look of horror flashed across her open face. 'Oh, jeez, I'm sorry, that was really tactless of me.'

'Let me give you the keys to the door, as it were,' said Gerald, seizing the chance to divert the conversation by reaching into his drawer for the keys. 'I'm sure you're keen to get over to Four Oaks and look around,' he added, with a nod towards Megan. 'Megan is more than capable of bringing you up to speed with the kennel operations.'

Suddenly the mental exertions of the past week caught up with Rachel, crashing over her weary head as they did every day, at three o'clock sharp. She felt overwhelmed with a need to be alone with a bottle of wine, under a duvet, and in a pair of pyjamas, instead of this Marc Jacobs skirt that was digging into her waist because it had been on sale and she was too in love with the label to size up, and professional single women in their thirties needed to be well-dressed, because they didn't have the excuse of puking kids to relax their wardrobes.

Gerald grimaced with perfectly judged sympathy as he handed her a large bunch of keys, with neat labels attached in Dot's meticulous print.

'And there's a letter, which Dorothy left to be handed to the executor with the keys, but I'll leave that for yourself to go through in private.' He passed her a thin envelope, which she tucked into the back of her notebook. 'As I say, we can arrange for the estate agents to pop round and do the valuations, send off the forms and so forth. If you could have a look through the property for any significant valuables – or we could just approach a house clearance firm to make the assessment?'

'No, I'll do that. But thank you.' Rachel looked between the two of them, wondering what she was supposed to say now. Val, for all her faults, was excellent at this sort of thing. She always knew the right tone of murmur to make. Funerals, weddings, will readings – her mother bustled into action at the drop of an elderly relative. She'd organised the whole funeral from a different county, and had Dot interred next to their parents, back home in Lancashire. It was, apparently, typical of Dot that she'd insisted that the will be handled in Longhampton, by the executor – Rachel.

Val was the only person Rachel knew who could be hurt that she *hadn't* been landed with a mess of administration.

The dog was gazing at her with its sad, icy eyes. It was sitting perfectly still, but at the same time it looked so forlorn that Rachel got the impression that, like her it would rather be alone in a basket with a bone, or whatever the dog equivalent of a bottle of wine was, instead of going through this charade.

Megan squirmed in her seat. 'Can I ask a favour, um . . . Ms Fielding?'

'Rachel, please. And sure,' said Rachel, more than ready to give her Gem to remember Dot by. But unfortunately, that wasn't what Megan wanted.

'Can I get a lift back to Four Oaks? If you're heading up there?'

'Of course. I'm not sure I know the way anyway,' said Rachel. She added a smile, because there was something about Megan that made it hard not to smile. Her face was eager and good-natured, still tanned despite the February gloom already darkening the sky outside. Megan clearly *was* a dog person.

Megan kept up a cheerful monologue out of the offices and into the car park and, when she saw Rachel's car, it bubbled right over into amazement.

'Oh, wow, this is yours?' she gasped, as Rachel bleeped the central locking on her black Range Rover. 'This is just perfect for Gem! Gem, just look at the gorgeous truck your new mum's got!'

Rachel winced again at the 'new mum' bit. 'He's a dog and I'm not his mother, OK?'

She rubbed a hand over her face and squeezed her sore eyes shut. She didn't add that now she'd walked out of her job, the Range Rover would probably be going back to London just as soon as the finance company she leased it from got wind of her newly unemployed status.

You'll just have to get another job, she reminded herself. Plenty of them about, with your CV. Even in a recession, people need positive PR. *Especially* in a recession.

Megan and Gem were looking at her expectantly, and Rachel wasn't sure who seemed more eager to please, Megan or Gem. She felt equally bad about letting them both down.

'Sorry. Look, I don't know where he should go. Will he be safe in the boot?'

'He'll be fine in a boot this size, lucky guy,' said Megan, opening the tail gate. 'Ooh, you're travelling light,' she observed, seeing Rachel's two small bags and her box of random junk that she'd thrown together when she'd left the flat. That was another depressing thing: how little she really had to show for ten years. 'How long are you staying?'

'I don't know.' Rachel raked her hands through her hair, remembered the white streaks, and sighed. 'I can honestly say I don't have any plans right now.'

'See how it goes, eh? Best way.' Megan patted the edge of the car. 'Up you get, Gem boy!'

Gem leaped obediently into Rachel's boot and curled up between her two leather Mulberry overnight bags. Already, Rachel could see long dog hairs settling on the black upholstery, but she was too tired to think about that now. Instead, she shut the boot and opened the driver's door.

'I appreciate the lift – the buses here are pretty unreliable, but that's the countryside for you, eh? I'll give you directions if you take the road out of Longhampton towards Hartley,' Megan was saying, climbing into the passenger seat. She had to jump a bit, being almost a foot shorter than Rachel. Megan wore practical boots over her old jeans and as she settled herself in, Rachel could smell dogs and Body Shop White Musk. 'It's not too far, out of the main town, but then you know that, don't you?' She paused, and listened. 'Is that your phone?'

Rachel knew it was her phone. The ringtone was 'Ride of the Valkyries' which let her know it was her mother on the other end. It was tempting to ignore it, and pretend she was driving, but Val knew she'd been to see the solicitor today and she would only keep calling. And calling. And calling. Better to get it over with.

'Yes,' she said, reaching into her bag, 'it is. Sorry, I'll have to pick this up. I'll just be a moment.' She slid out of the car, and put her mobile to her ear. 'Hello, Mum?'

'Are you out of the solicitors'? Was there a mistake in the will?' Val didn't mince her words. 'Your father and I have been discussing it, and he thought there might have been a letter from Dot, explaining how you were meant to divide everything up. When you got to the solicitors', I mean. He thought it might have been cheaper, for her to leave everything to you, and then have you share it with your sister, instead of involving someone official.'

Rachel breathed through her nose. This conversation had started four days ago. Val always picked up exactly where she'd left off last time. 'Mum, there is a letter but I haven't opened it yet. And can you stop making out that it's my fault? It's not like I expected this, you know. I'm sure I can find some things Amelia would like. I don't think Dot meant it as a *criticism*.'

'Don't get me wrong, I'm not blaming Dot,' her mother insisted, struggling to be fair. Val was always fair, and gave everyone the benefit of the doubt, even when she didn't actually believe them. Particularly when she didn't believe them. 'That's just the way Dot was – she was used to living on her own, with no ties or anyone else to bother about – but it's not just Amelia. Grace and Jack ought to have some keepsake from their great-aunt.'

Rachel resisted the temptation to point out that looking after a pack of assorted dogs didn't exactly leave you footloose and fancy-free. It riled her, this family assumption that not having children meant you led a life of nightclubs and riotous self-indulgence. 'Would they like a dog?' she suggested, only half-joking. 'Plenty left.'

She could hear the drawn-in breath of outrage, two hundred miles away. 'What? No! That would be totally irresponsible! What about allergies? You'd have to talk to Amelia first, Rachel. No, there'll be a nice silver brush set that would be appropriate for Grace, used to be our mother's, and as for Jack, I seem to remember Dot did a bit of fishing, I dare say there's an expensive rod somewhere.' There was a pause. 'And don't say I told you this, Rachel, but Amelia could do with a hand with nursery fees right now. It costs a fortune, childcare. I'm sure Dot left a nest egg that you could . . .'

'Mum, stop,' interrupted Rachel. 'I can put your mind at rest on that front. There's no money.'

'What?' Val sounded disbelieving.

'There's no money. There's the house, and the kennels business, but once the staff have been paid, and the solicitor, there'll be no cash at all.'

'But . . . how? She had half the money from Dad's house and no one to spend it on but herself!'

Rachel could hear the hurt bubbling up through the gaps between the words. It wasn't about the money, she knew that. Val was generous to a fault; in her own way, as much of a rescuer as Dot, but of people, not animals. She was always helping, resolutely putting other people first, carting old folk to the hospital in her red Fiesta, or doing laundry for bewildered widowed neighbours.

'She must have spent a lot of it on the dogs, Mum,' Rachel said, walking around her car. 'But that was her choice.' .

Val went silent on the other end of the phone, and Rachel knew she was counting up to ten, rather than say whatever she was thinking. She heard someone in the background, shouting something.

'What's that, Ken? Oh, your father says can you have a look for Dorothy's . . . Dorothy's what? Speak up! Dorothy's Acker Bilk albums.'

Rachel spun on her heel, and looked over to where Megan was still waiting in the car. 'This isn't a car boot sale,' she protested. 'Look, when probate's granted you can come and see what you want for yourself. How about that?'

'We wouldn't like to impose, and anyway, I've got commitments here, my hospice ladies relying on me and your dad – I can't just drop everything,' huffed Val.

*But I can*, Rachel added in her head.

'So. What are your plans?' Val went on. 'Are you going to sell it? A big house like that takes a lot of upkeep when it's just you. I always said to your father, it's a family house, far too big for Dot there on her own.'

Rachel stared at the other cars in the solicitors' car park, noting a silver Jaguar like Oliver's, and felt the band around her head tighten.

'Rachel? Are you still there?'

'Yes, Mum,' she said, squeezing her nose and closing her eyes tight.

'Are you staying there now? I tried you at the flat last night but there was no answer. You don't tell me anything any more,' Val continued, more gently. 'Some girls like to share with their mothers. Amelia's always dropping in with the kiddies, but I never even know if you're in the country or not.'

'I'm run off my feet with work, Mum,' said Rachel, determined to finish the conversation before it got back into the old, unproductive rut. She'd have to tell her about resigning at some point; at least she didn't have to tell her about splitting with Oliver.

Rachel had weighed it up some years back, and decided that it was easier to pretend to be single and deal with Val's nagging about 'finding a man to settle down with' than it would be to explain her complicated relationship with a man as unsuitable as Oliver Wrigley. Ironically, the only one of her family who knew anything at all about Oliver had been Dot, and even then Rachel had only told her the bare minimum.

'Work isn't everything in life,' Val reminded her, unhelpfully, Rachel thought, coming from a woman who'd been a full-time housewife since 1969, thanks to her dad's devotion to dentistry. 'You're not getting any younger.'

'Is anyone?' Rachel snapped and turned back to the car.

As she spun round, she came face to face with a pair of bright eyes. Gem was staring at her through the back window, and Rachel staggered backwards in surprise.

He sat like a sentry with one paw on her box of stuff, and tilted his head, as if he could hear the other side of the phone conversation. One black ear flopped down, while the other stayed pricked up, revealing tender pink skin, flecked with white hairs. He looked proud to be guarding her worldly goods, eager to be useful, unaware that his new owner had no room for him in her messy life.

An irrational surge of pity swelled in Rachel's chest and, to her surprise, she felt tears prickle along her lashes.

Maybe this was an early menopausal symptom, she thought glumly. Getting emotional about animals. Maybe this was what happened, your body telling you the final whistle was about to go and that you should stock up on cats.

'Rachel! Say something!' Val was still on the line, hoping for an Amelia-style outpouring.

'Mum, I'll call you later,' she said.

'There are things we need to talk about,' said Val.

'And don't forget the Acker Bilk albums!' shouted a muffled voice.

'And don't forget . . .' Val began to repeat.

'I know,' said Rachel. 'I heard him the first time.'

She hung up, and behind the glass Gem began to pant, his mouth drawn back into a smile, his pink tongue sticking out.

'Don't get too comfortable,' Rachel warned him.

# 2

As she shoved the front door open with her shoulder, it was fairly obvious to Rachel that the formal entrance wasn't the one Dot had used on a daily basis.

The wood had warped with disuse, and inside the dark entrance hall there were no signs of daily life – no pizza leaflets, or junk mail. Instead, there was a mahogany plant stand with a dusty aspidistra, a brass-faced grandfather clock and a series of prints on the crimson wallpaper featuring chocolate-eyed spaniels with limp game birds trailing from their soft mouths.

Rachel smelled beeswax polish, and lavender, but not dogs, strangely enough. Val always muttered about how Dot's house probably 'smelled like the inside of a wet kennel', but Rachel's sensitive nose couldn't detect anything too bad. The high ceilings dissipated any doggy aroma.

Nothing had changed since she'd last been here, on New Year's Eve seven years ago. It had been just after the first serious row she and Oliver had, in the days when she was still trying to persuade him to share the holidays with her, instead of leaving her to face the family festivities apparently all alone. Sick of Val's elephantine hints about settling down and fed up of Oliver's evasiveness, Rachel had booked herself and Oliver onto a skiing trip, which he'd cancelled at the last minute, the weasel, so rather than be at home, at the mercy of people's sympathy, Rachel had come over all Mother Teresa and called Dot, who had unexpectedly invited her to drop by.

Rachel did wonder almost immediately what on earth she was doing, driving miles on her own out to Worcestershire, when she could have been flirting in a Soho members' club, but the wilful desire to be unfindable spurred her on. Once in Longhampton, though, it had been different. Dot had ushered her into the warm kitchen, where she was listening to a Radio Four play, and she'd cooked a fish pie, as Rachel slowly found herself getting absorbed in the play too. They'd eaten in companionable silence, bar the snuffling of about seven assorted rescue puppies in a box by the Aga.

Midnight arrived and went by the log fire, toasted in with a vintage bottle of Krug. Dot didn't ask Rachel why she was on her own on a night when most women of her age were engaged in determined partying, just whether she was happy. The simple question had broken through Rachel's fake nonchalance, and she'd let more slip to Dot than she had to her own mother. Not everything though; just that Oliver was hard to pin down, and she was too proud to stay at home to be pinned herself.

'Men like to make themselves complicated,' Dot had told her, with something in her wry expression that said she knew what she was talking about. 'Don't let them complicate you. That's the thing about dogs – their affection is very straightforward. A walk, some food a bed . . .' She paused, and raised an eyebrow. 'Actually . . .'

Dot had looked decades younger in that instant and Rachel felt like a naive kid, not a jaded urbanite. But she couldn't ask. Val had told them never to ask Auntie Dot any questions about her strange lack of husband. Habits died hard.

Then she'd offered Rachel a whisky, and passed her some crystallised fruits from Fortnum & Mason, and they'd sunk back into their thoughts. Rachel wondered where Dot got Fortnum's crystallised fruits and Krug from. They didn't fit in with the image Val liked to paint of Dot at Christmas, sharing a bowl of Winalot with some holly in it.

Now she paused at the front door, as the memory of that night slid through her mind. She'd left first thing on New Year's Day, to prepare for a client meeting, and she and Dot never mentioned their shared New Year again. Their relationship of wry birthday and Christmas cards continued as before. From that New Year on, Rachel volunteered at a local homeless shelter, to teach Oliver a lesson. Not that he cared.

Rachel pushed her way into the hall. Dot clearly hadn't done any decorating since moving in some time in the early seventies, but the dignified shabbiness suited the country house. With a wash of pale paint and some vases of flowers, it would be a different place. It would be hers, to settle down in. Redecorate as she wanted. It didn't make Rachel as excited as it should have done.

'Would you like to freshen up first?' asked Megan, pausing at the foot of the carpeted stairs, one of Rachel's bags over her shoulder. 'Or maybe you'd prefer to come and say hello to the folks, get it out of the way? I've got to take out some of the dogs at five, so if you wanted to come for a walk, you'd be very welcome to join us, maybe give Gem some one-on-one time . . .'

Her voice trailed off as Rachel didn't reply. 'Sorry, it sounds like I'm welcoming you to a hotel, doesn't it? And this is your house now.'

'It's OK,' said Rachel. That wasn't why she was looking awkward; it was the idea of having to make small talk with strangers when all she really wanted to do was put on her Virgin Atlantic eyemask and try to block out the reality of what she'd set in motion back in Chiswick. Her phone kept buzzing in her pocket and she knew it would be Oliver. She didn't want to hear his messages; he'd be incandescent with rage by now, after what she'd done. 'Um, when you say *folks . . .*'

'Actually, I was meaning the dogs.' Megan grinned. 'Sorry, you'll get used to it. But George, the vet, is here, and I guess you'll need to talk to him about the kennels anyway?'

George the vet. The bath and a bottle of wine were beckoning, but Rachel dragged on her best PR meeting face. Better to get it over with.

'Good idea!' she said, rather hollowly, and felt a flicker of shame at Megan's eager, unforced smile as she set off down the hall.

'We have our team of volunteer walkers,' Megan said over her shoulder. 'Couldn't do without them, to tell the truth – they'll be in now, dropping the terriers off.'

'Walkers?' repeated Rachel, though she wasn't really listening. It was a client trick she'd learned from Oliver – if you don't want to talk or listen, just repeat the last word and let the other person chatter on.

'Yes, local owners who don't mind taking a few rescues out with their own dogs. And we've got some kids who aren't allowed a pet, some older people who can't take one on. Works out well for everyone.'

'Mm,' said Rachel, pausing by a photograph of Dot, straight-backed and white-haired, surrounded by a group of dogs leaping up to lick her face. Here and there were big portraits of frolicking greyhounds and collies in mid-leap, in much the same way that Val covered the walls of her Dustbusted living room with studio shots of Amelia, Grace and Jack.

'So what do you do?' Megan asked conversationally. 'Gerald said you worked in PR! Sounds very glam.'

'Oh, not really. Internet launches, mainly, new businesses, some web-based retailers, nothing too interesting.' Rachel felt something nudge against her heel and jumped.

Behind her, Gem was lowering his head to make gentle butts with his nose against her calf. He stopped, and looked up, tilting his head so his ear flopped.

'Gem! You bossy dog!' yelped Megan, outraged but obviously amused. 'You'll have to excuse him, Rachel, he's a real collie – always herding us around if he doesn't think we're moving quickly enough.'

'Was he a hand-in?' Rachel asked, making eye contact properly for the first time with her new dog. 'I don't remember seeing him when I was here.'

Megan's cheeriness drooped. 'No. He was her puppy. Dot got Gem when he was two weeks old. Our local policeman found him in a box down by the play area in the park with three of his baby brothers, just dumped there to die.' Her eyes widened. 'God knows what happened to their poor mum. The river froze over, so you can guess what sort of state these guys were in. When they came in, they were just clinging to each other for warmth. Their sister had already frozen to death in there.'

'That's awful,' breathed Rachel, jolted out of her self-pity. She crouched down to Gem's level, so she could stroke his neck.

Gem stared up at her, his bright eyes shining in the dimly lit corridor. His coat was so thick and strong, it was impossible to imagine him tiny and struggling for life.

'He looks amazing now,' she said.

'Yeah, well, that was Dot.' Megan leaned over and fondled his ear. 'She virtually kept all four in a sort of sling round her for the first week – they were far too young to leave their mother, so she had to feed them with pipettes and stuff. One little guy didn't make it – he'd got too thin. George did what he could, but even Dot couldn't keep him alive.'

There was a roar of male laughter from the kitchen, and Rachel wished she didn't have to face everyone just yet. Especially not now Gem's story had brought her back to the edge of tears. 'So what happened to them?' she asked, to delay the moment.

Megan bent down to Gem's level to stroke him better. 'Shem and Star went to a farmer up near Hartley, Spark went to an agility trainer in Rosehill. But she couldn't bear to part with Gem, so she kept him. Broke every rule in her book, she said, but he was worth it. And you loved her as much as she loved you, didn't you, poor sad boy? Eh? You're missing your mistress now, aren't you?'

Megan buried her face in his black fur and Rachel got the feeling she was paying him extra attention so she wouldn't see how tearful she was. Maybe they were both putting off the kitchen moment.

'Dot didn't normally take dogs for herself?' she asked. 'Wasn't that really hard, if she loved them so much?'

'No, she had to be tough – if we took all the sad cases that are handed in we'd be running our own dog rescues from home. She made me promise I wouldn't try to save all the dogs myself! The best we could do, she reckoned, was to make sure their second chance didn't let them down. We had to give the dogs their second chance, because they'd given us humans a second chance, despite how badly they'd been treated.'

'Don't,' said Rachel suddenly. 'You'll make me cry.'

Megan straightened up, and forced out a watery smile. 'Sorry. I don't know how we're going to manage without her, never mind Gem. He was with her, you know, when she had her stroke. At least he doesn't look out for her, like the other dogs do. He knows she's not coming back.'

Gem came forward with two delicate steps and this time nudged Megan's leg with his snowy muzzle until she broke off and looked down at him.

'Yeah, yeah, I know, tea time.' She raised her eyebrows at Rachel. 'Actually, I shouldn't say that. That was another rule. Don't pretend the animals talk like humans. They're bloody dogs, she said, about ten times smarter than we are. And ten times better company.'

'Well, that I can believe,' sighed Rachel, thinking of Oliver's silences and her mother's constant probing. 'But don't get any ideas,' she added quickly.

The kitchen was buzzing with hearty conversation when Megan pushed the door open, and it didn't die down as she went in.

'. . . and I said, here, have a poo bag, lad!' the old lady at the kitchen table was saying, nodding for emphasis so hard that her neatly set hair nodded with her. 'It's like I say to Ted, we should have training classes for the owners, not the dogs. Pippin *never* toileted anywhere inconvenient, did he, Ted?'

'He certainly did not.'

'He did not. He was a *very* clean doggie.'

'For a Yorkshire terrier, Pippin was a lavatorial miracle, Freda,' said the big man leaning against the Belfast sink, with a hint of what Rachel recognised as teasing, although Freda didn't.

So that's George the vet, she thought. At least he's got a sense of humour.

George looked like a country vet too, in a checked shirt rolled up at the sleeves, battered red cords, and muddy boots. He clutched his mug of tea with a large, chapped hand, not bothering with the handle. His hair was thick and blond, and, going by the casual confidence in his blue eyes and the way he was helping himself to a double slice of fruit cake, he seemed very much at home.

'Ah, Megan, you're back, love!' said the older man – Ted, was it? 'We've parked Mickey and Minnie in the kennels and we're fine to take out another two, if you'd like?'

'How about Bertie?' suggested George, and Rachel caught the shudder that went over the two elderly faces. Then he spotted her standing behind Megan, and his face changed, out of the relaxed bonhomie and into a more professional alertness.

Rachel thought she preferred the first, before he'd seen her looking; George's face was rugged, rather than handsome, and the red skin around his nose suggested he'd spent a lot of time outside in the cold air recently. But when he'd been gently teasing the old lady, the twinkle in his eyes made him look younger, and cheekier; as soon as he'd spotted her at the door, he'd seemed more like a senior vet, about her own age, she guessed, maybe a little older. A practice owner, not an employee.

'Hi, guys!' carolled Megan. 'This is Rachel Fielding, Dot's niece. She's the new owner of the house, the kennels, the rescue, everything!'

'Hello,' said Rachel, raising an awkward hand.

'Ted Shackley. And my wife, Freda. Our condolences, love,' said Ted. He rose to his feet and shook her hand, clasping it for a second in his. As he spoke, the creases around his forehead deepened. 'Not a happy occasion, this.'

'No,' echoed his wife. 'She was one in a million, was Dot.'

'One in a million,' sighed Ted.

'George Fenwick.' The vet pushed himself off the sink and switched his mug to the other hand, but didn't put it down. He was a good bit taller than Rachel, which was unusual enough for her to notice; she was nearly five foot ten, and hadn't worn heels since Before Oliver. He extended a hand, and she saw flecks of gold hair along his arm, disappearing into the checked shirt.

'Hello,' she said. His hand felt big and rough against her own smooth skin. Country hands against her SPF-protected city ones. 'Thanks for helping Megan keep this place ticking over since Dot's . . . for the last few weeks.'

'A pleasure. Dot was a client and a good friend.' George looked at her, his head on one side, scrutinising her. 'Don't tell me,' he said. 'You're not really an animal person.'

'Mr Fenwick!' exclaimed Freda, in a scandalised manner. 'How rude!'

'Well, a fancy black skirt in a kennel?' he said. His shrewd eyes didn't leave hers, and Rachel thought they weren't quite joking. 'I'm no fashion expert, but I'd advise you not to go anywhere near the runs until Megan's finished feeding time. You'll walk in with a smart black suit and leave with grey flannels.'

'I didn't dress for feeding dogs,' said Rachel. She couldn't be bothered with men who thought borderline rudeness constituted repartee. 'I dressed for meeting a solicitor.'

'Of course you did,' said Freda, soothingly. 'I'm sure you'll find something suitable of Dot's to pop on. And if you need any help, just ask.' She squeezed Rachel's hand. 'I'm here most days, helping out with the poor little souls. It's our way of remembering Pippin. Pippin was one of Dot's rescues, wasn't he, Ted? He was an angel sent to us from a higher place.'

'He was a Yorkshire terrier sent here from a puppy farm in Wales,' George corrected her. 'The failed stud dog in a harem of over-bred bitches, if I recall.'

Freda ignored him. 'George is an excellent veterinarian, but he's a way to go before he has his father's basketside manner,' she went on. 'Don't you listen to him, Rachel. I can see you *are* a dog person. Look how Gem's taken to you.'

Rachel looked down and realised that the collie had settled at her feet, his long nose resting on his paws. White hairs were drifting up her legs, settling on her dry-clean-only skirt. 'Oh. But I'm not, though. I've never had a dog. I travel a lot for work, and I don't have the time . . .'

*I don't want to be tied down. I don't want to be stuck. That's the great thing about me and Oliver, no ties, no boring commitment.*

*Was* the great thing, she reminded herself.

'Gem doesn't do that to everyone,' said Freda, as if she hadn't heard. 'He must know. They know, don't they? Pippin always could tell when it was going to rain. He'd pop his little head under the cushion and hide. He was a highly intelligent dog. Guided, we thought, didn't we, Ted?'

'We did.'

'Pippin did the National Lottery,' said George, catching Rachel's eye. 'Freda and Ted have Pippin to thank for their conservatory. He had his own sofa in there, didn't he? For watching the tennis.'

'Don't remind me,' said Freda, dabbing her nose. 'It's so empty without him.'

Ted reached for another slice of cake.

'I know you're not exactly dressed for it, but shall I show you round the kennels?' asked Megan. 'Then you can settle in a bit? Or whatever you want to do.'

Rachel felt bad for being so disorganised. They expected her to have plans. She looked as if she should have plans, coming here as the executor in charge of parcelling up Dot's life, dressed as if she was off to a power breakfast. But she had no plans at all. Her brain was so addled with shock and money worries and the things she should have said if she hadn't been so stunned, she wasn't even sure she could cope with a trip to the supermarket for food right now.

'Megan, just tell the dogs not to shed for ten minutes,' said George, with a fake bossy tone. 'And take an air freshener with you – these country smells can be a shock to sophisticated metropolitan types.'

Rachel was about to ask Megan for a cup of tea first, but she swung round at his words. There was a sardonic half-smile playing on the corner of George's wide mouth and, without warning, she felt riled, the first non-Oliver-related emotion she'd had since she walked out.

'You can always put scented candles in there,' he added, seeing her irritation. 'And have it feng shuied?'

That smug bastard's laughing at me, thought Rachel. He thinks I'm some London princess who's not fit to set foot in Dot's precious kennels. Just because I don't have some hairy animal in tow, he thinks he can take the piss. Well, he can't.

She put her laptop bag down by the table and pushed back the sleeves of her long cashmere cardigan.

'Working in London you get used to some unpleasant smells,' she said. 'Let's go, shall we, Megan?'

Megan looked between Rachel and George, her eyebrows raised a fraction, and then she put down the cup of tea Freda had poured and showed Rachel out of the kitchen to the dogs' domain.

The kennels were joined onto the back of the house by a covered passageway neatly tiled with black and white squares, and the walls decorated with happy photos of old dogs being united with their brand-new owners.

Long windows looked out onto the apple orchard, and the modest hills beyond that, and Rachel dimly remembered the will saying something about fourteen acres of land behind the house as they walked down the short corridor. There was certainly plenty of space for the dogs to run around in the wild gardens.

Megan pushed open the heavy fire doors to the kennels, and now Rachel really could smell dogs – a biscuity, oily smell of coats and hair, with a tangy top note of meat and bleach. It was strange, but not unpleasant. Over that, she felt as if she could actually sense the anxiety of the dogs' bodies, the tension and pent-up energy and confusion in the air.

Inside, everything was steel and concrete and glass, all spotlessly clean. As Rachel looked further in, she made out two rows of cage-fronted pens running either side of a stone-flagged corridor, with a little office to one side and a kitchen opposite. At the far end was a big old stable door; it let in sunlight and sharp fresh air when the top half was opened for ventilation, as it was now. Incongruously, the dogs seemed to be grumbling along to a panel discussion on the radio.

'So, here we are!' said Megan, cheerily. She threw her hands wide. 'Home sweet home for our waifs and strays!'

At the sound of her voice, the ragged chorus of yaps turned into a wall of barking – deep, booming baying with tiny yips cutting across the bass notes. It clanged on Rachel's unaccustomed ears.

'Shush!' yelled Megan ineffectively.

'How many are there?' Rachel asked, raising her voice to be heard over the cacophony.

'Fifteen, unless we've had any hand-ins while I've been out?' Megan was checking a book on the office table, and pressing buttons on the answering machine at the same time. 'Sorry, we often get phone calls from people at their wit's end with badly behaved dogs – wanting to dump them on us. I try to talk them round, rather than let them . . . Oh, not *again*. Sorry, Rachel, this nutcase in Madden's trying to palm off a couple of Scotties for, like, the tenth time this year. If she could get her arse to training classes it would save us all a load of . . .'

She grabbed a pencil and gestured towards the dog runs. 'Do you want to have a look at the guys? Put those wellies on, if you want. Walk very slowly, and don't put your fingers inside.'

Rachel realised she must have looked horrified, because Megan added quickly, 'They won't bite, but some of them are a bit peckish this time of day.' She chucked a bag of treats off the desk, and Rachel caught it. 'Give them one or two, but no more – it'll be their dinner at six.'

Rachel slipped her feet into the spare wellies parked by the door, and cautiously approached the first pen, not wanting to set off more barking. The smell of fur and dog breath intensified. As George had predicted, her skirt and opaque-clad legs were already turning grey with stray hairs.

I should have brought some jeans, she thought. In her rush to leave the flat she'd thrown the contents of her last dry-cleaning run into her bags, dumping the rest of her wardrobe in storage. Thinking about it, she wasn't sure what bits of her fashionable working wardrobe really lent themselves to kennel work. Most of it was dry-clean only.

Without warning a wet nose shoved itself up to the wire and she jumped as the front of the run shook with the impact of a big dog thrusting its paws up towards her.

'Oh, my God!' she gasped, grabbing her throat. 'Don't!'

But she couldn't help her heart melting at what she saw: a handsome red-and-white Basset hound with a softly wrinkled face, snuffling at her eagerly, one massive paw pressing up against the bars with a pleading gesture, so the solid pads pushed through the bars of the wire, revealing delicate tufts of hair between. Rachel had no idea how old the dog was, but it still looked to be growing into the huge knuckly paws and flopping ears, like a child wearing a set of clothes a year too big.

There was a tag attached to the top of the cage and she read it while the dog carried on sniffing out her interesting new scent. The note was in Dot's upright cursive handwriting, but the voice in the written words was clearly the dog in front of her.

'My name's Bertie, and I'm about twelve months old. My people took me for a walk in the park but then drove away. Though I tried to run after them, I couldn't run fast enough because as you can see, my legs are very short. I wish someone would come back for me, because it's rubbish being on my own. What I'm really looking for is a patient couple with a sense of humour who want a dog who's as funny as they are. PS When I'm big, I will like walks, even though I look like I prefer lying around by your fireside.'

Rachel's stomach tightened in a knot as the dog tried to lick her hand, eager for affection. How could anyone just abandon a puppy like this? How could you push a trusting dog away, stopping it following you home? She bit her lip as she fondled the dog's soft ear and tried not to think too hard about his sad story.

There were tags on each of the pens, she could see: Rachel wasn't sure she wanted to read them, but some awful curiosity compelled her.

She turned to the pen opposite the Basset hound's, where a little black poodle lay sadly in a basket at the far end of the concrete run, not even bothering to investigate the visitor. The cheery note was much brighter than the disconsolate ball of fur in front of her.

'Hello, darlings! I'm Lulu! Please ignore my bad hair day – underneath these knots I'm a beautiful show girl. My last owner didn't bother to brush me, or look after me properly, or even feed me every day. Luckily, now I'm here, Megan is going to give me a makeover, and soon you'll see just how gorgeous I am. I'm looking for someone clever enough to see that just because I'm cute doesn't mean I'm dumb – I'm probably the smartest dog in here (apart from Gem) and I want to use this brain of mine! Believe me, old dogs can learn new tricks.'

Were poodles smart? Rachel had no idea. The only poodles she'd seen were the silly shaved pets, prancing around show rings. But they had some spark, unlike this poor creature.

'Hello, Lulu!' she called through the bars, waving a biscuit, but the dog didn't even lift her long nose from the edge of her basket. Instead she cowered away from the voice, as if she was afraid of what Rachel might do to her. She had a shaved patch on her side, and the pale bluc-grcy suede of her skin seemed vulnerable around the pinched stitches holding a recent incision together.

Rachel turned away from the poodle, unable to bear it. This was just too sad. Where were the normal dogs? The ones Dot was boarding for people who actually *loved* their pets?

She leaned back against the wall opposite Lulu and closed her eyes, feeling weariness and sympathy swamp her whole body.

If anyone knew what it felt like to be shoved out of a life you knew by someone you loved, she did. How much she wanted a second chance. Dot couldn't possibly have known how ironic her will was. Or maybe she did. Maybe she'd remembered that strange non-conversation they'd had and decided Rachel needed not just *one* dog's worth of affection but *fifteen* . . .

'Watch out! Oi! No!'

Rachel jumped backwards as Megan came sprinting down the corridor, wagging her finger in the direction of the pen next to her. When she looked down she realised why: the Basset hound had stuck its nose through a gap in the wire and was half-licking, half-chewing one of the round horn buttons off her long cardigan.

'It's not a sweetie! Honestly, Bertie!' Megan directed a gentle swipe in the dog's direction and he dropped down, back onto his four enormous paws. 'Sometimes I wonder if there's a pig inside that Basset hound costume of yours!'

Bertie directed a plaintive, starving look at both of them, so that Rachel reached for the treats that she'd stuffed in her pocket.

'And don't give her that sad-eyed, *no one feeds me* look,' Megan went on. 'Sorry,' she said, turning back to Rachel. 'He's a naughty one, Bertie, but we love him.'

'But why's he still here?' said Rachel, shaking a treat out of the packet and offering it to him through the wire. 'He's beautiful!'

'Oh, Bassets,' sighed Megan. 'They eat, they sleep, they won't listen to you . . . Adorable puppies grow up into this huge dog. Bertie steals food, wasn't house-trained, cries when he's left alone, he chews.' She made a stern face that wasn't completely convincing, thanks to the soft way she bent down to tickle Bertie's draped ears. 'You're someone's project dog, aren't you, Bertram? You need someone who likes a challenge.'

'I saw his note,' said Rachel, nodding towards the tag on the door. 'I thought Dot didn't like dogs talking?'

'Well, she didn't. But she reckoned it was the best way of making people understand that they weren't toys to be picked up, or abandoned, that the dogs had feelings too, you know?' Megan's face darkened with protectiveness, and she chewed a hangnail. 'OK, so they don't do guilt or spite or emotional blackmail, but they get lonely. We wanted new owners to think really hard about what they were taking home – a life that depended on them.'

'Like a child,' said Rachel, with a pang. That was another ghostly thought, looming over her since her break-up with Oliver. Children. The children she'd never have now, even if she'd never wanted them before.

'Harder than a child,' said a new voice, and they both turned to the door, where George was standing, his arms crossed over his chest. 'A child can tell you what's wrong, whereas with dogs you've got to learn each other's language. Some people don't have the patience, but that's not the dog's fault. How's your designer outfit getting on? I see you've abandoned the Jimmy Choos.'

'I'm not afraid of a few hairs.' Rachel gave her skirt a cursory brush. She wasn't going to tell George that this'd be straight into the dry cleaners in the morning. 'I didn't realise there were so many rescue dogs here. The solicitor said Dot's business was mainly boarding kennels?'

'That's what they were *supposed* to be,' said George. 'But Dot had her own private mission going on, to rehome every lost soul in the area. If you ask me, you've got the potential to make a decent living here, if those kennels weren't full of rescue dogs. It's the only one in the area, there's room for a grooming parlour, plenty of space to expand – I know Dot had some offers to buy it off her over the years. I could probably put you in touch with the right estate agents.'

'That would be . . .' Rachel began, but Megan shot her a defensive glance that made her stop.

'Yes, but they wouldn't guarantee to continue the rescue, and that was Dot's *life*.' Megan turned back to the office, looking for paperwork to show her. 'We have to keep the boarders and the rescue dogs very separate – we had five boarders in, just before she died. Only I thought it was better to wind that down for a while, till we knew what was happening.' She paused. 'I mean, are you . . .?'

'Megan,' warned George.

Rachel wished her mother was here now, to see how much more complicated this was than everyone thought. Bloody 'get me the Acker Bilk albums'. Dot hadn't just left her a lovely six-bed villa with gardens and furniture – she'd left her a house that would probably take months to sort through, a business she didn't have the first clue about, forms to fill in before any of it could be sold or distributed, employees that depended on her, and fifteen reject animals that she'd be guilt-tripped into dealing with.

'Anyway, sorry to interrupt the tour, but I need to talk to Megan about clipping Lulu,' said George, briskly, and strode over to Lulu's pen as if Rachel wasn't there. He let himself in, and to Rachel's surprise the poodle perked up her head and allowed him to lift her. His manner with Lulu was a complete change from his manner with humans: firm, but gentle and almost tender.

'You're still not yourself, are you?' He turned back to Megan with the dog tucked into the crook of his arm, looking smaller than ever in his sturdy hold. 'Yes, on principle, once she's on her feet again, it's a good thing to get her tidied up, but you're not to make her look like some kind of ridiculous Hollywood handbag dog. And *don't* tell me about the course you've just done.'

'I'll do a traditional puppy trim,' said Megan. 'But she'd love to have some poms! Look at her, she's a show girl!'

'Megan,' said George again, and this time he sounded properly stern. 'She's not a toy, and I don't want her looking like one, in case she gets the wrong kind of attention.'

Lulu glared at Megan from the safety of her protector's embrace, her black button eyes shiny in the mass of matted fur.

'You *know* that's not what . . .' she started, then stopped as he lifted a warning finger. Rachel sensed an old banter between the two and felt awkward.

'Don't look so horrified,' George added, seeing her eyes fixed on Lulu's scar. 'She's just been spayed. We neuter all the dogs, or rather, I do.'

'George is very good about discounts,' explained Megan. 'Deep down he's a softie.'

'No, I'm not,' George corrected her. 'About this trim . . .'

Rachel let her gaze drift down the pens, where she could make out a brindled Staffie, and a couple of fat chocolate Labradors, a perky Jack Russell bouncing off the walls, and several Heinz 57, terrier-ish looking dogs with fresh eagerness in their brown eyes and a 'pick me!' wag in their tails. Other pens seemed empty, and she didn't want to look, in case their occupants were lurking miserably at the back like Lulu, unable to dredge up the spirit to hope.

How could you choose just one? Her throat tightened as if she'd swallowed cotton wool. How could you walk out, knowing you were leaving fourteen disappointed creatures to wonder what was wrong with them? When their owners would come back for them?

She looked down, and blinked in surprise. Gem had appeared silently, out of nowhere, to lie in front of her, his narrow paws placed neatly together while he waited for something to do.

'I'm not Dot,' she whispered, so Megan wouldn't hear her. 'I don't know what to do.'

Rachel, she thought, for God's sake don't start talking to the dogs. Get a grip.

'Megan?' Her voice cracked, despite her efforts to sound light. 'I'm going to have a bath. What's the routine for, you know, locking up?'

'No need,' Megan replied cheerfully. 'I've been living in? Part of the deal as kennel manager. Hope you don't mind – Dot let me have the whole of the second floor? It's got its own self-contained bathroom and sitting room. I won't be in your way.'

'Oh,' said Rachel. 'Right.'

So she had a lodger as well. Great. Actually, maybe that *was* great.

'Shall I sort you out some supper?' asked Megan. 'Freda's brought a casserole for you, and there's loads in the cupboards.'

'No, I . . .' Rachel didn't want to say, 'I don't want to talk to anyone', not when Megan was being so kind, but she really didn't. 'I've got some work to do,' she said instead. It was a catch-all excuse that had worked for so much in the past. Ironically, of course, she didn't have any work to do, unless you counted the letters to write to her ex-clients, explaining that she'd now resigned.

'No problem!' said Megan. 'I wasn't sure how you'd feel about sleeping in Dot's bed, so I've made up the spare room next to hers? There's towels on the heated rail in the bathroom.'

Rachel forced out a smile. 'Um . . . thanks. Thanks for everything you've done.'

Megan's smile increased. 'Really, my pleasure. Have a nice bath!'

'Good evening!' said George Fenwick, tipping his head in a deliberately old-fashioned manner. 'And let me give you the number of my dry cleaner!'

'You have a dry cleaner?' Rachel pulled an incredulous face. He smiled. 'Touché.'

But Rachel was too weary to enjoy scoring points off him. Instead she sloped off to Dot's roll-topped bath to soak away some of the weariness in her bones.

# 3

Johnny Hodge put his empty pint glass down between the empty crisp packet and the dish of pistachio shells and checked his watch.

Quarter past eight. Bill had been at the bar for twenty-four minutes, which was a record even for the Fox and Hounds, where service depended on whether Ray's darts injury was playing up or not.

Johnny knew he should have gone himself. Even when Ray was in the pint-pulling zone, Dr Bill's drink-buying always took twice as long as everyone else's on account of the locals treating it as a chance for some unofficial medical attention in the comfort of their own pub. That was the price you paid for being a doctor. Very few people, on the other hand, bothered to button-hole Johnny to ask about the GCSE History syllabus.

He glanced across at Natalie, but she was staring vacantly into the distance, an unfamiliar expression for her, and his heart sank.

Johnny could guess what she was thinking about: it was all she ever thought about now. She'd be calculating her fertile period and assessing whether it was worth hauling him back home early or leaving him for another hour with Bill. Ironically neither option – passionate sex with the most gorgeous woman in the bar, or an extra round with his best mate – filled him with the joy it should.

Bill might be a qualified doctor, but in Johnny's private opinion, when it came to human fertility he was a rank amateur compared to Nat. She did her best to keep the gory details from him, but when your wife started to seduce you for half the month then ignored you miserably for the other half, even a bloke like Johnny had to know something was going on. And he wasn't as daft as he made out. He'd seen the website she thought she'd hidden from him, the one that she plotted her morning temperature on. Nat thought she'd hidden that from him too, muffling the bleep bleep bleep of her thermometer before the alarm went.

These days it was less like making love and more like being a sperm courier.

Johnny tapped his foam-streaked glass against the table, more to distract himself than to get Nat's attention. 'How long does it take one man to buy a round?' he asked in a cheerful tone. 'What's he doing up there? Brewing the bitter?'

Natalie snapped out of her trance and looked towards the bar, where Bill was indeed pinned to a bar stool by an eager girl, in knee-high boots, who seemed to have something wrong with her neck going by the way she was encouraging Bill to peer at it. He didn't need much encouragement, bending his dark head so his hair fell into his eyes, making 'hmm' faces.

'No, I think he's doing one of his out-of-hours surgeries,' she said drily. 'Funny how many strange rashes seem to crop up in here. Ray ought to get the place fumigated.'

'I think she's requesting a home visit,' said Johnny.

'She'll be lucky,' said Natalie. 'There's a waiting list, isn't there?'

Bill was a handsome bloke, even Johnny had to acknowledge that. Tall, athletic, twinkly brown eyes – Bill had the sort of college rower good looks that meant he could wear polo shirts with the collar turned up and not look a total prat. He was exactly the kind of guy Johnny's mum had hoped his sister Becky would bring home – although Johnny was willing to lay money on Bill never actually reaching the 'meeting mum' stage, such was his endless turnover of adoring women. Three dates, or two weekends, was the average lifespan of a Bill girlfriend. And yet he always managed to break up so sensitively that they still cried on his shoulder and insisted to Johnny that he was 'the nicest man I've ever met'.

In Johnny's opinion, it was time Bill took this whole mating game more seriously. Not just because he thought marriage had a lot to recommend it, but because there were only a finite number of women in a small town like Longhampton.

'Do you think if he was less of a looker he'd stop playing the field so much?' mused Natalie, out of the blue. 'Do you think he's got too *much* choice?'

She often did that, slip inside his head, without him realising. Johnny slid his arm along the velvet booth, so he could pull her a bit closer.

'I think he looks at us, and wants what we've got,' he said, honestly. 'But what we've got doesn't come along that often, does it? I think how lucky I am every day, meeting the girl of my dreams in the comfort of my own school canteen. Twelve years down the line, you'll always be the cute sixth-former to me. With your Jennifer Aniston haircut.'

Johnny could have added, and every day you get more beautiful, and more amazing, and I can't believe that an ambitious, intelligent, gorgeous woman like you would pick someone like me. But he didn't, because Nat already knew how he felt about her.

'Lucky me,' he said instead.

She gave him a sideways look, her clever green cat's eyes glinting with amusement. 'Stop it. You'll make me nauseous.' But she leaned over and pressed a secret kiss in the hollow of his neck, quickly, so no one would see. Johnny's heart rate sped up and he hoped it meant they were heading into a Green Zone. It might be worth sacrificing a round for.

But Natalie's mind was back on Bill. 'Bill needs a girlfriend,' she said with a sigh, sinking back into the ancient burgundy velveteen. 'He can't keep on being so fussy. He can't keep on hanging out with sad marrieds like us. Why did he dump the last one?'

'She couldn't park her car.' Johnny returned his attention to the bar, where the brunette was laughing uproariously, and heaving her cleavage around. The first signs of rigor mortis were setting in on Bill's smile. 'Come on, the guy doesn't ask for much. He only wants a woman between twenty-six and twenty-eight, no baggage, no scary exes, good cook, blonde hair, taller than Kylie Minogue but shorter than Kate Winslet, likes the outdoors but also home comforts.'

'Who's perfect at parking.'

'Well, yes.'

'He's trying *not* to find someone,' said Natalie with a sigh. She knocked back the last of her Diet Coke while Johnny was racking his brains wondering what she meant. 'Should we leave him to his consultation or should you rescue him?'

They scrutinised Bill's body language; long legs crossed over each other, arms folded defensively over his chest. As they looked, he caught Johnny's eye and made a tiny shaky-head gesture.

'I'll rescue him.' Johnny rose to his feet, nearly knocking the small table over. He wasn't small, and the tables had got very close together since Ray had tried to upgrade the Fox and Hounds to a gourmet experience by shoving the drinkers into the snug to make space for a dining room. 'What can I get you?'

'A bloody Virgin Mary.' Natalie had sacrificed white wine at the same time as she'd given up tea, coffee and anything else that might interfere with her hormones. 'Johnny, I'm not nagging but don't you think you should ... have one too?' She bit her lip and looked down at her handbag, next to her

on the shabby velvet seat. She seemed more cross with herself
than him.

Johnny knew what she'd stopped herself saying: had he
remembered the advice about his own beer consumption?
Natalie never nagged; it had been one of their self-written
marriage vows, along with his promise to iron his own shirts.
But in this case she didn't need to; if it was a choice between
giving up the ale and giving Dr Bill's flat-shoed nemesis Nurse
Sonia the dreaded sample for analysis, he was willing to make
the ale sacrifice for a few months.

Twelve months, now, it had been since they'd 'stopped
trying not to get pregnant'. The longest twelve months of his
life.

Still, Johnny thought, it was really important to Natalie,
having a baby. And to him. Obviously. It was important to
them both, because whatever made her happy, made him
happy. But if it came to it, Johnny secretly thought that if it
was just him and Natalie for the rest of their lives, he'd be
happy enough.

'A Virgin Mary? Eeh, cocktails? At the Fox?' he said instead.
'Think I'll join you in that. Give Ray some sophistimacation
practice for those fine dining yuppies he wants to bring in.'

Natalie looked up and smiled gratefully, and he loved her a
little bit more.

Twenty minutes later, Natalie drained the tomato juice dregs
and shouldered her bag.

'I'd better be off,' she said, with an apologetic smile. 'I know,
party pooper. Sorry.'

'So early?' Bill looked disappointed. 'Does this mean we're
getting old? It's not even a school night. Mr Hodge is still
here, look!'

Natalie gripped the shoulder strap. 'No, I've just . . . I've
just got some reports I need to write up before the weekend

kicks in. I hate leaving it till Sunday night. Rather get it done while it's all fresh in my mind.'

Johnny started to reach for his jacket, but she shook her head. 'No, honestly, hon, you stay here and finish your drink. It's fine.'

'We'll share a cab,' offered Bill. 'Won't make it too late.'

'Before midnight's fine.' Natalie smiled. 'He turns back into a frog after that. See you later!'

She walked out of the pub into the night air, which had taken on an even sharper chill in the last few days. No sign of spring yet, she thought, clutching her hooded parka tighter as she blipped the central locking on their Mini Cooper and slid inside.

Natalie loved her Mini Cooper. Johnny got the bus into school most mornings, so this was really her car, for driving to the business park on the outskirts of town where she worked, and for the endless marketing strategy meetings she had to schlep all over the place for. Every time she ran her hands over the leather steering wheel Natalie felt good about her life. It was a new car, and a bit of a luxury, but it had been their big treat to themselves, her and Johnny, since they didn't have anyone to spend their money on but themselves, not like their brothers and sisters who spent every available penny on their kids.

She'd ticked the ISOFIX child seat fittings option, just in case, when Johnny was faffing around deciding on what type of alloys they should get. It was sensible anyway, for secondhand values. A rational decision. Not just because Natalie often imagined a chunky little Maclaren child seat there, in her rear-view mirror. With a chunky little Hodge inside.

As she pulled carefully out of the pub car park and onto the main road, there was a tight knot of moodiness in her chest, and she probed it ruthlessly. Since she and Johnny had officially started trying to conceive – Natalie hated the twee

TTC phrases but found herself using them anyway – she'd tuned into her body like it was a kind of radio transmitter. Every twinge and mood swing and break-out registered in some part of her brain.

Was it the pub? Did she resent not being allowed to drink on her baby diet? Not really. She missed the coffee more. God, she thought, you'd never believe women managed to get pregnant in the past, what with smoking and drinking and rare meat and what have you.

Was it Bill? Not really. She didn't mind hanging out, the three of them. Bill and Johnny were friends from college, and he was like an extra brother.

Was it work? The knot tightened and she knew she couldn't ignore it.

Yes, work was getting to her. The credit crunch had clamped its jaws around the multi-national food company she worked for, as a marketing executive in a new organics sector, and her boss, Selina, was sharpening her claws on her team every day. What had really set Natalie's nerves jangling was the way she already *knew* today's monthly strategy meeting hadn't gone well; Natalie was smart enough to see that other people's budgets were being cut, leaving even less room for them, but there wasn't much she could do about it, short of bailing out the World Bank.

With a sharper flick on the indicator than was strictly necessary, she indicated to turn onto the road up to the estate where she and Johnny lived.

But if she was being honest – and Natalie always tried to be honest – it was a guilty, less noble niggle passed down that chain of more reasonable work-related irritations that had caused the knot in her chest.

That morning, when Kay Lambert, the third pregnant woman in a twenty metre radius of her desk, had made her big announcement via the office email, something had burst inside Natalie, something hot and jealous and stinging. Kay was really nice, but she was thirty-seven and she already had two children. This one was 'a happy surprise!' She hadn't even been trying. She hadn't been on IVF or anything, just 'a rather naughty wedding anniversary in Bath!' It was so *unfair*.

Natalie's knuckles went white on the wheel. She hadn't let it show. She hadn't wanted to spoil Kay's moment, because she was happy for her, happy for *anyone* who was expecting a baby. In fact, she'd been the one to organise the collection and had bought the adorable sling she'd added to her own secret Mothercare wishlist.

So how come it's not *me*, howled the voice in her head, her mouth twisting with the effort of not crying. I'm only thirty, I don't smoke or drink, I love my husband, we have sex at the right times, I take folic acid every morning, I don't even drink bloody coffee any more! What's *wrong* with me?

Nothing, according to the doctors. Apart from impatience.

'Mother Nature doesn't like timetables,' the doctor (Dr Carthy, not Bill) had told her when she went to ask for some tests. He'd been rather dismissive, as if she was one of those pushy women who try to schedule their designer kids around their new kitchens.

It wasn't a to-do list tick for Natalie: it was a rush of yearning that shocked her, that longing to hold her and Johnny's baby in her arms. She felt as if the one thing missing now was their child, a melancholy ghost in their home. Natalie felt it so strongly she was almost embarrassed at how needy it made her sound.

She hadn't always been so broody. Up until her twenty-ninth birthday, she would have completely freaked out if the test had gone blue, but at some silent point something had clicked inside like a timed safe opening, and the yearning had rushed out, knocking her feet from under her with its irrationality. Now whenever she walked into Starbucks her heart flipped at the sight of the buggies and tiny feet in tiny socks. When the babies smiled up at Johnny – which they did, he just seemed to charm them somehow – Natalie's stomach churned with broodiness and fear and frustration that those women had managed something she couldn't. Might not be able to.

Calm down, she told herself. Remember all the fantastic things you have to be grateful for: nice car, nice home, independence, holidays, eight hours' sleep a night.

Natalie drove past the first few houses on their loop, drives parked up with Zafiras and CR-Vs, the yellow 'Little Angel on Board' shining smugly in her headlights, and she ached. She could remember what her dad had said at the wedding, seven years ago that June: she and Johnny were a happy family waiting to happen. Both of them loved kids. Between them she and Johnny had five godchildren – everyone, it seemed, had babies these days, apart from them.

Natalie reversed up their drive and parked. With anyone else but Johnny this would be a million times worse. He'd been so sensitive, right from the beginning, so optimistic and relaxed. At first, yeah, who wouldn't complain about being dragged into the bedroom every thirty-six hours, but lately, when she'd started tensing up when they missed a 'green day' because of family visits or having a cold, he'd managed to keep a sense of humour about it all. If it wasn't for Johnny, she thought, the whole process would be about as romantic as something from a vet programme.

They'd tried minibreaks, and yoga positions. Natalie had signed up for acupuncture and thrown away Johnny's favourite old pants. And yet nothing. Each month, when her temperature fell and the inevitable period came, there would be a bunch of flowers at work, or a special meal cooked in the evening, and Johnny's anxious eyes checking her crestfallen face, when he thought she wasn't looking. And she'd have to pretend that she didn't mind, because she didn't want him to think it was anyone's fault, least of all his.

It had been over a year. The next thing would be more tests. In case it really was someone's fault. Natalie didn't want it to get that far.

What if it *was* her fault? What if she couldn't give him the two point four children he deserved? What then for their marriage that everyone thought was so perfect?

Natalie got out of the car and grabbed her briefcase and laptop bag from the boot.

Inside their house that smelled of hyacinths and uncluttered adult space, she took a pink shopping bag out of her briefcase and went upstairs to change out of her suit into her loose yoga trousers. When she'd brushed her hair into a ponytail, she hesitated, then took the new silky nightie out of the bag and slid it under the pillow, ready for later. She'd never worn nighties, until sex had stopped being recreational and become procreational instead. Now she had to dress it up, to compensate.

Then, before she forgot, she put her basal body temperature thermometer within easy reach of her bedside table, under a paperback where Johnny wouldn't see it. She didn't want him to know.

Natalie stared at the bed for a moment – the perfect bed, brass-framed, white pillows, very Mills and Boon – and sighed. The pillows now went under her bottom immediately it was all over, to 'help' the swimmers into her uncooperative tubes, as she hooked her toes over the brass rails to nudge gravity along. Funny how the most romantic details got lost.

Then she turned on her bare heel and went downstairs to blitz her reports so she could put them out of her mind and be seductive when Johnny got back from the pub.

# 4

Zoe Graham gazed in wonder at her tidy front room and wished she could spray it with Elnett so it would stand a chance of still looking like this in an hour's time.

The house hadn't been this tidy since they'd moved in. The cushions were plumped in the corners of the un-squashed sofa, the Wii was in the big plastic trunk along with all the controllers and leads and games that usually littered the rugs, and everything smelled of fresh Hoovering. Even the beanbag where Spencer and Leo spent most of their time eating, drinking and squabbling in front of the telly was ketchup-free and inviting.

Zoe stood back and put her hands on her hips, and enjoyed the weird silence filling her home.

When it's tidy, it's a really nice house, she thought, almost surprised. When you got rid of the junk that went with two lads under eight, it almost looked like the house from the estate agent's original details: feature fireplace, big bay windows, period mouldings. What made it feel like home, though, were the masses of framed photos of her and Spencer and Leo on the royal blue walls, and the shelves where their toys and DVDs were stacked up next to her own CDs and the paintings they'd done together. A family house. That's why they'd bought it, for that family atmosphere, not that it had lasted very long.

Zoe shoved away that thought. It wasn't the house's fault that David had walked out; it was his colleague, Jennifer's. And David's, of course – it took two to tango off to pretend weekend workshops in Solihull. It was still a family home, she reminded herself, but that family was her and Spencer and Leo now.

Zoe pulled out her phone from the back pocket of her jeans, stepped into the doorway and took a photo of the unfamiliar show home she'd created, and texted it to her mum. Then she saved it as her wallpaper.

All done.

It was eerily quiet without CBeebies or simulated gunfire or the sound of squabbling, and Zoe found her brain was making up a fresh to-do list to distract herself from the nibbling curiosity about how much fun Spencer and Leo would be having with their dad. She knew she shouldn't sink to that level, but it was hard not to. The first few weekends had been miserable for everyone – tears when they left, tears when they came back – but now they were starting to look forward to 'Dad's' Friday nights.

But then, who wouldn't, she thought, tidying away the remote control car Spencer had come back with last time. It was like they both now had twenty birthdays a year.

According to the access they'd thrashed out after the divorce, nearly a year ago, David had them every other weekend, plus half the school holidays, Christmas Eve, birthdays and bank holidays. Zoe's solicitor had warned her that she was being a pushover, agreeing to David's demands, but she'd wanted to make it as easy as possible for the boys, caught in the middle of what had turned into a nasty split. That was her way of trying to ease it for them. David's way was to throw money at them. Money and the Haribo that she'd almost weaned them off.

*Maybe I should scrub out the fridge, like Mum's always telling me to.*

Zoe stared at her dishevelled reflection in the mirror over the fireplace. Her hair was even madder than usual: brown corkscrew curls tightening up with the effort of cleaning. 'Hello? What's wrong with you?' she said aloud. 'Cleaning, on your day off?'

She ought to be relaxing, she knew that. This was rare and precious 'me time', that the other mums at the salon were always going on about in the wistful way that other people talked about lottery wins. Didn't she spend every hour of every working day wishing she was putting her feet up at home? Didn't every hairdresser long to be horizontal and off their varicose veins?

'Me time,' she said aloud. Five more hours to fill before the boys came back – loads of time for . . . What?

Zoe's mind went blank. It used to be so easy in the days before motherhood, when she still read glossy magazines for fun, and not because they were lying around in the consultation area. Her Sunday nights had been a strictly timetabled facemask leg-shave hair-pack routine, and she could talk about books, films, minibreak destinations – the lot. These days she still made lists, but they always seemed to feature 'use up bananas' and 'wash sheets'.

She looked at her reflection again, and saw a sad woman, whose blonde streaks needed redyeing, whose eyebrows needed plucking, and who basically couldn't cope when she wasn't being frazzled to a crisp by two small boys.

'Oh, for God's sake!' said Zoe crossly, and went into the kitchen to help herself to the packet of Bahlsens she'd hidden from Spencer, who could smell a chocolate biscuit from across the street. They were her one secret treat, for the rare moments she got to indulge herself. It was the first time she'd actually eaten one before midnight.

I could phone Mum, Zoe thought, putting the newly descaled kettle on. Or Cal. But even as she thought it, she knew she didn't want to talk to either of them. Her mum and her best mate seemed to have joined forces in their campaign to get her 'back in the saddle' – a phrase that Zoe thought summed up the romance of post-divorce dating pretty well – and every conversation seemed to come back to the theme of when Zoe was going to start dancing lessons or going to book groups or whatever else you had to do to find yourself a date, second time around.

She told them that Spencer, Leo and Dr Who were the only men she had time for now, but if she was being honest, the whole idea of going out there again made her want to crawl into a hole and hide. David had crumpled up what little self-confidence she had, and as for the minefield of introducing a new man to the boys – if she got as far as finding one . . .

The kettle boiled and Zoe jumped. 'Me time' was all about tarting yourself up to find a new bloke. Right now, she preferred the idea of cleaning her house. That was what her inner 'me' really wanted: a carpet with no lurking Lego and a ring-free bath.

As it turned out, Zoe solved the problem of filling in the rest of the afternoon by falling asleep in her chair in front of *Come Dine With Me*, passively enjoying the sight of other people knocking themselves out over a social life she didn't have.

Some sixth sense nudged her awake at ten to seven, however, and she nearly bounced out of her chair at the distant sound of a big car engine at the end of the street.

'I think that's them,' she said aloud. It was weird, not having anyone around to talk to. She couldn't quite get out of the habit.

With one last, wistful look at her tidy sitting room, Zoe got up and began flapping round the kitchen, yanking off her pinny and checking the fridge. They'd need feeding immediately; David always took them to McDonald's, and then filled up the remaining spaces with sugar in as many forms as he could find.

The thought of David made her nervous too. Not that she still fancied him. God, no. The magic had worn off long before the unpleasant scenes at the solicitors'. But since bloody Jennifer had become a permanent fixture in his life, with her transatlantic accent and her bloody charity marathon-running, he'd started looking at Zoe with fresh pity in his eyes when she appeared, hassled to death, on the doorstep, and that made her feel smaller than any outright insult. Zoe had only met Jennifer once, at a work party, but she could tell she was the sort of woman who got up at six to go to the gym in full make-up. One of their friends let slip that Jennifer had insisted her husband keep the kids when she walked out. It made sense.

The car hooted at something at the end of the street, and she knew from the impatient tooting that it had to be David.

Damn, damn, damn, she thought too late, if only I'd put the facepack on while I was watching telly, I could have had intensive moisturisation and a hygienic kitchen. She ran her hands through her hair, then gave up and stuck a clip in it, and threw on the Domestic Goddess pinny her mum had given her as an ironic Christmas present. It hid the coffee stain on her t-shirt.

Zoe hurried to the front door in time to see David's huge new Chelsea tractor pulling up outside. Spencer, looking older than his seven years, got out almost at once, while David was still on the phone. Leo, just seventeen months younger, struggled a bit to get out of his belt, then jumped down onto the pavement after his big brother, and they scurried round to the back of the car, fizzing with excitement.

Zoe's heart swelled up with love at the sight of Leo's too-big ski jacket falling over his hands. As soon as she opened the door, Leo and Spencer stopped getting their bags out of the boot and hurled themselves into her arms, almost knocking her over in their excitement.

Until that moment, Zoe had thought she'd missed them, but in fact had had no idea quite how much. Just seeing them again was like stepping back into full colour, at top volume, and immediately she felt complete again, back to normal. They'd only been away a day; David had to 'be somewhere' on Sunday. Somehow he'd used that to get them next Saturday too.

'Hello! Hello!' she said, over the top of their gabbling about go-karting and burger bars in London, and – her heart swelled – how much they'd missed her.

'Don't go overboard, lads – you're making it look like we didn't have a great time!'

Zoe took a deep breath and looked up to see David unloading their bags with a triumphant expression.

If he wasn't such a git, she thought, he'd be a properly handsome man. Divorce suited David. He'd either been on holiday already or Jennifer had a sunbed – his face was glowing and his light brown hair was shorter than he'd worn it before, though the speckles of grey had miraculously vanished. Gone was the scruffy jumper and jeans weekend uniform he'd worn for the years they'd been married, and in its place he wore a fine dove-grey cashmere jersey over a t-shirt, and, yes, those were definitely Chinos and deck shoes. In February.

David had become a yummy daddy, just as he'd offloaded his childcare responsibilities. How ironic, thought Zoe.

'Hello!' she said tightly. She had an agreement with herself that she could be as foul as she liked about him in her own head, so long as Spencer and Leo didn't hear it.

'Hello!' he replied, leaning casually on the car. 'Been cleaning?'

'Yes.' *Yes, you bastard, although how would you recognise that particular activity? You never even so much as turned on the dishwasher for years.* Zoe's smile intensified.

David lifted an eyebrow and looked amused. 'Wow. Things *have* changed.' Then he frowned. 'You're not thinking of selling the house behind my back, are you? Because . . .'

'Mum!' Spencer tugged her sleeve. 'Mum, Dad's given Leo the best present *ever*.'

'Yeah!' agreed Leo. 'You're never going to guess what it is, it's so cool!'

Their faces were shining with excitement, and even as she smiled down, pleased to see them so happy, Zoe's heart sank. David's presents usually involved a lot of cleaning up for her. She hoped it wasn't going to be something that made them sick, damaged the house or turned her into Scrooge Mummy in comparison.

'Let me guess!' she said, making a reasonably good show of pretending to furrow her brow. 'Is it . . . a Tardis?'

'No!' howled Spencer and Leo.

'Is it . . . a Dalek?' Zoe cast a furtive glance over the car towards David. She half-thought it might be; she'd investigated hiring one for Leo's sixth birthday party the following week, only to discover she could get NASA to build her one for slightly less. It would be just like David to upstage her cunning cardboard approximation.

He shook his head dismissively. 'I don't think it's useful to buy into all that branding at their age. We need to talk about that, by the way. This Dr Who party business.'

*Aaaarrrrrrrrggggggghhh, shut up, you po-faced bastard.* 'Too late,' she said. 'I've already ordered the cake.'

'No, Mum!' said Leo. He was nearly bouncing with joy, his round face beaming up at her. He looked like a mini David, but with her brown eyes. Her heart twanged. 'Guess again, guess again!'

'Better than a Dalek,' said Spencer, scornfully.

Zoe hoped it wasn't a bike. Please, not a bike. Or a mini Ferrari or something.

'Is it . . .' She pantomimed putting her finger on her chin and looked at Leo with one eye closed. 'A speedboat?'

'No!' he cackled, unable to hold it in any longer. 'It's a puppy!'

Her jaw dropped, and this time there was no pantomime involved. 'Not a real one, though?'

'Yes a real one!' Spencer butted in, nearly knocking Leo out of the way. In the last few months he'd grown noticeably bigger than his brother, starting to look like a real boy. 'Look, let's get him out! He's in the boot. His name's Toffee and he's just like off the telly and he's going to sleep in my room during the week, and in Leo's at the weekend.'

'*My* bedroom!' howled Leo. 'He's going to sleep on *my* bed, Spencer! He's my dog!'

'No, I'm the oldest . . .'

'He's *both* yours,' insisted David in a calming, caring-and-sharing tone that made Zoe want to strangle him. 'Be gentle, Leo, Toffee's probably very scared after his journey.'

As the boys slipped into their habitual squabbling over who would get the puppy out, Zoe straightened up and glared over the top of the car. 'David. I can't believe you'd be so irresponsible!' she hissed. 'We talked about this at Christmas. You *knew* I've said they can't have a dog! It's impossible!'

He raised his hands. 'Nothing's impossible, Zoe. It's a question of what's *convenient*. We all have to make compromises and I really think it'll be good for them. Give them a sense of routine.'

Zoe could barely breathe for outrage. Routine? After he'd destroyed every scrap of routine they knew? There was so much wrong with this that she didn't know where to begin. The trouble was, she knew she had thirty seconds flat before he passed the buck onto her and screeched out of the boys' lives for another week.

'Maybe you should come in and have a cup of tea and we can talk about this,' she managed, but already David was looking shifty.

'I'd love to but I've got to make tracks. Jennifer's got plans for this evening. She's been away all week and we need to, you know . . . catch up.' He said it in an unnecessarily euphemistic way and Zoe felt her chocolate biscuit repeating on her.

'Oh? She's been away?' At least she wasn't muscling in on the boys' weekend, she told herself. At least there's that.

'Yes,' said David, meeting her gaze with a certain amount of smug confidence. 'But I thought it might be nice if she came along with us when we go to Alton Towers next time. We might even bring her two, though they're a bit older. Make it a family outing.'

Zoe's mouth went dry. 'We need to talk about that. About how we explain new relationships to the boys. Didn't the counsellor say it's best to leave it until they're OK with the idea of the divorce? Are you sure it's the right time? Do you even know Jennifer's children?'

'It's been a year, Zoe,' David interrupted her with a wave of his hand. 'We've all got to move on. And I don't like the implication that Jennifer is some kind of flash-in-the-pan rebound thing. We're very serious about each other.'

Zoe took a deep breath and tried to quell her rising panic. This wasn't the time. The boys were squealing, there was a whimpering noise coming from the back of the car, she hadn't even thought about the prospect of Alton Towers so soon after Legoland. There was enough hysteria in the house as it was. 'David,' she said, as emphatically as she could. 'This is something we need to discuss properly, not something you throw at me two minutes before you drop the kids off.'

The trouble was, Zoe was confrontation-phobic with a heart softer than melted ice cream. And David knew it – he'd always known it. That was precisely why he was doing this.

'Spencer! Come out of the road!' she called. 'Leo! Be careful! Get on the pavement, please. Both feet.'

The boys peered impishly from behind the back of the car. It was obvious something was up. How can I possibly take care of a puppy, as well as two kids and a job, wailed the voice in Zoe's head.

She looked at David. 'I can't deal with a puppy. Why do you always make *me* the one who has to say no?' Her voice sounded strangled.

'So don't say no,' said David, as if it was the most obvious thing in the world. 'Bye, boys! Are you going to come and give Dad a cuddle?'

'Mum! Look!' Leo thrust something into her arms and instinctively Zoe grabbed hold of the wriggling golden puppy. It was warm and soft, and heavy like a baby, with a seal-smooth coat and huge brown eyes that looked up at her with absolute trust. It made a whimpering noise and tried to lick her hand.

Oh no, she thought, doing her best to harden her heart. No. You don't get me like that.

'His name's Toffee,' said Leo. 'Isn't he cute?'

Spencer was saying his goodbyes to David, with hugs and hair rufflings, and Zoe's sharp ears caught more promises than she wanted to hear. The promises were worse than the sugar overload, in terms of comedowns.

She looked at Leo, who was gazing up at her expectantly from his still-too-big jacket. 'Yes,' she said. 'He's gorgeous. But, Leo, don't you remember we had a talk about dogs, and how it wouldn't be fair to . . .'

'Come and say bye-bye to your dad!' David was holding out his arms from the other side of the car and Leo rushed round, with a quick backwards glance of apology in her direction.

It broke Zoe's heart, watching the boys dole out scrupulously fair amounts of love to each parent on handover days.

The puppy whimpered again, and Zoe realised she'd squeezed it without thinking. She wondered if she was holding it right. How old was it? She'd never had a dog before. What were you meant to do with them?

The practical side of her brain, the side she'd never known was there till she had kids, was already making lists – did they bring a book? What about its stuff? Where was it going to sleep? – and she realised that the window in which she could make David take this dog back and have it live with him and Jennifer was rapidly vanishing.

Her beautiful boys were waving David goodbye, their eyes full of tears they weren't quite old enough to hide, and he was slinking into his car and revving the engine, and then suddenly, he was pulling away, and she was left with two hyperactive boys, all their washing and a Labrador puppy.

Zoe felt something warm and wet on her hands.

A Labrador puppy that had just weed on her.

Bloody, bloody David.

# 5

Rachel woke to the sensation of morning sun and warm breath on her face and assumed she was in bed with Oliver, in her own flat, in London. The house and the dogs? It must all have been a weird dream.

Her heart flooded with relief, but when she opened her eyes, it wasn't Oliver's come-to-bed expression she saw, but a long black nose, and – when her eyes focused properly – two ice-blue eyes.

Gem was standing with his paws on the duvet, leaning over her anxiously and making faint whiny noises. Rachel realised with horror that he'd been licking her. She could feel a dog hair on, or up, her nose.

'Urgh!' Rachel sat up, rubbing her face, and immediately he dropped back onto the floor and retreated to the far corner of the room, where he regarded her balefully.

'That. Is. Disgusting. Is that how everyone wakes up round here?' she demanded.

Gem said nothing.

Rachel sank back into the pillows and stared sightlessly at the chalk sketch of a sultry dark-haired woman that hung on the wall opposite.

She was definitely not in London. She'd been here three days now, and she hadn't even started on the sorting out, let alone reading the file on probate Gerald had given her. All she'd done was call the estate agent to value the house and lie to Val about searching for the bloody silver brushes.

Rachel let her gaze trail listlessly around the room, wondering if checking out the heavy Victorian furniture and unusual trinkets counted as getting on with sorting out the valuation of the house contents. Her attention was dragged back to the heavy-lidded femme fatale on the opposite wall, her proud expression burning out from under a backcombed bouffant of jet-black hair.

Might keep that, thought Rachel. It looked quite a lot like her, when she did the full make-up job on her brown eyes. It was signed with a squiggle, and Paris, 1966.

She wondered what time it was, although that wouldn't make much difference since everyone seemed to operate on Country Hours here. George Fenwick had dropped by at nine a.m. yesterday to give her a lecture about the importance of moving some of the rescue dogs out of the kennels and into new homes. She'd been in her pyjamas at the time, and Megan had had to drag her out of bed specially, but that hadn't apparently struck him as a reason to come back later.

'You can't afford to have them sitting here scoffing themselves silly,' he'd pointed out while eating the breakfast Freda Shackley had put under his nose. 'You're the PR expert – how hard would it be for you to do a nice little campaign to shift them on? It's what Dot would have wanted – new homes for her old dogs. That is part of your duty as executor.'

'I'll put it on my list,' Rachel had said. Her lists were now epic. But apart from lying on the bed feeling numb for hours on end, the only time she left the house – at Megan's suggestion – was to trudge round the fields outside the house with Gem, during which she'd rehearsed all the brilliant and devastating things she would say to Oliver if he ever dared show his face round here.

Rachel had made herself cry several times. Gem had said nothing but had lain with his head on her lap for the first time when they'd got in.

Downstairs, she could hear distant barking and the bang of the front door, which heralded the arrival of the volunteer walkers. In the brief flashes when she wasn't feeling sorry for herself, Rachel did feel bad about letting Megan do everything. But then seeing the volunteers in their bright parkas and boots appear and disappear from the kitchen, chatting away as the eager dogs hauled them towards Longhampton Common, made her want to hide away even more. They were all so nice, so sympathetic – and so sad that she was apparently so devastated about her aunt's death that she was laid up in bed with grief.

That was the worst part of her broken heart: she couldn't confess it to anyone. It was too messy. Worst of all, it was entirely her own fault and she'd made zero plans for the inevitable devastation to come.

Where am I meant to go? Rachel wondered, staring blankly at the cracked ceiling. What am I supposed to do now? What's the point?

There was a faint knock on the door.

'Rachel?'

It was Megan and the cup of tea she brought every morning to lure Rachel out of bed.

'Rachel, are you awake?'

Gem got up on his soundless paws and slunk to the door, cocking his head as if telling her to get the hell up.

'Um, yes.' Her voice cracked and she coughed. 'Yes, just . . . checking my emails.'

She hoped Megan wouldn't point out that Dot didn't have any sort of internet connection.

'Great! I've brought you a cup of tea. Thing is, I need a hand with the walking,' Megan went on. 'One of the usual girls is sick, and I can't take all the guys out at once. Do you mind?'

Rachel flopped back into the pillows. 'I'm not feeling great this morning . . .'

'Really?'

'I've got a . . .' Rachel's eyes skated around the room. 'I've got a stack of urgent emails. Um, it's the tax year coming up.'

'Ah, fair enough.' There was a pause. 'But fresh air's just what you need to clear your head! And I know the guys would appreciate it. And it'll be good for Gem to get an extra walk, you know? He needs his mind taking off . . . well, you know.'

Rachel could virtually see Megan's indefatigable Aussie smile through the door. She also spotted the way Gem's ears had twitched at the mention of the word 'walk'.

I've got to go to the bank, she thought. And I need some more wine. Might as well.

'OK,' she said, throwing back the covers so she had no choice. 'Give me ten minutes.'


Megan was down in the kitchen, checking rotas on a clipboard, when Rachel emerged in the least smart clothes she could find in her overnight bag.

On the big table was the biggest bacon sandwich she'd seen in years, and next to that was Freda Shackley, looking perky in a fleece-lined gilet and matching carnation slacks. When Rachel walked in she gave her a toothy smile.

'Hello, love!' she said. 'Ready to join the second shift of the day?'

'*Second* shift?' said Rachel. She glanced at the wall clock; it was only just past ten.

'Oh, yes, Ted's been round the park with me, and he's back in the café now. He likes to get a good lap in, first thing,' said Freda. 'Opens up his system, he says. Sends me back for round two, to get me out from under his feet!'

'What happened to those retirement plans?' asked Megan, highlighting something on her clipboard.

'He'll retire when he's dead, he says.' Freda sighed. 'Says Sunday's the best time to be open for fried breakfasts. Religion, DIY and a full English. Biggest Sunday sellers.'

'Ted and Freda have the Italian café in the high street,' explained Megan. 'With the black and white sunshade? Have done since when, Freda?'

'Since 1912. Shackley's served fry-ups through two World Wars.' Freda's plump mouth drooped sadly. 'Though some days I wonder how much longer, what with our Lynne in New Zealand and that new deli place opening up and me and Ted not getting any younger.'

'You'll see us all out,' said Megan. 'You just need a new doggie to keep you young.'

Rachel sensed another long-running conversation.

'There'll be no replacing our Pippin,' said Freda, decisively. 'It's not fair, with us being so old . . .'

'Get away with you. Rachel, that's for you?'

Rachel looked at the sandwich and felt her mouth water. 'For me?'

'Yeah! We make bacon sarnies for all the volunteer weekend walkers, it's part of the deal. Can't have you going out on an empty stomach.' Megan ticked her list, and dispensed some Bonios to the dogs. 'While you're eating that, let me give you a quick rundown of how it all works.'

Rachel hesitated. Normally she didn't eat bread – rather, she didn't let herself keep it in the house – but this smelled delicious. And after all, it wasn't like she'd be squeezing herself into any of Oliver's La Perla lingerie any time soon. Before she could stop herself, she'd picked it up and had taken a delicious, ketchup-oozing bite. Her tastebuds reeled in delight.

'You're OK with a couple of dogs, aren't you?' Megan went on. 'Gem's no bother, he doesn't need a lead, but he's training Tinker and Flash to walk to heel. They're just getting used to it, never been on a lead before. Came in from some woman in Rosehill, bit of a BYB, George reckons.'

'BYB?'

'Oh, sorry. Backyard breeder.'

Freda made a clucking noise, and looked up at Rachel, her kindly face wreathed in disapproval. 'Some of these poor mites that come in – never been for a walk in their lives. Barely even been out of the shed where they're kept, tied up like puppy machines. It makes me want to . . .'

'Freda, don't put Rachel off!' said Megan. She shot a glance at Rachel. 'We don't often get serious cases like that. These two aren't so bad, honestly. They're both Westies, George brought them over a few days ago. He sometimes gets a tip-off, about breeders wanting to offload dogs – not everyone who has dogs is a dog lover, sadly.'

'And he brings them here?' He's got a nerve, lecturing me about keeping an eye on the business side of things and not being a soft touch, she thought.

'Yeah, Dot always took them in. We love them, poor scared darlings. They just need a bit more TLC than your usual hand-in. Are you ready to go?'

Rachel realised she'd demolished the sandwich in about three bites. Until then, she'd had no idea just how hungry she was but now she thought about it, she hadn't had a full meal since . . . ten days ago. Since the quick supper she'd thrown together just before Oliver came round and set off the hideous train of events.

'There'll be more when you get back,' said Freda, arranging her *Dog World*, her mobile and the pot of tea next to her. 'Any emergencies, I'll call you. Have I got your number?'

She looked at Rachel, who started to say that her phone wasn't charged but Megan unplugged something from the wall and passed it over.

'I charged it up for you,' she said helpfully. 'Same one as mine. Coincidence, eh?'

Rachel turned it on, and immediately it bleeped with messages. Fifteen missed calls, ten texts. That was why she'd let it go flat. 'Um, thanks.'

'Off you go!' said Freda. 'Don't miss this lovely sunshine!'

Megan pressed some bits and pieces into Rachel's hands. 'Poobags, treats, whistle, lead, sweets for yourself.' She smiled. 'Welcome to the world of dog walking!'

Outside in the apple orchard, the air was crisp, and on the bare branches of the trees there were pale green buds, against a bright blue sky flooded with sunlight.

As Megan had predicted, Rachel did feel better for the fresh air filling her lungs, and though her legs initially protested, waddling along in Dot's spare wellington boots, she found keeping up with Megan's brisk pace pumped more than just blood round her body. It seemed to make her brain tick over, and for the first time in days one thought led to another instead of round and round in a constricting loop.

They were mainly thoughts about where she was putting her feet so as not to tread on the two nervous little white terriers, but it was a start.

Four Oaks sat at the top of the hill like a child's drawing of a house – a perfectly symmetrical box, with four big six-pane windows in white frames, two upstairs, two down, with a circular porthole above the red front door, and scribbles of climbing ivy all across the front. It had a panoramic view down towards Longhampton's modest spread of streets, and Rachel could see the Victorian town hall spire rising above the distant roofs as she and Megan headed out of the orchard onto the footpath.

Though the market town was quite busy, from what she remembered, the landscape quickly turned rural beyond the kennels: the lane running past the back gate went towards the town one way, and out into the thick woodlands the other, after which were fields of cows and the beginnings of some unassuming hills.

'We usually do this loop that goes through the wood, down to the town, around the park and back,' said Megan, setting off on a bridle-path hedged with rowan and gorse. She was steering four dogs on two double leads like a charioteer. 'If you want, I'll throw some balls while you have a quick run round, and do any shopping you need? Quite a few shops are open today.'

'Thanks.' Rachel looked down at her black Joseph trousers, now tucked into the boots for protection. 'I could do with getting some spare clothes. I didn't bring much that's up to dog walking.'

'I've got to warn you, the shops won't be what you're used to in London.' Megan smiled. 'Maybe you should ask George what sort you should get, since he's the one who seems so concerned about them?'

'I don't take fashion advice from a man who wears red trousers,' said Rachel, spurred into a better mood by the spring air. 'They've been illegal since 1938 in most parts of Britain.'

Megan giggled. 'I'll tell him that, shall I? It's about time he got a taste of his own medicine. Oi, Tinker! Out of there. Just pull him gently, Rachel.'

'His own medicine?' Rachel tugged Tinker out of a bush, terrified she was about to break him. 'Are you saying I'm as rude as he is?'

'No! I mean, sort of. Oh, George is terrible. I think it comes from living on his own.' Megan paused, waiting for Rachel to regain control of the terrier. 'But you should see Freda when he tells her how badly trained Pippin was. She goes all giggly.'

'That's probably because she's the only one old enough to remember the last time that rude charm thing worked,' said Rachel. 'Doesn't the fact that he lives on his own give him a clue?'

'Well, that's his choice. George isn't short of admirers, believe it or not,' said Megan. 'Some women round here love that rugged Daniel Craig the Vet look. And he owns that practice, so he's raking it in, with all the horses and farms round here. '

Rachel snorted in amusement. 'Daniel Craig! Is that what he thinks?'

'It's what everyone else thinks, especially since he turned up in a dinner jacket to Mrs Merryman's Christmas drinks. Rachel, this is the sticks. There isn't a whole lot of choice.' Megan stopped, put one hand on Rachel's arm, and widened her eyes in warning. 'Spend more than a year in Longhampton and you'll find yourself thinking Ted Shackley has a look of Paul Newman. Take it from me, you'd better start liking older men.'

Rachel laughed, and for a second, she almost forgot why that wasn't the least bit funny. When it did sting – that she always went for older men, stupidly thinking they were more reliable – the joke was still there, and she felt a sudden relief. Megan didn't know about Oliver. She didn't have to explain him, or omit him, or apologise for him, as she'd done for her friends in London, leaving herself with half a life at any one time.

Oliver was gone. She was starting again. In a weird way, it was like a weight lifting off her shoulders.

Rachel chewed her lip and grinned, and they set off down the hill.

The path sloped gently and Rachel worried for the Westies' little legs as they scampered on the uneven surface, but Gem seemed to keep them level, his calming presence stopping them from running too far ahead. It was sweet, she thought, watching the collie herd the two smaller dogs with instinctive care, as if they were  sheep.

'So, how long are you planning on staying?' asked Megan. 'Not prying, but at some stage we need to do a run to the supermarket.'

'I know,' said Rachel. 'There are bills. I think I'm supposed to pay them until probate's granted, then get the money back?' She started to run a nervous hand through her dark hair then realised there was a lead attached to her wrist, and that she'd nearly jerked a Westie off its surprised paws. 'Sorry, I'm a bit floored by all the forms and legal jargon. I don't know where to start, really.'

'Well, if you need any help, just ask,' said Megan. 'But in the meantime we need a top-up for kennel expenses and we're out of milk and bread too. And, this is kind of embarrassing, but I haven't been paid for last month and I'm a bit skint.'

Rachel stopped, embarrassed at her own self-absorption. 'I'm sorry, Megan. I'll call in at the bank and get some cash.'

I've probably got enough, she thought, making rough calculations. Somewhere between resigning from her job and learning that Dot's inheritance wasn't actually hers until this probate business was sorted out, Rachel hadn't given too much thought to how she was going to support herself. Saving wasn't really her thing; maintaining a 'happy to be unfettered and single' lifestyle to compensate for the complications of life with Oliver cost a considerable portion of her salary.

'Great! So how long do you reckon you'll be here? A month? A few months?' Megan made a clicking noise and the Staffie cross on her longest lead stepped back in line, by her leg. 'For ever?'

'I don't know,' said Rachel.

'I guess you've got your own flat in London, have you?' Megan's tone was conversational, not nosy, and so sincere that Rachel found herself responding honestly.

'No, actually, I don't have a flat. I've been renting, I've just handed the keys back. It was part of my job, you see, and I've just resigned. It's . . . complicated.'

Megan looked up, interested, and at the sight of her sympathetic face, the words tumbled out. Rachel hadn't been able to tell a soul any of this, not even her mother. Even her best friend, Ali, who'd warned her that exactly this would happen, over and over again from the comfort of her own marriage, had only had edited highlights.

'I've just split up with my boyfriend, about a fortnight ago. We . . .' Rachel hesitated, shaving off the less salubrious details to focus on the good, a PR force of habit. 'We'd been together a long time, we worked together in the same agency. Oliver was a partner, and I was the senior account director. My flat was above the office – I mean, I got a deal on the rent for being a keyholder – but when we broke up, I really needed to get away. Right away. I wanted to be somewhere Oliver wouldn't be able to find me. And then all this happened, and it felt like . . .'

'Oh my God.' Megan stopped walking and the dogs ran on, the leads extending. 'Was he violent?' She grabbed Rachel's hand, her face taut with concern. 'You can tell me, I won't tell anyone. But if he's looking for you, maybe we should tell Freda and everyone to be on guard? You should talk to the police station, they're so good here, it's not like London.'

It took a moment for Rachel to work out what Megan was saying, but when she did, her skin crawled. That hadn't been what she meant! She didn't want Oliver to find her because he'd be incandescent about the deliberate chaos she'd caused when she'd left, but also because one word from him, and she was scared she'd fall back into his arms like the sucker she'd been for so long.

'No, no, he wasn't like that,' she said. 'He was . . .' She stopped, searching for the right words.

But the trouble was, thought Rachel bitterly, you could only shave off so much inconvenient detail. Oliver Wrigley was her boyfriend, but he didn't belong to her. He wasn't, technically, hers to lose.

Oliver was married, to Mrs Kath Wrigley, and had been since 1989.

Rachel wasn't proud of being a mistress, but she had truly loved Oliver. OK, to begin with she'd taken his stories about Kath's lack of interest, and their outgrown shell of a marriage, held up by mortgages and school fees, with a pinch of salt, but there was a spark between them that she couldn't resist, and he swore he only felt alive when they were together. She'd insisted to Ali – the one friend she trusted with the details – that theirs was a genuine love affair, an arrangement that gave her freedom, and spared her the guilt of tearing a father from his family. She'd insisted that Oliver honestly loved her, and Ali had nodded, and said nothing, which was about as much as Rachel could have asked.

For a long time, it had been exactly what she wanted. Oliver and Rachel understood each other, they had steamy, spine-tingling nights together, and he never got under her feet on a Sunday or saw her hungover. Gradually, Rachel had stopped listening to the voice reminding her it was wrong. She'd never asked him to leave Kath, for fear of hearing the answer she already knew, and for years it had been fine. Until she hadn't been able to ignore what was in front of her.

Ali had told her it would end like this, two months after it began. Oliver was always going to go back to Kath. Tedious conversation and split ends notwithstanding, she was his wife. And now, of course, Rachel's real punishment was keeping her heartbreak secret, just like she'd tucked her affair to her chest.

'What happened?'

Megan was looking at her, a hundred domestic violence soap stories written across her face, and Rachel longed, wearily, for a few words of comfort. It was tempting. Her aching heart cried out for some sympathy. Yes she was a home-wrecking bitch, but one who'd only succeeded in wrecking her own home. Rachel's resolve slipped, just a fraction.

'I found out he was seeing someone else,' she admitted.

Which was true: Oliver had been seeing his own wife, but lying to her about it. You didn't take your wife for a dirty weekend in Paris while telling your mistress you were at a conference in Glasgow. Rachel had enough self-awareness to see the gallows humour in that.

'How did you find out?'

'A receipt. Well, receipts plural. He emptied out his wallet on my desk and . . .' Rachel gritted her back teeth, flinching inside at the memory. 'Oliver always shredded, made me shred too. And I found one for a hotel in Paris. He'd had a lot of room service, put it like that.'

The final straw had come on a bad day, a Sunday. Rachel had been feeling unsettled, wound up with PMT, conscious of a new crepiness in her cleavage that hadn't been there before, fed up because lonely Sundays were increasingly difficult to enjoy. It was a delicate, expensive balance, celebrating her independence and child-free existence hard enough not to see the other side. At first, Oliver's unexpected arrival at her door had been a real thrill – a sign that maybe he had more time for her.

Rachel's breath stuck in her throat. It wasn't. That bastard Oliver had said *nothing*. Just that he was sorry. Then *nothing* again. Nothing. Ten years of her life, ten years she'd given up to him, while he'd given nothing at all. And the expression on his face when she confronted him had shown her everything she'd tried to ignore. He'd almost looked sorry for her.

That's why she'd sent the keys of the flat back to Kath. With a note, telling her that if Oliver wanted his stuff, his spare clothes, his jeans that he was really too old to wear, his shirts that Rachel sent to the dry cleaners because ironing was his wife's job – either of them were welcome to come and get them.

'Oh God,' she moaned under her breath. She couldn't go back. Now the numbness was wearing off, the first licks of guilt about what she'd done to unsuspecting, golf-playing Kath were beginning to scorch her.

Megan took her arm, mistaking her moan for something else. 'Rachel, I'm so sorry,' she said. 'After all this with Dot too – you've been through the wars! I thought there was something up. My mum was just the same when my dad walked out, all zombie like. Slept for days, only talked to the dogs.'

'Can we talk about something else?' asked Rachel, trying to sound in control of herself. 'It's ... it's just ... not that interesting.'

'Sure!' Megan clicked her tongue at Gem and they set off again. The cheery yellow arrows directing them around Longhampton's Historic Canal Trail appeared at the edge of a wooded area, the wilder beginnings of Longhampton's municipal park scheme. They passed one or two other dog walkers, who smiled at them both in a comradely fashion, while the dogs sniffed each other's bottoms. 'What do you want to talk about? The kennels?'

'OK,' said Rachel. She'd have to talk about them sooner or later. 'Tell me about the dogs.'

Megan's animated explanation of the kennels' daily routine took them out of the woods and round the main town centre park, where old people sat in pairs on benches and straight regiments of daffodils lined up in the flower beds.

Rachel tried not to see the old couples. That was the thing about London; you rarely saw old couples together. Here they were like bookends, still holding hands at eighty, or however old they were.

'. . . the bank? Rachel, are you listening? Do you want to go to the bank?'

Rachel dragged her attention back to where Megan was limbering up with a scary-looking ball-chucking device. It looked like a giant plastic tongue.

'I can do some training with these guys if you want half an hour to run round?' she went on. 'There's only two main streets – try the side streets by the town hall for your trousers, there's one or two new boutiques opened?' She held out a hand for the two leads Rachel was holding. 'Gem, sit here and wait.'

Gem looked up at Rachel, and then dropped obediently into a sit by Megan's side.

'You tell him to wait,' she said. 'It'll help you bond.'

'Why would he take any notice of me?' asked Rachel. 'He didn't read the will, he doesn't know he's my dog. I've done nothing with him since I arrived. He just mopes around the place.'

Megan's face softened. 'Gem's grieving, Rachel. He lost the only owner he's ever known, and he's not a young dog, you know. He's seven, so he's like . . . fifty-something. He was with her when she died – came haring back here to tell me, just like Lassie. Poor soul.'

Rachel felt sad, and self-conscious. 'I'm not the right person to replace Dot.'

'All dogs ask for is a walk, and a pat,' insisted Megan. 'And the sound of your voice. Go on. Tell him to stay.'

Rachel looked awkwardly at Gem, who pricked up his feathery ears and wagged his tail along the ground, nearly knocking over Tinker the Westie.

'Stay,' said Rachel in a feeble tone.

'And point to where you want him to be.'

Rachel pointed to Megan's feet. 'Stay there.'

Gem wagged his tail harder, then dropped down with his head on his paws, still looking up at her, waiting for her smile.

He looked so grateful for the attention. So keen to please her. Something flickered in Rachel's numb heart. He wanted *her* attention. *Her* approval. He wanted to be owned and loved.

The other dogs scampered around, clearly thrilled to be out of their concrete runs and on the fresh grass, and Rachel made a decision; if she did one thing today, she was going to start the rehoming drive George had gone on about. It wasn't just about money – these sad dogs needed people to love them. She couldn't cope with the guilt if it was her inertia trapping them in the kennels.

Then maybe she could sell the house and kennels with a clean conscience. Dot couldn't ask much more than that.

'Good boy!' she said to Gem. 'Good boy.'

'Great! Good boy! And good girl!' Megan added, and tapped her watch. 'We'll have you doing agility in no time! See you back here at eleven? OK. Go!'

She hurled the first chewed-up tennis ball into the green space, and Rachel wasn't sure if she was talking to her, or to the dogs who hurtled off after it.

# 6

While the boys were getting their Monday morning school things from their room, and safely out of earshot, Zoe swallowed a mouthful of scalding coffee to make her voice sound croaky, and dialled the salon number from the phone in the kitchen. She didn't want them hearing the outrageous but totally necessary lie she was about to tell Hannah, the reception manager.

As it rang, Zoe kept one eye on the makeshift pen of cardboard boxes where Toffee was taking only his second nap in thirty-six exhausting, nerve-shredding hours.

At least, she hoped he was taking a nap. He could just as easily be shutting his eyes while trying to decide which bit of her house to destroy next. It was hard to say who was more excited – Toffee, or Leo and Spencer. Between them, they made an exhausting whirlwind of destruction. The sitting room looked as if someone had attacked it with a wrecking ball, and there were flakes of kitchen roll everywhere from the numerous 'accidents' she'd mopped up since Toffee had arrived.

Who knew a small puppy could hold so much wee?

'Hey, Hannah!' she said, when she heard herself being clicked onto speaker phone. 'It's Zoe, I don't think I'm going to be able to come in today. I've had a terrible weekend. Haven't slept a wink for two nights . . .'

Toffee began wriggling in his box, opened one eye and let out a happy squeal of delight to see Zoe. Her heart sank as he clamped his jaws around the edge of the cardboard box.

'You sound really bad, Zoe,' said Hannah. The salon was already rattling with early cleaning, the radio blaring in the background. 'Do you want me to rearrange your clients for today?'

'Would you? I'm sure it's just a bug, but I didn't want to spread it round,' said Zoe, reaching for the biscuit barrel, keeping one eye on the box and one ear on the racket upstairs. The boys were racing through their toothbrushing in record time, to get back to winding up Toffee. 'Listen, I'll let you know how I am in the morning, cheers.' She rang off, with Hannah's bewildered get well wishes still hovering in the air.

She caught sight of her guilty face in her clean oven door and felt terrible.

Zoe hadn't taken a sick day in years, and dragged herself into the salon through marital breakdowns, sleepless teething nights and snow. They owe me a few days' sick, she told herself, though the guilt didn't ease up. Neither did the bone-weariness spreading throughout her body. She was used to teething and nightmares but not night-long howling.

Zoe leaned out into the hall. 'Spencer! What are you doing up there? Come on, we're going to be late!'

As she raised her voice, Toffee began squealing in earnest again – a familiar sound that now went through Zoe like a knife.

She looked at him and Toffee made a whimpering noise.

Zoe knew what that meant and, abandoning the idea of putting bread in the toaster for herself, she grabbed the puppy, took four massive strides across the kitchen and held him out of the back door. Even then, she still ended up with most of the hot dribble on herself. She put him down and went to rinse her hands for the millionth time.

'Good boy,' she said firmly as Toffee sniffed around the back step. 'Good wee.'

That was something she'd learned in the ten minutes she'd grabbed to look up house training on the internet. Take them out every hour, praise them when they went where you wanted, introduce a non-embarrassing phrase they could associate with going to the loo. So far, Toffee would learn to 'toilet himself' every time someone yelled, 'Oh, for God's sake, not there!'

Zoe and Toffee regarded each other with mutual suspicion. 'Where am I going to leave you while I go to the shops to get all the stuff your stupid daddy didn't bring with you?' she demanded. How long could you leave a puppy for, anyway?

A thundering down the stairs indicated that the boys were on their way. Zoe could hear Leo yelling 'Toffee! Toffee!' which set the puppy off yelping in pure joy. She picked him up so he wouldn't run under their feet.

'We're going to have to get you to a training class,' she said to his perfect wet nose. 'And possibly your brothers as well. I reckon they need a bit of training too.'

She stopped as Leo and Spencer barrelled into the kitchen, all tousled morning hair and toothpaste breath. In Leo's case, most of the toothpaste was still round his mouth but at least it showed he'd tried.

'Tofffeeee!' squealed Spencer, making a grab for the dog and lifting him so his back legs dangled precariously, leaving the plump tummy exposed. 'Can we take him to school with us, Mum? Please? Please?'

'Yeah!' Leo jumped up, trying to touch Toffee too, but Spencer lifted him out of his brother's reach so only the wagging tail bounced in his face. 'I want to show Mrs Barratt!'

'You can't take Toffee to school,' said Zoe, reaching out to support Toffee's dangling back end. He didn't seem to mind, being busy covering Spencer's scrunched-up face in adoring licks. 'Hold his legs, Spencer, or else you'll hurt him! He'll be here when you get home.'

'Oh, pleeeease!' Spencer dragged his attention from the puppy and gave her an unsettling clear-eyed stare that reminded her of David at his most motivated. 'Dad said it would be cool to show our class. We could do a talk on puppies.'

'I suppose you'd be telling them all about the cleaning up and the feeding and so on?'

'Yeah,' said Spencer. '*Obviously*.'

Zoe was horrified at the new tone in his voice. It was cheeky, almost defiant. He'd always been the sweetest-tempered little boy, even with the baby brother who'd halved his attention time, but lately, since they'd been going off with David for weekends, there was a sharpness creeping into Spencer, as if he was testing her to see how far she'd let him go.

'Hey!' she said. 'That's enough of that. There's a lot more to having a dog than just playing with him. Do you know how big he's going to get? And how much walking he's going to need every day? Did Dad tell you about that?'

'I heard him crying last night,' said Leo. 'I think he should sleep with me.'

'He's lonely,' said Spencer, the dog expert. 'He misses his mum. Maybe we should get another one?' he added, as if he'd just thought of it. 'To keep him company?'

'Yeah!' said Leo. 'Two puppies! Toffee and . . . Fudge!'

'No!' Zoe put her hands on her hips. It made her look more in charge even when she didn't feel it. She could still smell puppy wee on her shoes. 'I haven't even said we're definitely going to be able to keep Toffee. This is . . .' Oh, God. She was such a pushover. '. . . just a trial.'

'But Mum!' The wheedling started at once, and Zoe felt herself caving in at the sight of Spencer and Leo's pleading faces, not to mention Toffee's chocolate-button eyes gazing up at her, his soft ears flopping onto his face. The dutiful, playful Labrador companion of a million kids' books.

Two boys and an Andrex puppy versus one harassed, guilty mother – it was hardly a fair fight.

Zoe struggled to get a grip. What about all the great reasons you had for not getting Spencer a puppy in the first place, demanded a voice in her head. What happened to them? The time? The mess? The fact that you have a full-time job?

As if he could read her mind – which he probably could – Spencer piped up, his attitude transformed from proto-teen to angelic boy-dog-owner. 'I'll look after him all evening,' Spencer begged. 'I'll clean his box and everything. Please, Mum! Please!'

The alarm Zoe set each morning to get them to school on time went off and she sprang into action.

'We have to go,' said Zoe, panicking that she'd be the last mum at the school gates *again*. Toffee would just have to stay in the kitchen with the door closed for an hour. How much damage could he do? All the plugs were still child-proofed. 'Put Toffee in the box, please, Leo, no, don't pick him up again. He needs to have a sleep after his breakfast. Shoes on? Coats on. Have you got your trainers for PE, Spencer?'

Spencer went to get his bag, but Leo was still leaning into the box, kissing the dog, and mumbling something into its double-velvet ear.

'Leo, come on.' Zoe hunted for her keys. 'We're already late.'

'I'm so happy, Mummy,' he said.

'Why, darling?'

'Because we've got a dog!' Leo looked up, his round face cherubic with delight. 'Dad said you'd make us send it back, but you haven't and I'm really excited! You'll let him stay, won't you?'

Oh God, thought Zoe. Even Leo knows what a pushover I am. And he's not even six.

\*     \*     \*

Zoe dropped the boys off at the school gate and raced – slumped in her seat while she drove past the Angel Hair and Heavenly Beauty salon – to the massive pet store on the industrial estate, her mind filling with visions of what Toffee might be destroying next. She was already one pair of FitFlops and a remote control down.

She pulled into the first parking space and tried David's mobile for the tenth time since the boys' return, but he wasn't answering. It didn't surprise her; David had got quite selective of late about which calls he decided to pick up, and which he ignored because he was 'in a meeting'. He'd always been like that, but now she was beginning to think he'd actually changed his phone.

Zoe sank back and felt her stomach jangle with the first tremors of panic. Time was ticking away. What was she meant to do? Who could she ask for help? None of her friends had dogs, and anyway, this wasn't *about* dogs, this was about her and David and the boys.

Zoe made herself take three deep breaths to stop the hysteria that swamped her chest, threatening to close up her throat. It came and went more and more frequently now, as David's desertion stopped feeling like some midlife crisis phase he'd wake up from, and hardened into stark reality, and it was getting harder to hide it from the boys. But she had to hide it. She had to look like she was coping as well as she'd done in the past.

She pulled down her sun visor and stared at herself in the vanity mirror, as if she were looking at a friend. 'Just get what you need for now,' she told her half-crazed reflection. 'Just enough to keep Toffee in one place, and happy. Then you can call David, tell him it's too much for you to cope with, and . . .'

She didn't finish. I've got to stop talking to myself, she thought. The wide-set brown eyes in the mirror lost their mad expression, and stared back at her with something approaching sympathy. She and her reflection both knew there wasn't going to be an 'and'.

The boys wanted the dog. It was unfair to uproot a puppy again. If she made David take it back, she'd look like Cruella de Vil. She'd just have to make the best of it.

The first thing Zoe spotted when she pushed her trolley through the doors was a magazine with a 'foolproof guide to Welcoming Your New Puppy' – and, falling on the first useful piece of information she'd had since Toffee arrived, she set off round the store with it propped open, throwing in whatever it told her to: a collar and lead, puppy food, a basket, a cushion for the basket, a crate for toilet training, chews, toys, cute snuggly things to stop Toffee feeling so lonely at night.

Fifteen minutes later, she was at the till, watching in awe at the amount a puppy cost, before you even took it to the vet's. This makes the kids look like a bargain, she thought, wondering if she'd really needed the puppy sleeping bag after all. She realised with a sinking heart that she'd have to call David anyway, for more money to pay for it. *If* she could get hold of him.

Zoe made herself remember how heartbreaking Toffee had been when she'd woken up in the watery morning light to find him nuzzled into the crook of her shoulder, his hot breath huffing into her ear and one paw pressed against her chest, as if she was his lost mum. They were both on the sofa, after his pitiful crying had dragged her downstairs. He was so vulnerable and soft, she'd forgiven him the puddle on the carpet.

He *was* adorable, she thought, stuffing the receipt into her bag without looking at it and pushing the trolley towards the exit. And how hard could it be to train a Labrador? They worked as guide dogs and turned off kettles for deaf people, didn't they? It was just going to take some organisation.

The alarm on Zoe's phone went off. The hour was almost up.

'Ah! New puppy?' asked the Australian girl standing by the noticeboards, five or six dogs clustered around her feet. They weren't playing up, despite being surrounded by treats and food.

Zoe stared at her pile of stuff. 'Actually, it's a hamster. With ambitions.'

The girl laughed, and the tall woman she was with finished sticking pins in her notice. It featured a photograph of a red-and-white Basset hound wearing a tragic expression on its wrinkly, hound-dog face. It *would* have been tragic, had it not also been wearing a Santa hat.

'*Is there room in your fridge for me?*' read Zoe, unable to resist. 'Aw! Shouldn't that be "isn't there room by your fireside"?'

'No, Bertie's priority is the fridge. Whoever his new mum and dad are, they're going to need to get a lock on it.' The Australian girl smiled. 'But I bet you could train him to do just about anything with half a bag of sausage – he's not stupid at all! They're the sweetest dogs, Bassets, brilliant with kids, really calm . . . I don't suppose your puppy needs a friend?'

Zoe laughed, and it came out rather manic. 'No! I've only had this one a day and already he's running rings around me.'

'Lovely! What is he? How old?' She sounded genuinely interested.

'Toffee's an Andrex puppy. I don't know exactly how old, actually,' Zoe confessed, 'he was a present.'

The two women glanced at each other, and Zoe thought the blonde girl's forehead flickered with exasperation.

She glanced at the poster's logo again, and realised that they must be from the rescue centre up on the Rosehill road – either Rachel or Megan, going by the phone numbers. The phrase 'Dogs deserve a future – don't give them as a present' was actually printed on the bottom of the page.

'No!' she said hastily. 'No, *I* didn't get him as a present, my husband . . . my ex gave him to the kids. I had no idea, I mean, now Toffee's here we absolutely adore him, I just wasn't quite prepared for not being able to leave the house for more than ten minutes.'

Zoe's voice trailed off. This wasn't making her look any better. Now she'd started reading, she couldn't take her eyes off the poster. *My first owners bought me as a Christmas present, but soon got bored of me and threw me out to look after myself,* she read. *I've got lots of love to give, in return for walks, food and the best sofa in the house, so I'm crossing my paws that you might have room for a little one. OK, quite a big one. Love, Bertie.*

'I'm going to take good care of him,' she heard herself say. 'That's why I'm here, buying up half the shop!'

'Of course you are,' said the dark-haired woman. She seemed quite brisk, and she had a folder full of notices ready to stick up. 'Megan just sees a lot of Christmas puppies around this time of year! I'm sure you're not going to be adding to our numbers. I mean,' she added, 'we're on a bit of a drive to rehome what we've already got. So we can make room for some paying customers in our boarding kennels. Aren't we, Megan?'

'Totally.' Megan sighed, and gave Zoe a friendly but firm look. 'The thing is, it's not the stuff so much as the constant attention, with a puppy. Has he been vaccinated? Have you got a number to ring the breeder, so she can tell you how old he is, and if he's had the right jabs?'

'Um . . . jabs?'

Megan looked worried. 'Toffee's not on his own right now, is he?'

'Um . . . yes?' Zoe glanced between them, registering Megan's disapproval and Rachel's amazing trendy bag. 'He's in the kitchen, it's totally baby-proof, I mean, I'm a single mum, I've had to leave him to get all this stuff, but what are you supposed to do with dogs? Get a babysitter?'

'Yes,' said Megan.

'You're joking, right?' Zoe asked hopefully.

'Would you leave your baby on his own while you went to the shops? Do you know how sharp his teeth are? They can chew through doors, cables . . .'

The reality of what David had landed on her began to sink in and Zoe felt the old panic rise up her, like an over-filling bath. 'Oh God,' she said.

'Look, she's got a crate,' Rachel pointed out. 'And a puppy book. And chewy stuff. Come on, Megan. Be positive. It's not like she's left him to play with matches.'

'Do you do training classes?' Zoe asked in a small voice. 'For owners?'

Megan's stern expression lightened. 'Yeah. We do, actually. Come up on Saturday and we'll talk you through the basics. I can give you the name of a vet too, get Toffee registered.' She scrabbled in her bag for a pen. 'Give us a leaflet, Rachel? George Fenwick, the clinic down by the fire station. Toffee's going to need shots and a microchip.'

'And if you want to come and do some volunteer walking, or help us with some fundraising, that would be great!' said Rachel, segueing effortlessly into sales patter. 'We're always looking for helpers. And donations. And if you need to board him for a few days, we have top-quality facilities.'

Zoe took the leaflet and tucked it into her trolley of supplies. She had a feeling she'd be sticking it on the fridge, right next to the phone.

'I think that went well,' said Megan, nudging her dogs back onto the bridle-path behind the industrial estate. 'That's the supermarkets, the precinct, and both pet shops. Just one more stop and we're done. And those are the highlights of Longhampton, as I'm sure you've realised!'

'So long as we're reaching every single possible new owner,' said Rachel. Her dogs weren't quite as well controlled, although Gem was doing his best to herd the smaller dogs into line for her. 'What did George say? You need to shunt ten non-paying dogs out and get ten dogs in before the end of the month, so he can get his bill paid?'

George's advice had been blunt, but free, and delivered over a pot of tea in Dot's kitchen. It had also revealed to Rachel that she wasn't the only one with dire cash-flow problems: Dot's money had run out, and so had the kennels'. Even if Rachel wanted to sell up, it would take a while to sort out the legalities, and in the meantime, the dogs needed feeding and suppliers, George in particular, needed paying.

He'd looked at her over the table with a sort of challenge in his blue eyes, as if he half-expected her to write a cheque and flounce away from the problem. Rachel hadn't told him that she didn't have any choice in the matter; with no job and no old life, it wasn't a matter of 'honouring Dot's legacy' – this *was* her job now. Until she sorted something else out.

'That's about the size of it. He speaks his mind, George.' Megan flicked through the clear plastic envelope of posters. 'Ah, we've saved the best for last – Chester. Look at that sad face! People'll be sobbing all over the surgery. I love these posters, by the way. You've really got a way with words.'

Rachel didn't tell Megan she'd spent the last six months working on a million-pound PR campaign for a new music download website; already that seemed like a different life. Instead, she allowed herself a wonky smile, and said, 'Thanks. To be honest, they made me cry a bit. Which I guess means they're working.'

The posters, made on the kitchen table the previous night, weren't flashy, but they were effective: handwritten 'wanted:

new owner' headlines, with Polaroids of the dogs, and pleas from them, partly nicked from Dot's tags. Rachel had used every shameless PR trick she could think of to pluck at Longhampton's heartstrings.

'And you're going to do us a website?' Megan went on, excited.

'I can't believe you don't have one already,' said Rachel. 'I can find someone who'll do that very cheap. It'll help with the boarding too.'

'You know, you're amazing, especially considering you've just come out of a bad relationship breakdown,' started Megan, but Rachel stopped her, embarrassed.

'Look, I really haven't done anything yet. Where next?' she asked, letting Gem off the lead so she could throw a ball for him, as a reward for his good behaviour.

'The surgery,' said Megan. 'I've put posters in there before – we have a cake stall in the foyer, once a month. And Dr Carthy, who's in charge, he's a big dog lover. Used to tell Dot that whenever an old racing greyhound came in, she was to call him. He's got two now. Used to have six. One used to sleep in a corner of his consulting room!'

'Wow,' said Rachel. Gem dropped the ball at her feet, pausing to pant at her, and she hurled it away again.

Her right arm was getting sore but, masochistically, she didn't mind. The look on Gem's face, just as eager every time, made up for it. Rachel couldn't communicate with Gem like Dot probably had, but this was a tiny way of offering something to their very unequal relationship, a small return for the patient nights he'd spent already, waiting by the door, listening to her broken sleep and making her feel a little less alone in the strange new life she'd found herself in.

Longhampton Park Surgery was a modern building with ramps and big windows and neat concrete boxes of red geraniums on every available flat surface. As Megan and Rachel approached, they saw a lanky girl in a white receptionist's uniform helping a wheelchair-bound lady down the ramp, bending over her like a mother hen.

Or a mother heron, Rachel corrected herself. She was all long arms and tanned legs.

'Oh, look at the lovely dogs!' the girl said cheerily, pushing back a long blonde ponytail. 'You had one of those Jack Russells, didn't you, Ida?'

'Till I moved into the home, I did.' The old lady stretched out her hand towards Bonham, the short-legged terrier who'd been dragging Rachel all round the park. He shied back, tucking his tail downwards. 'Hello, chap.'

Rachel felt awkward, as if he was a child showing her up in a supermarket. 'Bonham,' she said, 'don't be rude. I'm sorry, he's a bit grumpy.'

'Oh, he's fine, he just needs to have a sniff,' said the old lady, leaving her crooked fingers dangling, and sure enough Bonham began to edge forward, approaching her chair with tiny steps, until he was near enough for her to scratch behind the ears. 'There. Good lad.'

Rachel felt a lump in her throat at the way the lady's hunched shoulders seemed to relax at Bonham's wagging tail. Stop it, she told herself. It'll be a poobag belt next.

'He never does that for me,' she admitted.

'It's a knack,' said the old lady happily. 'Isn't it, Bonham lad?'

'Do you want to keep him?' Rachel joked. 'He's going spare.'

The sadness in the sigh was audible. 'Oh, I wish.'

'You know, Megan,' said the receptionist – Lauren, according to the badge on her chest, 'you should start bringing your doggies in for our oldies to play with. They'd really cheer up the Evergreens, wouldn't they, Ida?'

'Ah!' Megan reached into her bag and pulled out a poster. 'Funny you should mention that. We're on a dog mission as it happens.'

'Hang on,' said Lauren as a Ford Fiesta drew up next to the ramp. 'Here's your lift, Ida. Let's just get Mrs Harris here into her car. Ida, you're going to have to say goodbye to Bonham, sorry.' With a neat movement, she rolled the old lady down to her waiting lift, and helped the carer unload her, keeping up a stream of reassuring chat. Rachel had to resist the temptation to pop the Jack Russell into the back seat with Ida – Bonham himself seemed perfectly happy about stowing away.

'Lauren runs the surgery,' Megan whispered under her breath. 'She knows everything that's going on round here. She's the one who sells our cakes and does the book stall.'

'Does she want a dog?' Rachel whispered.

'Lauren!' A young man stretched his head out of the surgery doors, keeping his body inside in the warm. From the stethoscope round his neck, Rachel assumed he was a doctor, and from the dishevelled look of his brown curls and his anxious expression, she guessed there was a problem with something. 'Lauren, can you come and sort out the computer?'

Lauren straightened up and rolled her eyes at Rachel and Megan. 'You'd think doctors would be able to manage a simple computer, wouldn't you? But no! Just getting Mrs Harris away!' she called over the car.

'That's Dr Harper,' Megan whispered. 'You know I said you had to start fancying older men round here? Well, he's the exception. I mean, he's older for me, but not for you, I guess.' She went pink. 'Sorry, that came out ruder than I meant.'

'Don't worry,' Rachel started to whisper, then shook herself. 'Don't worry,' she said in a normal voice. 'I prefer older men, anyway. Ted's the one for me.'

'Right now, how can I help you two lovely ladies?' Lauren said, marching back towards them, ponytail swinging. 'And you lovely puppies?' she added, bending down to scratch some ears.

'We're on a rehoming drive,' said Rachel. 'Trying to find new owners for these dogs, and about five more just like them back at the kennels. Hello. I'm Rachel.' She jiggled back the four leads around her wrist and offered her hand. 'I'm Dot Mossop's niece.'

'Of course you are – I could tell that at once from your nose,' said Lauren. She shook Rachel's hand and smiled broadly. 'You're the spit of your auntie. I mean, we always said when she was younger she must have been a looker. Not in a traditional way, mind, but striking, you know. Sorry, that came out wrong, I didn't mean . . .'

Rachel wondered if she'd spent too long surrounded by PRs, or whether everyone in Longhampton was just incredibly tactless.

'Lauren!' The doctor at the door was pleading now. 'There are four people waiting at reception and I can't get into the appointment booking screen!' He dropped his voice. 'And I don't know who two of them *are*. I need your expertise.'

Lauren rolled her huge eyes. 'Now, here's a prime candidate for a new dog . . . Follow me, ladies. Dr Harper!' She strode inside, her long legs covering the ground in seconds. 'Weren't you saying to me the other day that we ought to be encouraging people to do more exercise?'

'Er, yes?' Bill glanced between Megan and Lauren, and winked at Megan. 'Hello, Megan. Nice to see you.'

Megan gave him a shy smile. Not, Rachel noticed, her usual hundred-watt Bondi beam. She looked away and busied herself keeping their small gaggle of dogs out of the way of the automatic doors.

'Well, look.' Lauren turned and pointed to Rachel. 'Rachel here's hoping to find some new homes for Dot's rescue dogs and weren't you saying just the other day that you were thinking of adopting one? To get you jogging again?'

'I'm a very busy man, as you know, Lauren,' Bill began but Lauren was having none of it.

'Come on, your social life doesn't take up that much time! You could bring it to work – you know Dr Carthy wouldn't mind – and then walk it at lunch, and set a great example about getting out and about. In fact, we could run some kind of lunchtime club – I know I'd come out with you.'

'Lauren . . .' Bill's handsome face took on an air of desperation, as if he'd tried and failed to stop Lauren in full flow before now.

'Let me give you a poster to put up,' said Rachel, seizing the moment and handing him her last poster. It had a photograph of Chester, an adorable springer spaniel with long brown ears and speckly legs.

'Aw! "I'm Chester",' read Lauren, to the small audience now gathering around them in the foyer. '"My owners moved to a flat that didn't have room for me, and so they left me behind on the street, tied to their old skip. I don't know where they've gone but I hope there will be someone else out there who wants some unconditional love. I'm happy to take you for walks, help you throw a ball and warm up your knee if you let me on the sofa at night. Please call Megan or Rachel and they'll tell you all about me."'

She looked up at Rachel in horror. 'They tied him to their *skip*?'

'Apparently.'

Lauren's wide mouth gaped. 'That's appalling.' She turned to the doctor, with renewed passion. 'He'd be *perfect* for you, Dr Harper. I can just see you now, striding across the park, with your long scarf on, and your faithful dog Chester, bouncing along by your side.' She paused, then continued, 'It's a great way of meeting people too, you know. You're always reading about how people met the love of their life when their dogs had a scrap in the park. Not that you need any help in *that* department,' she added, knowingly.

'You'll have to excuse Lauren,' apologised Bill. 'She watches a lot of Hugh Grant films.'

'Why watch films when you can watch what goes on in here, is what I say!' Lauren neatly snatched the poster off him. 'I'll put it up here, where everyone will see it. Next to the Walk for Life one.' She marched over to the Community Notices, unpinned some old posters and put Chester right at the centre of the board, directing all the yellow arrows towards him.

'Right. Great. Now can you *please* sort out the computer?' pleaded Bill, running his hands through his hair.

'Absolutely!' Lauren swerved around the table of magazines, and the stray toddlers in the waiting area, then slid behind the reception desk. 'Oh, you've gone into the wrong screen – you've re-ordered all the cleaning supplies.'

Bill opened his mouth to protest, but then raised his hands at Rachel. 'What can I say? I won't hear the end of it, but yes, I have been thinking about adopting a dog.'

'Wonderful! So, shall we see you up at the kennels?' asked Rachel, feeling more like her old professional, deal-closing self, and less like an inept amateur dog walker. 'I mean, if you're serious about getting a rescue? You can always come and have a chat. We don't bite.'

'None of our dogs do,' added Megan, in a squeakier version of her usual voice.

'It's his half day tomorrow,' Lauren called out from behind the desk. 'Sorry, Dr Harper, but you know what you're like. You need someone to get you organised.'

He turned round to roll his eyes at her, and Lauren raised her hands like a pair of puppy paws and looked sad. 'Poor baby Chester. He could be behind the desk with me,' she said. 'Guarding my biscuits. I need something to stop that Diane pinching them.'

There was a distant grunt of outrage from the dispensary.

'I'll give you a ring and arrange an appointment.' He held out a hand to shake Rachel's and she enjoyed the momentary sensation of his strong, dry clasp and direct eye contact. She recognised his handsomeness, but there was no tingle inside her, though. Just a note that no one wore nice shirts like Oliver's round here. 'Now, I'm sorry to dash off, but there are two as yet unidentified patients waiting for me.'

'Bye!' said Megan breathily.

Rachel nodded and smiled at him. 'See you soon.'

The dogs were fidgeting in the foyer, bickering under their breath like bored children – apart from Gem, who was waiting in his usual position, long nose on his white paws. 'Let's get you lot home,' she said. 'Come on, Megan.'

'I'll make sure I point out your poster,' added Lauren, giving them a sunny smile. Her fingers were clattering away efficiently on the keys as she spoke. 'We're very good at raising volunteers in this surgery. Captive audience.'

She winked, and as Rachel stepped out towards the automatic doors, the sun came out and made the golden daffodils glow in their grey flowerbeds.

# 7

Natalie was doing three things at once, something she'd got very good at since she'd been promoted to head of her team, and something she felt should stand her in good stead for motherhood.

She was simultaneously repairing her make-up in the space-age loos of GreenPea's fifth floor conference suite, and rehearsing the observations she was going to make to Selina about the pitches she'd just heard for the new all-organic cookie campaign, while keeping one eye on her mobile phone which was propped in her handbag, in case the last advertising team called back with the projected market share figures she'd asked for.

Natalie knew taking her phone into the loos was a shocking habit but everyone in marketing did it. They were all too scared to miss a call right now. Rumours were going round the kitchen – via Andrea, the office manager, who had ears like radar and a desk near the boss – that head office was 'restructuring', and Natalie was smart enough to know what that meant: redundancies.

She swiped her lip-gloss and checked her teeth for smears. Her team was good, and had been mentioned in the last three meetings, but it still wasn't safe, Natalie knew that. She handled most of the own-brand organic range GreenPea was developing, but in the last year, GreenPea had bought out a smaller company who came with a red-hot marketing director who'd worked with WholeFoods in the US. And from what

Natalie had heard from Andrea, Jason didn't intend to stay on the second floor for long.

Make-up done, Natalie turned to her fourth bit of multi-tasking. She took a quick look around the cubicles and, checking she was alone, slipped into the one furthest from the door and rummaged in her bag for an ovulation stick.

Trying to get pregnant robbed you of any Victorian modesty when it came to bodily functions. These days she spent more time pondering her various bodily fluids than any sane human being ought to. Natalie ripped off the plastic packaging and prepared to aim for the white test area, wondering at what point in the fertility obstacle course she'd lost the last bit of dignity.

She recapped the test, sat back and waited for the lines to appear in the tiny window. Natalie didn't really need to do the ovulation test – she knew from her obsessive temperature taking when the egg was about to drop, as Johnny put it – but secretly she liked seeing the double lines forming. You always got two lines on an ovulation test, unlike the pregnancy ones. Natalie had never seen two magic lines appear on a pregnancy test.

Well, apart from once. One Sunday morning, the third month after she and Johnny started trying, she'd sneaked out of bed, weed on a stick even though it was far, far too early to know for sure, and while she brushed her teeth to fill in the two agonising minutes, to her astonishment, two pink lines had appeared. Natalie had felt the bathroom floor go light beneath her feet as the blood banged in her eardrums. They'd done it! They'd made a baby!

She'd flown downstairs to show Johnny, but he'd already left to get the Sunday papers. Natalie dialled his mobile with trembling fingers, bubbling with the words she'd practised saying so casually: hello, Daddy! Or maybe, Is that the Longhampton Father of the Year? She couldn't decide.

The phone had rung in his pocket, and Natalie kept glancing at the test, unable to believe it – but while she watched, and the phone rang, the first line began to fade, fade, fading away until there was nothing there. It had gone! A chemical error, not a baby at all.

She hung up before Johnny could answer, and slumped down onto the kitchen floor, unable to raise her head for the crushing disappointment. Of course it was too soon to test. Of course these things happened. Of course it was early days. But still . . . Natalie didn't tell Johnny, when he came whistling through the door, knowing he'd say everything she already knew, albeit with gentle kindness. She'd never had a positive test again.

This month it would be different, she told herself, staring at the two pink lines that confirmed that an egg was ready to go. This month it *had* to be their turn, even the statistics said it would be. The lines had to match in colour to prove she was fertile. Were they equal or was that left one slightly darker? She held it up to the light to check, then jumped as she heard the door open outside.

'. . . call a meeting to discuss that, Kim. That's a pretty tough directive to share with my teams cold.'

Oh God, thought Natalie, her heart sinking. It was Selina. She had one of those Bluetooth headsets so she could be a bossy bitch in any hands-free environment, including the lavatories.

'Really? You're sure?' The taps ran and Natalie missed a bit. 'Uh huh. Uh huh.'

*Uh huh what?* Natalie strained her ears.

'Well, I don't look forward to making that decision, Kim. I hope it *would* be my decision . . . Yes, I understand that head office is taking a hard line, we all are in light of what's happening, what *I* think is . . .'

Her heart rate sped up, but just as Selina was about to reveal the key details of the call, her own phone began to ring, booming around the cubicle. Natalie scrabbled around in her bag to turn it off, but it had slid down to the bottom when she'd taken the test out and had apparently turned invisible.

Immediately Selina went silent.

Oh *shit*, Natalie panicked, feverishly unearthing it from a tangle of paper hankies. It was Johnny, and at that exact moment he hung up, and a strained silence descended over the loos.

'Let's talk later,' said Selina pointedly. 'Not a great moment.'

Realising she had no other choice, Natalie flushed the loo, and opened the door as nonchalantly as she could, not even looking in Selina's direction.

It's not my fault if my manager decides to conduct sensitive conversations in the *ladies' toilets*, she argued, but it didn't make her feel any less uncomfortable, or less curious as to why super-controlled Selina had sounded so, well, nervous. Natalie could see out of the corner of her eye though, as she washed her hands, that Selina was staring at her with an unfamiliar expression on her face, and she straightened up in surprise.

She dried her hands and wondered what the etiquette of awkward bathroom encounters was. Luckily, Selina solved it for her.

'You didn't hear any of that,' she snapped.

'Hear what?' replied Natalie, deadpan.

As soon as she was back in the comparative safety of her office, she called Johnny.

From the noise behind him, she guessed he was supervising the lunchbreak.

'Hey, gorgeous!' he said. 'Want to come and see a man about a dog tonight?'

'What?' Natalie tapped her pen against her chin. Cautious probing of Andrea had revealed that no one else knew what was going on at head office, which only increased her concerns. But listening to Johnny made her feel better about most things. He had that reassuring teacher manner about him, that everything could be worked out with some effort and application.

'A man about a dog. Bill's getting a dog from that rescue place on the Hartley hill, and he wants us to come for a second opinion.'

'But you're the one who's had a dog, not me.' Natalie kicked off her shoes under the desk and wriggled her toes. One of the benefits of a corner office, with window. 'I've only ever had a rabbit, and that was twenty years ago.'

'I know, but he values your female intuition. I'm just there to tell him what kind of dog to get, you're the one who's supposed to guide him towards what *suits* him. You know what Bill's like.'

'Yes. I know what Bill's like,' said Natalie. 'He likes a second opinion. And a third. And a fourth, if there's someone else around.'

'What time can you get away? By five?'

Natalie looked at her email inbox, already stacked up again from the thirty minutes she'd taken off to eat her lunch. And she had appointments all afternoon and a report to start compiling about whether 'getting into the veg box market' was working out for GreenPea's shortbread range.

As if he could read her mind, Johnny added, 'Come on, Nat, you worked late all last week. Can't Selina give you a gold star?'

'That's it, though.' Natalie dropped her voice. 'I think Selina's on the lookout for people who don't have gold stars. It's not a good time for me to be leaving early.'

'But Nat, I thought we could see this dog, have some dinner and then, you know, still have time for us this evening?'

They both knew what that meant. At least I didn't have to suggest it, Natalie thought, at least he knows. And cares.

'I'll do my best,' she said. 'Listen, I've got a call coming through – I'll see you there. Soon as I can after five?'

'Soon as you can,' said Johnny, dropping his voice so the kids around him couldn't hear his husky Barry White impression. 'Because I don't want Bill Harper and his canine girlfriend replacement eating into our special Green Zone time together, OK?'

'OK,' said Natalie happily.

'I still don't think I should be doing the actual interview,' said Rachel and pushed the clipboard back across the office desk towards Megan.

'Why not? You need to start sometime.' Megan pushed it back. 'And it's not that hard. All the questions are on there. Just tick yes or no. Simple as that.'

Rachel stared at the questionnaire, and tried not to think about how she was going to tell Megan that she had no intention of staying long enough to get experienced at dog matchmaking. It had been a bad afternoon. Lots of dogs, lots of barking, George Fenwick on her case about fleas, and the realisation that she'd never be able to walk into Topshop again without feeling like someone's grandmother.

'But it's *not* as simple as that, is it?' she whined. 'What about picking the right dog? What about the magic "Dot" moment when man and mutt meet and it's happy ever after? I can't do that.'

'Look, cross that bridge when you come to it. More than one no and he doesn't even *get* a dog.' Megan gazed at her over a huge mug of tea. The whole kennel seemed to run on tea, as far as Rachel could tell. 'Freda's done the hard part already – we know he's got the right kind of house, and he's not allergic to dogs.'

'I don't think Freda sees home checking as a hard part,' said Rachel, flicking through the extensive – some might even say nosy – report on Bill Harper's 'very pleasant conservatory, no expense spared!' and 'lovely gardens, about the size of ours, but not quite as well-organised, border-wise'.

'Well. Whatever. He's got a decent garden, fenced in, with no kids – that's the main thing. Just have a chat!' Megan tried to look encouraging. 'You've met all our dogs, you've had a walk with most of them now. You know what sort of owner they'd like, if they could talk to you.'

'Do I?' Rachel wrinkled her nose doubtfully.

Dot's famous 'dog whispering' hung over the kennel like a Turin Shroud/Jesus in the toast legend. People would expect to be matched up with the dog of their dreams and while Megan could probably pull it off, thanks to her experience, Rachel didn't believe for a second that she herself could.

Even though she and Gem were now coming to a sort of understanding, born out of their shared gloominess, she wasn't sure she had much of a rapport with the others. She certainly hadn't started talking to them, or imagining they could talk to her.

'Just imagine them in the park,' said Megan, helpfully. 'Do they fit, if you know what I mean?'

'No,' said Rachel. 'I don't.'

The kennel doorbell jangled and made them both jump. It was an old-fashioned housemaid bell from the old kitchens, and was loud enough to be heard from the fenced area outside the kennels.

'Right on time. That's a good sign. We like punctuality in our new owners,' said Megan as she pushed back her chair and went to let them in.

Rachel looked back at the form, trying to memorise the questions so they'd trip easily off her tongue. The goal, she told herself, is to have one less dog to worry about and one more kennel space to let out.

At the top of the form was a stern warning in bold italics:

**We're the only voice the dogs have! Please don't be offended if we seem intrusive or picky – we just want what's best for them. Some of our dogs have been badly let down by humans already, yet still want to trust us and give their love; we'd hate to see them back.**

Rachel's throat tightened, thinking of Bertie's eager, wrinkled face and Chester's anguished pacing every time someone walked past and wasn't his runaway owner come to get him. Please don't let me let them down, she thought, and raised her eyebrows in surprise at herself.

Megan's voice floated through to the office. 'Come in, come in.'

She looked up to see her ushering in Dr Harper, followed by a thirty-something couple who were looking round with great curiosity. The man was rubbing his hands excitedly, but the woman was more cautious, as if she was expecting the place to be overrun with slavering dogs.

'Now, can I get you guys tea, or coffee?' Megan was hovering. 'This is Rachel, she's going to guide you through the rehoming process!'

'Lovely. Tea, please, two sugars. I'm parched. Hello, I'm Johnny Hodge,' said the big man, extending his hand towards Rachel. He smiled, and crinkled up his friendly brown eyes. 'And this is my wife, Natalie.'

'Hello, Natalie.' Rachel noted that Natalie was wearing non-dog work clothes too, and felt an immediate sympathy for her smart black pencil skirt and fitted jacket. 'Come and sit over here,' she said, pulling out a chair, 'there's less chance of you getting hairy. I know. I go through a whole lint roller every two days.'

'So how does this work?' Dr Bill was looking around. 'I, er, thought you might have some dogs here?'

'What, like *Blind Date*?' joked Johnny. 'Bill would like to meet an ambitious dog, under three, with a good sense of humour.'

'We try not to let people see the dogs until we've had a chance to chat,' explained Megan. 'It can get rather over-emotional for everyone, seeing them in their runs, and them seeing you, coming to take them home. They all go a bit *X Factor*, trying to get your attention. But if you have specific ideas about what sort of dog you'd like, we can talk about that?'

'Oh, Bill's very specific about what he wants, aren't you, Bill?' Johnny turned to his friend. 'That's why he's still single!'

'Johnny . . .' Natalie frowned.

'I just like to know what I'm getting myself into.' Bill shot an amiable sideways glance at Johnny. 'I'm not that fussy really – I'd like something trainable, something that doesn't shed too much so I can take it into the surgery. And something with a bit of personality.'

'Is that the dog or the girlfriend?' asked Rachel.

Bill turned pink as Johnny leaned forward and said, 'Both.'

'Great! Shall we run through the questions?' Rachel suggested and glanced down. 'How often can you walk a dog, for a start?'

After twenty-five minutes Rachel had established that Bill could walk his dog about a mile to work and back, with a trot around the park at lunchtime; that he wanted something that came 'up to his knee' and was preferably black; that his mother had had a nippy Lakeland terrier and he definitely didn't want one of those; that Johnny loved dogs, and would have a Labrador, a pointer, a springer spaniel or just a 'fun little chap'; that Natalie hoped having a dog would get Bill out and about.

'So,' said Johnny, slapping his knees and looking at Bill. 'Is this where you go behind the screen and bring out date number one?'

'It is!' Megan pushed back her chair. 'If you guys want to help yourself to biscuits, be our guests. What happens now is that we'll have a chat, bring out a dog or two so you can have a play, get to know each other, and we'll take it from there. Come on, Rachel.'

Rachel glanced up from the paperwork. 'Sorry?'

'I need your expertise.' She beamed confidently as she hauled Rachel to her feet. ''Scuse us!'

Outside the office, Rachel turned to protest, but Megan carried on pushing her gently towards the kennels. 'OK,' she said. 'Away you go. Pop in there with that questionnaire and find Bill a dog.'

Rachel stopped in her tracks. 'No! Don't be ridiculous.'

'Come on, you can do it.'

'I can't! You're the kennel manager, not me! And you know *him!*' Rachel waved her arms. 'This isn't a game, Megan. I don't know enough about the dogs. It's not my job! I don't have that . . . knack.'

Megan put her small hands on Rachel's upper arms. 'There's no knack. It's logical. Just go in there, read the notes Dot left on the doors, and . . .' She paused and raised an eyebrow. 'Let the dogs talk to you. No, no! Before you say anything, I'm not being weird. Just let them . . . OK, maybe I am being weird. But keep really still. You'll hear it, inside.'

Rachel looked at her as if she were mad, but Megan gave her a firm push.

'Go on. If you bring out something totally wrong, I'll tell you.' Her face softened. 'I know you're not a dog person, Rachel. Don't tell me again.'

Rachel bit her upper lip and went in through the heavy door. Immediately the sound of conversational yapping and Radio Four ramped up a few notches, and the smell of warm dog and oily coats and dry kibble rushed up to meet her.

'It's just me!' she called out, without thinking. 'Don't go mad, come on, folks, calm down.'

Rachel walked slowly down the stone corridor between the pens, trying not to let her heart ache at the eager wagging and hopeful eyes that followed her. Instead she thought about the lanky doctor, and who would suit him, who would make a good companion? She passed by two collie sisters – trainable, but too energetic to sit in a basket. The Staffies, still barking up a storm at the sight of anyone who would play. Chester, the spaniel Bill had seen on the poster, was there, but he was bouncing around like he'd been bouncing since he woke up – that wouldn't work in a surgery.

Or then there was Bertie. Rachel smiled, seeing Bertie's tragic Basset hound eyes gazing up at her from his plastic bed, his long face wrinkling with hope.

'I have no more supper, so you can stop with the cupboard love,' she said aloud, but kindly. Bertie was gorgeous, but he wasn't right for Bill.

She stopped, without quite knowing why, in front of Lulu the poodle. Megan had given Lulu a rudimentary clipping that afternoon, still muttering about George's 'bloody sarky' instructions not to 'do anything stupid', and although Megan had just shaved off the knots, now Lulu's neat legs and bright eyes were visible under the black fuzz that had made her look more like a lamb than a dog.

Lulu would be perfect, said a voice in Rachel's head, before she had time to think. Bill wants a smart dog, who can be trained – according to the Dogs for Dummies book in the office, that's a poodle. And she won't shed her hairs over the surgery, and she's so easy-going and quick to learn new things.

Lulu's shiny black eyes fixed on hers and her tail, now almost a pompom, wagged for the first time.

But he wanted a big dog, she argued. A man's dog.

*Lulu's the right one.*

Rachel stood still as the dogs started to bark, curious as to what she was doing in there. She could hear the skitter of claws and then a warm body pressed itself up against her ankles. Absent-mindedly, Rachel bent and caressed Gem's ear. Gem's approval seemed to seal it, as near to Dot's help as she could get.

Lulu was the one.

'How about it, Gem?' she asked the collie, now wriggling his head towards the kennel door. 'Bill and Lulu?'

You're talking to a dog, Rachel reminded herself. That's not the slippery slope. That's the actual black run.

She pulled back the bolt on the pen door and Lulu came tiptoeing out, curious to see what was going on. She still wasn't perky, but since her trim she seemed to have regained some confidence. She certainly looked bigger than she had done when Rachel had first seen her, though that was more to do with her personality unfolding than the two good meals a day she was getting now.

'Hello, Lulu,' said Rachel, clipping the lead onto her collar. 'I've got someone I think you'd like to meet.'

She tried not to look back at the other dogs as she, Gem and Lulu made their way back down the corridor.

Megan was standing at the door, talking urgently into the phone.

'Sure, I can send our homechecker round in the morning,' she said. 'About eleven? Great. Where did you see the poster? In the post office? Oh, good on you.' She gave Rachel a thumbs up, and then turned her smile down to Lulu and did a happy double take. 'OK, I'll call you first thing. Bye now!'

Megan hung the phone back on the wall and dropped to her knees. 'Hey, Lulu!' Lulu nuzzled into her outstretched hands as she fondled her woolly black ears. 'Aren't you glad you had your haircut now, eh? Looking good!'

Rachel bit her lips. 'You think I've picked the right one?'

'Well, there's only one surefire way to find out.' Megan bounced to her feet and led the way back towards the office.

Bill and Johnny were joking with each other about something at the table, while by the window Natalie checked messages on her phone, but when Rachel walked in with Lulu on the lead, their attention snapped back to her, and then down to Lulu, who had hesitated at the door, confronted by three new faces.

'Is that a poodle?' said Johnny and laughed out loud. 'Mate, your ideal dog's a poodle!'

'Don't laugh,' said Natalie at once. 'Don't hurt her feelings.' She looked up to Rachel. 'Is it a her?'

Rachel nodded, touched that Natalie, who seemed quite brisk in her business suit, would think of the dog's feelings first. She tried to trot out what she'd gleaned from Dot's reference books. 'Lulu's quite a big miniature poodle – they come in three sizes, standard, miniature and toy, and we think she's the middle size. Her dad might have been a standard.'

'You think she's woolly now,' Megan added. 'I had to shave off knots like you wouldn't believe, just to see that snooty nose. Poor Lulu had a bit of a rough time on the streets before she found her way here.'

'Aren't poodles supposed to have pompoms?' asked Johnny, squinting critically. 'This one's all dreadlocked. Looks more like Slash from Guns N' Roses than a poodle!'

'Don't be daft. They're not born like that, it's *shaving*,' said Natalie. 'It's like saying, don't all men come with moustaches?'

She crouched down carefully in her tight skirt, and Lulu took a few steps towards her, lowering her tail as she sniffed Natalie's extended fingers. 'Hello, little lady,' she said. 'Those are clever eyes! Aren't you a smart girl? Yes!'

Rachel noted the neat pink nails and the shiny engagement and wedding rings with a pang of envy.

'Lulu's brilliant with new people, so friendly, even after everything she's been through,' said Megan. 'Rachel reckoned that'd be good for your surgery, right?'

'That'd be ideal,' said Bill. 'I can't have a snappy dog. But I'm not sure.' He scratched his chin. 'A poodle. I'd never really thought of a poodle as my type.'

'Hello!' said Natalie, softly, stroking one long ear with the back of a finger. 'Aren't you gorgeous? Bill, come down to her level. You're scary enough to most normal-sized girls, let alone a wee dog.'

Awkwardly, Bill hitched up his trousers and squatted down, holding out a hand. At once, Lulu swerved away from Natalie and trotted over to Bill, flirtatiously raising her bobbly head against his leg for a pat.

'Hello!' he said.

Lulu stared up at Bill with her bright eyes, and pushed her long nose into his hand. He reared back for a second in surprise, nearly toppling over, but he recovered himself, then smiled and rubbed her head. Lulu arched into his hand.

'Oh, she likes a handsome man, does Lulu,' giggled Megan.

'OK, so that's dog number one. Does Bill get to see any more?' asked Johnny.

'I don't know if we *need* to bring out any more,' said Natalie. 'Just look at the two of them. It's like love at first sight!'

Lulu had put her two elegant front paws up onto Bill's trousers and was sniffing around his collar, as he tried not to rear back too obviously. A crooked smile twitched on his lips as he struggled not to laugh in the dog's face, and he patted her as she wriggled to take in all his smell at once.

'Lulu! Have some dignity, will ya?' laughed Megan. 'I have seriously never seen her like this with anyone else. She's been so quiet up until now!'

'Bill?' said Johnny. 'Do you want to see any more?'

Bill didn't answer.

'I think . . .' Rachel started, but the rest of her sentence was drowned out by a deep baying noise from the direction of the kennels. It sounded as if the Hound of the Baskervilles had woken from a deep sleep, with a bad headache and possibly indigestion too.

'What the hell's that?' marvelled Johnny, sticking a finger in his ear and wriggling it around.

There was another howl, an echoing 'arrrroooo' that set off a volley of answering yaps, none as deep or sonorous as the original.

'Oh, it's just Bertie,' said Megan, pushing herself off the wall. 'He'll be thinking there's some supper going on in here.'

'Bertie? What's Bertie? A Great Dane or something?' Johnny had perked up. 'He sounds enormous.'

'He's not that enormous,' said Rachel. 'Although you'd think his stomach was the size of a St Bernard's the way he carries on.'

'Can we see him too?'

'I don't think we need to.' Rachel turned to Bill, who was now sitting back on his chair, with Lulu settled in his lap as if she'd been there since she was a puppy.

'I'll go and get him,' said Megan with a half-smile. 'Just so you know what trouble looks like, OK? You'll be begging us not to show you any more dogs.'

They could hear Megan and Bertie coming long before the door opened.

'Steady, steady, *heel*!' Megan was yelling, and Rachel knew how she'd be hanging determinedly onto the lead. It was Megan's mission to get Bertie walking to heel but he had a habit of slipping out of his collar when something really stinky was in range.

Bertie burst into the room, in a flurry of brown ears and wrinkly legs and wildly sniffing nose, with Megan clinging on for dear life. He stopped for a second to inspect everyone, and then plunged his nose back to the floor, like a canine vacuum cleaner, and carried on scenting whatever it was that was so interesting.

'Oh, my God, he is adorable,' breathed Natalie, unconsciously clasping her hands together with delight. 'Look at his face! And his stumpy legs!'

Safe on Bill's knee, Lulu barely turned her head, giving Bertie the faintest of superior looks before returning her attention to her new hero.

'How old is he? Where did he come from?' Natalie's words were tumbling over each other as she pushed her hair out of her face, and she bent down to stroke Bertie's velvety head. 'Hello! Hello there, Big Ears! Hello!'

To Rachel's horror, Bertie responded by sticking his nose into her designer handbag, followed by his entire head. But Natalie only laughed and pulled him out by his collar. 'You won't find anything in there unless you can unwrap Polos!'

'He can unwrap Polos,' said Megan. 'And sausages, and KitKats.'

'Oh, Jon, just look at these beautiful eyes!' Natalie nearly had her head buried in Bertie's neck. 'How did something so cute end up here?'

Megan gave Rachel a swift glance. 'Ah, Bertie's a sad story. I won't tell you because you'll want to take him straight home, and you didn't come here for your own dog, did you?'

Natalie looked up at Johnny, who was still sitting at the table. He had been smiling down at the clownish Basset hound, but something in his wife's face made his expression turn sad.

'No, we didn't come for a dog,' he said. He was speaking to Megan, but Rachel got the sense that his words were actually directed at Natalie. 'We both work full time and there's no way we could take him to work with us. I'm a teacher, you see, and Natalie's a marketing executive.'

'Does he need someone around all the time?' asked Natalie. 'Wouldn't he be OK if we popped back at lunch?'

Megan shook her head. 'Not a dog like this. Bertie's a hound and they can't stand being alone. He'd be howling like that all day, and he's not really house-trained properly, so he needs someone to show him the ropes. Put him in a routine.' She raised her eyebrows. 'That's probably why he ended up here in the first place, owners didn't have enough time for him.'

'Oh.' Natalie looked crestfallen. 'I suppose so.'

'It's for your sake as well as his.' Rachel felt bad, for treading on Natalie's enthusiasm. 'He'd be unhappy and you'd have your neighbours up in arms.'

'And your house trashed,' added Megan, pragmatically. 'Slobber up the walls, everything chewed.'

'I thought you were trying to rehome these dogs!' joked Johnny, but his voice was slightly strained.

'We are!' Rachel turned her attention to the successful rehoming of the night. 'And it looks like we've done OK here?'

Bill dragged his gaze away from Lulu, now curled up on his knee, her ears pricked to the conversation. 'Yeah, I think you have. I'm not sure I've really got much choice in the matter, though!'

'Come on, Bertie, you've had your share of tummy rubs now,' said Megan, pulling his front paws down from Natalie's knee. 'Back to barracks for the night.'

Bertie's eyes refused to leave Natalie's as Megan led him firmly towards the door, and he planted his feet so she had to haul him out, his paws dragging on the tiles as he gave a tragic whimper.

'It's like he's crying!' Natalie's voice cracked. 'He doesn't want to go back to his kennel!'

'Don't be fooled by this performance,' said Rachel. 'I know he's making out that we keep him tied up to a post in the pouring rain, but this one has a heated kennel, all the toys he can handle, a warm bed . . .'

'But it's not the same as a proper home, is it?' said Natalie with sudden emotion breaking her voice.

'Anyway!' Johnny slapped his hands on his knees. 'Lulu's coming home with Bill, I take it?'

'Tomorrow,' said Megan firmly. 'We like you to sleep on it. Make sure you're sure.'

Natalie was subdued as they drove home, and for once, so was Johnny.

Neither of them said much until she parked the car in the drive and pulled the keys out of the ignition. Johnny didn't leap out to get the door open and the kettle on as he usually did. Instead, he sat chewing a hangnail – which Natalie knew was a dead giveaway that he was preoccupied with something he found too hard to talk about.

'Are you thinking about that dog?' he asked eventually, as the cooling engine ticked in the silence.

'Yes,' said Natalie.

'Me too. But he'll find a good home. Didn't Megan say that pedigree dogs usually get rescued by the breed clubs? Someone'll come for him.'

'What if they don't?' She stared at the neat brick garage in front of them, and her eyes filled up with hormonal tears. All she could see was rows and rows of hopeful little faces, and wagging tails, begging for love. This was exactly the wrong time of the month to go looking in bloody rescue homes, she thought crossly, trying to regain some control over her lurching emotions.

'We can't have a dog, Nat,' said Johnny. 'You know we can't. We haven't got the time to give it.'

'Well, have we got time to have a baby?' Natalie knew she sounded irrational. 'I'll have to find time then!'

'That's not the same thing, and you know it,' said Johnny, and opened his car door. It was a full stop but a kind one. 'I'll make the tea tonight, shall I?' he added, trying to make up for it.

She knew he was right, but she still followed him in with a weight on her shoulders.

# 8

After three nerve-destroying days with Toffee, in which she'd barely left the house for fear of bumping into someone from work, Zoe thought she'd finally got the knack of watching him out of the back of her head. He was still far from toilet trained, but she was formulating a plan that would let her convince Marion the salon owner to bring him to work, until she got the phone call from her solicitor, and her carefully nurtured confidence was kicked down again.

Allen Howard had news about David's maintenance payments that made her forget everything, including puppy puddles.

'Sorry, can you say that again slowly?' she said, sinking to the kitchen chair. Her knees had given way. 'I thought he'd agreed to pay a lump sum – for the child support he didn't give me over the summer?'

'He wants the court to reassess his income in light of the recession. I know, it's ridiculous.' Allen Howard sounded embarrassed too. 'But it's within his rights.'

Zoe squeezed her forehead, and tried not to think about everything she'd stuck on her credit cards, in the expectation of David's lump sum. The more patient Allen's voice got, the more she wanted to cry. He sounded like her dad. Or rather, how her dad would have sounded if he were around to guide her through this horrible process. Part of her was glad he wasn't.

Zoe felt painfully alone. When had she turned into the adult who was supposed to have the answers? One of the few things she missed about being married to David was having that other person there to ask. No wonder she was talking to a four-month-old Labrador.

'Can he do that? *Why* would he do that?' She grabbed her hair and twisted, an old habit. 'He's taking them to gold-plated theme parks every other weekend and buying new cars!'

Allen sighed. 'You're asking the wrong person, Zoe. You'd be amazed what some people will do. Divorce isn't a nice business.'

Except for solicitors, she thought bitterly.

Zoe's attention shifted as she spotted Toffee emerging from behind a chair, looking sheepish. His jaws were moving in a manner she'd come to dread.

Allen was still talking, his voice now concerned, as well as patient. 'Zoe, I know you don't like being tough but we've really got to take a hard line about this. I suggest you come in and . . .'

'Hang on, Allen,' said Zoe and made a grab for Toffee as he sidled past. With the phone jammed under her chin, she scooped the puppy up – he seemed to grow every single hour – and, fearing what she might find, rooted urgently around in his mouth with a finger, removing, in the nick of time, a puppy-choking chunk of Leo's Lego.

Toffee gave her a baleful look and began chewing on her finger instead, his sharp teeth making red weals in her skin. Zoe bit her own lip to stop herself crying out.

'He could end up leaving you with nothing,' Allen went on. 'And to be honest, I'm worried about the noises his solicitor's making. Off the record, is he planning to settle down with this Jennifer?'

Zoe looked at the Lego, seconds from choking Toffee, then looked at her bitten fingers, which were throbbing, and then looked at herself in the glass of the kitchen cabinet. No make-up, wild hair, yesterday's t-shirt, bags under her eyes that she hadn't seen since her granny still roamed Barrow's bingo halls.

When the boys were here, it was easier to ignore things in the never-ending series of questions and snacks and washing. But without that comforting buzz of white boy-noise filling her head, sharp realities poked through.

*David's not coming back. I am a single mother and I'm only thirty. I'm letting him get whatever he wants rather than fight back because I don't have the energy to be vicious. And now Jennifer's lining up to be the next Mrs Graham.*

Zoe clamped her spare hand over her mouth, feeling sickness and panic rush over her. She put the puppy down, and he scampered to the other side of the kitchen, yapping uproariously, oblivious to her distress. 'Um ... sorry, I've forgotten the question.'

'Look, why don't you come in and see me?' suggested Allen. 'This morning – I've got a cancelled appointment. Jump in the car and we can go through this together. It's a lot to take in.'

'But I can't leave the dog!' she said automatically, panic filling her. This was going to take a lot longer than the forty minutes the book said she could leave Toffee without a loo break.

'You can't what?' Allen sounded confused.

No, thought Zoe, it's ridiculous. I can't be trapped in my own house by a *puppy*.

'OK. I'll be there.' She made a superhuman effort to pull herself together and began hunting for the hairbrush and Toffee's training lead and collar. I have to do this, she thought, through the frustrated tears flowing down her face. I have to sort myself out for the boys. Even if it hurts like hell.

She put the collar on a wriggling Toffee, then looked at her tote bag, which sat capaciously on the kitchen table. If needs be she could always line it with a supermarket carrier.

'Let's call this your first socialisation lesson,' she said bravely and he wagged his little tail.

As it turned out, it wasn't one of Zoe's better ideas.

Rachel had just finished putting the dogs back in their runs, and was heading for Dot's kitchen, mentally relishing a coffee to unthaw her freezing extremities, when she heard the sharp sound of raised voices in the front office, and for once, it wasn't the Staffies kicking off.

'You're not listening to me!' cried a woman's voice, shredded with distress. 'I'm telling you, I just can't cope! I can't *cope!*'

Rachel caught Megan say something in response, and it sounded so unusually sharp that she hurried into the office without even bothering to hang up the leads on their usual hooks.

The woman from the pet superstore was standing by the front desk half-clutching a yellow Labrador puppy in her arms. The puppy was yelping, and tears were running down the woman's face as she gabbled something to Megan and tried to push the puppy onto her.

Rachel racked her brains to remember the woman's name. Had she told them?

She strained to hear what was being said, but between the yelping and the crying, she could barely make out a word. Megan was doing her best to keep calm, but the woman was in hysterics and it was setting off the rest of the dogs in the runs. There was also a strong smell of urine – and possibly something more pungent.

Gem was sitting upright in his basket, his head on one side as if he was watching *EastEnders*.

'Please, please,' the woman kept saying over and over again. 'I've got to get back to work, my boys need me. You *have* to take him. I just can't look after him the way he deserves.'

'Let's be calm here,' Megan kept saying, to little effect. Zoe, 'just calm down . . .'

Rachel found herself taking charge, just to get the noise to stop.

'What's going on?' she asked pleasantly. 'Can I help you? Is this the puppy you were telling us about the other day? In Pet World?'

'Please, you've got to take him,' Zoe blurted out, before Megan could speak. 'He's a lovely puppy, and he deserves a good home but I just can't give it to him. I mean, I've done my best, but I can't take any more time off work to train him. I know it's cruel to leave him all alone.' Her face crumpled with misery. 'Don't make me feel worse than I already do. It's bad enough working out what I'm going to say to my boys when they come home.'

Megan glanced at Rachel with sympathetic eyes, and Rachel saw Lulu's fabulously empty kennel being refilled instantly, just as they'd managed to free it up. She shook her head, hard, at Megan and mouthed, 'No!'

'Then maybe you should give him back to your ex, and get him to return him to his breeder?' she suggested hastily, dragging up a handful of Dot's leaflets. 'Isn't that what you're supposed to do, Megan? Don't they have that unspoken code of conduct?'

'I don't know where he came from,' wailed Zoe. 'And I don't trust David – he won't even provide for his own kids, let alone a dog! I've just had a meeting with my solicitor that—' She sobbed. 'I'm sorry, I've had a really, really bad day.'

'Of course we'll take him . . .' Megan began, but Rachel interrupted.

'Megan, be an angel and put the kettle on? I'm frozen.' She rubbed her hands together and turned to the woman, who'd now sunk onto a chair, the baby Labrador still cradled in her arms. Zoe was obviously too upset to notice the damp patch on her coat, but Rachel spotted it. She spotted puddles everywhere. She was seriously considering a new *Dragons'*

*Den* career making puppy nappies. 'Can we make you a cup of tea? You look like you need one.'

Megan gave Rachel a warning look but Rachel nodded firmly towards the kitchen, and reluctantly, Megan left.

Rachel sat down next to Zoe, and lifted the puppy's paw up, as if they were shaking hands. The puppy gazed at her, his trusting brown eyes following her face. He has no idea he's about to be abandoned here, she thought. He thinks he's just having a trip out. A small pink tongue darted out and licked his nose, nervously. Rachel steeled herself not to fall for his cuteness.

'Hello, Toffee. You're a handsome chap!' she said, stroking behind one hot ear.

'Here, do you want to hold him?' Zoe said, and before Rachel had a chance to reply she'd dumped him on her knee.

Instinctively Rachel grabbed the puppy to stop him falling off, and he shuffled backwards into her lap.

He was a lovely warm lump, she thought, as Toffee sniffed her clothes and skin, but almost immediately he started chewing on Rachel's finger and she had to prise his jaws off her hand, trying not to wince.

'Is he going through a chewing phase?' she asked.

'All the time,' Zoe sniffed. 'Chews everything. I know he doesn't mean to, but I'm scared he'll chew through a cable while I'm at work and the kids will come home and find him dead in the . . .' She hiccupped and pushed her hair behind her ear, trying to sound calmer than she evidently was. 'Sorry. I've just had a very upsetting meeting. My ex is being a bastard.'

'All puppies chew,' Rachel said, in a reasonable tone. She hoped it sounded authoritative, and not as if she'd just read it, which she had. Years in PR had taught her the art of sounding knowledgeable on the basis of a leaflet. 'Just give him something to chew *on*. A Kong, or a teething toy. Pop him in his crate, and he'll be fine. Look, we do some advice on crate training . . .'

'I don't have time to do that!' wailed Zoe. 'I've got to get back to work to feed my kids!' She gazed miserably at Toffee, who was blissfully mouthing Rachel's fingers. 'He deserves more than we can give him. He needs to find a better home now, before he gets used to us.'

Rachel manfully ignored the pain in her fingers and focused instead on keeping the puppy out of her precious empty run.

'Could you pop back home at lunchtime? Or hire a walker?' she suggested. 'Do you have a neighbour who could pup sit? Or maybe you could take him into work? One of our new owners has done that, in fact – he's a doctor . . .'

Zoe half-laughed, half-sobbed, her composure now hanging by a thread. 'You must be joking! I know Toffee looks cute but he's a wrecking machine! He's trashed my house in three days, and it normally looks like a bomb's hit it already.'

Rachel furrowed her brow. 'So why did your ex think it would be a good idea to get a puppy, if he knew you worked?'

'Because David *doesn't* think!' Zoe sank her head into her hands. 'Spencer's wanted a puppy for ages, and it was easy for David to give them one, then let me deal with the shitty part. It's typical of David! He wanted a family – he had us. He wanted a bit on the side – he shagged someone at work. He wanted to have us both, but at least he's found out you *can't* . . .' A sob broke through her words, and she put her hand over her mouth, squeezing her eyes closed.

Rachel felt a squirm of shame about the bit on the side, but she pushed it away. Fresh start, she told herself. This is a fresh start, no Oliver, no secrets, no guilt.

'That's rough,' she said, and reached out a hand to pat Zoe's. 'That's a lot to deal with. I didn't mean to make you feel worse.'

'Sorry.' Zoe wiped her eyes roughly. 'God, this is so embarrassing. I had to take Toffee with me to the solicitors' and he just peed everywhere, on some cables or something

– caused a powercut to their computers, major disaster apparently.'

Her round brown eyes met Rachel's and there was a ghost of a twinkle in them. 'I mean, if it had been any other time, I suppose I'd have found it funny, but . . .'

She stopped, self-consciously, as Megan pushed the door open with her foot, and plonked three cups of tea on the office desk.

'Here we are, tea all round for us and a Bonio for the lad,' said Megan. 'Now, listen, I've had an idea.' She turned to Zoe with a reassuring smile. 'I reckon we can come to a compromise.'

Rachel eyed her with suspicion.

'Go on,' said Zoe, clutching her tea cup.

'If we take Toffee from you, he'll be rehomed in about five minutes flat,' said Megan sternly. 'No kidding. We've got people lined up for puppies, and once you sign him over that's it, no changing your mind when you get home. I'm sure you don't want that, not really. But I totally understand about your working, and it's very responsible of you to know he needs more company. So have you thought about doggie daycare?'

Each time she'd paused for breath, Zoe and Rachel had opened their mouths to interrupt but Megan hadn't let them. Now Rachel jumped in before she could do it again.

'Doggie what?'

'Doggie daycare,' said Megan, as if Rachel should know exactly what she meant. 'Like daycare for kids, only here? You drop your pup off on the way to work, we walk him, feed him, let him socialise, then you collect on the way home, spend the rest of the day together and do your training with your boys.'

'Really?' Zoe's eyes lit up. 'That would be the *perfect* answer.'

'Would it?' Rachel beetled her brows at Megan. 'I didn't know Dot did that kind of . . .'

'It's a fairly new idea.' Megan busied herself breaking up another Bonio into small pieces for Toffee. 'We were just, you know, trialling it. Seeing if it would be popular. And clearly, it would be!'

Zoe looked from Megan to Rachel. 'That would be OK?'

'Yes,' said Megan at the same time as Rachel said, 'Megan, can I have a quick word?'

'What about?' Megan beamed brightly.

'Er, the tea' said Rachel. 'Let me show you how I like it. Can I leave you here with Toffee for a second?'

She steered Megan out of the office and into the kennels kitchen. From the patter of claws on lino, she knew that Gem had followed them, as if he was part of the team.

'What on earth was that about?' demanded Rachel in a low tone. 'We don't offer doggie daycare!'

'It's a great idea!' Megan insisted. 'It's an easy way of making some cash! Look, it's not much more work – puppies that age don't need walking, he could be in the office with Freda, or round the house with you.'

'Yes!' hissed Rachel. 'Peeing all over the place! '

'Ah, we'll have him trained in no time, he's a Lab. They're smart. You just have to be firm.'

Rachel sighed. There wasn't much point in arguing with Megan, she knew that already.

'Well, I suppose it's a way of keeping that run clear,' she conceded. 'And we can charge her something. Although if she hasn't got any money for a walker, I don't suppose she's going to have much for doggie daycare?'

Megan folded her arms. 'Rachel, I don't know how much you know about these things, but let me tell you, pedigree Labrador puppies like that don't come cheap. If the stupid two-timing bastard ex can afford to sling several hundred quid for an Andrex puppy, he can deffo afford the babysitting.'

'How do you know she's got a two-timing bastard ex?'

'Fine, so I was eavesdropping.' Megan looked sheepish. 'All the stuff about not wanting to upset the kids, I know where she's coming from, she's obviously a good person.' She shrugged and her plaits bounced. 'We should cut her some slack – she wasn't expecting a dog. All first-time owners freak out for the first few weeks. They're like new mums.'

Rachel looked down at the sink, where piles of metal dog bowls were stacked, ready for tea time. It was terrifying, the speed at which the kennel routine had imprinted itself on her brain. 'Yes, fine. Fine. OK, well, let's go and talk to her.'

'Thanks!' said Megan. 'I appreciate it!'

'What for? It's your great idea.' Rachel gave Megan a reluctant smile. 'Look, if you want to set that up, you can, you know, run it. I won't tell George you're angling to get even more dogs in here.'

'Oh God, don't do that!' Megan slipped into her George impression as they made their way back to the office. '"You have to say no and mean it, Megan! You'd say no fast enough if it were peeing on your leg, wouldn't you? Think about it!"'

'That's not a bad local accent for an Aussie,' said Rachel.

'I hear it often enough,' Megan replied with a grimace. 'Especially the "think about it!" part.'

By the time Zoe and Toffee left, several cups of tea later, Rachel was convinced the business world had missed a ruthless star in Megan.

In return for a week of doggie daycare, she'd persuaded Zoe to pay them for two days in cash (which Megan would pocket), and then give both her and Rachel one free haircut per month plus some 'colour guidance' in lieu of the rest. Zoe would also volunteer for the dog-walking efforts on Saturday and teach Megan some tricks of the trade about shampooing.

Everyone was happy. It wasn't so different from the dodgier deals Rachel had done herself at work, to get her computer fixed.

'I reckon she got herself a bargain there,' said Megan, as they began measuring out the evening kibble, rattling it into the metal bowls.

'She didn't. You have no idea how high maintenance my hair is.' Rachel had to raise her voice above the excited baying. 'It takes a lot of work to get it looking so casual.'

'The grey streaks are highlights?'

'Shut up, cheeky.' Rachel gave Megan a nudge. 'Leave the fashion tips to Mr Fenwick.'

'Well, I guess this means you'll have to stay now, to get your money's worth,' said Megan. 'What? At least two months?' She looked innocent, but Rachel detected a hint of nosiness under her usual demeanour. Freda had doubtless put her up to it.

'Suppose I will,' she said, then sighed. 'There's so much to do.'

There was, as well. She'd only just got round to calling an estate agent to value the property, and hadn't even opened the letter Dot had left her, no doubt outlining all the irritating minor bequests she'd have to sort out. And then there were the cupboards. Dot hadn't had Val's obsession with annual clear-outs and lining paper.

Of course, when it was finished, that's when the real decisions would have to start. To sell, or stay? To go back to London or move on? To start again . . . where?

When you put it like that, sorting out Dot's creaking Victorian sideboards wasn't such a terrible alternative. The problem was, how long could one house take to sort?

# 9

Natalie's bad day started with someone else's good news. Johnny's mother called before she was even properly awake, to inform them that his sister Becky was pregnant with her third baby.

There were moments when Natalie honestly thought she was some kind of fertility totem, but just for other people. Everywhere she went, babies popped up in her wake, like mushrooms.

'I'm going to be a granny again!' Sheila screeched down the phone, clearly on her fourth coffee of the morning. 'I've told Becky I want a girl, because I've got drawers and drawers of pretty clothes to pass on! And that would make two of each, which is nice and neat, isn't it? Due on Jacob's first birthday too! As I said to our Michael, talk about the Hodges – only have to wink at each other to have us all down at Mothercare!'

At that point, Johnny had seen her face and wrestled the kitchen phone off her, but it was too late. Natalie knew she hadn't made the right noises, so she'd had to send twice as big a bunch of flowers to prove she really was happy for Becky and Steve. Yet another nephew or niece, yet another bloody christening where she'd have to hear all those 'you ought to get a move on' and 'it'll be your turn soon' comments.

She left Johnny talking on the phone, and busied herself making complicated coffee in their shiny espresso machine, but Natalie couldn't stop her ears tuning into the muted conversation he was making. After all this time, she could fill in the blanks with depressing ease. It was a conversation he and his mother seemed to have a lot – not so much a conversation as a game of polite chess.

'Yes . . . things are absolutely fine . . . Not the best time to talk about this, is it, Mum! . . . Of course not . . . She's very busy at work, well, we both are . . . Mum, Natalie's just been promoted, it wouldn't be . . . Come on, you *know* that's not true . . .'

Natalie's shoulders slumped. *What's wrong with Natalie*, that's what Sheila would be asking. It's what everyone was asking, when they weren't making jokes about whether she and Johnny were actually remembering to have sex. Talk about making a choice – was it better to look like a selfish career bitch, or a barren sex-avoider?

Natalie's lip trembled, but she looked at herself in their hallway mirror, stylish in her new suit, and reminded her reflection that there was more to her than just her uterus. She'd single-handedly brought in more business in the last year than anyone else in her department. Without stamping on any toes or resorting to sneaky lunches. That was something to be proud of, wasn't it? Didn't supporting your family and establishing your career count for anything any more? Was this what feminism had come to?

'Look, Mum, just tell Becky we're both thrilled for her and Steve and I'll give her a call when I get in from school tonight . . .'

Johnny's voice got louder as he walked back into the hall with the phone. Natalie blinked hard to squeeze back any tears, and she put on a bright smile that she already knew looked fake.

'OK.' He strode past the kitchen, making loopy gestures around his head. 'Yes, it's wonderful. We'll see you at the weekend, then? Yes, Nat sends her love to you too. Bye, Mum. Bye.'

'Coffee?' said Natalie, holding out a mug, her voice a little too high. 'It's decaf.'

Johnny looked at her for a second, a strange expression on his face, then silently he took the mug off her and put it on the side.

Natalie gazed back at him, trying not to cry. 'I'm really pleased for Becky,' she began, but Johnny cut her off, holding out his arms so she could bury her head into his chest.

'Come here.' Johnny wrapped his arms around her so tight she thought her ribcage might crack. They stood, swaying slightly, in the beautifully decorated hallway, not saying anything for a moment or two.

'I love you,' he murmured, burying his face into her freshly blow-dried hair. 'I'm sorry. It's not fair. I know. But our turn will come, I promise.'

Natalie didn't say anything, because she could feel an unusual grimness about his love for her and in her bleak mood, it warmed her in a way that his sweetness wouldn't have done. The harsh realities of life that made her hurt inside just seemed to glance off him: Johnny was one of those honest souls who believed everything would work out, eventually. She couldn't see life like that.

This morning, though, he seemed to sense her despair, and she felt closer to him, like they were clinging together on the same lifeboat. It didn't matter how hard they tried or how much they wanted their baby – it was in the hands of something else.

'Come on,' she said, pulling away after a few moments. 'I need to get to work. Something's up with Selina – I got an email at seven this morning asking for a confidential meeting.'

He held her at arm's length, examining her face. His boyish face was confused. 'Are you OK?'

'Could be a promotion?' Natalie went on, brightly. 'Or a transfer?'

If I can't have a family, she thought, I'm going to have the best possible career. I am going to *fight* these job cuts.

Johnny smiled sadly.


'Redundancy?'

Natalie stared across the desk, and furrowed her brow. This wasn't the way she'd anticipated the meeting going. At least, not within the opening minute of the conversation.

Selina made her non-binding nodding gesture of agreement, the one that Natalie had seen her make to so many unsuccessful new clients, most of whom didn't even recognise it as a brush-off until they were leaving.

'Regrettably, yes. But you have to look at it in a positive framework – you're getting a very generous redundancy package, and with your references and connections . . .' She emphasised the shrugging gesture, as if she was actually rather jealous of Natalie's situation. 'It's more than a lot of our staff are looking at, Natalie.'

'Can I ask . . .' Natalie swallowed as her heartbeat went into panic. 'Can I ask why you're letting *me* go? My appraisal at the end of last year was really positive. I've achieved all the goals we discussed, and I thought—'

Selina held up her hand, as if she didn't want either of them to be embarrassed.

'I don't need to tell you that we're suffering from the global downturn. It was an impossible decision, working out where we could make staff cuts. We had many factors to consider – length of contracts, financial responsibilities, long-term team players . . . And then there's the maternity leave issue.' Selina paused. 'We could hardly make Fiona redundant halfway through her maternity leave – we'd be sued to high heaven!'

'But you could let *me* go,' said Natalie incredulously. 'Because what? I *don't* have dependants?'

'Because, off the record, you are the candidate who will walk straight into another job.' Selina turned over her palms, as if she were presenting Natalie's future to her like a gift. 'It's a small industry. I have no doubt I'll be seeing you again before too long. And in the meantime, have some fun! Relax! Take this as an unexpected sabbatical. You've got holiday outstanding, haven't you? You could be in the Maldives by the weekend!'

And that was it. Her whole career, from fast-tracked graduate trainee until now, condensed into a five-minute 'chat'.

Natalie felt sick, and for once she didn't bother to count it as a possible pregnancy symptom.

She didn't call Johnny straight away.

He would just tell her it was Fate and a lucky break in disguise, and Natalie, who didn't believe in luck, just bloody hard work, wanted to wallow in the sheer unfairness of it for a few hours. So she got in her car and drove to the park, where she sat on a bench and stared at the mid-day Longhampton she'd never had time to see before. Old couples, kids eating chips on their lunchbreak, and – of course – herds of mummies ranging like fertile wildebeest across the park with their Bugaboos.

The mummies felt like a personal slap in the face. Why'd she been worrying about taking maternity leave at the right time when she should have been worrying about her *job*?

Maybe Johnny was right, thought Natalie, feeling a masochistic tug as two toddlers wobbled towards the Jubilee fountain. Maybe it was Fate – grabbing her and telling her to relax on full pay for five months. Everyone else was. When they weren't telling her to drink grapefruit juice, get a pet, book a holiday, drink cough medicine, have sex every day, have sex every other day . . .

No, she decided, *just relax* was the worst. It was irritating on so many different levels. There was nothing in the world less relaxing than living at the mercy of your luteal phase. Anyway, Natalie wasn't a 'relaxing' sort of person; one of the things she loved about Johnny was the fact that he didn't mind trailing round castles and markets on holiday instead of baking on a beach.

The takeaway tea had gone lukewarm in her hand as the questions went round in her head. What was she supposed to do? Go nuts trying to find a new job, work flat out for a year to get maternity leave, and then start trying again with thirty-five staring her in the face? Or just grit her teeth, do the tests and try to fix whatever it was while time was on her side? How much did she and Johnny want kids? Enough to risk everything, if one of them turned out to be infertile?

Natalie shivered, despite the sun glinting off the fountain's jets. Marriage, career, house, friends – she'd taken all of it for granted. And now, suddenly, none of it was certain any more. All it took was one person, telling you one thing, and everything could stop.

She watched as a pack of dogs came into view at the far end of the park, the side that led up to the woods. Through her numbness, she recognised the woman leading them as Rachel, from the rescue shelter.

Was that Bertie, being dragged along at the back? She'd thought about him often since Bill had been to get Lulu, wondering if the right person had come, hoping that he hadn't been taken away by someone careless or cruel.

Nat's heart had twisted at the idea of him sitting howling alone, pacing his kennel, waiting for his owner to come back for him, still loyal despite everything. Still willing to give unconditional love.

Maybe that was what she should do, instead of beating herself up about her substandard womb. Give a stray dog some of her time, and love. Johnny really wanted a dog, she could tell. It was just her job that was standing in the way, and now she didn't have one. If she couldn't give him a baby, maybe a dog would be the next-best thing.

Natalie imagined Bertie curled up happily between her and Johnny on the sofa, and made a decision. Rachel's green jacket was vanishing into the trees – she was too far away now to catch up with, and anyway, Natalie didn't want her to think it was a snap emotional reaction. This was *her* one thing that was going to change everything.

She wiped the smudged mascara from under her eyes, and got out her mobile phone.

Rachel realised something astonishing, halfway up the hill towards the house on the return leg of the walk: she was actually starting to enjoy the daily dog wrangling.

She'd nearly got the knack of keeping the dogs together at the same pace, and the landmarks around her circuit were now getting familiar – the shimmering bluebell banks towards the town, the halfway stretch where the rough bridleway turned into the smooth path of the municipal park, the church spire and town hall tower rising into view.

Megan obviously thought her dog skills were improving, because this morning she'd entrusted her with Bertie, who had not – Rachel looked back to check that he was still moving and not sniffing his way into the hedge again – played up too badly, probably because Gem was on hand to nudge him into line, and even Rachel had realised that none of the dogs had the effrontery to resist Gem's gentle commands.

Even better, through a complicated system of mime, she'd got the deli to bring her a takeaway coffee outside, so she could recaffeinate herself for the way back. It was a tiny taste of London, that double espresso hit, and it only made her feel half-homesick.

Rachel took a deep breath of the fresh air and closed her eyes against the sunshine, letting the dogs lead her uphill.

'Things might work out, eh, Gem?' she said out loud, with only a shred of self-consciousness.

When she'd turned into the orchard behind Four Oaks, and returned the dogs to their runs, Rachel found a welcoming committee at the kitchen table.

Megan was chatting away to a possible new rehomer on the cordless phone and making notes on her clipboard, while Freda sat drawing circles around the obituaries in the local paper.

George Fenwick was also there again, drinking tea and polishing off a fruit cake donated by one of the WI, while a couple of shy teenagers hovered by the dog basket where Zoe Graham's Toffee was busy demolishing three cardboard rolls.

Rachel felt a small ripple of anticipation, seeing George leaning up against the Aga, his sleeves rolled up despite the cold air outside. George brought the outside in with him; he looked as if he'd recently been manhandling a cow or mending a horse, or some other manly countryside vet business. Rachel was a bit hazy on the details.

'Ah,' he said, when she walked in. 'Longhampton's most stylish dog walker.'

'Don't you have a business to go to?' Rachel enquired, hanging the leads back up. It was quite flattering really, that he could be so taken in by one Marc Jacob skirt, reduced.

'I do,' he agreed. 'I just called in to check on a couple of your inmates, and to see how your clearance sale was going.'

'Not so bad, so far,' said Rachel. She scrutinised his craggy face for signs of sarcasm, and found an infuriating mixture of amusement and something she couldn't put her finger on. 'Lulu's gone to Dr Harper as I'm sure Megan's told you . . .'

'And Chester's had a couple of visitors,' added Megan, hanging up the phone. 'Nice couple from Hartley and a woman from Rosehill. Phone's been red hot all morning, hasn't it, Freda? We haven't stopped since you went out!'

'It's those posters, Rachel. I saw your poster in the library, love,' said Freda. 'Very touching. Had the gardening club in *floods*.'

'Good,' said George. 'Get the blue-rinse brigade matched up with those shopping-trolley-sized terriers, and sent straight over to me for vaccinations, please.'

'George!'

'He's a businessman, Freda,' said Rachel, shaking her head. 'Don't let that James Herriot routine fool you.'

'And you'll be pleased to hear that Bertie's going to have a home check too,' added Megan. 'Who wants to do it?'

'Anyone we know?' Freda looked nosy.

'The couple who came along with Dr Bill, actually.' Megan was scribbling down the details. 'It was the wife who rang – she seemed really excited. Natalie. There,' she added, handing her the note, 'they live on that new estate down by the canal. Can you do it tonight?'

'No, I can't.' Freda sighed. 'Oh, shame, it's my bowls night, I wouldn't have minded a look around one of those houses. Lovely, they are. Executive.'

'You can do it, can't you, Rachel?'

'What?'

'You just look round the house, check they've got fences, secure gates, that sort of thing.' Megan made it sound a doddle. 'I've got a checklist you can use. And just think about how happy you're making Bertie! He's been pining for a new home since he arrived.'

'Well, yes, I'm pleased Bertie's on his way out of here!' said Rachel. 'He really seemed to take to the wife – it was like he knew her from somewhere. It was like they clicked.'

Freda wagged a finger. 'See? We told you you'd get the knack!'

'No, Freda,' George corrected her. 'Rachel's just a ruthless businesswoman too, she wants her runs cleared so Megan can get some fee-paying boarders in. Did she tell you about the new scheme she's running? Adopt one dog, get one free? Like Tesco, but with the smaller dogs. Your Ted's thinking about getting a couple of replacements for Pippin.'

Freda's face registered shock, then crossness, and then she swatted George's arm. 'You're having me on! He wouldn't do that. Not without telling me. Ooh, you're an awful man.'

George winked at Rachel, who stifled a smile, then furrowed her brow in disapproval. 'Says the man doing two-for-one testicle removals.'

It was hard not to respond to George's pantomime grumpiness. She wondered why she was the only one who bothered pitching it back to him – he seemed to like it.

'But you should think about a dog, Freda,' said Megan persuasively. 'It'd be good for you, honestly. You *and* Ted. Help him to think about retiring.'

'It'd take a very special little dog to replace Pippin,' said Freda. 'Did I tell you, Rachel, how he used to—'

Rachel's mobile rang in her pocket and she flinched when she heard who was calling: her mother.

Val and Oliver had called daily but now he seemed to have given up, presumably to fix his marriage, but Val hadn't. Rachel knew what she'd want to talk about as well: the current progress on the probate, and the whereabouts of silver brush sets and Acker Bilk albums, neither of which she'd quite got around to locating.

'Would you excuse me?' she said, grabbing the solicitor's file, still largely untouched, off the breadbin. 'I'll just take this call.'

Conversation started up as soon as she reached the stairs, with George's hearty laugh booming over the top, but she ignored the voice in her head wondering if they were laughing about her.

'Mum, how are you?' she said. Rachel knew she should have phoned earlier but there was a limit to how much red-hot news of new teeth and bowel movements she could stand.

'I'm fine, Rachel.' Val sounded slightly off. 'How's it going? Have you made any headway with the sorting out?'

'Not really, I've been busy with the kennels.' Rachel crossed the landing, and turned towards Dot's bedroom at the front of the house. 'Listen, I'm going to get those brushes now, all right? But I'm not supposed to dish anything out until probate's cleared and I've paid the first bit of inheritance tax. It could take six months, you know.'

She threw the file on the bed, and began searching for the letter Dot had left for her. Val would be bound to ask about that. She'd forgotten all about it, assuming it would be specific bequests to the dogs. Instructions to leave Gem in charge of dog matchmaking or something. Files and accounts tumbled out until it appeared, and Rachel clamped the phone under her ear while she slit it open with a finger.

It was only one side of Dot's neat handwriting, and didn't seem to contain any bequest details at all.

Oh *great*, thought Rachel, but her mother was speaking again.

'I wasn't just ringing about that, Rachel! But are you managing? Do you want me to come and help you sort things out?'

'No, I'm fine, Mum. These brushes, where do you think they'd be? Did she use them? Or will they be in a drawer?'

Rachel had only put her head around Dot's door so far; it felt rather odd, poking around someone else's most personal space when their toothpaste was still fresh. The dressing table was as Dot had left it, with her gold-cased lipsticks and tissues scattered about, and a dry-cleaning bag hung on the back of the door. Two tweed skirts, and a jacket.

The room smelled of old ladies, thought Rachel, looking around. Stylish old ladies, not the crumpled husks of women Val shunted from day centre to table-top sale. Dot's room smelled of woollen clothes and old-fashioned perfume and powder compacts.

She twisted up the nearest lipstick, expecting to see a sugar pink colour: it was a deep carmine red.

'They'd be on her dressing table,' Val added. 'They were my grandmother's, family heirlooms. *Our* grandmother's, I should say.'

'They're not here,' said Rachel. 'There's just knick-knacks and some photos.' She picked up the largest, in a silver frame, and studied it with interest. Everything downstairs showed Dot in her old age, surrounded by animals, looking somewhat weatherbeaten. This, though, was a young Dot at a formal function, looking positively sultry in a satin shift dress, leaning up against a handsome man in a sharp suit.

A *very* handsome man.

Rachel frowned with surprise. Was that actually Dot? This woman was quite a stunner. Her exotic dark looks were perfect for the dramatic sixties style; she was striking, like Eleanor Bron or Alma Cogan, and wasn't afraid to play up her bold features with false lashes and jet-black hair piled high on her head.

And the man was pretty sexy too: full lips, thick hair, a sort of Mick Jagger-ish twinkle in his eye. He was glancing sideways at Dot with a proud expression on his face – with good reason, Rachel thought. He looked as if Dot had just cracked a particularly witty joke.

'Who would this man be on Dot's dressing table, Mum?' she asked. 'I thought Dot never had a serious boyfriend.'

'Where did you get that idea?' said Val, evasively.

'From you?' The frame was heavy too, hallmarked solid silver. It must have been someone special to have warranted the frame, as well as the prominent place.

'Well . . . I'm sure I never said that.'

Rachel's skin tingled as she looked into Dot's hooded eyes, so like her own, and the penny dropped. *Dot* was the woman in the spare room chalk drawing. She hadn't recognised her, because the only photo she remembered of a younger Dot was the one at Amelia's christening, in which Dot looked like the lost Supreme in a tangerine trouser suit that her mother still clearly took as a personal affront.

There was a gap in her mother's photograph albums – Dot appeared as an ankle-socked child with Val, then as a lanky teenager off to university, and then pretty much nothing until she hovered in the background in a few weddings and funerals, white-haired and clearly uncomfortable.

This was the Dorothy who was missing – a Dorothy who hadn't always lived in tweeds. A Dot who'd been quite clearly adored by someone hot enough to give Oliver a run for his money.

'Oh my God, Mum,' said Rachel. 'Why did you never tell me about this?'

'Because it's not something we liked to discuss,' said Val. 'I'm not sure I want to talk about it now, actually.'

Which was possibly the worst thing she could have said.

'You have to,' said Rachel.

## 10

Val's shifty tone immediately alerted Rachel that there might have been more to her mother's frequent phone calls than a simple interest in Rachel's house-clearing skills.

Was she worried that some family secret was about to come to light, she wondered with delicious curiosity. Because it obviously was.

'Come on, Mum,' she said. 'This is news to me. I thought the whole point was that Dot lived the life of a nun, but with dogs instead of singing children and a guitar.'

'I didn't say she didn't *ever* have a boyfriend . . . I said she was too picky to settle down with one.'

'Well, she doesn't look as if she did too badly with this bloke,' said Rachel, examining the photograph more closely. 'Who is it? It must be, what . . . mid-sixties? In what looks like a hotel bar?'

There was a pause on the other end of the line. 'It would probably be Felix, I expect,' said Val. 'Tall, curly hair? Bit of a dandy?'

'Yes, I suppose so. Looks like an expensive suit.'

'Mmm. Felix Henderson was his name.' Another pause. 'He and Dot were . . . Well, I can't pretend I know what went on there. They seemed quite serious about each other, but it all fizzled out for some reason. I didn't like to ask, in the end. Dot thought I was very old-fashioned about relationships, but then I was married at twenty-one years of age.'

Rachel's brain was busy putting two and two together,

very rapidly, given her own experience of complicated relationships. Was this what Dot had meant, when she said men liked to be complicated? Was this Felix already married? Was he someone Dot had worked with? She wasn't even sure she knew what Dot had done for a living. Val was very vague about anything that went on in London.

'But they were quite serious, though?'

'Well, they courted for a good few years, went on holiday together, that sort of thing. He never managed to get a ring on her finger, though, poor Felix. She was daft to let him go, if you ask me.'

'Maybe she didn't want a ring on her finger,' retorted Rachel, automatically. Dot's fingers in the photograph were noticeably covered with plenty of other expensive jewellery. 'Maybe she *preferred* being single.'

'Preferred suiting herself, more like.' Val sounded vexed. 'But that was Dot. Wouldn't be told anything.'

'So how come I don't remember this Felix?' Rachel turned the photograph to the light. 'He's really handsome. They both are. They make a great couple – Dot looks like a model in this.'

'Oh, you wouldn't have met him – Dot broke it off when you were a toddler. I never got to know him, not really. She didn't trouble Felix with our family functions, said he was too busy with his job.' The short pause added, *which even your father didn't believe.*

'Which was?' she prompted.

'He was a businessman of some kind. Dot met him when she was working as a secretary in the City, I think.'

'But you met him, though?' Rachel was curious now. 'What was he like?'

'I just met him the once. Amelia's christening was the only time our side of the family ever met him. In eight years, would you believe. Anyone would have thought he didn't *want* to meet us.'

Not going to family functions was a hanging offence in Val's book; Rachel had been hauled over the coals about it herself in recent years. Naturally, she hadn't been able to explain that holiday opportunities with Oliver were like hen's teeth and had to be grabbed with both hands, even if they did coincide with other people's wedding anniversaries. Especially since weddings and wedding anniversaries weren't Rachel's family occasions of choice.

A gossip bell rang in a distant part of her memory, and she frowned, trying to dig out a half-heard grown-up conversation. 'Did something . . . happen at Amelia's christening, Mum?'

There was a pause. 'Not that I'm aware of.'

Rachel rolled her eyes. That meant something *had* done. Val was a skilful brusher-under-the-carpet. If she didn't want to talk about something, it might as well never have happened.

Rachel, on the other hand, had all the imagination Val and Amelia lacked, and a secret knowledge of the complications illicit relationships brought. Her mind whirred.

Felix was a good-looking guy. Had there been some sisterly jealousy? Her dad was a nice man, but he thought a good night out involved bowls and a lock-in at The Bull and Bishop. Felix, on the other hand, looked as if he *was* the good night out. Like Oliver. Suave and confident. A man who could have you in a cab in ten seconds on a rainy night, and into bed in sixty.

'So how did they meet?' she persisted, curious. 'Come on, Mum – I can't believe you've never told me about Dot's gorgeous bloke. I thought she was a lonely old spinster!'

'Well, if she'd sorted herself out and married Felix she needn't have been! Not that I ever really knew any details.' Val was sounding really shifty now. 'Rachel, it's never nice to speak ill of the dead. It wasn't any of our business at the time and it's still not.'

'Mum, I'm in her house! I'm going to find out anyway, once I start going through the eight million drawers!'

There was a reluctant sigh. 'He did something financial,' Val said. 'He had a big house in Chelsea, I know that much, when she had some poky studio flat. Felix either came from money, or had made a lot of it, because he had some very fancy friends, and a nice sportscar that he gave Dot when he got bored. I remember your father was very jealous of Dot getting to drive around in it . . .'

Rachel moved slowly across the room, and picked up other smaller framed photographs, kept in a shrine-like cluster on the mahogany chest: Dot on a continental quayside in big shades and Capri pants, Dot and Felix at another black-tie party, Felix on his own, posing against a white Jaguar E-type, his tight shirt open and an uproarious smile lighting up his face, as if some passer-by had just mistaken him for Tom Jones – and he didn't really mind.

No wonder Dad was jealous – he was schlepping us around in an Austin Allegro, she thought. Yelling at Amelia not to spill pop on the seats.

'But they just split up? Didn't she tell you why?'

She could almost hear her mother's lips purse. 'We didn't talk about things like that.'

Rachel stopped in front of the window, which looked out over the small gravel drive, towards Longhampton, the spires and towers visible in the far distance, and the sheep-bobbled fields in between. So different from the London scene Dot had obviously been a glittering part of. The photos downstairs and the photos in this room could be of two totally different women, two totally different lives.

'And you never asked?' Rachel had never quite understood her mother's fundamental lack of curiosity.

But scrupulously fair or not, Val wasn't afraid to go on the counter-attack. 'Do you and Amelia talk about private things?

Has she ever asked you why you and that nice Paul split up? Because he was a nice chap, Rachel. We hoped that might . . .'

'Paul and I were never serious,' Rachel began, and then stopped. Paul – a thoroughly pleasant solicitor friend of a friend – had been an attempt to prompt Oliver into some kind of . . . well, she wasn't even sure what she'd expected. It hadn't worked. Paul wasn't right. Oliver knew it. She'd gone back to him before nice Paul had had a chance to get attached.

Oliver. God, he had made her behave in ways she really wasn't proud of.

On top of the chest, on a lace runner, was a faded colour photograph that she'd never seen, but she recognised the occasion from the clothes: it was herself, about two years old, in Dot's arms at Amelia's christening. Dot was wearing a fashionable tangerine orange trouser suit, complete with trailing headscarf, and she was wearing a pair of tiny dungarees. They were both beaming at each other with great delight, big nose to miniature big nose.

We do both have strong noses, thought Rachel, rather sadly. I suppose I'll end up with all that white hair too. And the house, full of dogs, and no man, while my sister brings up her kids and organises Boxing Day sherry parties and drives everyone up the wall sending birthday and anniversary cards.

She felt her skin prickle. History was repeating itself. Dot had messed things up with a man, and now she had too. Maybe it was inevitable, a character trait. Like Dot's isolation.

'Amelia thinks . . .' Val began, but Rachel interrupted her.

'That doesn't mean I don't *love* Amelia, though,' she blurted out. 'Just that our lives . . . our lives are very different. She's got Grace and Jack, and she thinks I'm . . . well, it doesn't matter. I never know what to say. Just because someone's related to you doesn't mean you automatically get on.'

There was another pause on the line, but it was different to the previous ones. Rachel thought she could detect a sigh.

'Well, exactly.'

She stood still, in front of the big double bed for one, wondering whether handsome Felix had ever pulled Dot to his bare chest in this room. A shiver ran through her.

'Have you tried in her wardrobe?' suggested Val, in her 'changing the subject' tone. 'Because now I think about it, you should have a look for some of the jewellery Felix gave her. Some nice pieces there, I'd say, might be something you could give to Amelia and Grace for when she's older.'

'But I can't send them to you until probate's been granted.'

'You can look, can't you?'

Rachel opened Dot's modest wardrobe, ready for a blast of mothballs and old coats, and blinked at the unexpected flash of emerald and cherry red. Satin and brocade dresses and jackets gleamed from the dark interior, tucked between dark wool suits like jewels in a case. Elegant hat-boxes and tissue-stuffed shoes lined the bottom while drawers of gloves and folded evening scarves filled up one whole side.

Her great-grandmother's silver-backed brush and mirror set sat at the top of the drawers, stashed carelessly on a box from a Mayfair lingerie shop.

'Are they there?' Val enquired, clearly wishing she was there to do the job properly.

Rachel grinned. I bet Mum expected her to have them on the dressing table like a dutiful spinster ought, she thought, liking Dot even more. Not hidden away on top of a gift from her rich lover. I wonder if Amelia would prefer what's in the box?

'I've found them,' she said. 'Tell Dad I'll look for his Acker Bilk albums this afternoon.' She pulled out a silver maxi dress that rustled seductively in her hands like snakeskin. It still smelled of Shalimar.

Dot! thought Rachel. What *did* you get up to before you hid yourself away here? The prospect of beginning the sorting-out process suddenly didn't seem so bad.

'Good girl,' said Val, sounding more like herself. 'Have you got time off work? They ought to be understanding, what with it being a family bereavement.'

'Mmm.' Felix must have taken Dot to some smart places, she thought, stroking the soft velvets and crisp moiré satins. Maybe the same places she'd gone with Oliver.

'Mum, listen, I'll call you back, shall I? I've got to go,' she said, making a mental vow to tell Vall all about her resignation next time they spoke.

Then she sank down on the bedspread and read Dot's letter properly.

*Dear Rachel,* Dot wrote.

*If you're reading this, then I'm long gone, you've seen the solicitor, and now you're beginning the uphill task of sorting out my house. Poor you! I want you to know that I've left you in charge because you're the only member of our family whom I think really understands secrets. In the course of sifting through forty years of junk, you're going to come across things that are precious to me - and some of those are secrets I've held on to for many years. Not all of them are mine. It's up to you what you do with them, just as it's up to you to decide what to do with the house.*

*Here's our first secret. I've made a bit of a mess of saving for inheritance tax - you're going to get clobbered. But in the butter dish in the fridge there is a necklace I've never worn. Wear it so everyone thinks it's yours, and then, if needs be, you can sell it. I have a feeling your 'complicated' relationship means the odd diamond necklace here or there isn't unlikely.*

*And here's another. Your mother and I fell out some years back, and she thinks it was her fault. It wasn't. It was mine, as you might see when you go through the house. If you can find a way of explaining it to her, then I'll be eternally grateful. I would have explained it to her years ago, but I made a promise that I couldn't break. Maybe you can.*

*I hope you'll find everyone you need in this house. I did. I hope, too, that by the time you read this, you're more settled than you seemed last time we met. If all else fails, my advice - for what it's worth - would be to take the dogs for a walk. Even if the answer never comes, you've made someone else happy in that time, and I find that counts for something in the bigger picture.*

*Love, Dorothy*

*PS Please take good care of Gem. He took great care of me.*

Rachel sank back onto the bed, winded by the unexpectedly vivid tone of the letter. It felt as if the younger Dot, not the elderly lady she thought she knew, was in there with her, winking in a conspiratorial manner. Secrets? Where? And how was she meant to find them, let alone parcel them out like silver hairbrushes?

There was a scratching at the door, and Gem's long nose appeared, followed by the rest of his ghostly body. Without making eye contact he skulked to her side, as if she couldn't see him, and lay down a few feet away.

Rachel felt cornered, her imagination interrupted. It was like having a toddler following her about – she couldn't even shower without Gem scratching the door. Was she ever going to be alone here? 'What do you want now?' she snapped, then remembered Dot's note and felt guilty. 'Do you need feeding? A pee? A quick Sudoku? Help me out here?'

Gem raised his head but made no sound. Rachel clicked her tongue, and got up to go downstairs. Silently, he followed her.

Rachel was relieved to find that Megan and George's gathering had relocated to the kennel office. The kitchen was empty, and she crouched down to reach right into the back of the fridge, where a Clarice Cliff butter dish was rammed behind many sticky jars of local WI jam.

Rachel pulled it out, sceptical. The more she thought about it, the more it sounded as if Dot had started with Alzheimer's – necklaces in butter dishes? Honestly?

Half expecting to find a lump of rancid butter, she lifted the lid and her mouth slackened in shock.

Heaped up like any old jumble-sale tat was a collar of fine diamonds, interspersed with sapphires the size of her little fingernail. Rachel sat back on her heels in shock, and held the chilled jewels up to the window, letting shards of pure wintery light dance through onto the paw-marked floor tiles. Her unmanicured fingers felt too shabby to be holding something so lovely and when she put it around her neck she gasped at the sensation of the cold settings against her skin.

Rachel looked at herself in the oven door, pulling her hair back off her neck for full effect. There were thousands of pounds-worth of stones, just lying on her collarbone. There was no way she could pass this off as hers to anyone who knew her – or Oliver. She was a minimalist, and he'd always kept his gifts untraceable: flowers, dinners, cash 'to treat herself'. This was a flamboyantly romantic gift, a necklace to adorn someone equally precious, given by someone very generous, or very in love.

Rachel wasn't given to bouts of self-awareness but, for the first time ever, she could have kicked herself for her selfishness. Why hadn't she taken more time to talk to her aunt? Why hadn't she built on that awkward but comforting New Year's Eve? Why had she been so glib as to swallow Val's version of the bonkers old unloved dog-martyr, even when she was mature enough to see it for what it was – an old family argument gone bad?

Dot hadn't been quite real to Rachel, growing up so far away; she'd seemed more like a character in a book, surrounded by her dogs and decorated with Val's mutterings. Only now was Dot starting to come to life, in a bizarrely close shadow of Rachel's own experiences, and it was too late to ask her anything.

'Bollocks,' said Rachel and on cue, Gem slid silently into the kitchen, sitting down next to the hook where his lead hung.

# II

Johnny would have guessed something was up even without the five missed calls on his phone. But now, as he strolled round the corner towards their house, he spotted Nat's Mini parked in the drive.

He did a double take and checked his watch. Natalie was rarely at home before seven at the earliest. It was their running joke, that he was the part-timer who had the tea ready on the table when she threw her laptop bag into the hall well after the nightly news had finished.

Johnny quickened his step. Though she'd rung several times while his phone was off in class, she hadn't left a message for him, which made him hope for the best. Maybe it was a bedroom summons. According to his vague reckonings (based around Birmingham City home matches) they were entering a critical time; maybe Nat had come home early to waylay him at the door in her beige mac and last year's anniversary underwear?

That had been something of a highlight a few months back.

Johnny smiled as he loosened his tie and swung his bag of marking onto the other shoulder. If Nat'd now managed to pinpoint her ovulation down to exact hours it wouldn't surprise him. Last summer, she was the one who'd learned basic Finnish in the time it had taken him to remember the name of their hotel properly.

The front door was open when he pushed it, and he could hear the sound of Hoovering inside.

Hoovering? Now that wasn't so much like Natalie. Johnny frowned. Maybe his mother had finally cracked and broken into their house to give it the spring clean she kept hinting that it needed. Nat's calls were for back-up.

'Nat? Is that you?' He dropped his school bag by the door and shrugged off his thick coat.

The vacuum cleaner was turned off, and Natalie appeared in the sitting-room door. She was bright-eyed and still wearing her navy suit, but her feet were bare and her bob was messed up with static so it rose in a blonde halo round her head.

'Are you *cleaning*?' Johnny asked, bewildered. 'But Mrs Landon came yesterday, didn't she?'

'She did. But I'm doing it again.' Natalie trod on the cord winder, and the plug spun back at high speed into the machine, flicking dangerously near her slender ankle. 'I've done downstairs and I'm just going to—'

'Stop! Stop!' Johnny grabbed her by the arms. 'Are you OK? You look . . .' He peered at her, not sure how she looked. She looked a bit pissed, if he was honest. Her eyes were bright and she was hot. 'You look a bit flushed.'

Natalie bit her lip and wiped her forehead with the back of her hand.

'Do you want to sit down?' Johnny asked, wondering if it had something to do with his sister's baby news that morning. 'I think you should. Come on, let me make you a cup of tea.'

He realised he was talking to her as if she was an escaped mental patient, but Natalie didn't seem to mind as he steered her into the kitchen, and sat her at the table.

There were documents strewn across the table, Johnny noticed, along with various Mr Sheen-type products he didn't recognise. Cleaning wasn't his forte; it wasn't Nat's either, hence the weekly ministrations of Mrs Landon. He put the kettle on for a cup of tea; his instincts told him to open a bottle of wine, but wine was on Natalie's hit list for both of them, at least until her period arrived each month.

'Johnny, I've got good news and bad news,' announced Natalie. 'Which do you want first?'

'Er, the good news?'

Her eyes shone with enthusiasm. 'You know those lovely dogs we saw up at the rescue, the night we went with Bill?'

'Yes,' he said guardedly.

'And you know you've always wanted a dog?'

Johnny couldn't see where this was going. 'Yes, but didn't we decide that we couldn't have a dog while we were both working full time?' He scanned her face. 'We *did* decide that?'

'I know. I know, but things change, and I've been thinking about Bertie, that lovely Basset hound, and anyway, I've arranged for Rachel, who runs the rescue, remember?, to come and do a home visit tonight – hence the cleaning – and if that's OK, then we can take him out for a walk tomorrow, and see how we get on!' She smiled up from the table, and though she looked happy enough, Johnny felt a sinking sensation in the pit of his stomach.

Something was wrong. He wasn't sure what it was – he wasn't sure he was ever going to follow Natalie's much quicker brain – but something was definitely off-balance.

'Nat,' he said, 'what do you mean, things change? What was the bad news?'

'I've rung Bill and he's going to come with us, because he's picking Lulu up to bring her home tomorrow,' Natalie went on, sorting through the papers and banging them against the table top. 'We don't need to take anything with us, apparently – they've got leads and . . .'

The kettle boiled behind Johnny, but he ignored it. Slowly, he went round the table and sat down next to her, not letting her break his gaze. He lifted the paperwork out of her hands and glanced down at the familiar logo – it was her contract.

Or rather, it wasn't her contract: it was an official letter about . . . redundancy packages?

'Nat?' Johnny looked up at her, and her manic smile faltered. 'Tell me the bad news. Now.'

She bit her lip. 'I've been made redundant. They're merging two departments, part of a cost-cutting measure. I've got five months' pay and as many letters of recommendation as I want. Oh, and obviously plenty of time to walk a dog.' She blinked, hard. 'I've decided that I've got to make the best of it. Treat it like a sabbatical.'

Johnny was lost for words. He wasn't sure what she wanted him to say – this wasn't the calm reaction he'd have expected from a woman who lived for her job, who treated each promotion like a badge of honour.

'Right,' he said. 'How much notice have they given you?'

'No notice. I've got three weeks' holiday outstanding, from last year, so they've asked if I want to take it now, and finish today.'

'Today?' He couldn't make sense of it. 'So . . . you're not going back on Monday? That's it?'

Natalie nodded. 'Me and half the department. At least I get my holiday pay. And I don't have to organise any of the leaving parties, so it's not all bad news, hey?'

Johnny racked his brains and wished he understood the subtleties of women's minds better. It couldn't just be the job that was making her like this – a bit mad. Was this something to do with his mum calling about Becky this morning? But that didn't make sense – getting sacked and someone else getting pregnant in one day would surely bring anyone to tears?

'OK,' he said, standing up and playing for time. 'Shouldn't you be a bit more . . . upset? I mean, I don't *want* you to be upset but . . .'

'Johnny?' Natalie stretched her hands across the table, so he had to sit back down again. 'I've spent the afternoon being upset. I've *done* upset. I've *done* how bloody unfair it is. I don't want to waste any more time on stuff I can't change. I want to do things for us, from now on. Stuff I *can* change.'

Johnny looked at his wife. She looked so small and determined, like a little girl in her work suit, that he was filled with a desperate urge to make her happy. 'It's going to be OK, Nat. If you want to adopt a dog, then great! Let's do it! Weekends in the park, training, whatever! Fantastic!'

Natalie glanced down and seemed to be gathering herself for a second confession. 'When I say stuff we *can* change, I mean . . . Johnny, let's go to the doctors and have those tests done. I know you're not keen but I think we should. So we're not just waiting and hoping.'

'Tests?' Johnny squirmed at the thought of waiting rooms and test bottles and Natalie even more keyed up than she was right now. 'But can't we just . . . I don't know . . . take more iron?'

'I need to know,' said Natalie. She spread her hands out on the table, and looked at her fingers, with her wedding and engagement and eternity rings sparkling. 'Every month, I try to do everything right, and I hope against hope that this time, it'll work, and it's not. It's not working. And it feels like I'm failing. Every single month.'

When she looked up, Johnny realised her mascara was smeared, where she'd been crying. He felt ashamed that he hadn't realised just how miserable it was making her.

'I just need to know why,' she said, in a small voice. 'What's wrong with me.'

Johnny's heart lurched. He was so lucky. So incredibly lucky. He didn't ask for much in life – a wife, a job, a house with a garage, a few pints down the pub with Bill every so often – and he had it all, without even trying. A baby on top would just be a bonus, though he couldn't really tell Nat, not when she was sitting there, breaking her heart. *She* was all he wanted.

'Of course,' he heard himself say. 'Make the appointment.'

Her face flushed with gratitude, and he felt mean that it was obviously such a big deal for her to ask. She grabbed his hands, and entwined her slim fingers round his. 'Thank you.'

'But on one condition.' Johnny tightened his grip and felt her wedding ring nip his skin. 'Whatever these tests say, we still have each other, right? And we can be happy, just us. We're not going to turn into those couples who go to dinner parties and talk about their . . .' He cringed just thinking about it. '. . . their sperm samples or whatever.'

'Of course not!' Natalie's eyes were shining, either with tears or something else. Determination. 'Don't be daft. But this time off . . . It'll give us a good chance to try.'

In that moment, Johnny had a rare flash of intuition: that while they were both saying the same thing, Natalie was already thinking something two or three steps ahead of where he was, and it worried him that he had no idea what that was.

The front doorbell rang and she sprang to her feet. 'That'll be Rachel from the rescue now. Do you think I should be in my suit?' She wrinkled her nose. 'Does that make it look like I'm too fussy to have a dog? Hang on, I'm going to get changed. You let her in, and show her round. Make her a cup of tea or something.'

Natalie darted out of the room and Johnny heard her stockinged feet thumping up the stairs.

Johnny stared after her, bewildered. How on earth did women manage to go from emotional meltdown to worrying about the right clothes for a rescue shelter, in the space of ten seconds? How could she be more worried about whether the house was clean enough for a dog than she was about being made redundant? Shaking his head, he went back out to the hall and opened the front door.

On the front step stood Rachel Fielding, clutching a clipboard. Johnny thought she looked a lot younger in her off-duty clothes than she had when they'd met earlier that week; her dark hair was ruffled out of its neat crop and she was wearing jeans, boots and some kind of shiny sixties jacket, and very little make-up apart from a slash of matte red lipstick.

Johnny immediately felt nervous. Rachel wasn't the sort of woman he was really used to; she had a London sort of gleam to her, something to do with the haircut (which Natalie loved and he thought looked weird), and the confident manner. She had a huge handbag, big enough to stow a small child in, and so weirdly studded he suspected it was fashionable. Nat would know.

'Hi,' she said, raising a hand – with dark blue nails. They looked freshly done. 'I'm here to check out your house to see if it's Bertie-proof?'

'Come on in.' Johnny stood back to let her pass and wondered when the assessment was going to start. Had it started already? 'Should we have a catch on the door?' he asked.

'No! I mean, I don't think so. Please don't look so worried,' she added. 'It's really not a big deal, just a quick look round.'

'Try telling my wife that,' said Johnny. 'She's Hoovered everywhere.'

Rachel gave him a sympathetic look. 'Seriously? Her Hoovering days are just beginning. I could restuff a sofa with the amount of hair Dot's collie sheds in three days. Look.' She showed him the checklist; question three was, 'Does the new home have white carpets?'

Johnny raised his eyebrows. 'Is that a good thing or a bad thing?'

Rachel's wide red mouth twitched humorously. 'Megan says that anyone with white carpets and visible evidence of a Lakeland shopping habit should be gently steered towards getting some goldfish.'

'Oh, good.' Johnny let out a deep breath. 'Because between you and me, we're not exactly . . .'

'Not exactly what?' Natalie came bounding down the stairs in a pair of jeans and a soft red shirt she'd had since college. 'Hello, Rachel! Thanks for coming out so quickly!'

'Well, thank you for ringing up about Bertie – we're quite keen to get the dogs rehomed, as you know.' Rachel smiled, glanced round the room, and made some swift ticks on her clipboard. 'This really isn't going to take up too much time. I don't want to ruin your Friday night.'

'Oh, that's not a problem, we were staying in anyway,' said Natalie, surreptitiously moving a breakable glass ornament off the telephone table.

Johnny peered over Rachel's shoulder to see what she was ticking but Natalie shot him a 'don't!' glare.

'Do you want a cup of coffee while you're looking round, Rachel?' she asked sweetly. 'Or a glass of wine?'

'Thanks!' Rachel followed Natalie into the kitchen, peering around as she went. 'You'll have to bear with me – this is the first check I've done. Normally you'd get Freda assessing your living conditions. I'm sure Bertie would be very happy to move in to this house. I know I would. Is that your garden? Sorry, but I've got to check for fences. Ooh, what a gorgeous kitchen!'

Natalie beamed with pride. 'Course, go ahead. Johnny, show Rachel outside while I make some coffee.'

Johnny pretended to salute his wife, and extended his arm towards the back door, flicking on the outdoor lights. 'After you.'

Rachel walked round the perimeter of their flowerbeds, scribbling on her board as she went. Johnny followed her with a torch, and wondered how she was managing to walk on the grass in her boots, but kept his questions to polite enquiries about exercise and routines.

Natalie was waiting with three perfect cappuccinos on the table when they got back in, the velvety foam neatly dusted with chocolate. She was proud of her coffee.

'Wow!' Rachel pulled an appreciative face as she took a sip. 'That is the best coffee I've had since I got here.'

'You should try the deli in town,' said Natalie, always eager to help with information. 'It looks a bit rough from the outside, but inside it's much nicer. They've gone organic.'

'I.e., they've put their prices up by fifteen per cent and they tell you the name of the cow who made the milk for your tea,' explained Johnny. 'Everything comes in a paper bag and is made by people called Rollo in Crediton.'

Rachel smiled and somehow looked more like the girls Natalie saw at the book club. 'Yes, but the problem is they don't let dogs in. And I always seem to be dragging at least four around with me.' She winked at Natalie in a long-suffering way. 'Megan should say on this form of hers, what a great credit-crunch asset dogs are – you can't go into shops any more! You're going to be spending a lot of time at home or at the end of a lead!'

'Fine with me!' said Natalie. 'I'm on sabbatical, as of Monday.'

Rachel looked between them and tapped her pen against her lips. 'I don't mean to sound negative, but you don't know how long that's likely to be for, do you? It could be six months, or six weeks, or . . .'

'It's not going to be less than six months,' said Natalie decisively. 'I've got a couple of projects I want to work on.'

Rachel turned her form sideways, so they could see what was written on it in Megan's large handwriting. 'Don't take this as a personal slight, but Megan's suggested you foster Bertie, since you're not going to be at home for him full time. It's just as helpful,' she added quickly. 'He hates being in kennels, and getting some house training will mean he'll be much more adoptable. Is that OK?'

'Of course.' Natalie's face was bright at the prospect of the challenge. 'If it gets him out of the kennels, we'll have made a difference to him.'

Johnny glanced at her, concerned. 'Nat, that's not going to be so easy, you know. Having to give him up, if someone else . . .'

'We'll cross that bridge when we come to it.'

Rachel looked pleased. 'We'll miss him, but he needs one-on-one attention. And rules. Like, strictly no counter-surfing, and definitely no sofas,' she added, pointing at the notes. 'Megan says you've got to be firm because his bones are still growing. No stairs or sofas until he's two.'

'Course. And will there be the option to keep him permanently? If things change?'

Rachel nodded, then stopped as Johnny turned the clipboard to read something.

'What's this?' he asked, pointing at Megan's asterisked note. '"Ask about kids"?'

'Oh, nuts. Sorry.' Rachel grabbed the board back and her cheekbones turned red under her porcelain make-up. 'I have to ask, but it feels a bit rude and I'd go mad if someone asked me. But Megan said I have to.' She sighed. 'Are you planning on having children in the next year or so?'

Johnny and Natalie looked at each other.

'I mean,' Rachel went on, not quite seeing the unspoken exchange, 'you're a bit younger than me, but sometimes it feels as if the one thing people feel utterly at liberty to ask a woman is whether she's having a child, whether she's leaving it a bit late, whether she feels her career or her ability to have kids is more important. They wouldn't ask about your religion, would they? Or your weight?' She directed her eye-roll towards Natalie, who rolled her eyes back, sympathetically.

Natalie hesitated, unable to tell a direct lie. 'The thing is . . .' she began.

'Shall I make some more coffee?' asked Johnny.

'Yes, please,' said Natalie. 'Make mine a decaff. No, actually, go mad – I'll have a full-caff one.' She passed him her cup and went on talking to Rachel. 'You don't have any then?'

Rachel shook her head. 'No,' she said. 'I don't. But anyway, I still think it's intrusive, and I'm only asking because Megan says dogs can get very upset at being pushed down the pecking order, and we'd hate to be making a complicated situation worse.'

'Mmm, quite,' said Natalie. 'But it hasn't bothered you, the kids thing?'

Oh, Nat, shut up, thought Johnny but Rachel's face didn't change too much. There was just a brief pause, before she answered.

'Sometimes,' she admitted. 'But not for long. I work in PR, and there's lots of travelling, short-notice stuff. I like my independence, doing my own thing.' She grimaced, semi-seriously. 'I've got to tell you, having a dog's made me realise just what a pain in the arse it would be to have a baby. At least I can leave Gem with Megan. And I only need to pick up his poo twice a day.'

Natalie laughed, her full throaty laugh. Johnny realised, as he gripped the espresso handle, that he hadn't heard her laugh like that for months.

'But you are thinking of kids?' Rachel went on.

'Yes, we are,' said Johnny, before Natalie could leap in. He wanted Nat to know he'd meant it, about the tests. Even if it wasn't what eager-to-please Nat thought Rachel wanted to hear for her notes. 'But obviously it wouldn't be for nine months,' he added. 'So that wouldn't affect the fostering idea, would it?'

'Not at all. Lovely,' said Rachel. 'Well, good luck!'

She bowed her head to make a quick note, and Johnny wasn't sure what he saw in her face.

He knew what he saw in Natalie's, though. Real happiness.

And when he saw that, the faint cloud in Johnny's heart lifted, and he smiled his guileless, loving smile across the kitchen.

On the other side of town, in the terraced houses near the canal, Zoe glared at David's new car and wondered where in Milton Keynes he was living, that he now needed a four-wheel-drive, all-utility sports vehicle that looked as if it was about to crush her battered Polo beneath its mighty wheels.

David had arrived at eight on the dot to collect Leo and Spencer, and their new yappy best friend, along with all their stuff and the surprising amount Toffee needed too. It filled the boot of his flashy midlife-crisis-mobile, not that David seemed to mind, as the boys clamoured around his legs with news about school and their mates but mainly their puppy.

Toffee was sitting in the boot, silently yelping his head off, and – Zoe hoped –having a clandestine wee on the upholstery. Toffee liked weeing in new places. According to Megan at the rescue, he'd weed in a few corners of their office, but was responding well to the strict on-the-half-hour programme she'd put him on. Since he'd been attending daycare, he'd already learned not to wee *on* people. He'd also learned the word 'No'.

Megan had taught her that, with Rachel. The three of them had practised saying, 'No!' and making policeman hand gestures, until even Zoe had managed to quell Toffee's worst noises. Her 'No!' was now rating a 4/10 on Megan's scale.

'You've got to be firm,' she'd said when Zoe reeled at the unfamiliar voice of authority coming out of her mouth. 'Make boundaries. Stick to them! It's what he needs.'

Boundaries weren't Zoe's strong point, though. Now she drew a deep breath and forced herself to raise one with David.

'I need some daycare money for the dog,' she muttered, still trying to maintain the cheery expression the boys could see.

'Daycare? For a dog? Speak to my solicitor.' That was David's new catchphrase, along with, 'We need to go through the proper channels.'

Zoe's determination flagged. She'd been deflating slowly since last night, with Leo and Spencer's eager discussion about the amazing rides they'd be going on with Dad. But she saw Spencer looking at her anxiously through the tinted glass, and reminded herself that she had every right to expect David to follow through on his stupid gestures.

Zoe remembered Megan's 'firm voice' pep talk, and made herself press on. 'He's a baby, he can't be left alone all day, and you know I've got to work full time. Well, clearly you know I've got to work full time since you've just halved our maintenance.'

David turned to her, with his placating smile spreading across his face, and put a hand on her shoulder: a gesture that used to make her feel safe and protected. The 'everything'll be fine' gesture that now, she realised, meant absolutely nothing.

'Don't be ridiculous, Zoe, it's a dog! Can't you just get a neighbour to look after it? I mean, come *on*,' he said. 'It's hard times for everyone. I *bought* the thing – you have no idea how much one of those things costs!'

'Toffee's not a thing,' snapped Zoe. 'He's a dog.'

David half-smiled. 'OK, whatever. He's a dog.'

Zoe forced herself to sound brisk and reasonable, like Rachel had when she'd told her what to say. 'David, I've done a deal with the local kennels, for half the cost, but I need you to contribute. I can't take it out of the maintenance, unless you'd rather I fed the dog, rather than the boys?'

He reached into his pocket, and before she knew what he was doing, he'd pulled out his wallet and slapped a hundred quid into her hand. 'There. Is that what you want?'

'It's not about that—' she'd started, but he was opening the driver's door of his brand-new car and, getting in, was ready to drive the boys away for their weekend of delights.

'So,' he called into the back, 'who's ready for a weekend at Alton Towers?'

An awful thought struck Zoe as he slammed the door and started the engine.

'Stop!' She hammered on the window, and David buzzed it down, crossly. She could hear Radio 1 on the stereo, too loud. Too young and too loud.

'What now?'

'Who's going to be looking after Toffee while you're living it up at Alton Towers?' she demanded breathlessly.

David widened his eyes so the boys wouldn't be able to tell he was giving her his 'shut up' face. 'What do you mean, who'll be looking after him? We'll take him with us, and leave him in the car in his cage thing. He'll be fine. We're only going to be there until, I don't know, three-ish . . .'

'He won't be fine! He needs to go outside every hour at least.' She had a horrible vision of a frantic Toffee, overheated, scared and lonely, sitting in his own mess in the back of David's stupid new car, or worse, being dragged round on a lead, terrified by the crowds.

David's jaw dropped. 'It's a dog, Zoe, for God's sake!'

'Exactly! He's not a toy! I'm sorry, but Toffee will have to stay here,' she said in a properly firm voice now. 'I should have realised. Open the boot.'

I can't believe you're doing this, Zoe told herself. You were about to have a dogless, childless weekend of almost complete sleep.

'What? Don't be so—'

'Open the bloody boot!' she roared.

David's expression hardened, and then he turned round in the car. 'Sorry, boys, Mum says Toffee has to stay here with her. He can't come too.'

There was a howl of protest from the back seat. 'Muuuuuuum!'

Zoe steeled herself. 'I'm sorry, Spencer, but it's too noisy for Toffee. He'll be here when you come home.' She struggled to open the heavy tailgate, and lifted Toffee's travelling box from the back of the car.

Two adoring brown eyes gleamed at her through the wire mesh of the crate and she felt a stab of relief that Toffee wouldn't be trapped in there for the rest of the weekend. He'd have cried, she knew. And had to sit in his own vomit and poo, and done all sorts of things that would probably have ruined Jennifer's house in hundreds of satisfying ways, but which her soft heart couldn't let him go through just to teach David a lesson.

Spencer gave the back of David's seat an almighty kick. 'It's not fair!'

'Spencer! Don't kick the seat! It'll mark!' snapped David, then, in a change of tone, he added, 'Please, mate.'

That's not half of what one hyperactive puppy would have done to it, Zoe thought.

She walked round to the driver's window, feeling a strange new determination. 'And if they come back here with so much as a plastic duck, I will be on to my solicitor,' she hissed, then raised her voice so the boys could hear her.

'See you on Sunday, lovely boys!' she called. 'Be good for Daddy!'

Spencer had his arms folded tight in a sulk, his chin pressed down into it, but Leo was waving his fat little hand, near the window, so she could see. 'Look after Toffee, Mummy!' he called out.

Zoe's heart tugged as she waved back, and she had to force herself to hold her smile. Then David floored the accelerator and they vanished into the night.

Shivering, Zoe lifted Toffee's crate so he was at eye level.

'So, Toffee,' she said. 'Just you and me. Got any plans for the weekend?'

Toffee licked her nose through the bars and yapped to be let out for a wee.

Which was progress of some kind, thought Zoe.

# 12

'Be kind to me, Megan,' pleaded Rachel. 'In real life, at this hour, I'm not even awake yet, let alone standing up fully dressed.' She peered at the rota on the table. 'And about to organise volunteers.'

It was a Saturday morning, Rachel's first proper experience of the volunteer walking club's main day. Megan had woken her up with a cup of tea outside her door, and then Gem had woken her up more insistently by removing the covers from her bed.

Rachel told herself that at least he'd packed in the licking her awake as if he was trying to raise her from the dead routine.

'You're doing great!' said Megan, who looked far too cheerful for someone who'd been up for two hours already and had mucked out all the kennels. 'Why don't I put you on bacon sandwiches?'

She steered Rachel over to the Aga, where two loaves of bread were stacked up next to several packets of bacon and a bottle of tomato sauce. Rachel had raided her emergency savings account to replenish the kitchen cupboards, pay Megan and deal with the most urgent bills; the rest of the bills were scary enough to make sorting out the probate forms more of a pressing matter.

She'd made a new list, anyway. Getting started on asset listing was a job for the afternoon.

'Fry the rashers, put them in the warming oven, make sandwiches when walkers come back. Repeat all morning.

We usually get about ten or so regulars turning up,' Megan explained. 'And your poster campaign's worked a treat.'

'I warn you, I don't really do cooking.' Rachel lifted the heavy old pan gingerly onto the hot plate. 'I'm more of an eating-out girl.'

'Hello? Am I too early?'

They turned round to see Zoe Graham standing at the kitchen door, Toffee under one arm. When Toffee spotted Gem in the basket by the Aga he wriggled happily and squirmed out of Zoe's arms to greet his grown-up friend.

'Please don't tell me you've come to give him up?' begged Rachel.

Zoe shook her head. She was wearing a blue knitted hat that squashed her reddish curls around her face. 'No, my ex has got the kids for the weekend – house seemed a bit weird and quiet, and I got all the hints Freda was dropping about weekend walkers, so . . .' She raised her hands and her eyebrows theatrically. 'Here I am! You should put up notices in the solicitors'. Get all the weekend-off single parents down here.'

'You told your ex, did you?' Rachel said. 'About the daycare?'

'And you said, "No!"' added Megan, making the policeman hand gesture. 'To him *and* Toffee?'

Zoe's eyes clouded. 'Sort of. I told him he couldn't take Toffee and leave him in the car all weekend. I'm going to, honestly, soon as they get back. David gave me some cash, look, so let me give you something up front.'

'That's brilliant!' Rachel took the notes off Zoe before Megan could wave it away. Fifty quid, right now, was fifty quid towards food. Her savings schemes were set up for new season fashion, not kennel support, and they were already running low. 'Call that Toffee's first month's fees, introductory offer. I'll get you a receipt.'

'It's a start,' said Megan encouragingly. 'I mean, not about the money, about you setting him straight. It's about not letting him ride roughshod over you!'

'Why change the habits of a lifetime?' sighed Zoe. 'Like I'm not letting that one there ride roughshod over my life.'

'Dogs are different,' said Megan, looking on indulgently as Toffee climbed all over Gem, tugging at his ears while Gem stared at his paws.

Rachel tucked the cash into the back pocket of her jeans. 'Megan, why don't you give Zoe a couple of dogs to take out, then by the time she gets back, I might have worked out how to make a bacon sarnie?' She examined the packet doubtfully. 'And don't rush back.'

On the other side of Longhampton, Natalie and Johnny were sitting in Natalie's Mini, watching Bill emerge from his front door, in his new role as a dog owner.

Natalie was biased, but she thought he looked like a Boden model, all cheekbones, and chunky parka, and knitted hat. And black poodle accessory.

Although, having said that, Lulu did seem to be using Bill as her handsome owner accessory, the way she was strutting over to the car.

'Only a guy as good-looking as Bill can carry off a poodle,' said Johnny. 'So to speak.'

'I think he looks gorgeous.' Natalie waved at Bill so he'd see them waiting. 'He'll be fighting them off in the park. There's nothing girls love more than a man with a dog.'

'Are you going to be saying that when I'm walking Bertie around the park?' Johnny gave her a cheeky look, and she nudged him.

'I'm going to be *with* you. We're going to be walking him *together*. Anyway,' Natalie settled back in her seat, ready to go,'just make sure Bill talks to that nice Megan at the kennels.'

'What? Oh, now I get it ... This isn't just a simple volunteering job at all, is it?'

'We're going to meet Bertie again,' Natalie insisted. 'But I thought, while we're there, that Megan was very much Bill's type.'

'In what way?'

Bill was fussing around his front door now, checking he'd got the right keys. Obviously he hadn't, because he turned and waved his hands at them, tied Lulu to the front door and vanished inside. Lulu sat down, patiently.

'In that she seems the nice organised type,' Natalie went on. 'No baggage, good with dogs, well-travelled, cheerful . . .'

'How do you know all that? You've only met her the once!' Johnny rounded his eyes.

'We had a nice chat on the phone when I rang up about Bertie's home check. Anyway, you can tell.' Natalie smiled through the windscreen as Bill came out, now in a different coat, with a different lead. 'I can see them really hitting it off. He just needs a bit of a nudge in the right direction. The settling down one.'

'Well, you've been nudging for the last three years,' said Johnny. 'But you know what a bloody perfectionist he . . . Hi, Bill!'

'Hi, Natalie, Johnny!' Bill lifted up the poodle and put her under his arm.

'Hi, Lulu!' cooed Natalie.

'Hi, Auntie Nata—!' Bill began to reply in a poodle voice, until Johnny gave him a look and he stopped.

Johnny got out of the front seat so Bill could slide his lanky frame into the back.

'If you see, there's a little clip there you can attach Lulu to,' said Natalie, leaning over to point it out. 'Yes, that's it.'

'It's for Bertie. She's got all the gear already,' said Johnny over the top of the car. 'We've come via Pet World. As if seven hours on the internet last night wasn't enough to learn every fact about Basset hounds, we now have the whole kit, including something called a clicker, with which Nat's going to start her new career as a dog behaviourist.'

Bill raised his eyebrows. 'The full Natalie special.'

'Yeah,' sighed Johnny. 'Well, it's a bit more complicated, mate. Get in and she'll tell you more than you ever wanted to know.'

Megan had paired Zoe up with Bertie and Treacle the labrador, on the grounds that they were about the size Toffee would eventually grow up to be, and told her to be firm, remember her "No!" and if the worst came to the worst, issued her with some biscuit bribes.

And then she sent her out on the Three Mile Lap, as shown on the photocopied handout the weekend walkers were given.

All the way down the hill, and round the first side of Longhampton Park, Zoe could see herself like an advert for shampoo or something, smiling happily at other dog owners enjoying the crisp weekend morning. The dogs were demented with joy to be out of their runs into the open air, and so was she. It was the first new thing, Zoe realised, with mild horror, that she'd done on her own since the boys were born. And it seemed to be going OK.

In fact, it was more than OK. It was like being on holiday – on her own. She felt free and light and released. And better than that, the dogs seemed to be taking her seriously, keeping pace with her steps and occasionally looking back with a touching need to check she was still with them.

But as soon as they hit the wilder part of the park, on the way back, Bertie and his nose got wind of something and he shot off like a pony, pulling out the whole of the extendable lead in one surge.

'Slow down!' yelled Zoe, ineffectually, as she felt the lead click out to its maximum extension, and then, with a yank, it nearly tugged her arm out of its socket. She began to walk faster, to stop the collar choking Bertie, who was trotting now, so fast his ears were flapping. 'Slow down! Heel! Heel!'

What were you meant to shout? She scoured her brain for dog instructions. 'Stop! Heel! Stay!'

Nothing worked. Bertie was hauling her determinedly across the common towards some other people – and their dog.

Now she was almost running. Zoe looked down at Treacle who had begun to trot next to her, ever obedient, despite the strange new direction the walk was taking. 'Sorry,' she gasped, but the docile Labrador didn't seem unduly bothered.

Zoe felt something vibrating in her jacket pocket – her phone was ringing. The sense of freedom vanished and her brain immediately started to throw out lurid scenes of amusement park accidents, motorway pile-ups, Leo taking ill on some ride.

She looked ahead to where Bertie was heading – it was a fairly clear patch of grass with no bushes or hedges to fall into – and decided to risk it. She switched the lead to the other hand, still running, and rummaged around in her inside pocket for the phone. It slipped out of her fingers. As she was grabbing for it, her foot connected with a loose molehill of earth, and she lost her balance, stumbling forward towards the wet grass and a metal drain cover she hadn't seen until it was hurtling towards her forehead.

Zoe threw out her hands but it was too late to break her fall. She dropped her phone and the leads as she skidded along the ground, cracking her head against the drain. Stars exploded behind her eyelids and she could hear the sound of jubilant barking, as Bertie galloped free. Everything seemed a very long way away.

'Ow!' she half-sobbed, tasting the iron tang of blood where she'd bitten her lip. In a moment, she knew, there'd be a sudden burst of pain from her forehead and her skinned palms. This was the part she tried to talk the boys through, so they wouldn't notice.

The phone rang twice more, out of sight, and then stopped.

Zoe tried to sit up, but everything was spinning. The dogs! Where had the dogs gone?

She looked up to see Bertie bouncing with delight around the three people with the dog, who were staring over towards her while their poodle skirted Bertie's advances like an unwilling woman being chatted up in a club. Treacle meanwhile was hovering protectively over her, wagging an uncertain tail and drooling.

'Bertie!' yelled Zoe, scrambling to her feet. As she did, little stars of pain shot up and down her palm, her leg, her shoulder, and she felt her knees give way beneath her. She slid back onto her hip. 'Oh, God.'

This was painful and embarrassing. And now, she could hear the people coming over to her. She shut her eyes and put a tentative hand to her forehead. Her hat had come off, and there was an enormous lump there where there definitely hadn't been one before.

'Are you OK?' a man called. 'Don't move, we've got a doctor here.'

'Can you grab the dog?' she yelled hopefully. 'Please?'

'I've got him,' shouted a woman.

The sound of running footsteps got louder and turned into heavy breaths, some of which weren't Treacle's.

'That looked painful,' said a wry voice. 'And very *You've Been Framed.*'

Zoe opened her eyes and saw a man standing over her. He too was wearing a woolly hat pulled down over his ears, and tufts of black hair stuck out over his dark brown eyes. Even a bright red wind-chilled nose didn't diminish the effect of faint weekend stubble and long dark lashes.

Why do you only ever meet hot men when you've just made a total fool of yourself, she wondered through the dull roar in her ears.

'Um, I'm no expert, but I think you might have ripped your jeans,' he added. 'I'd get up quite carefully if I were you.'

Zoe groaned inwardly, then realised she'd actually groaned aloud as the sensation returned to her grazed palms.

His manner became more professional as he squatted next to her and held her chin in his hand, so he could stare into her eyes. Embarrassed, Zoe tried to look away. 'Now, don't take this the wrong way, but can you look into my eyes, please?' he asked. 'Don't worry, I am a doctor.'

'Yeah, yeah, I bet you are.' Zoe managed a fat-lipped smile. 'You don't just hang around the park waiting for dog walkers to fall over so you can hypnotise them?'

'Nah.' His eyes were gorgeous, thought Zoe, like Toffee's on a good day: huge and brown and melting. She wondered if her pupils were going black as A Sign of Attraction, like the teen magazines had said. 'Not worth it in this weather. Nope, I don't think you're concussed. You didn't black out?'

'No.'

'Good. But you're going to have an amazing bruise for your boyfriend to explain away in the morning.'

'Lucky I don't have one then, isn't it?' said Zoe, without thinking.

He didn't drop her chin, but grinned. Why, Zoe asked herself, had she chosen that morning not to bother with make-up? Not even mascara?

'Do you feel OK to get up?' he asked, checking her over for other injuries. Zoe was sorry to say she didn't have any for him to find.

'I'm hurting more about ripping these jeans. They're my favourites.'

As she lurched to her feet, Zoe saw the other couple approaching, with their own dog, the black poodle, as well as Treacle on her lead and Bertie, who was now bouncing happily around the woman, easily reaching up to her hip at full stretch.

'Lean on me,' said the man, slinging his arm around her shoulders for support. 'That's it, put your arm round my waist if it helps.'

'Hello, I'm Zoe.' Zoe offered him her other hand to shake, since they were now in closer contact than she'd been with any man since before David. He smelled of clean washing and his wool overcoat, and he was keeping her upright as if she weighed nothing.

'Oh, sorry. I'm Bill,' he said. 'Bill Harper,' he added. 'I think we might have met at the surgery? I'm terrible with names.'

'We haven't. I'd have remembered. Hello, Bill,' she said, and they shook hands gingerly. Even Zoe could tell it was just an excuse for them both to touch hands and suddenly she felt a bit too warm, despite her polar jacket.

I shouldn't be fancying random men in the park, she reminded herself. Ten seconds ago, I was panicking that my kids were hanging upside down from a roller coaster!

'My phone—' she began, and Bill scrambled to look for it on the ground just as she bent down too. Their heads bumped and she yelped.

'You're not from one of those Personal Injury ads, are you?' he asked, rubbing his forehead through the woolly hat.

'No,' said Zoe. 'Just a bit clumsy right now.'

'Everything OK?' The blonde woman hurried up with the three dogs, passing the leads to the other man so she could pick up Zoe's mobile. 'Johnny, grab that, would you? Here, is this your phone? Anything broken?'

'That was quite some flying leap,' the other man – Johnny – agreed. 'Bertie's got some apologising to do.'

'You know him?' Zoe looked between them, surprised. From the way Bertie was sniffing and wagging round the woman, he certainly seemed to.

'We're on our way to give him a walk, actually.' She reached down and fondled an ear. 'Hopefully we're Bertie's new foster parents. Natalie, and Johnny. Hi!'

'Lulu's from the rescue too,' Bill explained. 'I think she and Bertie have some history. Oh, man, you've made a right mess of your hands. There must have been glass down there or something.' He reached into his pocket and pulled out a red hanky. 'Just press this over it, OK. And keep your hand above your head.'

'To stop the bleeding?'

'No, to stop you punching me by accident.' Bill grinned and Zoe felt a smile appear on her own face. A rather stupid one, she suspected.

'Shall we head back up to the kennels?' suggested Natalie. 'We parked down here to give Lulu a walk first – didn't want her to think we were taking her back so soon after Bill getting her!'

'Is the chocolate Lab yours?' Bill asked as Zoe took Treacle's lead back from Johnny, and they set off towards the path.

'No, but I've got a Labrador puppy. Or rather, I've been landed with a puppy,' she said. 'I work during the day, so he's in doggie daycare with Megan. He can only do fifteen-minute walks at his age.'

'Fifteen minutes?' He pulled a 'fancy that' face. 'I thought puppies were hard work?'

'Hard work?' Zoe dragged her stinging hands down her face. 'Oh, the crying. And the drama! I've been sleeping on the sofa just so I can let him out twice a night to go to the loo. I don't know who's training who.' She pulled Treacle away from a tempting rubbish bin and winced at the pain in her forehead.

'How's the head feeling now? Any worse?' Bill glanced up

at his friends who were being hauled at a much brisker pace up the path by Bertie, who had decided enough was enough.

'I'll be fine. Do you want to catch them up?' Zoe asked, quickly. 'Don't feel you've got to hang back.'

'No, no, it's not a problem. It'll do them good to bond with Bertie. Show them what they're in for.' He smiled, showing square white teeth. 'If you don't mind me saying, I think you should be lying down and taking it easy for a few hours.'

'But we've only just met!' said Zoe without thinking.

His smiled increased. 'Let me get you back to the kennels,' Bill went on. 'I'm sure they've got somewhere you can chill out for a while. And some ice to stop the bump swelling much more. Are you rushing back anywhere?'

'No,' said Zoe, seeing her weekend alone stretching out. 'Now now.'

'Good.' Said Bill.

There was a tiny pause, in which Zoe realised she was actively flirting and being flirted with. Wow. She could still do it! And someone still wanted to do it with her!

'Come on,' said Bill, putting a very light hand on the small of her back. 'Don't rush.'

They set off up the hill, with Lulu trotting next to them, and Zoe basked in the unusual feeling of being looked after for a change.

'That went well,' said Natalie, pulling out of the car park slowly, so as not to upset her newest passenger, securely fastened on the back seat in a truss-like harness.

'If you mean, have you convinced those rescue women that you've done your research, then yes, I think it did,' said Johnny, evenly. 'That Rachel was asking *you* questions in the end.'

Natalie turned to him. 'I just want to make sure we've got everything right for Bertie. I don't want us to let him down.'

'You're not going to let him down.' Johnny grabbed her knee and held it reassuringly. 'You're going to be a great dog owner. And he loves you. Don't you?' He wriggled round in his seat and let Bertie lick his fingers.

'Careful, Jon, don't want to make him sick,' she said, glancing in her rear-view mirror. Bertie had taken some convincing to get into the car, and it had only been when Megan hid a sausage on the back seat that he'd finally jumped in.

Bertie looked tragic, sitting there now in his harness, as if he was getting ready for a parachute jump. Natalie reminded herself that he'd looked just the same shortly after getting back from the walk, and stealing a bacon sandwich – it was his default setting.

'I saw the way you signed us up for next weekend,' Johnny went on. 'Was that for the bacon sandwiches or to make sure Bill and Lulu go too?'

'A bit of both.' Natalie turned the car round and hid a little smile.

'Now *that* plan seems to be working,' said Johnny. 'Man plus dog definitely equals romance.'

'You think they're getting on?'

'From the way they were chatting away in the kitchen? I'd say so. I've never seen Bill so animated.'

The weekend volunteers seemed like a friendly bunch – the three of them, and Zoe, whom they'd met in the park, some nice old dears and one or two teenagers from Longhampton School, whom Johnny knew. Rachel Fielding, in a pair of jeans topped with some gorgeous cashmere, was making bacon sarnies and Megan was holding a sort of advice clinic about handling puppies. Everyone was chipping in, offering advice, mainly about getting dog hairs out of your washing machine filter. It felt nice, Natalie had thought. Like joining a club, but without the competitive element that made her book group such a trial.

Natalie had kept her eye on Bill, and he seemed to be chatting to Megan quite a bit, about Lulu's grooming routine.

'I hope so,' she said. 'I like her a lot – she's so funny and friendly.'

'Mm,' said Johnny. 'Bit accident-prone but if he's a doctor, could be a good thing?'

'What?'

'Zoe. Didn't you see the way she nearly fell over Bertie, when he was waiting by the door? Thought Bill was very quick to see she hadn't concussed herself again.'

'I didn't mean *Zoe*,' said Natalie, shocked. 'I meant Megan. It's *Megan* who's perfect for Bill.'

'What's wrong with Zoe?' Johnny pulled his 'I don't understand women' face. 'She's pretty, and young, and has that adorable puppy! What's not for Bill to love?'

They were stuck in the traffic now, and it was starting to drizzle. Natalie turned on the windscreen wipers and tried to work out what it was about Zoe that wasn't right for Bill. She was perfectly sweet. Just not someone she'd ever have imagined Bill 'I couldn't date someone who didn't like Hitchcock films' Harper with.

'I don't know,' she said finally. 'Maybe it's because Bill's always been so specific about what he wants.'

'And he's done a *great* job finding her so far.'

'He fell in love with a poodle when he went up there for a spaniel, didn't he?' observed Johnny. 'And look how that's turned out.'

'True.'

'And we didn't go there for a dog at all, and now we've got Bertie the canine waste disposal unit back there. People never know what's right for them until they meet it. Life always turns out right in the end.'

Natalie stared into the rainy evening and thought about the other dogs lying, head on paws, in the kennels, wondering who was going to come for them, hoping they'd be someone's surprise choice when the door opened. Johnny always believed things would turn out OK because he never even thought about the alternative.

'Or maybe I'm just lucky that I keep running into all the right things,' he said, softly.

She felt his hand cover hers on the gearstick, and told herself that it was about time she starting thinking the same way.

# 13

On Wednesday, Megan asked for the evening off – her first night off in over two months.

'Do you mind?' she asked, over breakfast. 'I usually get three nights a week off, but you know, with Dot and everything . . .' She lifted her hands apologetically. 'I'm just going into town with some mates – it's a birthday party? I won't be far away, if there's an emergency.'

Rachel hardly felt she could say no, given that Megan had mucked out the kennels already that morning – and she was still waiting for a small bequest from Dot, which couldn't be released until Rachel filed the probate application. Which she was definitely going to get finished that morning. Definitely.

'Of course! It's no problem,' she said, checking through the morning's post for ominous bills. 'I will be just fine. Watch me.'

'Brilliant. And you've applied for the boarding licence?'

'Yes,' said Rachel, even though she hadn't. She would have done by the end of the afternoon, though, she told herself. Today was going to be a very efficient day.

She took another slice of toast from the huge pile in front of her – her bread drought was well and truly over – and opened Dot's Christie's auction catalogue, from one of a selection of very upmarket mailing lists Dot seemed to be on.

'Can you pass me the marmalade, please, Megan?' she added.

'Have you applied for the boarding licence?'

Rachel looked up from the glossy pages of the Fine Art sale and saw Megan withholding the sticky pot of Longhampton WI marmalade, just out of reach.

'Are you training me?' Rachel demanded. 'Like one of the dogs?'

'Have you filled in the form?' Megan repeated. 'Because the council are fine about it for a certain period, but they're going to start kicking up a fuss if there are dogs on the premises and no licencec.' She waggled the marmalade. 'It'll take you two minutes.'

Rachel didn't like to put her thoughts into words: she hoped that she'd be out of Longhampton and back in a world with no white hairs and slobber well before the council got round to inspecting the new ownership. But even as that went through her head, she had a sinking feeling that getting another job, after Oliver had dined out on her very un-PR-like behaviour, wouldn't be so easy. Even if her confidence *wasn't* at an all-time low, and the recession was closing down PR agencies left, right and centre.

Megan fixed her with a bluster-piercing look. 'It doesn't mean you *have* to stay. It just means we can do some business till you make up your mind.'

Rachel wilted. What was the point? Megan knew her too well already, after hardly any time at all. Either Megan had acquired Dot's skill for mindreading dumb animals, or Rachel had just got horribly easy to read since she'd left London.

'Yes. Yes, I will fill in the form this morning. Now can I have the marmalade, please?'

'Good girl!' Megan's smile broadened and she handed her the marmalade.

The dogs were listening to *The Archers* when Rachel pushed open the door into the kennels, clutching Megan's scribbled instructions.

'Evening, all,' she said, stepping out of her heels and into the wellies positioned by the door. Talking to the dogs was now automatic, but she was still a bit squeamish about the hair/poo/disinfectant cocktail that sloshed around the place before the cleaning started.

There was a little barking, but not too much – the dogs were sleepy after their supper and most were curled up in their baskets, heads drooping over the sides as if they were concentrating on the Ambridge gossip.

Gem slunk silently at her side as she pinned Megan's list to the noticeboard for easy reference. It wasn't long:

*Check and refresh water bowls, sweep out kennels (don't use broom near the Staffies at the end – they're scared of brooms, bad experience probably), disinfect where necessary, check blankets, change radio to Radio Three or Classic FM for night time.*

Rachel pulled on a pair of plastic gloves and opened the nearest mesh door to let out the first dog – Chester, the stir-crazy springer spaniel – while she stepped gingerly inside his run to pick up his water bowl.

To her surprise, he didn't bounce out as if he'd been released from a catapult. Instead he lay in his basket, his eyes vacant, his liver-spotted ears flopping lethargically over the edge.

'Hey, Chester!' said Rachel, tipping his water down the drain. 'Are you feeling OK?'

She went back to the dogs' kitchen to rinse and refill the bowl. When she returned he hadn't moved, and Gem was sniffing around like a nursemaid. Chester didn't even bother to swipe Gem's nose out of the way.

Rachel looked at Gem, the first ripples of unease spreading across her chest. 'Is he all right?'

Gem stepped delicately out of Chester's space, and sat down in the corridor between the kennels. At the far end, two of the Staffies were barking for some attention, but even that didn't rouse the spaniel.

'Shh!' She stepped forward to hush the Staffies, and felt panic rising as Chester emitted a low groan.

Megan had only left the premises for what? A few hours? And already Rachel was out of her depth. She had a quick brain, and she'd been absorbing some dog-care basics from Dot's hand outs in the office, but she hadn't a clue about canine first aid. Even so, she'd known Chester long enough to realise that anything short of mild hysteria was wrong in a working springer spaniel like him.

Rachel sniffed. Something in Chester's kennel smelled pretty disgusting – a quick look confirmed there was a puddle of yellow diarrhoea right at the end of the run, as far away from his basket as he could manage. It was a long puddle, as if he hadn't quite made it.

'Oh, my God,' she said, taking an involuntary step back. These weren't her best trousers, but they weren't her M&S dog-walking ones either, and she'd never be able to get toxic dog slurry out of them.

Was Chester seriously sick? Was he going to give the other dogs whatever he'd got? What if he died? Was she liable?

Rachel closed the kennel door as fast as she could, trying to get away, but then she caught sight of Chester out of the corner of her eye. He was gazing up at her with dull eyes, pathetically trying to wag his tail with what little strength he had left.

Suddenly, she got a flash of what Dot must have felt and her squeamishness evaporated. It was up to her to help Chester – he didn't have anyone else. And the fact that he trusted a human to help him, after the owners he'd loved had thrown him out like an unwanted sofa, was more than she deserved.

Rachel ripped off her gloves, stepped back in and stroked Chester's soft ears, crouching down next to him as he tried to lick her hand. There were flecks of runny poo on his feathery back legs and she tried not to notice what they were doing to her trousers.

'I don't know what's up, Chester,' she whispered, irrationally worried the other dogs might hear. 'But I'll find someone who does, OK?'

She stood up, locked his door with trembling hands, and made her way to the office as fast as she could, not wanting to freak out the other dogs. The cordless phone by the door had several speed dials on it, and Rachel's finger hovered between 'Megan Mobile' and 'George Mobile'.

She didn't want to spoil Megan's night, but if Chester was ill, Megan would only ring George anyway, so . . .

Her finger pressed 'George Mobile' before she could think, and it only rang twice before he answered.

'What's the problem, Rachel?' he asked. 'Fluff on your skirt? Or are the dogs not matching?'

'No, it's Chester,' she said, too worried to rise to his teasing. 'I think he's sick. He's got diarrhoea and he's just lying in his basket.' She walked back to the pen, where Chester hadn't moved. 'He's just lying there, like he's about to die.'

'Hang on and don't panic.' George's tone changed to calm authority. 'Has he vomited? Does he feel hot?'

'I don't know,' said Rachel. She felt powerless, and scared for the little dog. 'What can I do? Is it something I've done?'

'No. Well, I don't think so. It's probably nothing serious, but I'll come and have a look. Just keep an eye on him, make sure he's got some fresh water, and I'll be right with you.' He hung up and Rachel stood for a moment, feeling weak at the knees. She'd never experienced such total inadequacy, and utter panic. How could George be so calm?

She grabbed a clean blanket from the pile in the store cupboard and went back into Chester's run, tucking it around his small body. Beneath his feathery coat, he was shivering, but when he felt her nearby his tail managed a pathetic wag of gratitude, and her heart wrenched.

'George is coming,' she said, in a soothing tone. 'I'm going to carry on sorting out everyone else, but I'm not going to take my eyes off you, all right? Please don't die before he gets here!'

Chester wagged his tail again, but it was even more feeble than before, and now even the Staffies in the far pens were quiet.

# 14

For the next fifteen minutes, Rachel refreshed water, cleaned runs and checked bedding like she'd never done before. She kept her sight fixed on Chester, who flopped listlessly in his basket, not even watching her. The other dogs were hushed, sensing something was afoot, and before *Front Row* had finished on Radio Four, the fire door opened and George's familiar broad frame appeared, filling it up.

Rachel had never felt so glad to see him.

'That was quick!' she said, brushing her hands clean and rushing up to the door.

'Well, I was passing, as they say.' George already had his bag open. 'So, where's the patient?'

'In here.' She opened the kennel, and hovered anxiously outside as George went in and knelt at Chester's basket. 'Is he going to be OK?'

'Good God, Chester, what have you been eating? Now, then, old chap, let me have a look.' George murmured cheerful, soothing words to the spaniel, which had the side effect of soothing Rachel at the same time. 'Let me guess, was it a rotten bunny? Or have you been at the dustbins again?'

Rachel watched as his hands moved expertly over the dog's head. It was mesmerising to watch, and, to her surprise, quite sexy – the combination of skill and tenderness in the way he opened the dog's eyelid, and checked over his small body. Eventually he stood up.

'What is it, do you think?' she asked anxiously. 'Will they all get it?'

'I shouldn't think so.' George wiped his hands with anti-bacterial gel. 'More likely to be something he helped himself to while he was out today. But there's no harm in keeping an eye on him, just in case – you've got those isolation crates in the utility room, haven't you? We could pop him in there tonight, so you can check up on him.'

'You're sure it's not infectious?' Rachel's eyes were round with concern and she was grateful that, for once, George didn't try to poke fun at her inexperience.

'Pretty sure. The ones who've come in off the streets can't resist scrounging. It looks a lot worse than it is, and there's no blood. I can give him something for the dehydration, and he might have to be on rice and chicken for a few days.' George lifted the whole basket up in one easy movement, and moved it to one side. 'We should get this slurry cleared up though. Had you got as far as getting the buckets out? I'll give you a hand.'

Rachel opened her mouth, to tell him he didn't need to, and George smiled.

'Come on, don't look so panicked,' he said, patting her arm. 'This happens all the time.'

He had a smile that changed his face from craggy and rather fierce, to a familiar gentle giant-ness. She could see, briefly, where the Daniel Craig wishful thinking came from amongst the town's female owners.

'I'm more worried about you,' he went on. 'You look like you've seen a ghost! Is it the state of your trousers that's given you a funny turn, or Chester here?'

'It's Chester,' Rachel confessed. 'I was really ... worried about him.' She put a hand on her chest, only half-joking at her racing pulse. 'I thought it was my fault.'

'And you not a dog person,' George huffed, amused. 'I think we can stop saying that now, can't we? Rumour has it you've even been out walking Gem when you don't have to.'

'How would you know that?' Rachel demanded. 'How small is this town that other people's dog walking passes for entertainment?'

George raised his hands, then turned away to start the hose. 'Just a guess, that's all! I know there's nothing like a long walk with a good companion to get your problems aired to a sympathetic ear.' She couldn't see his face, because he was sluicing out the pen with practised sweeps of water, but his voice was conversational. 'They're great listeners, dogs. Never try to give you advice, unlike people.'

Rachel stared, open-mouthed.

'You can add it to your PR campaign for the rehoming.' He lifted one hand to draw an imaginary headline in the air. 'Get a dog, skip the therapist. Better than a useless boyfriend.'

Now that was too close to home. Rachel stopped changing the water in the Staffies' pen. Had Megan said something? About her leaving her job? About – her skin crawled – about Oliver?

I've got to put her straight about that, she thought, but even as the idea of confessing was passing across her brain, Rachel saw her lovely clean slate slipping away and she pressed her lips together. I'm not that old Rachel any more, she reminded herself. As of now, I'm just any other single thirty-something, making a fresh start.

And that fresh start began with focusing her attentions on men who were definitely not attached. Few men came as definitely unattached as George Fenwick.

'Better than a useless girlfriend too,' she retorted, arching her eyebrow. 'Megan says there's a space going by your fireside – have you met my gorgeous friend, Treacle the chocolate Labrador?'

'I have indeed. Met her, whipped out her bits, put her on a diet. She's a lovely girl, but not really my type.'

'And what is your type?'

He paused, with the Westies' water bowl in his hands. 'Something with a mind of its own. Labs are lovely, but they're a bit . . . passive. I don't mind a bit of independence, now and again. A bit of cussedness, even.'

'In that case, I should be introducing you to our broad range of grumpy terriers.' Rachel gestured towards the yappy end of the runs, like a gameshow hostess. 'Any colour you fancy, all very cussed.'

They were both standing clutching water bowls now, and Rachel wondered if the thermostat had gone onto night mode, because she was feeling a little hot.

'I didn't say I wanted grumpiness,' said George. 'Just a bit of a spark.' He paused, and added, with a hint of a wink, 'And good hips.'

The Daniel Craig thing was quite pronounced now. Either that or the overhead lighting was very flattering indeed, she thought.

'By which I mean, no hip dysplasia,' he added. 'Bane of my life. Now, is that it?' He turned his attention back to Chester, and lifted him and his basket up in one easy go. 'We should get this chap somewhere quiet, and get you a drink. It looks like you need one.'

Since it was now going on eight, it seemed only fair to offer George some of the embarrassingly basic supper Rachel had planned to make for herself, and when he elbowed her out of the way, to 'improve' her attempts, she happily stood back and opened a bottle of wine, and watched him, impressed.

George moved around the kitchen with the same capable air he'd shown diagnosing Chester, who was now curled up in the crate in the warm utility room off the house kitchen. As George chopped and threw bits of garlic and salt and wine into the pan, he kept up a stream of questions – how was she finding the house? Had she been round the agility course with Gem? Had Freda told her the story about how Pippin once saved Ted's life by carrying his heart pills into the bedroom when he forgot? And did she believe it?

Rachel sipped her wine and let the conversation ebb and flow naturally between them, feeling more and more at ease in his company. George actually listened to her answers, often firing off second and third questions. It was brisk, sometimes, but she liked it; she'd encountered plenty of closed-off people who used questions as a way of not revealing anything of themselves, but he wasn't like that. George was happy to talk about his work in Longhampton, and made her laugh with his accounts of what the locals and their animals got up to – although, she noticed, he glossed courteously over names.

For every good-humoured jibe – 'I could tell you were a big restaurant goer as soon as you tried to measure that spaghetti on the scales,' he'd observed, rolling up his sleeves – there was a softer question, wrapped up in a gruff delivery.

'How are you getting on with clearing out the house?' he asked, setting down a piled plate in front of her. It smelled delicious. 'Dealing with the kennels is bad enough, but it must be quite a strange job to tackle, sorting through your aunt's personal life. On your own.'

'I wish I'd known just how weird it was going to be.' Rachel picked up her fork, and tried to tell herself to eat just half of the mammoth helping. 'I always knew I didn't know Dot very well, but now I wonder how well any of us knew her. If you know what I mean.'

'Sort of. Aren't you meant to be a professional wordsmith?' George tucked into his spaghetti with gusto.

'No, I'm a professional spinner and creator of good news,' said Rachel. 'Anyway, I can see now why people have children. You just tell them they can have half each and let them get on with stripping the house to the bones. It's like my mum used to say – one cuts, the other chooses. I reckon that's the fastest way to get probate done. If Dot had left half to my sister Amelia, there'd be removal vans and BBC *Cash in the Attic* experts lining up down the orchard.'

George laughed. 'That's the best solution I've heard so far.' He looked up from his plate, and tipped his head to one side, suddenly serious. 'If you need a hand, though, you'll ask? Not just with the heavy lifting either.'

'Yes.' Rachel felt touched.

'So, have you any future help lined up in that direction?' he asked casually. 'Children? Boyfriend? Partner . . . whatever you call them in London these days.'

'No,' said Rachel. 'No kids.

Oliver had made that very clear; there would be no 'accidental' babies on his watch. His nappy days were behind him, he said, even though his third child – Jensen, stupid name – had arrived a year after he insisted he and Kath were no longer sharing a room. That had caused a legendary row. That was when she should have left, when she was just thirty-four, and still had time.

Her hand hesitated on the stem of her glass, as the memory cut across her mood, and George topped up her wine, taking it as a hint. 'Not a baby person *or* a dog person, eh?'

'Oh. Thanks. No, I like babies you can hand back.' Rachel twisted her spaghetti round her fork with an expert knack. 'I always say my biological clock must be digital, because I've never heard it ticking.'

It was a smart answer; one she'd given her mother before. And it was true, as far as she wanted to examine it. Since he'd asked such a personal question, Rachel felt entitled to bat it back. 'How about you?'

George shook his head. 'I hear you need to find a wife first? I do a eighty-hour week – it's like I said, it wouldn't be fair to get a dog, let alone a relationship. But I knew that when I went into vet school, so, unless I meet another vet . . .' He shrugged. 'I think that's why vets used to have housekeepers.'

Rachel thought George's answer sounded as well-practised as her own but he met her gaze as he trotted it out. 'It's an anti-social life,' he went on, his blue eyes twinkling in the dim light, 'probably a selfish one, but—'

'You enjoy it. I know.' Rachel knew exactly what he was hedging around. 'It's like you're supposed to feel *ashamed* because you like your childless, high-pressure existence. I get it all the time. And when you try to explain that actually it's very satisfying to work all night to bring in a major client, or be able to go to Venice at the drop of a ticket, or . . .' She cast about for an equivalent vet thing. 'Or save a sick pony or something, people just give you that sympathetic, "Oh, it's because you don't have children, you're looking for a substitute in your work" look.' She took a large sip of wine. 'Well, hello. I'm sorry, but it's not a substitute. It's what I want.'

'Mmm.' George looked amused at the other end of the table. 'Maybe without the Venice trips. Have you seen the Longhampton canal? Very picturesque.'

'You'll have to take me.'

'I'd love to.' He lifted his glass. 'Can't promise gondoliers, but I can buy you a Cornetto.'

'That's a date.' Rachel smiled and had to look down when he smiled back, because the crackle in the air when their eyes met was too much.

She glanced at him, taking in the sardonic half-smile and the defiantly unfashionable checked shirt. The wine and the mood and the easy conversation was making her feel relaxed, and yet not very relaxed at the same time.

George gestured towards the pasta. 'Is it OK? It's been a while since I cooked for two.'

Rachel's lips tingled as she met his gaze and she felt conscious of herself – her expression, her clothes, her mouth –

in a way she hadn't for a long time. George wasn't handsome, not like Oliver, but he had something that made her feel they'd known each other before.

'How long have you been cooking for one?' she asked casually.

'Oh . . .' George pretended to think. 'Years.'

'Doesn't show in your cooking. This is delicious.'

'I'm flattered. You're the sort of girl who's always being taken out, rather than cooked for, right?'

'My ex didn't cook,' she said. 'And yes, I prefer being taken out, as you can probably tell by my kitchen skills.'

'Serious, this ex?' George's tone was light, but Rachel knew they were dancing around important details they were both keen to know, but without wanting to seem like they were too interested in finding out.

'Quite serious,' she said. 'Work colleague. We split up a few weeks ago.'

'Ah.' He tried to look sympathetic, but his expression was more complicated. 'Sorry to hear that.'

'Don't be,' she replied quickly. 'It wasn't going anywhere. I should have called time on it, but . . .'

'Men can be idiots,' said George, and took a sip of wine before she could read his face.

Rachel was racking her brains for something witty yet flirtatious to retort with when the phone rang on the wall. 'Sorry,' she said, pushing her chair back. 'Let me get that.'

When she picked up, she had to concentrate to hear over the background noise of a pub.

'Hi, Rachel, it's Megan. Is everything OK?'

'Hello, Megan. Everything's fine. Well, sort of. Chester's eaten something he shouldn't and put the fear of God into me, but I think we're fine. George is here.'

'Is he?' Megan sounded a bit too surprised, Rachel thought. 'Great! Well, listen, I'm not going to be able to get back tonight

– my mate Jules has kind of overdone it on the happy hour and I've said I'll stay with her tonight. Are you going to be all right there? I'll try to get back for first thing, so you needn't worry about—'

'Are you suggesting that I can't cope?' said Rachel.

George got up from his seat and gestured at the phone. 'Give me that. Hello, Megan? Megan, you'll be pleased to hear that Rachel has mucked out the kennels as well as you could yourself. Yes, everywhere. Total pebbledash job.' He glanced up at Rachel; the phone lead was short, so they were standing quite close together, and she felt conscious of the solid warmth of his chest through the shirt.

I wonder what it would feel like to be pressed against that, she thought, with a shiver. I wonder what George's body looks like underneath his clothes. Muscular, definitely, from the heaving around of cows and horses, but hairy? Smooth? Golden?

She shook herself and George glanced at her quizzically.

'She's fine. So, if there's anything else? No? Great. Goodnight, Megan.' He hung up, but didn't move away immediately, and she found herself unwilling to move either.

'So,' he said quietly, and Rachel braced herself for the next move. Oliver would have trotted out a seductive line about now. Or just gone straight in for a confident kiss.

Instead, George said, 'I don't supposed you've got any pudding, have you?'

Their eyes met, and the smile in his eyes changed to something more intense, and this time Rachel had to step away, as sparks tingled up and down her skin, in a way that made her feel about eighteen.

'No,' she said. Her voice didn't sound like hers. 'But I think Dot might have some whisky?'

George tipped his head to one side, as if he was considering. 'Are you suggesting we make a night of it?' Then his brain seemed to catch up with the meaning and he looked embarrassed. 'I mean, in drinking terms, I wasn't trying to—'

His confusion was endearing, but the suggestion that the other, dirtier thought was passing through his mind suddenly charged the atmosphere, and it hung between them like a question.

Rachel's breath caught in her throat as she realised just how much she wanted to kiss him. He wasn't going to make the first move, he was far too decent. But she'd had just enough wine to be reckless, if not properly drunk, and slowly she saw her own hand reach out and cradle the strong line of George's jaw, her fingers long and delicate against his scratchy stubble, her navy nail varnish jarringly urban next to his old-fashioned face.

He kept his darkened eyes trained on hers, not resisting but not exactly helping either, until she pulled him gently towards her and brushed her lips against his, feeling the surprising softness of his warm mouth. The hesitation lasted for two, three seconds, in which Rachel felt she was suspended in mid-air, and then his strong arm went around her waist while his other hand slipped into her hair, cradling her head while their mouths parted, and she tasted the wine on his lips, and his own taste that was instantly, dizzyingly familiar.

Rachel's head began to spin, not with the alcohol, but with longing, burning in the pit of her stomach. Without knowing exactly what she was doing, she wrapped her arms around George's neck and let herself melt into his body, thrilling at the substantial feel of him, perfectly capable of supporting all five feet ten inches of her without complaint.

George broke off for a second, kissing her nose, around her eyelids. 'Don't get me wrong, Rachel,' he murmured. Kisses fluttered along her cheekbone. 'This is . . .' The word was lost as he pressed his lips under her ear. 'But are you sure . . .?'

Rachel grabbed his face again and kissed his mouth, leaving him in no doubt about what it was she wanted.

And then George did something that would have swung the balance anyway. In one easy move, he picked Rachel up and carried her through to the sitting room, and Dot's enormous velvet sofa.

Down the hill, on the other side of Longhampton, Johnny was kissing Natalie's neck and winding his arms around her, snaking inside the soft t-shirt she wore in bed. She'd had it since school and it was paper-thin, and sexy in an innocent way. He much preferred it to her new range of seduction nightwear, which made him feel as if he was making love in the window of Ann Summers.

Natalie stiffened under his touch, and he smiled, knowing he'd hit the magic spot on the back of her neck, the point that made her wriggle and sigh, the opening bars of something more passionate.

Encouraged by her reaction, he did it again, this time with more urgency, but she batted his hands away and lifted her head up off the pillow.

'What?' said Johnny, caught off stride.

'Can you hear that?' she hissed.

'Hear what?' He strained his ears and made out a now-familiar sound – a long, sorrowful groan, more like a dying man than a sulky dog. 'Oh, that.'

'Don't sound so annoyed.' She turned on her side so she was facing him, their bodies still tantalisingly close together under the warm duvet. 'He's crying.'

Johnny eyed the tempting swell of Natalie's breasts under the t-shirt, and her nipples hardening against the thin cotton, and moved his hand to her hip, unwilling to give up so quickly. Untimetabled sex was something of a rarity.

'Nat, I know he's crying.' He smoothed his hand over the sweeping curve of her waist. 'He's knows exactly what he's doing. You can't keep going down to him. Didn't Megan tell you – he's going to do this. He's testing us.'

She turned back and they lay nose-to-nose in the dark, listening to the horrible groaning noise echoing through the house. It sounded like someone playing a double bass in boxing gloves.

'That's not crying,' whispered Natalie. 'He sounds like he's in some kind of pain. Do you think he's hurt himself on something in the kitchen?'

'It's the same noise as he was making last night. And the night before that.'

'Is it? Oh! Did you let him out before you came up? Maybe he needs the loo.'

Johnny groaned and rolled onto his back. 'What about me?'

'What about you what? You don't need to ask to use the loo, Johnny. Feel free.'

'Nat.' He pulled her hand so she rolled on top of him, and then gripped her round the buttocks, squeezing her to him in a way she normally found irresistible. She could feel how aroused he was, surely. 'Let me take your mind off the dog. What was it you read on the internet? The more sex you have, the better your chances are of—'

'I ovulated days ago,' said Natalie, a wry smile twisting up the corner of her mouth. 'Your sperm would have to have a Tardis to make a baby this month.'

Johnny flinched. 'Maybe I didn't want to make a baby. Maybe I just wanted to make love to you.'

Downstairs Bertie added an extra quaver to his plaintive howl. It sounded almost supernaturally awful.

'I can't stand it, I'm sorry.' Natalie squirmed free, threw back the covers and leaped out of bed. 'I'm going to go down there before the neighbours call the RSPCA.'

Johnny watched in acute frustration as she hunted around for her dressing gown, her long slim legs gleaming in the pale light from the clock radio.

Was that it now? If it wasn't a green day, it wasn't worth it? He felt hurt. Even if she was joking, which he hoped she was, it still showed there was a timetable in her head, even when she was pretending to be spontaneous.

He sank back into the pillows. Frantic sex on demand for half the month, nothing for the rest of it, and the dog putting up this dying routine until he was allowed on the bed – and then no sex at all?

Johnny jumped as Natalie leaned over him and kissed his nose. 'Don't sulk,' she said. 'I'll be back in a second. And just think – it's all good practice for sleepless nights with the baby.'

'If we ever have a baby,' he muttered, but only once Natalie was out of the room.

Natalie padded downstairs in her slippers, knowing she was breaking all the rules in the book by giving in to Bertie's howling, but at the same time, telling herself – as the same book said – she was powerless to resist a 'where are yooooouuu?' pack-locating howl developed over hundreds of years.

It was nature. And anyway, he was still settling in. Bertie had been through a lot in his short life. Plenty of time to get tough once he knew they weren't going to abandon him too.

She opened the kitchen door, and immediately the howling ceased, and the Basset hound rocketed into her arms, wagging his tail so hard he seemed to be jointed in the middle.

How can you resist so much love, Natalie wondered, bending down so she could hug his warm, wrinkly body to her.

'Hello, Bertie!' she murmured into his neck, revelling in the adoring snuffles he was lavishing on any exposed skin. His coat had a biscuity smell that she was just getting used to. Megan had warned her that 'hounds stink' and had washed him before he left, but even with air fresheners in every room, you could still tell exactly where he was.

Natalie didn't mind. She could forgive Bertie anything when he gazed up at her like he was now, brimming over with love and gratitude for his new home, new attention, new start.

He made her heart brim over too. At least now she felt as if all her maternal longing was going somewhere, touching another life and making it better.

'Oh, you daft dog! You've got your bed all rucked up!' In his distress at being left to sleep alone in a top-of-the-range leather basket, Bertie had dragged the cushion out, and left it near the door. Natalie bent down to tuck it all back in, and when she turned back, Bertie had vanished.

She looked round for a second or two, confused, then heard the tell-tale clatter of claws on hardwood flooring. Natalie darted out of the kitchen, just in time to see the white tip of Bertie's tail vanishing up the stairs.

She set off after him. He wasn't supposed to go upstairs – it was bad for his back. Not to mention their superiority as pack leaders.

'Nat, is that . . .? Ooouf! Bloody hell!'

That would be Bertie landing on the bed, she guessed, with a wry smile. It turned out that having legs like a piano stool's wasn't any obstacle to reaching up to grab titbits off the kitchen counter, or springing onto the sofa.

Natalie entered the bedroom to see Bertie lounging regally on top of the white duvet, regarding her with adoring, if still tragic, eyes. She still couldn't get used to his doleful face. Even when, as now, he'd got exactly what he wanted.

'You let him upstairs!' Johnny's muffled voice was coming from somewhere beneath the dog. 'I thought you said they weren't meant to go upstairs? In your big book of rules?'

'I know.' She glared at Bertie who gazed back sadly. 'It's bad for your back, Bertie. And you might fall off and hurt yourself.'

Bertie said nothing.

She slipped into the bed, and the dog filled the gap between them before she could cuddle Johnny to her. Bertie stretched out his long neck onto the pillow so he lay between them like a bolster, his long brown ears splayed on each side.

Not very hygienic, thought Natalie, but so lovable she couldn't bear to move him. He obviously hadn't had many pillows in his life up until now.

'Just this once,' she told him. 'Tomorrow night, you sleep in the kitchen.'

'And tonight he snores in our faces.'

'He won't snore,' said Natalie, just as Bertie stretched out his legs and punched her in the face. She pushed them away. 'Or rather, he won't snore much worse than you do.'

'All right for you to say that. You don't have work to go to. You're a lady of leisure.' Johnny wriggled so his head was visible over Bertie's. His hair was tousled and his face had a sleepy crossness that was almost as cute, in its own way, as Bertie's.

'Well, in that case do you want to waste more precious hours listening to him crying downstairs?'

'No,' said Johnny and rolled back onto his back, grabbing what duvet there was left underneath Bertie. 'But I can't cope with two duvet hogs.'

Next to him, Bertie exhaled with supreme satisfaction.

Zoe was listening to the sound of puppy breathing too, but she wasn't asleep.

She couldn't sleep, which was why she was sitting on her sofa in her fleecy dressing gown at two-thirty in the morning, her hands cupped around a mug of cold coffee while she watched Toffee's soft stomach rise and fall in his basket by the fireplace. It would have been nice to have him on her knee, but Zoe was trying really hard to follow the rules Megan had given her.

Boundaries, she kept saying. Puppies and kids need boundaries. Zoe wished she had Megan's easy authority with either or, ideally, both.

At least he was asleep. It was typical that on the rare occasion she could drop off, safe in the knowledge that Toffee wasn't trashing, chewing or peeing on something he shouldn't, her head was buzzing with dilemmas that made it impossible for her to shut her eyes for more than a minute. Zoe had a lot to think about, all tangled up in her head like a knotted necklace and impossible to unravel.

Bill. She couldn't stop thinking about Bill, for a start. It was ludicrous to have a crush on someone you'd just met but once he'd installed her on Rachel's sofa, they'd basically spent the rest of the afternoon chatting – to prove she wasn't concussed, of course. He'd talked as much as she had, with plenty of non-concussion-related eye contact, and dropped some tentative hints about meeting up again with the dogs, maybe for lunch. Zoe wished she could just enjoy the first shivery daydreams of what could be something new, but a cloud was hanging over her.

When she and Toffee had left, she'd realised that she hadn't mentioned Spencer and Leo once. Should she make a clean breast of it about being divorced, with two boys? Or would telling him about the kids make it look like she was jumping the gun?

The longer she left it, the more of a glaring omission it was going to look when she did get round to telling him. And the insidious night-time voice couldn't help reminding her how luxurious it felt to have that brief hour when she was just Zoe. Not Mum or anyone's ex. Just her again, for the first time in years.

She pushed that to one side and took out the phone from under the cushion where she'd hidden it from herself.

It was Spencer's mobile, the bribe David had given him just before he left, even though Zoe had protested he was far too young. Her fingers moved on the keys before she could stop herself and there they were again: the Alton Towers snaps of David having as much fun as money could buy with the boys. They were bad enough on their own, but several of them featured Jennifer too, grinning away in the background, clearly trying really hard to be their best mate.

She had very bad highlights. Zoe could tell they were expensive but cack-handed.

Stop looking, she told herself, but it was useless. It was like picking a scab. Now Zoe knew the images were there, she couldn't stop herself. Leo seemed happy enough, but Spencer's face was shadowed with a gloom she knew very well, when he was trying his best to go along with things like a big boy, but was still too young to hide his discomfort.

She forced herself to turn it off. David had taken those photos knowing she'd see them. The conniving sod had framed his new girlfriend with his old sons, knowing Spencer would show her, to remind her that she wasn't part of this family unit any more.

Zoe put her hand to her mouth to stifle the painful sob that came out.

She didn't love David any more. She didn't want to be with him; Jennifer and her bad highlights were welcome to him. But she didn't want to lose her boys, just because she was too nice to fight dirty, like David did.

She couldn't bribe them. She couldn't afford to. All she could do was love them, and how long was that going to hold up against weekends away, and puppies on demand?

Toffee stirred, hearing the noise, and raised his soft head above the plastic rim of his bed. He looked sleepy and adorable, with his nose and eyes wrinkled up against the faint light.

Zoe got up quietly, scooped the puppy out of his basket and brought him back onto the sofa, where she lay back with him in her arms. Instinctively, he snuggled into the crook of her neck and breathed his hot puppy breath into her ear.

'Sometimes I think you're the only simple thing in my life,' she whispered. 'You're the only one who understands "no". Even if you don't always take any notice of me.'

Toffee licked Zoe's ear. She felt better.

# 15

The next morning, Megan's tea knock on the door came, as usual, at half past seven, only for once Rachel didn't spring upright. Something invisible was anchoring her to the pillow and it wasn't Gem.

It wasn't the worst hangover she'd ever had, though the inside of her mouth felt parched and she wasn't sure she should move her head without due consideration. It didn't take much to lay her low these days. But despite the rough edges, Rachel felt a lingering sense of happiness, a flutter, almost, a bit like a birthday morning. What on earth had she got to be happy about?

She rechecked, keeping her eyes shut.

Oliver, dumped. Job, none. Probate, now done, but with a massive bill to come any moment. Kennels, nightmare of sick dog. George . . .

Her eyes snapped open, and the good mood fluttered out of her grasp like a butterfly.

George. Last night. It had been perfect, a real, promising date, right up until she'd got drunk and hauled him off to bed like a teenager home alone for the first time.

Rachel sat up, ignoring the warning swells in her chest, and checked out the room. There was no sign of George, and her jeans and shirt from last night were piled onto the chair by the door. She looked down, and saw she was wearing an old yoga t-shirt that she'd thrown over the chair a few nights ago.

Fragments of the previous evening drifted back across her cringing mind. The free-flowing conversation. Feeling like she'd known George for ever. That amazing, knee-melting moment where she'd kissed him, and felt his strong arm wrap around her waist when he kissed her back.

And then it went blurry. She hadn't been *drunk*, just that it has happened quite fast . . .

Rachel dredged her memory ruthlessly for details. Now was not the time to go blurry.

He'd carried her up the stairs, she still shivered at the thought of that. And when she'd pulled off the checked shirt, she'd been delighted that her guess about the cow-wrangling muscles had been spot on. And for a man who allegedly hadn't had a girlfriend in years, he'd touched her with a confidence that had reduced her to a series of inarticulate gasps. But there were gaps. She didn't remember falling asleep, for one thing.

Oh God. Rachel covered her face. She hadn't had a reckless one-night stand since she was at university. What kind of rebound cliché was she?

There was another knock at the door.

'Rachel? Tea?' Megan sounded chirpy. 'I've put two sugars in it this morning. Case you need it!'

Rachel stared in horror as the sultry Dot on the wall seemed to wink at her. What time had George left? Had Megan seen him on her way in?

'Or would you prefer a Berocca?' Megan went on, in her helpful tone.

I've got to get up before she thinks I'm a drunken slapper, thought Rachel, and with a superhuman effort, she hauled herself out of bed, grabbing her cashmere dressing gown and slinging it on in one movement.

As she moved, she nearly fell over Gem, who was lying in his usual place by the door.

Rachel's stomach rolled. 'Oh, great,' she said, aloud. 'Don't tell me you were here the whole time? That would be . . . just weird.'

She yanked open the door, and Megan handed her the mug of tea. She looked fresh as a daisy in a clean version of the sort of t-shirt Rachel was wearing, and cut-off denim shorts and Uggs. Sleeping over at her mate's hadn't affected Megan's tea deliveries.

'Morning!' she chirped. 'Looks like you had a good night!'

Rachel ran a nervous hand through her hair, which she could see from the big oak-framed landing mirror was sticking up at all angles. How much did Megan know about last night? 'Meaning?'

'The pans! In the sink! Kitchen looks like a bomb's hit it. I never had you down as a cook.'

'I didn't cook. George stayed for dinner and refused to eat what I was making,' said Rachel, before any hinting could be done. 'He stayed for a drink afterwards.'

'Great!' Megan lifted her eyebrows in what looked worryingly like an 'And?' gesture to Rachel.

Pause.

'And?' prompted Megan.

Rachel's head throbbed, but underneath her embarrassment at what George must have made of her, she could still feel the delicious Christmas morning glow. The tiny smile at the corner of her lips gave her away, even if she hoped she sounded cool.

'And nothing. We had a nice chat. He's . . .' *He's absolutely gorgeous.* 'He's very good company.'

'You mean he didn't spend the night winding you up?' said Megan. 'Blimey. Listen, I'll stick a bacon sarnie on for you.' She turned to go. 'Freda's downstairs, wants your advice about seeing a show in London for Ted's birthday, seeing as you're our expert. Nothing with nudity or sudden flashes, please. Sets off his angina.'

Rachel clutched her tea and leaned against the doorway as Megan trotted down the stairs with Gem. When she caught a second glimpse of her own reflection, she saw a dishevelled but happy woman she hadn't seen in a while.

By the time Rachel came downstairs, freshly showered and feeling more like herself, Freda had done all the washing up and had moved onto polishing the glassware. Rachel boggled at the array of pans now on the draining board, but knew the price of this domestic favour would be a rundown on the previous night.

Megan was mixing up some rice and chicken for Chester, who was sniffing around the kitchen, significantly perkier than the previous evening, and she gave Rachel an apologetic smile in advance for the cross-questioning to come.

'Did you have a nice night in?' asked Freda, hanging the damp towel over the Aga rail.

'Very, thanks,' said Rachel. 'Ooh, is that fresh tea?'

'I hear George Fenwick popped over?' Freda persisted with her casual expression.

'Mm. He did. Chester wasn't too well. How is he this morning, Megan?'

'Oh, much better, actually! He was—'

'I hear that's not the only one George was looking after last night,' Freda burst out, unable to resist any longer. 'Good for you, love!'

'I didn't tell her,' protested Megan as Rachel squawked. 'She guessed. From the pans. She didn't think you'd use that many to heat a Pot Noodle, no offence.'

'So?' Freda raised her plucked eyebrows.

Rachel lifted her mug to her lips and had to smile at the expectant faces: Freda, Megan, Chester, and now Gem. 'So, nothing. George cooked me dinner and stayed over because it was late.'

Freda clapped her hands together. 'Lovely! Oh, you deserve a decent man, love, if you don't mind me saying, after what you've been through!'

Rachel started to demur that Dot's death really wasn't that much of an ordeal, but saw Megan try to shush Freda and knew she'd confided in her about her 'abusive' relationship. Her heart, which had lifted at the friendly delight they'd taken in her night in, sank. So much for her fresh start.

'Don't be cross with Megan for letting on, you're among friends here, Rachel. Good for you for leaving,' Freda went on, to both Rachel and Megan's chagrin. 'You can't find Mr Right while you're with Mr Wrong, as I said to our Lynne. In the days when I still saw her to advise, that is.'

Rachel looked at Freda's homely lined face, brimming with sympathy, and felt shabby. From now on, she told herself with determination, it's honesty all the way. Apart from this.

'We had a nice evening and I enjoyed getting to know him,' she confessed, 'but I don't think George and I are at that stage yet. We just had dinner, that's all.'

'Well, I think you're a good match, you two,' said Freda. 'You're the first one I've met will be able to give him what for. The only one he'll let, too.' She winked. 'You might have to tell us the details, love, because we're not going to get any out of George.'

Megan suppressed a gurgle of horror, and Rachel aimed a friendly 'tsk' in her direction, surprised at how nice it was to be able to talk about her evening, instead of pretending it never happened, as she'd always had to in the past.

It wasn't her kitchen, not really, but she was starting to feel strangely at home.

Throughout the morning, fragments of the previous evening floated back as Rachel's thick head wore off, making her stop mid-kennel check, or mid-phone call, with a bittersweet tingle of pleasure mixed with mortification. It made her feel like a teenager, but even so she kept checking her mobile to see if he'd rung.

He didn't. He was, she told herself, running a busy veterinary surgery. And even if he wasn't busy, George didn't seem the type to follow up dinner with a bunch of flowers. Although, she argued, he didn't seem the type for a one-night stand either – she didn't know him well, but she felt quite sure of that much.

In her new spirit of honesty, Rachel decided the best course of action was to take the bull by the horns herself and sort out where they stood. She didn't want to go from gazing up in awe at his broad naked shoulders to discussing some puking spaniel over the kennel table. Her skin was already crawling at how embarrassing that would be, especially with the obligatory audience of Megan and at least two dogs.

So just after lunch, Rachel pulled into the surgery car park only to see George's muddy Land Rover swing in at top speed on the opposite side.

She took a deep breath, pinned a smile on her face and jumped out.

'Hello!' she said. 'Have you got two minutes?'

George's face was friendly, but guarded.

'I have, yes. Good timing,' he said, a little stiffly. 'I'm only popping back to get supplies – full day today. Lots of lambing dramas.'

They scrunched up the gravel to the surgery and he held the door open for her to go in. It was a modern reception room, decorated with lots of flea control posters, and, Rachel was pleased to see, a whole notice board of rescue pleas, which Megan must have photocopied for him.

A couple of clients were waiting with carrying baskets and cardboard boxes, and they smiled as George walked past. He ushered her rather formally into his office, where he opened a filing cabinet and carried on checking through some files.

'Do you mind if I carry on?' he asked. 'I've got to be out again in ten minutes.'

'Not at all.' Rachel suddenly realised she didn't quite know what to say. It was like seeing the first boy she'd snogged at a school disco in class the following morning.

George turned round, and she saw that he was as awkward as she was.

'So, what have you come to talk to me about? Or are you worried I've upped my call-out rate?' His voice was light, but he wasn't as easy as normal.

'Listen, I wanted to come and see you, because . . .' Rachel was turning red, despite her best efforts to behave like a mature woman. 'Because these things never go well when you try to do it over the phone.'

George raised an eyebrow and Rachel's insides fluttered.

She put her hands on the back of the chair. 'I came up to say thank you for cooking me supper last night. I had a really lovely evening, but I got a bit drunk, as you probably noticed, and, um, I just wanted to say that I don't normally . . .'

How to say she didn't sleep with men on the first date, without sounding like a prude? She was nearly forty years old. But for some reason, his opinion mattered to her. Whether they started a relationship or whether it stayed as a friendship, Rachel wanted things to be right this time.

George took pity on her blushes and rolled his eyes, looking more like the George she remembered from the previous night.

'No need to explain,' he said. 'I don't generally, either.'

'Oh, right. Good!'

'Good!' George looked at her and the tension between them crackled again. 'Right answer?'

'Yes. Absolutely. ' Rachel steeled herself for the next question. 'We *did* . . .'

'We did.' George nodded. 'Maybe you've blotted it out, but you nearly fell off the bed, searching about in your overnight bag, and tried to make me use a handiwipe from a sushi restaurant as a contraceptive.'

Rachel froze, then spluttered. It wasn't funny, but there was something about the solemn way he said it, and his straight face. 'Did I?'

'You did.' He sighed. 'Obviously we both need to go back to school on that front, because it wasn't the most textbook demonstration. That's what happens when enthusiasm gets in the way of experience.'

'Well, it definitely was enthusiastic.' It was quite endearing, really, she thought – the two of them, at their age, agonising over this like a pair of horny, drunk teenagers.

They looked at each other for a moment, and Rachel wondered where she was supposed to steer this conversation next. For a rural vet with apparently little female service history, George seemed to be doing a much better job of handling this than she was.

'But now we've got that out of the way,' he went on, 'would you like to go back about ten paces, and have dinner with me some time this weekend? I'm old-fashioned, you see. I think if we go forward any more steps I'd have to propose.'

Rachel realised that she hadn't been expecting this reaction: the simple, we've-started-something calm. No subterfuge, no need to think up reasons not to do it. It felt like putting one foot on an icy lake and finding it solid enough to skate on.

'Yes!' she said. 'Yes, that would be great. Shouldn't I cook you dinner, though?'

'No, thanks,' said George, 'in the kindest possible way. I think we know each other well enough already to know that's not a great idea. How about this Saturday? Got any plans?' He paused. 'Or is the whole point of being ageing singletons in the middle of nowhere that we don't have to pretend about stuff like that?'

'Quite,' said Rachel. 'My diary is empty. I am desperate. I'll come over for dinner.' She smiled because she could see how much, despite their words, they were both rather looking forward to the prospect of another evening's talking.

It had got to two o'clock and Natalie still hadn't managed to do anything on her to-do list, thanks to Bertie and his incessant, child-like demands for attention.

If this was what kids were like, she thought, removing his paw from her leg, she wasn't a hundred per cent sure it was a good idea any more.

Not being at work wasn't as easy as she'd imagined it would be, either. The day had started when she'd woken at seven, as usual, but instead of getting into her suit and charging off to the office, she'd got up, let Bertie out and begun *his* routine, which seemed to include fifteen minutes standing in their garden with a poobag, waiting for him to perform.

Johnny had gone off to school at eight, and now she and Bertie were in her study downstairs, where they'd been locked in a battle of wills all morning. Natalie was strong, and very focused on her sabbatical to-do list, but she couldn't type with a Basset hound leaning on her right forearm, begging for attention.

'Down!' she said, in the firm tone the books recommended, but Bertie didn't give up his position at the side of her desk. Instead he lunged for her nose with his, to administer a bump. Natalie jerked her face out of reach at the last minute but, undeterred, he shuffled even further forward on his sturdy back legs.

Stretched out, Bertie could reach desks, kitchen work surfaces, Natalie's dressing table and any other surface with edibles like a canine extending ladder.

'That's lovely, but *down*,' she said again, more firmly, pointing at the floor. 'Down!'

He lunged for her face again, this time banging his nose against hers so hard it hurt. It still hurt from the first time he'd done it – when Johnny had roared with laughter at how cute it was and thus cemented it in Bertie's repertoire of attention-seeking tricks.

'Ow! No! Bad!' She pushed the dog down so she could cover her nose, which felt like it might be bleeding.

Bertie dropped onto all four paws and gazed up at her sadly. She knew what he wanted: he wanted her to sit on the floor, so he could sit on her lap, then go to sleep. Sometimes Natalie wondered who was training whom here.

'Bertie, just because I'm home doesn't mean I haven't got loads to do. How am I going to get my CV updated if you keep interrupting?' she demanded through her hands.

So far, all she had managed to do that morning was to have a shower, and that had been a speedy operation, since she only had the amount of time Bertie could be distracted with a treat-stuffed Kong. Otherwise, he appeared at the shower door, making his unearthly grumbles for attention and padding around the place looking devastated.

Apart from the recommended hour's walk, which actually took up nearly two hours if you counted all the bribery required to get Bertie off the sofa in the first place, Natalie had spent the first days of her new life chained to the house, because she wasn't sure she could leave him alone safely. Johnny thought she and Bertie were home watching daytime TV and having a whale of a time, but in fact, if Natalie was honest, it was a bit, well, limiting. Not that she was going to tell him that, or let Bertie see.

'You can't have Mummy's attention all the time,' she informed the dog.

Bertie let out a low, melancholy moan and Natalie's heart melted. She was being mean. He'd had so little attention in his last home, no wonder he wanted to make sure she wasn't going to abandon him too.

'Right, well, we'll go for a walk, shall we?' Natalie gave up on her CV and reached for her list instead. Her sabbatical, as she was now thinking of it, had only made her more determined not to waste a second; her goals were to get pregnant, train Bertie and chill out completely.

Walk Bertie was on there, so it counted as something to tick off.

Poring over the Longhampton street map at the weekend, Johnny and Natalie had worked out some nice varied routes for Bertie's daily leg-stretch, all ending up at the big park, where he could have a run around and chase some balls.

That was the idea anyway. Natalie had read that Basset hounds could be trained to retrieve, if you were patient and persistent enough, but so far she'd thrown the ball twelve times and had to collect it herself. She was starting to feel a bit stupid when Bertie finally showed some signs of animation and bounded off towards the trees on the edge of the park.

Natalie grabbed his extending lead, and shaded her eyes against the light. Bertie's excitement had nothing to do with her. He'd spotted Rachel from the rescue heading towards them with four dogs of varying sizes.

She waved and Rachel came over, followed by Bertie, bouncing around the others as if he hadn't seen them in years.

'Hi! Fancy seeing you here!' joked Rachel, transferring all her leads to one hand with some difficulty. 'I see you've joined the daily walking cult?'

'I guess this is what the school run mums feel like,' Natalie said. 'Same time, same place, same manic behaviour.'

'Yeah, but if you're a school-run mum, at least you can go for coffee!' Rachel hurled a manky tennis ball from her plastic thrower, and all the dogs – plus Bertie, to Natalie's surprise

– hurtled off in pursuit. 'Have you tried getting in anywhere with one of these in tow? It's killing me. I had a four-a-day espresso habit back in London. Now I can't even get into a café. Oi, Lucy! Bring me that ball! Now!'

Lucy, a brindled Staffie, scampered up with the ball lodged in her powerful jaws, followed by the others, and Rachel bent down to hurl it away again.

'You know what we need? A dog-friendly coffee shop,' said Natalie, as a rosy vision started to form in her mind's eye. 'With hooks and bays so you could park the dogs like the mummies park their buggies – inside, so you'd know no one was nicking them, obviously.'

'And Bonios free with every coffee and water bowls at different heights.'

'And a park and escape facility, so you could drop them off for half an hour with a friend, and go and do your chores,' Natalie went on, thinking of the blood test she really needed to organise at the surgery. 'Bertie's perfectly clean, you know. Much cleaner than half the kids I see in cafés.'

'Sounds like a great idea.' Rachel smiled. 'You should set it up.'

'Want to go halves, with fifty per cent profits to the rescue?' Natalie hurled the ball for the dogs. 'You could be selling those bacon sarnies, you know. Johnny said he'd happily pay three quid for one – apparently they're worth going on a long walk for.'

'Really? Don't joke,' said Rachel. 'I need to rustle up some extra funding for the kennels. My aunt Dot wasn't exactly a financial genius and you wouldn't believe how much those dogs eat. It's like they're making up for lost time.' She chucked the ball again. 'I've got to confess I'm a bit clueless when it comes to that sort of thing, but I'm going to have to come up with something fast if the kennels are going to stay open.'

'Well, if you need some ideas, I've got a lot of marketing experience and plenty of free time. As long as I can bring my dog with me.' Natalie couldn't help offering. There was something about Rachel she liked – not least the fact that she was in her late thirties, hadn't had a child, and seemed pretty happy nonetheless.

Stop it, she told herself. That's not what defines anyone. And, anyway, the blood test was a positive first step. Natalie looked wistfully at Bertie, now wrestling a passive Treacle. There was no way she could leave him in reception. 'Is he ever going to be OK to leave on his own? I mean, at home?'

'He'll never be great, according to Megan, but who knows?' Rachel turned to her. 'Is he stressing you out already? Have you changed your mind about fostering him?'

'No! No, not at all,' said Natalie quickly. 'It's just that I've got to go to the surgery to get a blood test done, and do some stuff round town, and I can't leave him on his own till Johnny gets back from work.' She bit her lip. 'I've got to get my bloods done today or tomorrow.'

'Nothing serious, I hope?' Rachel looked concerned.

'No, it's . . .' She hesitated, then it poured out. 'Johnny and I are trying for a baby, like we said at the home check, and it's not happening as fast as we hoped, so I need to get my hormone levels measured, to see if I'm ovulating. I have to do it today, ideally.'

'Oh, God, right,' Rachel murmured sympathetically, then said, 'Look, I'm going to be here for at least forty minutes, chucking balls and walking them – do you want to leave him while you do your chores?' She nudged the crowd of dogs around her legs. 'One more won't make a difference.'

'Really?' Natalie felt as if she'd just been let off the lead herself.

'Sure. Just bring me an espresso and a cake on your way back.' Rachel wrangled the ball out of Lucy's drooly mouth, fitted it back onto the thrower with squeamish fingertips and hurled it extra hard towards the woods. 'Actually, make that a double espresso. And can you get me the latest *Vogue*?'

'No problem. Oh, my God, Rachel, you are a lifesaver!' Natalie tucked Bertie's lead onto the hook on Rachel's belt and set off for the surgery, her mobile already out to get Bill to pull some nurse-related strings.

Rachel got back to the kennels at four o'clock, after the final round of walking, put the dogs back into the runs, and went through to the kitchen, humming happily to herself.

From a rubbish start, today had turned into something truly enjoyable. The sun was out, she was at the beginning of a relationship that she could tell the world about if she wanted to, the dogs were actually coming back when she yelled for them, and Natalie Hodge was going to help her work out what to do about raising some real money for the kennels.

It was a relief to have someone help with that, she thought. A rough calculation of the inheritance tax had left her rather panicky – even with her dodgy maths, it was going to be a lot. Dot's 'secrets' didn't seem to include the magic formula for how she'd managed to make ends meet over the years.

There was the necklace, of course, currently at the old jeweller's in Longhampton, being valued 'for insurance'. Hopefully it would go some way to clearing the probate but after that?

Rachel paused, her hand on the fridge door. She'd checked all the other condiments pots for further diamonds, but there weren't any. What she really wanted to find, though, was some explanation for that amazing necklace – a gift? From mysterious Felix? Or something else?

She made herself a cup of coffee, letting her imagination wander romantically over the possibilities. Dot and Felix lurked at the back of her mind a lot of the time. No further clues or secrets had turned up in the course of her sorting out, so she'd had to embroider her own version of events, based not-very-loosely on her own experience with Oliver – the late nights at the office that had turned into snatched brasserie dinners, that had turned into something more.

At least Felix had taken Dot out in public, if those photos were anything to go by, she thought, with a twinge of regret. There were no records of her years with Oliver, because he'd swerved out of any snaps with the instinct of a spy. At least Dot had had *proof* of her relationship.

All in the past, she told herself, heading through to the kennels office to see what had been going on. It works both ways – it didn't exist for him, so it needn't exist for me.

Megan was at the desk, chewing on a pen and going through the daybook. Freda had been on afternoon phone duty and as usual had left a stack of scrawled missives for Megan and Rachel to decipher once she'd taken herself off home to make Ted's tea.

'Hey!' Megan pointed at the Dundee cake on the table. 'Freda left this. Help yourself. You look like you've had a good walk.'

'I have,' said Rachel. 'Treacle's recall's improving. I did the whistle and reward thing you told me.'

'Excellent. Well done you.'

'I've got to admit, it's a nice feeling when it works.' She peered over her shoulder at Freda's notes. 'Looks like it's been a busy afternoon here too. Any messages for me?'

'Couple of home checks for Freda or you to do in the next few days, for Tinker, and Treacle.'

'Yay!' said Rachel, pretending to punch the air like a cheerleader. 'Four down, eleven to go!'

'And we've had three calls about doggie daycare, which is money in the bank, isn't it? Oh, and a personal call for you.'

'A personal call to the kennels?' Rachel frowned. Her mum would have called her mobile, as would Oliver. Then a depressing thought struck her: her probate estimates would have reached the Inland Revenue by now. 'Was it someone from the solicitors' about the probate forms? Oh God, have I ballsed them up?'

'No, it was on your mobile. You left it here in your other coat, apparently. Someone called . . . Freda's writing is so awful.' Megan squinted at the cramped note. 'Someone called Kath Wrigley. She wanted to talk to you about . . . Oliver? Oh, Rachel.' She looked up with a worried expression on her face. 'That's not your ex, is it?'

Rachel's good mood curdled. Kath. In her blanket ignoring of Oliver's calls, she'd somehow forgotten that *Kath* might try to get hold of her. It seemed so obvious now – how could she not have imagined that Kath would want to have her moment of absolute rage?

'Is that all Freda wrote?' Her voice wobbled. 'Kath, calling about Oliver?'

Megan nodded, her eyes wide as saucers.

'Did she say she'd call back?'

'I don't know. Freda said she gave her the kennels' number, in case she wanted to try you here.' Megan looked guilty. 'I didn't tell her any names, you know, when I, um, filled her in on your break-up. I don't think she'd have made any association. She probably thinks Oliver's a dog.'

Rachel swallowed. Thank goodness for that. The thought of kindly Freda's face when she realised she'd been sympathising with an Other Woman was too shameful to contemplate.

'Listen, I can call her back and tell her you're not here,' said Megan. 'We can block her calls!'

'No,' said Rachel, bravely. 'If she calls again . . .'

It's part of your punishment, she told herself, even though she was terrified. You've got to speak to her. She probably needs to yell so she can move on. It's the least you can do.

Megan saw her discomfort and changed the subject. 'Oh, and George called – wanted to know if you're allergic to pheasant?' She grinned. 'I take it you're seeing him for another dinner?'

'I am. At the weekend.'

Megan clapped her hands together in delight. 'Go, you! Looks like everything's really starting to happen, eh?'

Rachel's incipient smile faltered. So long as she could keep her past well out of her future.

# 16

Zoe didn't normally take her lunch hour, preferring to book clients through and finish early so she wouldn't be rushing for Spencer and Leo, but today she made sure Hannah knew she wasn't around for any walk-ins, and almost power-walked down the high street to get to the surgery for one o'clock.

Her plan had been very clear in her head on the way – she was going to take Bill some tulips from the market stall near the salon to say thanks for the Red Cross act and then go – but once she actually arrived at the desk, something weird came over her, and she couldn't quite get her words out. Or at least, not in any order that made sense.

'So you don't have an appointment?' Lauren the receptionist clarified, her head tilted helpfully on one side. Behind her, Zoe could see Lulu curled up in a basket in the corner of the office, watching everyone with sharp black eyes that missed nothing. 'You want to see Dr Harper? But not for an appointment?'

'Um, yes,' said Zoe. 'These are for him.' She held out the flowers, and as she spoke, she could hear how stalkerish that sounded, and began to backtrack in embarrassment. 'Actually, I suppose I could just leave them with you . . .'

Lauren shook her head vigorously. 'No! No need, he's just with his last patient before lunch. Why don't you take a seat and he'll be out in a minute? He needs to take Lulu out for a walk.' She gestured affectionately towards the dog. 'Doesn't he? You're about ready for your walk, aren't you?'

As she spoke, Zoe spotted a male figure entering the back of the office, and from Lulu's instant reaction – ears pricked, up on her neat paws – it was obviously Bill.

She felt something twitch nervously inside her stomach, and almost wished she hadn't come. How clichéd did it look? Turning up to give him *flowers*? He'd just been polite, she told herself. She was making something out of nothing.

But before Zoe could change her mind and slink off, Lauren had accosted Bill. 'Dr Harper? There's someone to see you in reception!'

He looked up, and Zoe's butterflies went into overdrive. Oh, God, how Mills and Boon – he had an actual stethoscope round his neck. He scanned the reception across the desk then, when he spotted her, sitting there with her knees clamped anxiously together in her unfamiliar skirt, his expression changed from puzzled to a smile of recognition.

Don't say anything stupid, she warned herself. Just keep your brain engaged at all times.

Bill was coming out through the office door now, with Lulu prancing next to him, heading straight for her. Zoe pressed her lips to check her lipstick was still roughly where she'd put it, then smiled, hoping there was none on her teeth.

'Hey, Lulu, look who it is!' he said to the dog, with a nod towards her. 'Your new hair stylist! I see the lump's gone down! Have you come to be checked out?'

'I'm fine! I mean, I'm a bit wonky and I'm off the marathon training, but I seem to be managing!' gabbled Zoe. 'Hi, Lulu! How are you? Been rolled over by any big dogs lately?'

Oh shut up, Zoe, she thought.

She distracted herself with a moment's ruffling of Lulu's ears.

'We're just off for a walk round the block,' said Bill. 'Do you want to join us? Um, unless you're here to see someone?'

Zoe looked up, straight into Bill's brown eyes. His keenness to see her was now mixed with a spot of embarrassment, and it just made him even more handsome. 'No, actually, I came to give you these.' She held out the tulips, red with yellow streaks, a bit like her own hair this week, after the trainee's session. 'Just to say thanks. For looking after me. It messed up your Saturday but I really appreciate it.'

Bill looked genuinely taken aback. 'My pleasure. And I don't think anyone's ever given me flowers before. That's so kind of you. Look, why don't you walk us to the park and back? I can see how your mobility is. You've obviously worked out the quick way to get private treatment on the NHS.'

'That would be great.' Zoe grinned.

Limp a bit, said a wicked voice in her head.

Zoe had to hold Lulu while Bill rushed into Shackley's greasy spoon to get them a cup of tea each, and she couldn't help feeling that she was being assessed in the manner of a suspicious mother-in-law. Lulu sniffed her legs delicately and circled around her, peeking up from under her curls, and standing quite still when Zoe tried to pet her.

'Can you smell Toffee?' Zoe asked, to make conversation. Talking to dogs no longer bothered her. She got more conversation out of Toffee than she did out of Spencer at the moment. 'He's smaller than you. Not so fashionable. You'd like him.'

'Like who?' Bill handed her a polystyrene cup.

'Toffee. My puppy.'

'I know who Toffee is.' Bill sounded as if he hadn't forgotten, which was either true, or a skill doctors learned, thought Zoe. 'How's he coming on? Eaten any more house plants?'

Zoe felt a tiny thrill that he'd remembered her horror stories from the weekend.

'Almost. It's the discipline I have trouble with,' she sighed. 'It's like Megan at the kennels says, I just don't have that commanding voice. I have to keep practising saying "No", like I mean it.' She put her hand out, and barked, 'No!' so sharply Bill jerked his cup back in shock, spilling tea over his jacket.

'Sorry! Oh, my God, did you burn yourself?' Zoe turned to him, aghast, and began patting him down with her napkin.

'I'm fine, fine.' He grinned. 'What's an outdoor coat for, if it can't take some outdoor action? Shall we?' He set off walking towards the park, and Lulu fell into step between them.

'So, are you walking the dogs again on Saturday?' he asked.

'Probably. Between you and me, Rachel and Megan are doing me a bargain rate on the daycare, so I feel like it's the least I can do. And I really like it, to be honest. It's good training for when Toffee's old enough and I'll have to control six stones of prime Labrador.'

She turned her head and caught Bill looking at her, with an interested sort of expression on his boyish face.

'You'll have to come out with us,' he suggested. 'Get Lulu here to teach Toffee to walk like a show dog.'

'I'd love that! I bet she would too! Are you two going on Saturday?'

'Definitely.' Bill made a huffing noise. 'Even if I didn't want to, which I do,' he amended, 'I wouldn't have a lot of choice. My best mates, Johnny and Nat, you know, the couple who've fostered the Basset hound, are signed up for the full morning's walking. It's Nat's new obsession. She's a born-again dog owner. Seriously. It's all she talks about now.' He grinned. 'I guess I'm probably as bad, though.'

'They do take over your life,' agreed Zoe. 'Everyone at work keeps telling me horror stories about how I'll never leave the house again, how he's this massive tie. But I like it! I'm always taking Toffee places – Megan's given me a socialisation checklist – and I've met loads of new people.'

'Tell me about it. It's like you turn into this magnet for everyone in the country who's ever had a poodle or a Lab or whatever.' Bill let Lulu trot ahead a little, so they could admire her perfectly straight show walk. 'Doesn't it feel like you're in a kind of club – it's definitely easier to talk to someone when they've got a dog with them. I mean, you already know how much you've got in common.'

There was a brief pause between them that flickered with unspoken words, until Zoe broke it with a stream of gabbling.

'Oh, totally, and there's the fresh air aspect too! Until I had that total disaster with Bertie I was just thinking how nice it was to be out there walking with the dogs, and letting my head clear completely! It was the first time all week I'd had a moment to myself, don't you find that? You can just have some proper space.'

'Yes,' said Bill. 'I know exactly what you mean. The only downside I've found – like just now – is that you can't meet up for lunch and walk the dog at the same time.'

They were in the park now, alongside the fountain with the cavorting granite mermaids. Lulu was doing her best to ignore the sniffing of a rather forward Yorkshire terrier, and as Bill stopped to shoo him away, he met Zoe's eye, and she realised he was struggling to look casual.

'I mean,' he went on, 'unless you know a spot two dog owners might be able to . . .' He was turning pink now, with the effort of not making a big deal of things. 'Um, meet for a drink after work?'

'Oh. After work?' Zoe shook her head, sadly. 'School nights are completely out for me, sorry.'

'Of course, you've got Toffee,' Bill cut in, before she could explain. 'Stupid of me. Lulu's OK to leave, but yeah, you can't really leave a puppy for the evening.' He smiled. 'But you'll be at the walking club on Saturday?'

'Absolutely,' said Zoe before she had a chance to think.

*     *     *

Zoe only started to feel properly bad as she was leaving the salon to pick up Spencer and Leo from school. The lingering warmth of chatting with Bill, and the prospect of seeing him again on Saturday, had lasted through her boring afternoon of highlighting, at which point her conscience had started throbbing like a big spot.

Somehow, she hadn't told Bill she was the mother of two children. Again.

Back at home, making tea for those two children, her tingling lunchtime walk felt a long, long way away.

'Muuuum!'

The familiar sound of a Spencer–Leo quarrel jolted her right out of her daydream. Spencer's howl was only just louder than Toffee's renewed barking. He didn't need to move from the sofa to be heard, either.

'Mum! Leo's teasing Toffee with my Dalek and he's been sick on the sofa!' he announced, sounding more annoyed at the mess than any distress caused to the dog.

'Spencer let Toffee pee on the sofa! Spencer didn't do his pee rota!'

'Leo is a little bastard!'

Zoe's mouth dropped open with outrage. She put her mug down and was in the sitting room in a flash.

'What did you just say?' she demanded, grabbing a puky-looking puppy off the cushions. 'And what have you been doing with Toffee? Who was supposed to be taking him out to the loo?'

She looked between her two sons, who immediately stared down at their shoes, mutinously. But Zoe wasn't going to be beaten on this one. When it came to Toffee's house training, she wasn't going to be a pushover – not just because of her rapidly deteriorating soft furnishings, but because of the little dog who was trying so hard to learn the rules.

Zoe pointed to the alarm clock set up on the mantelpiece, and the star chart next to it, another of Megan's suggestions to get the boys involved in Toffee's training. 'Spencer, look, it was your turn! You were supposed to take Toffee out to the loo at five.'

'I was watching something,' he shrugged, and Zoe felt more than annoyed.

'How would you like it if I locked the bathroom door when you needed a wee?' she demanded. 'Toffee's only a baby. He needs to go out every hour, on the hour. We talked about this, didn't we?'

Spencer shrugged again and Zoe grabbed the remote control.

'No more television until six,' she said, turning the set off.

Toffee squirmed in her hands, and she put him to her shoulder, so he could see over the top. His body was warm, and he was nearly too big now to be carried around easily.

The boys groaned but Zoe held her ground.

'I'm really disappointed in you,' she said firmly. 'I thought you were going to look after Toffee properly. Not treat him like a toy.'

''I'm going to my room,' said Spencer, defiantly.

'Good,' said Zoe. It took her a second to realise Spencer had out-foxed her again.

## 17

Compared with Rachel's first numb days at Four Oaks, when her aimless mood had made the clocks stop ticking in the spare room, the time started to fly past.

She didn't miss her old routine as much as she'd thought she would: the blur of frenetic daily meetings, followed by time-wasting evenings, treading water until the precious Thursday night with Oliver (his 'gym' night). The sneaking around had made her weeks oddly lopsided. Professionally, Rachel had a bursting contacts book, but her lonely evenings and weekends echoed with silence, so she'd stuffed them with shopping and yoga classes and anything else that made her feel busy.

Now, Rachel's day started at seven-thirty in the morning, when Megan left a cup of tea outside her room, and finished at eleven at night, when she turned in, exhausted by miles of dog walking and talking to unfamiliar people about the relative merits of Staffies versus collies. Rachel's sponge-like mind soon refilled itself with dog facts and training tips, where she used to store London restaurants and sample sales. Slowly but surely, the dogs began to inch their way into her 'non-dog-person' heart; when the fifth dog left the kennels in the arms of loving new owners – Flash, the shy and scruffy little Westie – she realised her eyes were streaming, along with the openly weeping Megan and Freda.

With Megan or Freda at her elbow all day, she had no time to think about Oliver, but Rachel allocated one hour in the early evening for wallowing in her private misery. Megan thought it was sweet the way she wanted to spend time walking Gem on his own, to bond better, but she couldn't hear Rachel as she circled the orchard and the huge fields around the house, railing at herself, at Oliver, at the unfairness of the human heart, but mainly at her own stupidity. The first week, it had taken an hour to get through her monologue of regret and recrimination. By the end of the month, she found herself using the last twenty minutes to wonder more about Dot and Felix or how she was supposed to pay the electricity bill.

One drawback of life in Longhampton, however, was that her mother now knew exactly where to find Rachel, and she could no longer pretend she was 'in a meeting' as she had in London, especially since Megan and Freda were more than happy to put Val through.

Rachel was sitting in the kitchen with Natalie, brainstorming fundraising ideas, when Val called for 'an update'.

'There's nothing to update you on, Mum,' said Rachel, rolling her eyes apologetically at Natalie. 'Unless I can interest you in a Schnauzer?'

Natalie grimaced back. She'd been there since just after feeding time, with Bertie in tow. Either she had a burning desire to help Rachel work out ways to fund the kennels, or else she had nothing better to do with her time.

'Of course I don't want a Schnauzer, Rachel. What did the estate agent say about the house?' Rachel could hear Hoovering in the background, and wondered if Val was multi-tasking or if her dad had now been dragooned into housework.

'He said it was a nice house, but it needed a lot of work doing to it. Something about structural underpinnings.' Rachel's brain had zoned out at that point, while she argued internally about whether she wanted the house to be worth a fortune, so she could maybe buy something somewhere else, or worth nothing so she wouldn't be liable for an enormous tax bill.

'And what does that mean?'

'I don't know. He's sent off the valuation to the solicitors' and I'll get the bill in the post. No, I don't know when,' she added before Val could ask. 'But Gerald Flint says you can have the Acker Bilk albums for Dad. Apparently they're not likely to affect the final valuation one way or another.'

'Rachel says you can have your Acker Bilk albums, Ken.' The vacuum cleaner was turned off. 'What? Your father says he'd like a word, Rachel. Here you are.' There was a muffled exchange, which included the words 'proper coffee', and then Rachel's dad came on the line.

'Hello, Dad,' said Rachel. She hoped he wasn't going to say anything about her resignation. Val hadn't taken the news well in their last call. She had sounded bewildered, as she had every right to be, given Rachel's apparent decision to give up the career 'she'd sacrificed her thirties for' to run a kennels.

'How are you, love? Coping OK?' Ken sounded concerned. Rachel hoped he wasn't going to give her his 'whatever you do, we'll be proud of you' speech; it always reduced her to tears.

'I'm fine, Dad. Are you OK?' Rachel mouthed 'thank you' at Natalie as she passed her a fresh cup of tea. 'It's just that I'm a bit busy . . .'

'I won't keep you,' said Ken. 'I was just . . .' his voice dropped, 'just wondering how you were getting on with Dot's things.'

'Um, fine.' What was that supposed to mean? 'There's a lot of stuff to go through, if that's what you're getting at.'

'I was really meaning her . . . personal effects.'

'Dad,' she said, heavily, 'if there's something in particular that Mum wants and is too polite to ask for, then either tell her she's welcome to come and have a root around, or tell me what it is I'm looking for and I'll—'

'No, no!' Ken sounded as if he was having his thumbnails pulled out. 'All I'm saying is ... you come across some peculiar things when you're going through houses. Personal things. Letters. You know.'

'Actually, I *don't* know.' Rachel racked her brains for whatever it was Ken was too embarrassed to say. Did he know something about Felix? Surely not; he barely liked to talk about his own marriage, let alone other people's relationships. She was struck by sudden inspiration. 'Is this something to do with the fall-out Mum and Dot had? Are you saying there's some kind of letter?'

Now that would make sense. A stinging letter from her mum, listing all Dot's selfish ways, something she'd always regretted sending – Val's conscience went back years.

'Not exactly.' Rachel could hear her mother's voice in the background. 'Anyway,' Ken went on, in a higher tone, 'forget I said anything. It's not important. I'm sure. Your mother wants another word. Bye, love!'

From the confused mutterings on the other end, Rachel got the impression her mother didn't want a word, because when she came on the line, she didn't put up any sort of conversational fight, and Rachel was able to hang up within minutes.

'Family problems?' asked Natalie.

'I don't know.' Rachel lifted her shoulders, baffled. 'Who can tell with parents? My mum and Dot had some minor spat going on, you know, typical sisters falling out. I wouldn't call it a feud. I think Dad thinks there's going to be some secret cache of family voodoo dolls or something.'

'Oooh,' said Natalie. 'Intriguing!'

'No. Not ooh. More like Dot stole Gran's secret lemon curd recipe in 1974, and Mum never forgave her. Or Dot's boyfriend wore stacked heels to my sister's christening and the vicar complained. Anyway, where were we?'

'Sponsorship!' said Natalie. 'We were talking about how you need to get business sponsorship to cover the rescue kennel costs.' She wrote *sponsorship* at the top of the page with a flourish. 'I had another look at your figures and I reckon this is what you need to run each kennel space, per year. It's not a lot, is it? I've made a list of all the businesses I think you could approach on the industrial estate, plus the high street solicitors and accountants and the *Longhampton Gazette*.' She drew a confident ring around Rachel's wonky sums. 'And normal people – you can put a collection box in the surgery, and get the primary school to get involved.'

'And in return?' Rachel tried to stoke her brain up to Natalie's speed, but it wasn't co-operating. Despite the blissful eight hours of silent countryside sleep she was enjoying each night, she still needed more than strong tea to get going this week. 'Um, sorry, my mind's gone blank.'

'Are you OK?' asked Natalie, peering more closely at her.

'Yeah, I'm fine.' She rubbed her eyes. Megan had a cold – it was probably that. 'You know what? I think my London germ immunity's finally wearing off. I thought the day would never come.'

'It's probably delayed stress,' said Natalie. 'Having to deal with the house, and your break-up and everything all at once. You've done an amazing job so far. '

'Oh, I don't know. But thanks.' Rachel wasn't sure she should really take the sympathy, but it felt nice, the sad way Natalie was smiling at her.

She wouldn't if she knew you were a husband-stealer, she reminded herself. Even a failed one.

'OK, um, sponsorship.' Rachel made her brain swerve away from that uncomfortable topic. 'What if we make updates from the dogs to the sponsors, to put on their office kitchen wall? Like I did with the posters?'

'Exactly! And you and Megan take the dogs to the school to do talks about keeping pets responsibly. Take the least licky dogs to the old folks' home for an afternoon's stroking. We can talk to Lauren at the surgery about therapy dogs – she's already got a poster up about dog walking for health.'

'You've really thought about this, haven't you?'

Natalie shrugged modestly. 'I don't have a lot else to think about right now. Turns out I'm not as good at relaxing at home as I thought I'd be. Have you decided what you're going to do about the boarding kennels, though? Because you might as well relaunch the whole lot at the same time. Presumably that was how Dot was funding the rescue operation? From the boarding fees?'

Rachel wasn't sure. From what she could make out from the accounts, the kennels had barely been turning a profit and for all she knew, Dot was paying for everything from her diamond necklace tree in the garden. But whether she decided to stay, or sell, it made sense to get things up and running.

'Yup, that's a good idea,' she said. 'Now we've got the internet coming to Four Oaks, a mere decade after everyone else.'

Natalie looked amazed. 'There was no internet before? No website?'

'No website. I've been on email detox since I arrived. But there will be from this weekend,' said Rachel. 'I'm calling in some favours. I reckon that should get some tragic mutts moving.'

'What you need is an Open Day to get everyone up here to see what you do.' Natalie drew a large cloud around the words Open Day and started jotting out spikes. 'When they see the dogs, they'll just melt like we did, and when they see how nice your kennels are, they'll all want to book their pets in this summer. Double effects! Now, what do you need to make people fall in love with Four Oaks Boarding Kennels? You're the PR expert,' she added, generously.

'Face-painting,' said Rachel, solemnly. 'And maybe a hog roast. That's what the website geeks used to like, anyway.'

Natalie's expression froze, until she realised Rachel was joking. 'Oh, very funny. I was thinking more of competitions everyone can win. Like, Scruffiest Ears, and Most Loving Pet. You have to have a Pet Most Like Owner competition, just so Bertie and Johnny can win it. I don't know who spends most time lurking round the fridge.' She pointed her pen at Rachel. 'I've got it. Super-tear-jerking – invite all the happily rehomed pets back for a reunion with their old friends!'

'You are a marketing genius, Natalie.' Rachel nodded approvingly. 'That will make the best local newspaper story *ever*.'

'So, when?'

'Ah.' Rachel pulled a face. 'That's a problem. Not until I've got probate – there's a huge bill to pay on account, then they give me the keys officially. But we can get it all planned and then launch it onto an unsuspecting public as soon as I get the go-ahead.' She pushed the plate of chocolate biscuits nearer Natalie. 'I don't want to take up all your time, though. I'm sure you've got much better things to be doing than helping me run dog shows.'

'You're welcome. Don't tell Johnny but I'm glad of a distraction,' sighed Natalie. Now Rachel looked closer, there were bags under her round green eyes and she seemed strained.

'Is it Bertie?'

'No! No, he's lovely.' Natalie hesitated, then rushed on. 'No, we're waiting for the results of some tests. You know, the bloods I had to go for the other day, when you minded Bertie for me? I probably said, we're trying for a baby and this is the next step.'

'Oh, right,' said Rachel. She never knew what to say when it came to trying for babies. She'd spent most of her life going to some lengths not to get pregnant; it seemed perverse how hard it seemed to be when you actually wanted one. 'Have you, er, been trying long?'

'Over a year. Feels like longer.' Natalie bit into a chocolate biscuit. 'Sorry, it's not really something to chat about but it sort of takes over your brain.' She smiled weakly. 'Sorry. Bit too much information.'

'You'll be fine. The tests'll be fine.' Rachel wanted to be encouraging. Natalie looked so crestfallen, compared to her sunny confidence when they'd been mapping out the Open Day.

Natalie sighed. 'I don't know, though. We've been so happy, me and Johnny. I don't know how he'll cope if I can't . . .'

Megan announced her presence with a huge sneeze. 'Rachel, sorry, it's—' She sneezed again, into a big white handkerchief. 'There's someone to see you – she came round to the kennels, but she said she wanted to talk to you.'

Natalie pressed her lips together and Rachel felt bad that the moment had gone. She turned round reluctantly. 'Did she say what about?'

'No, but she was looking at the dogs.' Megan smiled, wrinkled her nose to hold back the sneeze, then sneezed again. 'Seemed quite interested in Tinker, actually. She looks like a West Highland White sort of woman.'

'Which is what?' Natalie raised a curious eyebrow.

'Oh, you know.' Megan wiped her nose. 'Middle-aged. Nicely dressed, well-spoken. Gilet.'

'Sort of woman who likes a dog to be about the same size as her largest bag,' added Rachel. 'And with hair that won't clog her Dyson. Natalie, don't look at me like I'm a psychic, you get to read the types very quickly.'

'And me and Johnny – were we obviously Basset types?' asked Natalie.

'No,' said Megan. 'I thought you'd go for Treacle, the Lab. Johnny's more of a Labrador kind of guy and you're . . .'

'Go on,' said Natalie good-humouredly. 'I can take it.'

'All right, Megan, you stay here and dig yourself out of that.' Rachel got up from the table, and felt her head swim. She made a mental note to get some Berocca on the next grocery run, before Megan's cold took hold. 'Listen, Natalie, can you hang on for ten minutes? This won't take long.'

'No problem.' Natalie settled back and at once Bertie stirred from his slumber by the Aga and began to gaze hopefully at the biscuits. 'So, Megan. You were saying.'

When Rachel pushed the office door open, the woman visitor wasn't flicking through leaflets or peering around to see the dogs as most visitors did. She was simply waiting, arms folded across her sheepskin gilet.

'Rachel?' She stepped forward, looking her up and down.

'Yes, hello.' Rachel offered her hand to shake. 'Sorry, Megan didn't give me your name!'

Megan was right – this was a classic Westie owner. The lady was dressed in stylish jeans that were a fraction too high-waisted, with a camel polo neck the same colour as her highlighted mass of hair.

'Kath.' Her shiny pink lips curved into a smile of quiet amusement, as she took Rachel's hand and gave it a limp squeeze. 'Kath Wrigley. How funny. I thought you'd be younger.'

In all her walks with Gem, rehearsing the things she would say to Oliver's wife if they ever met, Rachel hadn't planned for this.

She'd planned for Kath raging out of control, Kath tragically telling her how she'd nearly wrecked her marriage, Kath smugly reminding her she'd pulled it back from the brink. Usually Rachel apologised beautifully but maintained a dignified defence that she had loved Oliver, no matter how wrong it had been.

She hadn't planned for Kath turning up and giving her a pitying but not aggressive once-over, as though she was a curiosity, not a threat.

'And I always imagined you'd be blonde,' Kath added, more to herself than to Rachel.

Rachel withdrew her hand, and tried to recall some of her better lines, but she couldn't. '*Always* imagined?' she blurted out. 'How long have you known about me?'

'Oh, years. Years! Don't take this the wrong way, Rachel,' said Kath, 'but it's rather naive to think a wife wouldn't notice her husband of twenty-two years is having an affair. I could tell from the difference in aftershave which days he was seeing you. Thursdays, wasn't it?'

The simple intimacy sliced through Rachel like a paper cut and the wounds she thought had begun to heal over stung again.

'I even know when your birthday is,' Kath went on. 'July the nineteenth. He wasn't as clever as he thought. I mean, come on! The mysterious long weekend with clients, when they're all on holiday? And then the shirts you preferred, the tiffs you had, the *moisturiser* you gave him that he pretended his PA got . . .'

Rachel couldn't bear any more. Kath was making it sound so trivial – her ten-year love affair with the man who'd been as much hers as Kath's. 'So if you knew, why didn't you say anything?'

Kath's eyebrows raised in mock surprise. 'Why didn't I say anything? Why would I want to?'

'You didn't mind someone else sleeping with your husband of twenty-two years? You minded enough to drag him back. Why wait so long?'

Rachel's heart was pounding despite her vow to keep cool. It was worse than when she'd actually broken it off with Oliver. Now she felt rejected *and* humiliated. She'd prepared herself to put on her sackcloth and ashes, but Kath was talking as if she didn't even want her apology. Didn't care one way or another *what* Rachel felt.

'I didn't *wait.*' Kath sighed. 'Oh, dear. I was wondering on my way here whether you'd be one of those cynical gold-diggers who was just in it for the minibreaks, or whether you'd be a silly romantic who thought he'd leave me for you.'

'You never thought I might actually be in *love* with him?' Rachel struggled to keep her voice under control. 'Or that he might have been in love with me?'

'No.' Kath looked at her with beady eyes and Rachel saw several years' worth of expensive Botox in her forehead. 'Especially not at *your* age. I thought you'd at least be smarter than that. I mean, come on, darling! You work in PR! Aren't you used to people spinning you a line? Oliver's lying was what paid for our houses.'

Rachel summoned up what little dignity she felt she had left, given that she was wearing a pair of mud-streaked jeans and not enough make-up for a face-off with her lover's wife. Ex-lover's wife.

'Fine. You've had your gloat,' she said, tightly. 'I'm sorry for what happened. It's over, as you now know. You've got Oliver back, I've left my job, so can you please leave?'

'Oh, but I haven't got the little shit *back*,' said Kath, surprised. 'What on earth made you think that?'

The Staffies had started to play fight with each other, but Rachel didn't hear. 'But he went back to you. That's why I sent you the flat keys.'

'Oh no. No, no. He's dumped us both, Rachel. Oliver and his midlife crisis has skipped off with Tara, his tennis coach.' Kath spoke slowly. 'It's all over our village, the stupid, thoughtless bastard. I'm going to have to divorce him now, and that means all hell breaking loose. Oh, it wasn't so bad with you,' she went on, as Rachel's jaw dropped. 'I didn't have to see you. You kept him out from under my feet, kept him amused. You were the reason I got my own holidays after fifteen years – I didn't mind *you*.'

She said it with such distaste that Rachel felt cheapness spread over her like a rash. She'd been an itch-scratcher, nothing more.

'But he never even mentioned a Tara,' she whispered. A sudden insanity to know what this Tara looked like gripped her, what Tara sounded like, whether she was better, thinner, funnier than her.

Kath saw Rachel's distress and patted her on the arm. 'You don't need to imagine very hard, sweetie. Just imagine what a midlife crisis looks like. She's blonde. About twenty-five. Flexible – in all sorts of ways, I should think.'

'Is he going to . . . marry her?' Rachel's voice was almost a croak.

'More like is she going to marry *him*. I doubt it. Especially once she realises how little he'll have left after everything's split fifty-fifty, less school fees. But it's his own fault. He could have stayed with you, seen his middle age out, retired in some comfort but now . . .' She shrugged. 'I came to give you these back.'

She dropped the flat keys into Rachel's hand. Rachel stared at them with dull eyes. Her own Tiffany keyring was still on there, the one Oliver had given her for a thirty-fifth birthday present. She saw it for the first time: a tiny silver house, so perfect and safe. A house probably very like the one he'd driven back to, after making love to her.

'Thanks for sending them. I just wish you'd seen his face when I worked out what was going on. He thought it was so neat and tidy – you'd finished with him, leaving him free to carry on with his bimbo, and me none the wiser about either of you. As it was, you tipped me off – so I thought the least I could do was to set you straight as well.' She leaned forward and Rachel got a noseful of Chanel No. 5. 'I don't know if Oliver ever told you, but that flat belongs to him, not the agency. And if I were you, I'd get back in there and claim squatter's rights or something. Because there won't be much left once my solicitor's had a good go.'

Rachel stumbled back into the house, trying desperately to stop the tears, but they flooded down her face and sent great choking waves up her throat. These would be proper hiccupping full body sobs in about a minute's time, and she knew there was no way of stopping them.

She knew now she'd been coasting through on shock alone. All her grief now wasn't for Oliver, it was for the mess she'd made of her own chances, and it made her want to curl up somewhere like a wounded animal, and die.

Oh God, she thought, Natalie was still in the kitchen. How could she get rid of her?

Too late. Natalie had heard her coming back into the house and was already approaching with last week's *Longhampton Gazette*.

'I've had a look through here and I reckon you could take out a whole page ad for virtually nothing,' she said, eyes shining with project-managing zeal. 'It would look . . . Rachel? Are you OK?'

'Just had some bad news,' gulped Rachel.

'Sit down.' Natalie shepherded her back into the kitchen and pushed her into a chair. 'Oh my God, you've gone white. Do you need tea? A whisky?'

Rachel laid her head down on her arms and let the pain in her heart spread to the rest of her body.

The irony of it made her sick. Oliver was going to be divorced. Free. As simple as that – and he was doing it to be with someone else. Someone he'd *just met*! All those years she'd never asked about marriage because she'd believed his sob story about hating to hurt his kids by leaving – gone, like the worthless stacks of old newspapers she'd chucked out from the utility room.

She'd never be thirty again, never have that time again – when her bare legs didn't need tights and she could drink all night – to find someone better. And this year she'd be forty.

'Is it about your ex?' asked Natalie, hovering anxiously. 'Megan said you'd had some horrible experience . . .'

For a moment, Rachel considered which bits of the truth she could shave off, and not lie outright, but then she realised that it was over. She didn't have to apologise to Kath, or feel bad, because Kath was pitying her. She was the only one who'd managed to come away with nothing.

What she had to risk now, though, was the warm new atmosphere there'd been round the table, when Natalie had started to confide in her. But what was the point? Friendships couldn't be based on secrets. She'd only be worrying *when* Natalie would find out.

Rachel lifted her head and summoned up what little self-respect she had left. 'That was my ex's wife. She came to tell me that he's left her *and* me for some blonde airhead.'

Natalie's green eyes clouded. 'What? Wife?'

'I know. I don't deserve any sympathy, but—' Rachel gulped again as a fresh realisation hit her. Maybe this Tara was pregnant.

In that moment, she realised just how hard she'd suppressed the idea of carrying Oliver's baby, as the bitterness sprang up like an oil strike. Oh no. That would be too cruel. Too unfair.

'Get it off your chest,' said Natalie. 'Come on.'

Rachel braced herself. 'I was with Oliver for ten years,' she said. 'On and off. We worked together, and it started off as an office romance, but it was more than that. I thought he loved me, but . . .' Rachel stopped. She could hear the lies she'd told herself blaring out of her own words, and couldn't bear to hear them any more. She didn't sound smart or independent, she sounded like a total fool. 'Anyway, I finished it, and now his wife's come to tell me she's divorcing him, because he's gone off with another woman. He's cheated us both. I've been . . .' she shuddered, 'so stupid.'

There. It was out. And Natalie just looked sorry, not disgusted. Her kind face scrunched up with sympathy.

'Oh, Rachel. I don't know what to say.' She reached out and stroked her hand. 'I'm so sorry.'

'You shouldn't feel sorry for me. I don't deserve it.'

'You do. Whatever the ins and outs were, you loved someone and they've let you down. I'm not a judgy person,' said Natalie. 'I know there's never a black or white answer to stuff like this. But you're a beautiful woman, with a great sense of humour and . . . and so much going for you. Was that really the best you could do? A man who let you dangle around for ten years while he had it both ways? I can't believe he was the only man you could have dated.'

Rachel shook her head, as big sobs gripped her ribcage. 'He was the one I loved. And don't tell me what a cliché that is, because I know.'

'But it's over now,' said Natalie. 'That's in the past. You're free to meet the right guy now, someone who *can* give you what you want.' She made it sound so matter-of-fact, another project that could be arranged and achieved. 'I know Longhampton's not exactly a hot spot for talent, but there are some nice guys here. Come out to the pub quiz, with me and Johnny. You know Bill already – Lulu's new dad – the doctor and my book group girls, if you don't mind getting competitive about 'Friends' trivia. Is that a smile, or what?'

Rachel had to acknowledge it was. Just a watery one.

Natalie smiled back and squeezed her hand. 'My mum always told me that you should look at your problems as if you were advising your best friend, and not be so hard on yourself.

Like, when I beat myself up for not getting pregnant yet, I say, no, if it was a mate I'd tell her to give it time. Not to take it as a personal failure, but just one of those things.'

She paused, her face soft with sympathy. 'And you should be the same. This, whoever he was, Mr Love Rat, wasn't the right man. It just took you a long time to work it out but now . . .' Natalie shook her hand. 'Now you're like the dogs in there. Waiting for the forever man to turn up and choose you.'

Rachel gurgled. 'Thanks!'

'Well, one of the nicer dogs. One that won't be here very long. In fact, from what Megan's let slip, there might even be a certain vet making house calls already, hey?'

Natalie looked up under Rachel's fringe to check her face, and the child-like gesture made Rachel feel wobbly with gratitude.

She understood now why the bedraggled strays wagged their tails so pathetically, the first night they were brought in and shown some affection. Rachel had an address book to rival the Yellow Pages, but she'd never been able to relax completely with any of her friends, for fear of letting something slip. Even her best friend didn't know the complete truth – but then Ali was married, and made it clear that she didn't want to know too much. For all their envy of her untethered life, she had the feeling they were just waiting for her to reap the whirlwind.

But Natalie, so secure with her lovely husband that she could feel sorry for the Other Woman, was telling her it didn't matter. That she could have a fresh start here. And even more touching, that she'd help her make it.

'Thank you,' said Rachel, and slid her hand over the table to hold Natalie's.

'My pleasure,' said Natalie.

# 18

It took a lot to get Johnny prised out of bed before nine on a Saturday morning, but Bertie's breathless arrival on their pillow at seven had done an excellent job of waking both him and Natalie up.

'How does he get up there, with such short legs?' Natalie wondered aloud, as Bertie delivered effusive morning licks.

'He's using that mini trampoline you got from QVC. Can't you train him to make a cup of tea?' Johnny complained, pretending to be cross from beneath three stones of Basset-y wrinkles. 'Instead of just drinking out of any mugs left lying around?'

'Give me a chance – I haven't managed to train you to pick the mugs up, have I?' said Natalie. She threw back the covers, cocooning Bertie with his master – a situation Bertie responded to by closing his eyes in delight and rolling onto his back. 'You've got five minutes and then we should get going – we need to drop him off at the kennels with Rachel before we go to the clinic.'

'The clinic?'

Natalie turned on the shower in their en suite. How could Johnny forget stuff like this? She tried to make her voice sound casual, and failed. 'We're getting the results. Of the tests.'

'Oh.' There was a snuffle from the duvet. 'Nat, let's not make this into a big deal . . .'

'I'm not! It was Dr Carthy who told us to come in as soon as we could. Together.' She pulled off her t-shirt and stepped into the shower, not wanting Johnny to see her anxious face. 'Five minutes, Johnny.'

There was another, lower *aroooo* from the bedroom.

'You're with Dr Carthy, in room six. I've squeezed you in,' said Lauren with a wink. 'Must be important news. D'you want to take a seat?'

Natalie made herself look round the crowded waiting room at the bright posters for ante-natal groups and Stop Smoking clinics, but her brain couldn't stop running through the reasons Dr Carthy wanted to see them so soon.

Maybe she was already pregnant. Maybe her bloods had shown it, against the odds. It happened like that in magazines. As soon as you signed up for fertility treatment, or bought a really expensive pair of jeans, you got up the duff.

She cast a sideways glance at Johnny, who was skipping through a year-old copy of *Top Gear* magazine, as if they were waiting for a bus, not waiting to hear the verdict on their future family plans.

She wondered if everyone else could tell what they were in for. Johnny and Natalie Hodge. Can't make a baby. Aren't having enough sex. Aren't having the *right* kind of sex. Aren't talking about what's going to happen if there's more of a problem than just getting the dates right.

Natalie stared at a poster for baby vaccinations and felt her stomach churn. Johnny was always going on about what a natural 'mum' she'd turned out to be for Bertie. But what if nurturing wasn't enough? What if she physically couldn't complete the happy family he had in his head? If gory childbirth put men off sex, what on earth was IVF going to do to his rose-tinted visions of Natalie Hodge, Supermother?

Their names appeared on the digital display: Johnny Hodge, Natalie Hodge, Room Six. And an arrow.

'Ah, that's us.' Johnny dropped the magazine back onto the table, oblivious to her tension. He even grinned at Lauren as they went through.

Dr Carthy was sitting at his desk when Johnny breezed in with a cheery hello, and he motioned to the pair of chairs next to him. Natalie took the one nearest, so Johnny would have room to cross his long legs.

'Hello, Natalie! Johnny!' the doctor said, shuffling through their files. Natalie had been seeing Dr Carthy since she was about twelve, which made this even more awkward. It was like discussing her periods with her dad.

'Now, I've asked you to come in because I've got the results of your tests,' he began.

'But I've only done one blood test,' Natalie pointed out. 'My day twenty-one test – I haven't done the day five one. Was it the internal scan? I thought I could feel something like fibroids maybe, on my uterus? I've been reading something on the internet about . . .'

She trailed off, seeing his lack of response. 'I know,' she apologised. 'The internet's a dangerous thing.'

Dr Carthy coughed. 'No, I'm glad you've been getting to grips with what's a very complex topic. You'd be amazed how little some people know about their own bodies. Actually, your ultrasound came back very healthy, Natalie – no polycystic ovaries, no endometriosis, nothing.' He went through his papers and took out a sheet. 'I'm afraid we're going to have to get another sample from Johnny, though.'

'Another sample? Why?' Natalie was confused. Next to her, she felt Johnny straighten in his chair.

'Well, the results have come back with rather a low count, which might just be a blip – one in ten tests does come back with abnormal levels and then turns out to be fine.'

'Abnormal?' said Johnny, his voice a strangled echo.

Dr Carthy looked up at the pair of them and Natalie was horrified to see that 'better deliver this news fast' look in his eyes. 'A standard sperm count is about twenty million per millilitre. Yours was quite a bit less than that. We need to do another test to be sure, but even if it is the case, there are various options we can consider.' He opened up a new screen on his computer. 'Better to get the ball rolling sooner rather than later.'

Natalie started to prepare herself for those complications, but Johnny was still reeling.

'That can't be right. I've never had a day's sickness in my life,' he protested. 'I don't smoke, or drink . . . much. And I do loads of exercise.' Again, his nervous laugh. 'I do rugby coaching! I mean, I cycle to work sometimes. Is that it? Because I can stop.'

Dr Carthy was properly sympathetic now. 'Low sperm count's not always caused by outside factors, though you can cut back on caffeine, wear looser underpants, see if that helps. Now.' He looked at his notes. 'There can also be genetic reasons – I'll take a blood sample, so we can rule out a few hormonal possibilities, and I can refer you to a urologist at the hospital for a karyotype profile. Let me book you in for a second test.'

As the keyboard clattered, Johnny turned to Natalie, bewildered by the turn of events, and she felt sorry for him. After the cervical smears and chlamydia tests she'd already had done, Natalie was used to this feeling of falling into the NHS system like a ball in the lottery machine, her reproductive system reduced to a series of symptoms. Johnny wasn't. He said nothing, but 'what's going on?' was written all over his face.

She wished she had something to tell him, something positive, but she'd only scanned the male infertility sites. She'd been so sure it was her, holding things up, that she hadn't really absorbed the details of male problems.

'Is this right?' he whispered, as if he trusted her expertise more than Dr Carthy's.

Johnny's boyish, scared expression was so heartbreaking that Natalie almost wished the scans had showed up fibroids or blocked tubes. She was geared up for things not working, whereas Johnny . . . it was so much harder for Johnny. His ego was crumbling in front of her.

'Might there still be ovulation issues?' she asked Dr Carthy. 'I mean, you haven't finished testing me.'

He glanced up. 'Well, it's unlikely. You did one of those over-the-counter egg reserves tests, didn't you? They're not perfect, but if that came back fine, as you said, then it's unlikely to have changed.'

Johnny's head swivelled. 'You did a home test?'

She nodded. 'A few months ago. I just wanted to know.'

'You didn't tell me.' He sounded hurt. Yesterday he'd have sounded tolerant, she thought. Yesterday he thought she was worrying too much, with her temperature charts and her green tea.

'There wasn't anything to tell. It was fine.' Natalie bit her lip. How could she explain the top-of-the-roller-coaster moment when she'd turned over the little stick, then the rush of relief when it told her that her eggs weren't the issue? Or the flutter of relief now that it still wasn't?

'You never said.'

'I didn't want you to think I was getting obsessive about it.'

Dr Carthy was an old-school doctor, not one of the newer GPs. She wasn't sure he offered relationship counselling along with prescriptions. Even now he was assembling a selection of leaflets from a file in his drawer.

'Things are moving on all the time,' he said briskly. 'And there's always ISCI, IVF, DI, if it comes to that and you decide to go down that route.'

Natalie froze. 'I don't think—'

'DI?' asked Johnny. 'I'm not as clued-up as my wife here.'

'Donor insemination. It's just the same as a woman using donor eggs, really. You use donor sperm instead.'

There was a painful pause.

'No, it isn't the same,' said Johnny. 'It's not the same thing at all.' He looked at Natalie and she recoiled from the naked humiliation in his face. 'You're not going to have some stranger's baby, Nat. I'm sorry. I can't.'

'Johnny, this is a long way in the future and it certainly isn't something you have to rush into,' said Dr Carthy, gently. 'Lots of couples have a tricky path to parenthood, but they get there, and you two are still very young, aren't you, really? You just have to relax and make sure you're getting all the help you need. Try booking a holiday – that's what my daughter did. She'd been trying for two years, more or less given up, and—'

'How the hell is a *holiday* going to help Johnny's sperm count?' demanded Natalie, unable to contain herself.

Dr Carthy had the grace to look embarrassed.

That was the trouble, thought Natalie. People who've never known real problems getting pregnant just love those fairy stories about relaxing and booking a holiday. Even bloody doctors.

She glanced over at Johnny, who was now staring out the window, shellshocked. He was only just starting to discover that.

Outside the sun was still shining, but Natalie felt a chill that went straight through her coat.

She unlocked the car, but Johnny shook his head.

'I don't want to go up there just yet,' he said. 'I need to ... I need to get my head around this.'

Natalie could understand that – Bill knew where they'd been, and could probably guess why. Not that he'd ask about the test results – male friendship rules forbade it – but Johnny's face would give it all away.

She followed him as he set off down the high street, past the charity shops and mobile phone stores, his long legs covering the ground quickly. Natalie walked fast but she couldn't keep up and eventually admitted to herself that the sight of Johnny's broad back in his cord jacket was more comforting than his furrowed forehead.

When they reached the park, Johnny walked past all the benches to the secluded bandstand, where they'd all got pissed on Martini pinched from Bill's mum's drinks cabinet as sixth-formers. He sank onto the side, and put his head in his hands. Thick locks of blonde hair stuck out between his fingers.

Natalie hesitated, then sat down next to him, leaning into him with her head against his shoulder.

Eventually, he spoke, and his voice broke with emotion. 'I'm so sorry.'

Natalie didn't know what to say so she said nothing and reached out to take his hand, but he pulled it away.

'No. It's my fault. I've ruined everything. I wanted us to have a family. One boy, one girl. Then a surprise. I wanted to see you with our baby in your arms at the hospital, and to drive you home, and to look after you both. And I can't do that. I can't give you that.'

'You *can*. Don't be silly.'

'Nat, this is the worst thing anyone has ever told me.' He raised his head and she could see his eyes were red. 'I never realised until now how much I wanted us to be a family. And now you might need some stranger to give us that. I just feel so . . . inadequate. I feel like someone's cut my balls off.' He gulped. 'I suppose they might as well, for all the fucking good they are.'

Hot tears burned Natalie's throat at the sight of the big strong man she loved, struggling with humiliation. 'Johnny, *you're* my family. You . . . and Bertie now!' She tried to smile, but she knew it was a TV sort of smile, too shiny and not convincing.

'I promised you I'd give you everything you wanted,' he said, his voice thick with pain. 'And I *can't*.'

'Come on. It's one test! And didn't Dr Carthy say there are all kinds of things they can do? As long as I've got you, that's all I need. All I want. If we can't have a baby, then . . .' She made herself say it because she couldn't bear to see Johnny so despairing. 'Then so what? We've got each other. That's more than most people have.'

Natalie knew he knew her heart wasn't in it, and she hated herself that she couldn't make it true. How could they both want something so much and pretend it didn't matter? There would always be an echo at the heart of their marriage, something they both wished was there.

But she didn't want a baby more than she wanted Johnny. Instead, she pulled his head onto her shoulder and let him cry, for only the second time in their whole marriage, and the first time sober at that.

Zoe took Spencer and Leo to Saturday football, and decided that today was definitely the day she was going to drop the small matter of her children into the conversation with Bill. Not because she necessarily thought it was the right time, but because if she didn't do it now, it would look even more dodgy than it already did. Plus, she couldn't stand the endless to-ing and fro-ing in her brain about when, if ever, there would *be* a right time.

Somewhere over the past week, she and Bill had crossed an invisible line between two strangers meeting for a chance coffee into two strangers actively seeking reasons to bump into each other. Every time Zoe's phone buzzed, she felt her own skin buzz too, and the prospect of 'something' was hanging in the air between them.

It had started, after that first lunchtime walk, with a text from Bill about some shoes he was looking at in town – he needed a woman's opinion, apparently, which made Zoe wonder why he didn't just ask Natalie, since they seemed to be such good friends. She'd replied, not expecting a further response, but those texts had spread out over the next day into enquiries about Toffee, which had turned into enquiries about Lulu, and a casual reference to seeing each other on Saturday, and then whether she'd be around for lunch on Tuesday.

She had been. They'd eaten baguettes while walking around the park with Lulu and this time Zoe had consciously kept the conversation on Bill so she wouldn't have to bite her tongue. The topic of families hadn't come up, so she hadn't mentioned it. But since he now knew her least favourite foods (blue cheese and carrots) and she knew he had a scar on his elbow from a moped accident on his gap year, it would look pretty bad if they got to discussing anything more trivial, and she hadn't mentioned the small matter of her previous marriage and two sons.

It was part of the positive action in her life, instead of reacting the whole time, she told herself, as she parked outside the kennels. Firm with Toffee, firm with the boys, firm with herself – which in this case meant facing up to stuff, like her failed marriage, and moving on.

Like her friend Callie at the salon said when she confided in her, if Bill was a decent man he'd understand, even if he hadn't been there. Plus, was Zoe planning on living alone until the boys were twenty? Thirty? And what sort of impression was she giving them – that Daddy was allowed to find a new friend, but Mummy wasn't? Callie had all the answers. But then she was onto her second husband already.

Rachel was serving up a round of bacon sandwiches when Zoe walked into the kitchen, with Toffee on his training lead.

'Ah! Just the woman!' she said. 'I've got an old friend who's been looking forward to seeing you.'

She pointed to where Bertie was doing his lugubrious best to beg Freda's sandwich out of her hands, and if Bill hadn't been sitting at the table looking pleased to see her, Zoe wasn't sure what her reaction would have been.

'Oh, great!' she said, eyeing him. 'I'm just about recovered from last time.'

'Bill's looking after him until Johnny and Natalie get back,' Rachel explained, handing her a roll. 'But he'd love to go out with Treacle, if you don't mind? You can leave Toffee here for us to have a fuss over.' She dropped down to stroke the puppy's soft head. 'It'll be your turn soon, sweetie. Just a few months more and you can go out with the big boys.'

'Shall we go?' Bill sprang to his feet, brandishing Lulu's lead. 'Unless you want a coffee first?'

'You've changed your tune, Dr Harper!' said Freda. 'Weren't you just saying you'd hang on until . . .'

He cast a shy look in Zoe's direction and she smiled back, feeling her stomach flutter. It was quite nerve-racking to see Bill again in the flesh, after their flirtatious texting. He'd had his dark curls cut and had a tousled weekend look in his off-duty big jumper and jeans that was different from his weekday doctor clothes.

'Well, no, might as well crack on – if Zoe's taking Treacle out, I should probably go with her, in case of any accidents.' He winked, and when Zoe glanced down, out of pleasant self-consciousness, she saw he was wearing the new shoes she'd advised him to get, and her stomach flutter turned into a warm glow.

Once out of the kennel yard, they took the lane out of the orchard, down towards the park, Zoe steering Bertie and Treacle while Bill took Lulu with Tinker the Westie trotting by her side.

'Nice shoes,' observed Zoe.

'Why, thanks. I had expert advice,' said Bill. 'Good week?'

'Not too bad.' She steered Bertie away from a stray crisp bag. 'Toffee's had a bit of a breakthrough with the house training. Three clean nights in a row! And I didn't have to get up at all last night.'

He beamed at her with new dog owner delight. 'Congratulations! That's a real step forward.'

'I'm glad you think so – everyone at work thinks I've gone mad, getting excited because my puppy no longer covers me in wee. How's Lulu?'

'Oh, fine, thanks. Lulu!' He clicked his fingers to get her attention. 'Lulu, show Zoe your new trick. Watch this.'

They stopped, and Bill fished around in his pocket for a small treat, which he balanced on the poodle's elegant nose. 'Wait,' he said, in a warning tone, and raised his hand. Lulu's eyes followed him until he said, 'OK!' and she flicked it into the air and then ate it off the ground.

'Good girl!' Bill looked slightly disappointed, and whispered towards Zoe's ear, 'Normally she catches it in one go. But I don't want to discourage her.'

'It's very good anyway,' said Zoe, enjoying the sensation of Bill's breath on her neck. 'Did it take you long to teach her?'

'Not long. I think she knew some tricks before, because it only took an hour or so to get her to sit and stay, and all the usual stuff. We're onto advanced tricks now, aren't we, Lulu?'

'Or else you're a very good teacher?' suggested Zoe. For some praise and a pat from Bill, she thought she'd consider balancing biscuits on her nose. Just for starters.

'Ah, you're too kind.' He shrugged and set off walking again. 'To be honest, my social life tends to revolve around her now. You know what it's like,' he added, with a sideways glance. 'What is it everyone says? Dogs, they're such a tie!'

He said it in a way that made it pretty clear that it was a tie he didn't mind, and Zoe knew what he meant. She'd heard the same 'they're a tie!' line at work, from the other walkers, from everyone, including the mums who shared the school run with her.

'Yeah, as if kids aren't!' she said without thinking. 'I can't say my social life was exactly rip-roaring before. I've met more people since I've had Toffee than I have in the last three years.'

Bill laughed, and she realised that he thought she was speaking figuratively.

'Yeah, I guess it is a way of breaking yourself in for parenthood. The training, the timetable – I suppose that's what Nat and Johnny were thinking.'

This is it, she told herself. This is the moment to say, I have no social life because I have two children. She took a deep breath.

'Don't get me wrong,' he said, before she could start, 'I've never been into going out much – Johnny and Nat are always trying to drag me out, but to be honest, I'd rather be at home, teaching Lulu how to balance stuff on her nose. She loves it. I do too.'

'Really?' Zoe couldn't help it. There was something so charming about the way his face lit up when he smiled at Lulu – a man that cute should be busy fighting off women with a stick, not getting his companionship from a poodle.

'Yeah, really.' He sighed. 'You must get this a lot too – I appreciate their concern, but don't you get sick of being match-made by married couples? I mean, I'm not saying I don't want to meet someone,' he went on, hurriedly, 'you know, settle down at some point, but they're always on at me to meet this girl or that girl who's exactly my type, but how do they know what my type *is*?'

Bill suddenly seemed to realise he'd said too much, and coughed.

'Anyway, speaking of going out, I know you said it's hard to get away during the week, and I know what you mean, because obviously I've got the same problem with Madam here, but I was talking to Rachel . . .' He slowed his pace until they were more or less at a halt. 'She said she'd be happy to do some babysitting one evening this week, if you'd like to come out with me and try that new Indian place, near the shopping centre?'

Zoe's pulse quickened. He was asking her out for dinner. On a date! A proper date! But as soon as that registered, she felt the weight of responsibility on her again. She had to tell him now.

'I'd need to arrange babysitting too,' she said.

Bill nodded. 'I asked her about Lulu, but I'm sure she'd be happy to look after Toffee too.' His smile faltered. 'Sorry, have I . . .?'

'Aroooo!' Bertie let out a blood-curdling howl, and then yanked so hard on the lead that Zoe stumbled forward. As she did, she saw that the reason for his excitement was the two figures coming towards them up the hill: Johnny and Natalie.

'Just let go!' Bill laughed, as she staggered to keep her balance, and managed to unclip the lead so the Basset charged adoringly to his owners, ears flapping with the effort of running.

'That's love, right?' gasped Zoe, watching the joyful leaping that nearly knocked Natalie over.

'Reckon so,' said Bill, and gave her a look that she wished she could freeze and look at later.

As the Hodges came nearer, Zoe could see Natalie was putting a brave face on something: though she was smiling, her eyes kept darting towards Johnny, who seemed to be sleep-walking. His face was blank and he barely managed to acknowledge them.

'Hi, Bill! Zoe!' said Natalie, with strained cheerness. 'I hope Bertie's not been any bother?'

'No, he's been fine. Till now anyway. I think he just likes pulling me over. Have you thought about getting him a sled?' Zoe handed her the lead. 'Do you want to carry on walking, or are you heading up for breakfast? We were on our way back.'

Natalie glanced at her husband. 'Um. Why don't we head back? I think Johnny could do with a cup of tea. Couldn't you?'

Johnny didn't respond.

'Mate, are you OK?' asked Bill.

'Fine.' It was more of a grunt.

Natalie turned her attention to Zoe and started steering her back towards the path. 'So, Zoe, did Rachel tell you about the Open Day she's planning to relaunch the kennels? She's looking for some volunteers – could you do some face-painting or something? Or those hair braids?'

Zoe could tell when a subject was being changed, and she was happy to make small talk with Natalie, while Bill and Johnny fell behind. Natalie kept glancing backwards, and Zoe strained her ears, trying to work out what the men were discussing – well, what Bill was discussing. Johnny wasn't saying much, but she heard the word 'test' once or twice.

Driving test? Or, wasn't Johnny a teacher? Maybe it was a school thing.

At the top of the hill, she and Natalie paused to let the others catch up. Zoe was promising to run a stall of some kind when Bill touched her arm to get her attention.

'Weren't we just saying, Zoe? Plenty of time to settle down yet.'

'What? Sorry?' Her arm tingled under her coat where he touched her.

'We're all too young to be getting tied up with babies and stinky nappies and all that. Dogs are enough of a tie for the

moment, aren't they?' He smiled at her, with an added 'help!'
in his eyes, but though she instinctively wanted to help him
out, Zoe felt her heart sink instead.

Great. Not only did he not know she had kids, but he didn't
want them yet himself. How to sink a promising relationship
in three seconds.

It's not about *you*, she told herself guiltily. You shouldn't
even be thinking that, not when Spencer and Leo are still
missing their dad. What kind of mother *are* you?

'Bill, there's no need to . . .' Natalie began, but Bill was
obviously on a roll.

'People get too hung up on starting a family, just because
everyone else is. Bertie's more than enough, isn't he? You can
practise the sleepless nights, and cleaning up after him . . . It's
pretty much the same thing.' He looked between Johnny and
Zoe. 'Right?'

'No, it's not!' Natalie burst out, and Zoe saw pain flash
across her face. 'It's *not* the same thing. God, Bill, for a doctor
you can be incredibly insensitive.'

There was clearly something more going on here, but if
Zoe hadn't been feeling so disappointed, she might have been
more embarrassed at the private drama she'd stumbled into.
But just then, her maternal instinct was over-riding everything.

'She's right – kids *aren't* the same as dogs!' Zoe heard
herself say. 'They're far more than that! I mean, they're hard
work, yes, and they can drive you mad, but they're the best
thing that ever happened to me, and I wouldn't swap them for
the world.'

Bill's brown eyes clouded over with mortification. 'I didn't
realise you . . . Oh, God, I'm so sorry.'

'Don't be sorry. I've got two, actually,' said Zoe. It tumbled
out of her once she started, as if she couldn't say enough to
make up for her silence. 'Two boys – Spencer, he's seven, and
Leo, who's just turned six. I'm not saying it's easy, because it

isn't, not when I'm bringing them up on my own. But they're amazing and I love every moment I have with them, even when they are driving me berserk. They're the best gift in the whole world, children.'

Her mouth was dry and her tongue seemed to be sticking to the roof of her mouth. As she spoke, Zoe saw Natalie stifle a sob. Johnny had – oh *no!* – tears in his eyes, which he was trying to blink away. It suddenly occurred to her that the tests hadn't been school-related at all – and if Bill had been trying to cheer Johnny up, maybe her little outburst had only made things worse.

Zoe wished the ground would open and swallow her up.

She touched Natalie's shoulder awkwardly. 'I'm really sorry, Natalie. I hope I haven't said anything to upset you. I think I should, um, just go. You've got things to talk about, and, um . . . Sorry.'

'Zoe, listen,' Bill started, but she just gave him a quick, tight smile.

She might have made a fool of herself, but she had to admit it: if he'd been right for her then he'd never have said something like that. Better now than after the romantic Indian meal, when her hopes had been properly raised.

Zoe grabbed hold of Treacle's lead, then turned and marched up the hill, to collect her puppy first, and then her sons. And if they wanted to go to McDonald's, for once she wasn't going to beat herself up about not being able to say no.

# 19

Johnny didn't talk to Bertie in the car as he usually did on the way home. He didn't talk to Natalie much either, except in direct response to questions, and when they got home, he took himself off for 'a walk'. She and Bertie weren't invited.

Natalie waited until he was out of sight, and then got on the internet, methodically winkling out all the information she could find, all the message boards, all the helplines. Bertie lay at her feet, his nose pointing towards the door. Neither of them moved for a couple of hours, and when they both heard the scrape of Johnny's key in the lock, Natalie slammed her laptop shut, and Bertie sprang to his sturdy feet.

Natalie prepared her face to look calm and sympathetic, but Johnny went straight upstairs and they heard the bath running.

Bertie gave Natalie a sideways look, and slunk out of the room, to follow Johnny up the stairs, if not into the actual bath.

'No, Bertie,' said Natalie, getting up to grab his collar. 'Daddy doesn't want to be disturbed now. He's sad.'

As soon as the words were out of her mouth, she bit her lip. They'd started calling each other Mummy and Daddy in front of Bertie as a joke – they weren't *really* the sort of people who'd use a homeless dog as a baby substitute.

Except they were. That had to stop.

'Let's get some supper!' she said, and at the sound of the words, the apparently untrainable Basset hound dropped into a sit that would have amazed Cesar Milan, and Natalie's heart pinched with love for him.

Johnny's brooding silence lasted all evening, but by Monday morning, he was at least talking again. Just not about the tests.

'Look, I'll go and do another one,' he said, raising his hand to ward off her tentative questions at breakfast. 'Don't go on at me, Nat. I'm still getting my head around it all.'

Natalie noticed that he didn't look her in the eye as he left, and though he muttered the usual 'I love you' as he went, she could feel something different between them, and it made her cold inside.

'Right, Bertie,' she said, when Johnny had left the house and the day stretched endlessly ahead of her. 'Let's get you walked.'

They took their usual route along the canal, past the ducks and swans that Bertie arooed at, and into the park, but once there, Natalie's legs still twitched to walk further. She wanted to walk off some of the tension that Johnny's unusual mood had coiled into her.

'How about a visit to the kennels?' she asked, eyeing the route up to the hill. It would double their normal outing, but what did she have to get home for? As if someone was reading her thoughts, she saw Megan heading down into the park with an assortment of terriers, trotting perfectly on their leads.

Natalie waved as if she'd just arrived herself, and was strangely consoled when Megan cheerily called her and Bertie over.

An hour and a longer walk later, Natalie was back in the warm kitchen up at Four Oaks, Bertie was in a basket by the Aga with Gem, and she was helping Rachel insert copy into the new Second Chance Dogs website.

It was like being in an office and being at home at the same time – a pretty good combination, Natalie thought, helping herself to another biscuit.

They'd made heartwarming profiles for Treacle the Lab and Lucy the Staffie – making each other well up with tears at the messages they were posting on behalf of the dogs – when Rachel took a break to make them some elevenses.

Natalie had only taken a sip of her coffee when Rachel pulled a face and stopped her. 'Sorry, don't drink it! The milk's off.'

Natalie smelled her mug. 'Is it? Tastes perfectly fine to me.'

'No, it's foul. I thought there was something wrong with it on my Weetabix this morning, so I opened a fresh pint but this is the same. It tastes really nasty. Eurgh.' She shuddered dramatically. 'It actually turned my stomach. I thought it was that bug of Megan's making me feel puky, but it's the milk.'

Natalie scrutinised her. Rachel seemed even paler than usual, and drawn, as if she hadn't slept. Cogs began to turn in her mind, little boxes that she'd tried really hard to check herself each month, starting with that elusive metallic taste, ironically brought on by folic acid tablets.

*It wouldn't be fair. It would be so unfair.*

'It tasted sort of metallic?' she asked, unable to resist.

'Yes!' Rachel pointed with her pen. 'Like someone had left ten-pence pieces in it. Can you taste it? Is it just local milk or something?'

*Was she being obsessive? Should she say something?*

'What?' Rachel demanded. 'Why are you looking at me like that? You think I'm going mad, don't you?'

Natalie shook her head. 'Don't take this the wrong way, but do you think you might be pregnant?'

Rachel laughed. 'No! I don't. Why? Is it a sign? Milk tasting like spare change?'

'Yes,' said Natalie and watched as Rachel's face fell. 'Is your period late? Do your breasts feel too big for your bra? Are you spotty?'

Rachel's hand went automatically to her chin, which was, Natalie noticed with a sinking heart, caked in the palest concealer she'd ever seen.

The number of spots she'd almost celebrated, wanting to believe they were a hormonal shift inside.

'No,' said Rachel, almost to herself. 'Oh . . . no.'

Silently, Natalie reached into her handbag and pulled out her emergency test, the one she hid in the zip pocket for moments of total weakness. 'Easy way to find out.'

Rachel was shaken out of her bewilderment by the foil-wrapped sachet. 'You carry pregnancy tests around with you?'

'When you've been trying as long as we have, you have to hide them well away from the loo,' said Natalie. 'How late is your period?'

Rachel gazed at her with big, scared eyes. Natalie thought she'd never seen such long lashes – round and dark, real sixties go-go girl eyes.

After a moment's pause, she laughed lightly and said, 'I don't know. Isn't that awful? I don't really notice. But, Nat, it's not going to be that. I'm nearly forty – I thought it was pretty much impossible to get pregnant at my age, unless you were on IVF and shipping in eggs from students.'

'Apparently not.' Natalie chewed her lip in an effort to stop it wobbling. 'Cherie Blair, Mariella Frostrup, Jerry Hall. All older mothers.'

'Have you been researching into . . .' Rachel stopped. 'Oh, Nat, you're only thirty! You and Johnny are going to have kids any minute now!'

'No, we're not!' Natalie tried, but she couldn't stop it bursting out of her. She had no one else to tell, who wouldn't give her a hard time. 'We got the results at the weekend. Johnny's not . . .'

She couldn't. That was too private. And saying it out loud made it more real. They were going to need help to conceive.

Natalie looked down at the First Response pregnancy test in her hands and felt something stab through her heart as she remembered the times she'd held her breath, waiting for the magic line to appear. All those months! All those tests and charts and nerves, when every single time there had been absolutely no chance of the lines turning blue, because there weren't even any sperm to try. The money she'd wasted on tests when there had never been a thing there to test.

'Here,' she said, pushing it towards Rachel. 'Have it. I don't need it any more.'

'Natalie.' Rachel stared at her, lost for words.

'Please.' Natalie tried to smile. 'You'll know one way or another. And honestly, I won't go mental if you are. I haven't reached that stage yet. I can still be happy for other people.'

Rachel opened her mouth, as if she was about to say something, then thought better of it, and slipped out of the room.

Natalie made herself focus on small details to block out the darkness creeping up in her chest. The radio was playing 'Clocks' by Coldplay, and there was a bright jug of lemony daffodils on the windowsill, catching every ray of morning sun. Bertie was gazing at her, with two dark rings around his eyes like liner, and two bright orange eyebrows above his mournful eyes.

She stretched out her fingers to him, wanting to feel his soft head.

Bertie ambled over, thinking she was about to offer him something to eat from the table. Instead, Natalie held out a hand so he could shove his cold wet nose into her palm, and as he did, laying his trusting head against her knee, a fat tear dropped from her nose onto his.

'Oh, Bertie,' she whispered. 'You're going to have to be our baby now.' She stroked the warm velvet of his ears and loose dewlap and her head tightened against the sheer unfairness of life.

Bertie took the opportunity to spring up and put his massive white paws on Natalie's knee, and for once she didn't push him down, or tell him she was worried about his spine. Instead she hugged him exactly as she'd have hugged a toddler to her and squeezed her wet eyes against his ears.

It suddenly occurred to Natalie that Bertie would have to go on the website too, so a full-time family could find him. She'd have to write a really amazing page for him, so someone would take him home and love him just as much as she and Johnny did already. She wasn't prepared for the wrench in her chest at that, and had to hug Bertie even tighter.

Natalie clung motionless to her dog until the song had finished, then she put on a stern face and made him drop back down to the floor. 'Not good for your back, Bertram,' she said.

Somewhere deep in the house the ancient pipework announced the flushing of a loo, and after a moment, Rachel appeared in the door, looking sheepish.

'Didn't work!' she said, marching over to the side to put the kettle back on.

Natalie quickly wiped her eyes. 'What do you mean, it didn't work? It's really simple, you just have to . . .'

'I know, pee on the stick. I think I peed on the wrong bit.' Rachel waved her hands disparagingly. 'Sorry, Nat, I'm not used to controlled urination. But I'm sure there's nothing – I'm so old it's probably the menopause, not a baby. My periods have always been a bit irregular, and there's been all this stress.'

'Mm.' Natalie looked at her closely. There was something not quite right about Rachel's face but right now she didn't want to deal with it.

'You'll go to the doctor, though?' she said, because she had to say it.

'What? Yes, absolutely. Yes. Another cup of tea?'

'Um, I'm OK, thanks.' Natalie turned her attention back to the screen and the dogs who needed homes. She put Bertie to the bottom of the list. 'OK, who's next? Chester? Have you got some photos of Chester?'

When Natalie and Bertie had gone home, Rachel dragged on her trainers and set off across the fields.

She wasn't even sure if Gem was following her to begin with. She wasn't sure where she was going either, only that she needed to run and run and not think. The trouble was, she couldn't stop thinking. The same thought stuck in her brain, not getting any more real: she was pregnant.

She'd lied to Natalie. The test *had* worked; she hadn't even had to wait the three minutes for the blue cross to appear in the window. It had pinged up there at once, as if it couldn't underline enough how stupid she was not to know already.

Rachel had lied partly because she couldn't get her own head around this startling new fact, and partly because she hadn't wanted to put poor Natalie in the position of having to react one way or the other. It made Rachel feel even worse than she already did: Natalie wanted a baby so much and couldn't have one, while she, who'd never even allowed herself to imagine her own baby while her heart was tied to a man who made it very clear a secret second family wasn't on the agenda, had managed to do the statistically improbable and get pregnant without even trying.

It wasn't that she hadn't thought about children over the last ten years. She'd often wondered what it would feel like to say those words that seemed to reduce everyone else to tearful ecstasy: 'Darling, I'm having a baby.'

But Oliver, the lying bastard, had been clear that he had all the family he wanted already. 'I'm not some Tory politician who secretly likes the idea of fathering kids everywhere,' he'd said, the first time the conversation had drifted within discreet distance of the topic, 'so don't ever put us in a position where we might have to have a conversation neither of us will like.'

That had been the choice: their affair, or her having children. If she was honest, Rachel had never felt broody enough to sacrifice the easy life she had. Whether that was self-protection or not, she didn't know. She'd never allowed herself to go beyond imagining the mess and disruption, just in case it turned out to be dangerous.

Rachel ploughed on across the field, making her lungs burn with the effort of running on the uneven ground. It wasn't real. It couldn't be real.

If it was real, shouldn't she feel different somehow? She hadn't been fudging the truth when she'd told Natalie she wasn't sure how late her period was. She never bothered to keep track, since stress at work often threw her off, as did stress with Oliver. Recently, her whole body had gone haywire, but with the benefit of that little cross, she saw other signs: the itchy, sore breasts that she'd put down to – Rachel almost laughed at her own idiocy – cheap washing powder. And that sickly feeling in the morning she'd assumed was Megan's lurgy – apparently not.

She stumbled over a molehill and broke her stride, coming to a staggering halt. Gem suddenly shot forward from his discreet following position, and bounded ahead to check she was all right, anxiously circling her as she bent over to get her breath back. Her heart was pounding and she felt aware of every part of her body now, except her stomach, which felt no different at all.

You couldn't hide anything from your body. Even now, that solitary cell was dividing into heart, fingers, hair, making decisions, moving on while she stood there unable to take it in.

Running away, thought Rachel, wasn't going to change anything. This was one decision that she couldn't duck out of. One way or another, she would have to deal with it because it was actually happening inside her.

She straightened up and looked out over the fields to the thick pine forest behind Four Oaks' neat Mr Men house façade, and tried to make it feel more tangible. She dredged through her half-forgotten biology knowledge, ashamed at how little she actually knew. When? How?

Well, not how *exactly* . . .

A tiny fantasy crept into her head like ivy. What if it was Oliver's?

Their Last Time, though she hadn't known it then, had been the week before she'd found the Paris receipts. That made it . . . Rachel tried to work backwards. Time seemed to pass differently here. Six weeks ago? But Oliver had always been so careful. Despite his claims to the contrary, he really wasn't a spontaneous man. Even when they'd done it on his desk in the office, there were condoms suspiciously to hand.

But what if it was his? Did that trump Tara the tennis coach – or Kath, and his three existing kids? Rachel tried to play the scene in her head but it was too messy. She just couldn't imagine Oliver melting with delight; she'd tried for years to picture that, but he'd made it hurtfully clear he wouldn't. And what about Kath? She couldn't keep up that patronising 'you're so old!' routine if she was pregnant with Oliver's baby. She'd fight tooth and nail to stop Rachel getting any money.

Rachel's breath burned in her lungs and she sank down onto the grass. Gem lay down near her, waiting, and without thinking she reached out a hand and laid it on his neck. His coat was rough, not silky like some of the more pettable dogs, but it was warm. Gem had the tough coat for the country rain and muddy fields; he wasn't a sleek town creature, he was a survivor. He'd survived long enough for Dot to rescue him from his cardboard box.

The first tears welled at the corners of Rachel's eyes.

Inside, she knew it was George's baby, not Oliver's. Sod's Law alone would have made it him. The man she barely knew, on the one night she'd been too drunk to check he'd sorted out the condom properly – but then, as her mother had warned her at sixteen, two careless minutes was all it took.

She closed her eyes and felt sick, but with regret, not hormones. George was the first proper, promising relationship she'd had since she was twenty-one, with a man who, from what little she knew of him, seemed to be exactly what she needed: amusing, decent, as stubborn as she was. What was he going to say when she told him? Either he'd feel morally obliged to stand by her, or he'd react with Oliver-like horror and demand that she get rid of it. Which was worse?

The truth slowly sank into Rachel's bones, as the cold from the earth crept through the material of her trousers. She wasn't the person she'd been yesterday. But she didn't even know who that person was. She hadn't reacted in the way she'd have predicted: no shrieks of horror, no immediate phone call to the nearest discreet clinic. She wasn't weeping tears of broody joy, sure, but she wasn't running around desperately trying to get rid of the tiny parasite growing inside her. She felt suspended in mid-air, unable to decide what she felt.

What did she want? It was so long since she'd seriously asked herself that.

'Gem,' she said. 'What am I going to do?'

The dog leaped up, thinking she wanted him to do something, and then when he saw her despairing face, he dropped to his belly, to lie with his nose on his paws, waiting. Rachel patted the space next to her, and eagerly, Gem sidled over like a crab, to lean in against her side. Slowly, she lay back on the ground and looked up at the clouds drifting across the china-blue sky, feeling the hardness of the field beneath her and the heat of Gem's body comforting her.

Even in the wide open air Rachel couldn't ignore the sense of being trapped by something huge and invisible. The responsibility. The timetable. The emotional tie she'd never be able to sever with George and Longhampton and this spinsterish inheritance.

No one knows about this baby but me, she thought. No one knows. And it's not a baby yet. It's just a few cells. I could go back to London for two days, no one would bat an eyelid. I could put the world on pause, come back, and be exactly the same. She let the idea spin round in her head, as the puffy clouds drifted without urgency.

Gem might think I've abandoned him, she thought. I can't leave him. I can't take him with me. I can't go. That's it. I can't go.

*And it wouldn't be the same.*

An image drifted into her head from nowhere: of Dot carrying Gem and his brothers around in a sling for days while they were still too little to be left. That was a woman who'd replaced her chances of her own biological children with dogs, but had not been able to replace that need to love, and nurture.

Do I really have that, Rachel wondered. Maybe I am as selfish as everyone makes out. Shouldn't I know what I want? Didn't Mum say she cried with joy when she found out she was expecting me? And Amelia, announcing it at some poor upstaged cousin's wedding, because 'she couldn't keep her happiness in'?

'What kind of bloody awful mother am I going to be?' she said aloud, and stretched out an arm. Gem laid his head along it, waiting patiently.

*    *    *

Back in the house, Megan was making up some special scrambled eggs for a half-starved pregnant Doberman bitch as if nothing was any different.

'I saw you and Gem up in the orchard,' said Megan, when she let herself in. 'Are you going to start doing some agility with him?'

'Agility?' Rachel looked at the phone messages, her eye skimming for 'Oliver' as it habitually did. She blinked it away.

'Yeah. He'd be great. You could do some at this Open Day. There are posts and little jumps in the shed – you want me to get them out? It'd be good for the Staffies too, get some of their energy worked out and it'd make a good display for visitors. I had a look at Natalie's plans, hope you don't mind.'

Rachel could see the notes Natalie had left on the kitchen table. She had clear, precise handwriting, and had marked out boxes and flow lines. That seemed like a long time ago.

Natalie. Rachel felt a wrench inside, remembering the miserable expression on her face when she'd handed over the test. It's just one test, she told herself. It's really early days. It might be nothing. I might have got it wrong.

'Megan, are you registered at the surgery?' she asked. 'Who's your doctor?'

'Dr Carthy.' Megan didn't react to the sudden change of topic. 'I'm trying to get on with Dr Harper, obviously.'

'Is Dr Carthy . . . nice?'

Oh, shut up, Rachel, she thought crossly. Nice? Unlikely to shout at single women who manage to get pregnant on a one-night stand like a stupid teenager, do you mean?

'Er, yes? Quite old-fashioned, though. There are some female doctors there – Dr Powell is very friendly, Dot fitted her up with a sweet old Cavalier King Charles spaniel a few years ago.' She smiled hopefully, then her face clouded over. 'You're not ill, are you?'

'No, no. Just . . . just thought I should get registered.'

'Good,' said Megan. 'Cup of tea? I was about to put the kettle on. Freda's left all sorts of notes to work through – and lots of juicy gossip from the café. She thinks Ted might finally agree to retire this year! Can you believe it? She reckons she'll be able to prise his hands off the fryer now Dr Carthy's got him on statins. I reckon we should find her a dog.'

Rachel felt a sudden need to be on her own, in complete silence, where she wouldn't have to pretend everything was the same. There was too much going on in her head to fake an interest in Ted Shackley's cholesterol levels.

'Megan, listen, I hate to leave you with Freda's notes, but I really need to get cracking with the sorting out,' she said, with an apologetic shrug. 'Orders from my mum – an hour a day of junk-sifting, until it's done.'

'No problem,' said Megan. She carried on stirring the scrambled eggs. 'Give me a shout when you want a cup of tea.'

Rachel made her way upstairs, and stood for a moment on the landing, looking into the big mirror that hung over the stairs, wondering when Dot's face had changed from the one looking back at her to the white-haired dowager in the photographs.

She knew she should really tackle the spare rooms, all of which were full of heavy Victorian furniture from her grandparents' old house, according to Val – they'd need to go to the sale room, once she'd emptied them of whatever was inside. But instead she felt drawn to Dot's room, and that lovely wardrobe of clothes and secrets. She wanted to see the glorious evidence of her aunt's single life, before she let the routine of Four Oaks swallow her up.

There were two wardrobes in Dot's bedroom. The one nearest the bed was filled with simple tweedy skirts and the basic, hard-wearing clothes she'd worn to tramp the dog-walking loop each day. Rachel shifted the hangers back and forth, checking there were no mysterious boxes stashed at the back. Bar an unworn pair of Marks & Spencer Footglove gold sandals with the receipt still inside, it was exactly the collection of heathery separates a middle-aged dog-lover would own.

But the other wardrobe – that was a different life altogether. Rachel's skin tingled as she trailed her hands across the hangers, trying to feel the occasions and memories clinging to the clothes. Shimmering satin gleamed out from between fur-tipped wool coats, bright slashes of bold orange and burnished cerise that only a woman with dark eyes and a long, lean frame could carry off.

Rachel laid each hanger over the bedstead until the frame was thick with clothes, each one a night out, or an office party in. There were wool suits with A-line skirts and cropped jackets that made Rachel suspect that Dot's job in the City hadn't been as menial as Val seemed to think. She let her fingers creep into pockets and into bright crocodile-skin handbags, and pulled out fragments of Dot's swinging London world – bus tickets and taxi receipts into Soho, a dry-cleaning bill for three dinner jackets, a shopping list including champagne and eggs, headache tablets and dance cards, one from a New Year's Ball at the Dorchester in 1969.

Every dance was full, but 'Felix' featured in every other slot.

Were these the secrets Dot meant in her letter? she wondered. The secret, independent life that Val had never bothered to ask about? Had she, in fact, made some money of her own, and then retired to look after her dogs – maybe that was what had broken her and Felix up, her ambition?

Rachel could imagine Val turning her head away when Dot tried to tell her what she'd been up to, who she'd met. Her own sister Amelia did it to her. 'Oh, I couldn't keep up with that sort of life,' she'd sniffed at Christmas, when Rachel had started to tell them about the last big launch she'd organised, as if Rachel's manic success was something to be ashamed of. It had irritated and stung Rachel in equal parts, not that she'd given Amelia the satisfaction of seeing either.

Once the hangers were all removed, and the rail was left bare like a winter tree, Rachel could see a mountain of shoeboxes stacked behind, some with price labels still stuck on, in pounds, shillings and pence.

'You were a woman after my own heart, Dot,' she sighed, and began to lift them out. Dot had long, narrow feet, and though Rachel tried to squeeze her own toes inside a square-toed turquoise pump with a patent bubble on the toe, Dot was at least a size smaller. She sat back against the bed, disappointed. The clothes fitted – she was wearing a Courrèges bronze-and-cream blazer – but it was the shoes she'd have loved to have walked in.

They were all in such immaculate condition that Rachel didn't know whether to eBay them or offer them to a museum. Some had obviously never left their tissue wrappings. She put the turquoise pump back and began opening the other boxes, until the carpet was covered in heels, flats, pumps and boots. Several had the handwritten receipts inside, others had notes – one pair of beautiful oyster satin stilettos had a card in them. Rachel took it out and her heart skipped: it was Felix's business card, with his St James office numbers. She turned it over, and on the back was a note in fountain pen – *For Cinderella! X*

She sighed. The shoes were perfect, too perfect for the average man to pick. It was the sort of fabulous gift Oliver would have sent; he always knew exactly what she liked, how she looked best. But obviously Felix didn't care whether Dot towered over him or not.

Rachel reached the final box with a sense of sadness, but as she pulled it out, she realised it was much heavier than the others, and her curiosity prickled with excitement. She lifted the lid and saw that it was full of letters, and on the top was an old-fashioned manila envelope, with no address.

Love letters! How romantic, she thought. Email had ruined that. You couldn't sigh over an email, even if you printed it out. But what was in the bigger envelope? She unclipped the metal wings at the back and a jewellery box slipped out.

Cartier. Rachel swallowed, holding her breath as she prised it open, wondering what on earth Dot had done to have a stash of Crown Jewels amongst the dog biscuits.

But inside there was no necklace. There was an envelope, a folded piece of document paper, and a Cartier card, with 'for my wife' in the same flowing handwriting as on Felix's own business card.

Rachel's heart stopped. Dot had been his wife? She and Felix had been married?

She unfolded the document carefully, oblivious to the darkness falling in the room. It seemed to be a marriage licence of some sort, or at least the application form for an emergency register office ceremony between Felix Anthony Carlisle Henderson and Dorothy May Mossop. It was dated 3 September 1972.

It obviously hadn't taken place. There were no signatures anywhere. But the intention was quite clear: Felix had wanted to sweep Dot off her feet properly.

Rachel tried to place the date in her family photograph album. Amelia was born in February 1972 – this maybe wasn't too long after the family christening, with the big fall-out.

The last thing in the jewellery case was a letter, addressed to Dorothy on the front. Rachel fumbled over the thick writing paper, pale duck-egg blue and engraved with a London address. It read:

*Darling D, please know that I understand. It's a lot to ask, and I realise that your response is out of love for me, rather than yourself. As always.*

*But if you change your mind, there's still time. There will always be time, because I'll always be waiting, and hoping.*

*Will you keep the necklace? It's precious, but really nothing compared with what I've lost today.*
*All my love,*
*F.*

Rachel sat in the darkness and felt a tear drop onto her bare arm. She wasn't sure whether she was crying for Dot, or for herself.

# 20

Since Toffee had crashed into her life, Zoe had really started noticing the number of clients who brought their handbag dogs into the salon. One of them even bought the same expensive highlight shampoo for her Shih Tzu as she did for herself.

Zoe surreptitiously massaged her aching feet as one of the juniors ushered her last client, Mrs Naylor, out of the door with her Jack Russell tied to her shopping trolley. Marion, the owner, had reluctantly admitted that so long as the dogs were 'small enough, quiet enough and clean enough', she'd turn a blind eye.

Zoe thought about Toffee's slow obedience progress, and went back to the appointments book with a wry sigh. It'd be nice to bring Toffee to work, but it could be years before he could be trusted in a room with so many Velcro rollers.

'You got a walk-in while you were finishing Mrs Naylor,' said Hannah the receptionist. She was juggling two phones, while changing the CDs in the player, and still didn't look flustered. 'I've put them in the spare seat – looks like a quick one. Is that alright? Everyone else has gone off on their break, or they're sneaking off early.'

'That's fine.' Zoe swigged back the Red Bull she'd left behind the desk and headed back into the brightly lit 'consultation area' of the salon.

'So, what's it going to be today?' she said, checking in her bag for her comb. She could tell from the back of the head that it was a bloke – she liked blokes at lunchtimes, because they never over-ran or talked much, leaving her free to plan the evening meal and sort out chores.

'An apology?'

Zoe nearly jumped out of her seat when she checked in the mirror and saw the face looking back at her.

Bill didn't look quite as sexy as usual with a black nylon cape around his shoulders but it made his dark eyes stand out even more. They were very contrite. 'And then a quick lunch?'

Zoe fiddled with her scissors to disguise her nerves. 'I try to work through lunch. I've got clients until two.'

'Yes,' said Bill. 'Me. Twice. I booked in for something very complicated.' He tried a smile. 'It's going to take me about fifty-five minutes to explain, and you five minutes to cut my hair.' He ran a hand through the dark curls. 'Which is four minutes more than I normally spend on it.'

She tried not to meet his eyes in the mirror.

'Where's Lulu?' she asked instead. 'I hope you're not abandoning your dog responsibilities to get your hair cut.' She didn't add that he hardly needed a cut – last time she'd seen him, his hair had looked freshly done.

'No, no. Lauren's walking her. There's a queue to walk her most days.' Bill paused. 'It's just me that has a vested interest in going to the park. If I'd known you normally work through lunch then I wouldn't have been spending a whole hour circling the place. She's sick of it, to be honest. Prefers the shops.'

Zoe couldn't stop herself looking up, and as their eyes met, she felt a pang of regret mixed with longing. He was gorgeous, and obviously wanted to explain, but she couldn't just push away the things he'd said about kids – and the things she *hadn't* said about her own. It didn't do either of them any favours.

'So, just a trim?' she said, in a businesslike fashion. 'Or a restyle?'

Bill hesitated, hoping she was just joking around, then when he saw she wasn't, he said, 'I'm in your hands, Zoe.'

'Great,' she said, and her voice wobbled.

Manda the trainee appeared to do the backwash but Zoe waved her away. She wanted to do it herself – she rarely washed hair any more but when she did, Zoe used the shampoo time to let her brain work out the cut while her hands went through the familiar lather-rinse-repeat routine. Today, though, it was the chance to touch Bill in a way she probably wouldn't ever get to again.

She settled him in the chair, smiling to herself at his awkwardness at being settled between two old lady regulars who persisted on discussing their latest medical symptoms, then lathered up the shampoo, massaging the bubbles into his scalp with her fingertips. As she rinsed his hair clean with warm water, she admired his neat ears and the thickness of his dark hair, enjoying the private intimacy while the salon bustled around them.

She knew he was enjoying it too, from the way his tense shoulders relaxed and his head sank into the backrest. Zoe was the best in the salon when it came to the conditioning head massage and she spent even longer than normal raking and pressing his scalp, watching the tension melt from Bill's face.

It was such a *shame*, she thought. If only I'd said something. Or if only I'd said something better. Something more noble than 'I'm a mum with responsibilities.'

She dried off his hair and when his face emerged from the towel, surrounded by day-old-chick spikes, Bill's expression was earnest.

'I have to explain,' he said, 'and you're not going to stop me.'

Zoe said nothing but began combing.

'The thing is,' said Bill into the mirror, 'Nat and Johnny are trying to have a baby and they'd just had some bad news. Apparently it's going to be a bit harder than they thought.'

'You really don't have to tell me this,' Zoe interrupted, blushing. 'It's none of my business.'

'But you deserve an explanation. In fact, Nat *wanted* me to explain, since I put you in such an embarrassing situation. All of us, for that matter.' He pulled a scared face, and Zoe got a brief flash of exactly how much Natalie had told him to apologise. 'I really didn't handle it very well, and I'm sorry.'

Zoe started sectioning Bill's hair, weighing up the first cut. She didn't want to take any of it off, but she couldn't not cut it, now he'd made the appointment. 'It's fine. You're entitled to your opinions. Kids aren't for everyone.'

'Look, that came out all wrong too. I would *love* to have kids, one day. They're great. But in my stupid, tactless bloke way, I just wanted to say something to stop Johnny looking like someone had burned his house down.' He gazed at her, appealing for forgiveness. 'He didn't give me the full story until we got home. I mean, I'd never have said what I did if I'd known that . . . well, how hard it's going to be for them.' Bill paused. 'And obviously if I'd known about *your* children, then I wouldn't have said it either.'

It was Zoe's turn to look embarrassed. 'Well, that's my fault. I should have mentioned it right from the start.'

'Why didn't you?'

She made the first crisp slice across the edge of the curls, trying to put her incoherent thoughts into words. 'Because I didn't want to make a big deal of it. I'm not very experienced in single-mum dating etiquette.' Zoe caught herself. 'I mean, not dating, that's just it, I wasn't sure whether we were, you know . . .'

'Having a date?'

'Well, yes. I didn't want to make it into something if you were just walking your dog. With me.'

They looked at each other in the mirror, and Zoe's heart flipped over at the way Bill's eyes met hers, as if there was no one else in the salon.

'Well, for the record, I've never dated a single mum, either,' said Bill. 'But I didn't meet a single mum. I met *you*.'

Zoe didn't know what to say.

'Shall we agree that we were?' suggested Bill. 'Having a date, I mean?'

Zoe's hands wobbled, and she moved the scissors away from his hair, to be on the safe side.

'If it makes you feel any better,' Bill went on, 'men aren't exactly encouraged to discuss their family plans either. I assumed, because you were single, and you seemed happy with your puppy, that . . .' He trailed off, and Zoe realised he was as flustered as she was about what to say next.

She thought of Megan, telling her to take control of the situation with her attitude. Calm authority worked on both Toffee and her, when she found him covered in something he shouldn't be. Zoe took a deep breath. It was time to move on with her life. Time to move into the unknown.

'I've been divorced from Spencer and Leo's dad, David, for nearly a year now,' she said. 'He has them alternate weekends, and holidays. I love the boys to bits, wouldn't be without them, but sometimes it's nice to have an hour to myself.' She paused. 'I felt like I was just being me, when we first met. I wasn't sure who you thought I was.'

'Well, I'm Bill, I have no children, no significant exes and some people, by which I mean Natalie, feel that's even worse than being divorced at my age. Which is thirty-four. I also have a breadmaker, but I've only used it twice.'

'Good,' said Zoe. 'I have an ice-cream maker and a chocolate fountain.'

'Brilliant. So, now we've got that out of the way, can we talk about that Indian meal? I think Rachel's babysitting offer still stands. I mean, for Toffee.' He hesitated, as if reality was creeping in. 'I guess it's a bit more complicated, with the children. I don't want to, you know, make things difficult.'

Zoe tried not to look at Bill's face. Was he asking because he felt he had to now? Doubt crept around the edges of her buzzy mood, and she reminded herself he was right: her first responsibility was to look after her sons, not set up dates with sexy doctors.

'Maybe we should stick to dog walking,' she said, more breezily than she felt. 'It's not really fair on the boys. David drags his new woman into the picture constantly and I don't honestly think the boys are as happy with it as he thinks they are.' She sighed. 'Spencer's already pushing me harder and harder. He knows he can get away with murder because I feel so bad about what's going on.'

'I get it.' Bill seemed almost relieved, she thought, sadly. 'You know where I am every lunchtime. And every Saturday morning.'

'I'll look forward to that. And so will Toffee.'

They smiled crookedly at each other, and Zoe made herself carry on with the haircut, stretching out the sections between her fingers to check she'd got the lengths right.

'At least you're going to get a decent haircut,' she said, stroking his thick curls for a little longer than she strictly needed to. 'Where do you normally go? Your mum?'

He caught her eye again, and she knew he was enjoying the bittersweet sensation of her hands in his hair almost as much as she was.

You're doing the right thing, Zoe told herself. Boundaries. Rules. That's what you need. Things could build up from friendships, whereas a date – that could go badly wrong.

'Zoe?'

Hannah, the salon receptionist, was hovering behind her, with the portable phone pressed against her chest. She looked worried, not her usual competent self.

'Is there a problem?' asked Zoe.

'Um, there's a call for you, from the school? It's Spencer. He's . . .' Hannah glanced at Bill. 'Maybe we should go into the staff room.'

Zoe put down her scissors at once, patted Bill on the shoulder, and almost chased Hannah into the tiny room the stylists used for coffee breaks and emergency bitching sessions.

Hannah kept the phone clamped to her chest and widened her eyes. She was wearing a lot of blue kohl – as only a twenty-year-old could – and the effect was dramatic. 'You've got to go and pick Spencer up. There's been some kind of *incident*.'

'Oh, my God.' Zoe grabbed the phone off her, a thousand grisly possibilities flashing through her mind. 'Hello?'

'Is that Mrs Graham?'

'Yes.' Zoe recognised the voice: Mrs Barratt, Spencer's class teacher. The last time she'd seen her was six months ago when she'd been singing his praises at a parents' meeting. She'd sounded a lot happier then. 'Is there a problem? Has there been an accident?'

'Yes. I'm afraid there was some trouble at lunchtime, and Spencer's been rather upset. As well as very naughty.'

Zoe felt the blood drain from her face. 'What sort of trouble? Is he all right?'

There was a worrying pause. 'Spencer's all right now, yes,' said Mrs Barratt. 'But I'm afraid Callum Harris isn't quite so well. Would you mind coming in to get him? I think it's best if he goes home with his mum now.'

'Oh, God,' said Zoe. 'I'll be right there.'

Zoe barely remembered the drive up to the school, or the near-sprint towards the head's office, with the school secretary struggling to keep up with her. Her salon FitFlops seemed to clatter horribly down the corridors, and when she saw Mrs Barratt waiting outside the office, her heart sank.

Mrs Barratt had always reminded Zoe of a lovely story-book mum, right down to the handknitted cardigan and homely smile. To see the disappointment in her brown eyes now cut her to the bone. Zoe felt as if she was being summoned to the head's office, just as much as Spencer was, for failing as a mother.

'It's just so unlike him to be so *angry*,' Mrs Barratt whispered in disbelief as they went in.

As the door opened, Spencer spun round with relief plain on his tear-streaked face, and Zoe felt a tug of maternal protectiveness towards her little boy.

He'd obviously been crying his eyes out, but his lip was jutting as if he defied anyone to tell him so. Lunchtime with Mrs Kennedy had put a lid on whatever attitude had got him into trouble, and now he looked ready to throw himself into his mum's arms for a cuddle.

Zoe resisted the temptation, and instead arranged her face into a disappointed expression.

'Is Daddy here?' Spencer peered behind her, as if he expected David to be following.

'No, your daddy couldn't come,' said Mrs Kennedy. She was poised behind her desk while Mrs Barratt hovered anxiously somewhere between Spencer and the door. Like a stern owl and a mother hen, thought Zoe.

'We called him too – our new secretary wasn't sure from your file who was the custodial parent,' explained Mrs Barratt. 'I'm very sorry about that, I hope it hasn't caused any trouble.'

'No, no,' lied Zoe. She didn't want to think about what David would say. Another triumph in his 'better off with me' campaign. 'We share . . . all parenting matters.'

'Is Daddy going to come?' Spencer persisted, his face suddenly eager.

'I don't know,' said Zoe. 'Shh.'

'I'm very sorry to have to interrupt your working day, Mrs Graham,' said Mrs Kennedy. She gave Spencer a reproachful glance, and added, 'There will be people going without their haircuts because Mummy had to be here to collect you, Spencer.'

'I'll fit them in somewhere,' said Zoe hurriedly. 'What's been going on?'

Spencer immediately lost his eagerness and looked down at his shoes, which were, Zoe noticed, scuffed.

'Hit Callum,' he mumbled.

'We can't hear you,' said Mrs Kennedy calmly. 'Be a big boy and tell the truth.'

Spencer looked up at Zoe with a heartbreaking expression. It was like the one Toffee gave her, when she saw him wee in the kitchen – guilt and frustration that he couldn't help doing it. Zoe had to bite her lip not to reach out and hug him. 'I hit Callum.'

'Why, darling?'

He shook his head and stared at his shoes again.

'He won't say.' Mrs Barratt leaped in. 'I've asked them both, and Callum says he didn't say anything, but I rather think he did, because Spencer gave him a real thump. Nothing broken, but we can't have any hitting here. It's not very nice and Spencer's going to have to miss his playtime tomorrow.'

'Spencer! We never hit people!' Zoe was horrified. 'Never ever!'

'Spencer, would you like to go with Mrs Barratt to collect your coat?' suggested Mrs Kennedy. 'I'd like a word with your mum.'

Spencer slid off his chair without looking at Zoe, and took the hand Mrs Barratt offered him. When they reached the door, he turned around and looked Mrs Kennedy straight in the face. 'Sorry, Mrs Kennedy,' he said in a rush. 'Sorry, Mrs Barratt. I didn't mean to be naughty.'

Zoe felt her eyes water.

'I'm sorry too, Spencer,' said Mrs Kennedy. 'But we'll start with a clean slate tomorrow, won't we? Come in with a happy face. That's a good boy.'

Her expression turned more serious once he'd left the room.

'I wouldn't normally send a little one home, but Spencer had such a tantrum even Mrs Barratt couldn't calm him down. He was really inconsolable. He broke up the model he'd been making all this morning. I thought it was best if he went home and the two of you worked through it together.'

'Of course,' said Zoe, now mortified as well as distraught. 'I'm so sorry about the hitting – he's such a gentle soul.'

She stopped. Spencer had got more physical lately, smacking Leo in play, but never seriously. Never to hurt. Her eyes welled up again. Was it her fault? Was it something she wasn't doing? Wasn't it enough, without David's male influence to set him right?

Mrs Kennedy passed her a box of tissues. 'If you don't mind me saying, Mrs Graham, it's not unusual when parents separate for children to act up, for attention.'

'But he gets plenty of attention!' Zoe blew her nose. 'And it's not like it's news – his father moved out over a year ago now. We're really careful to be nice in front of him and Leo, to make it as easy as we can.'

'Are there . . . Again, I'm sorry if this seems a bit personal, but we do see a fair bit of this sort of behaviour.' Mrs Kennedy's voice was kind, but she chose her words carefully. 'Are there new partners on the scene? That can set a child back in coming to terms with a separation.'

Zoe looked up at her. 'Well, yes. He did go away with his dad and his new girlfriend the other weekend. But he seemed fine about that.'

'Well, not if he was secretly hoping the two of you might still get back together. It would be so much easier if we could just tune into little ones' heads like a radio, wouldn't it?' The head teacher lifted her eyebrows with a world-weary sympathy. 'I'm sure you can get to the bottom of what happened today. Let Spencer know we're not angry about it, but as we say, it's better to talk with your mouth, not your hands.'

'Of course.' Zoe stood up and her knees felt weak.

And that was the end of any daydreams she might have had about sexy doctors.

Spencer was worryingly silent until they were out of the school gates, and then, when Zoe turned up the hill, away from their usual route, he came to life again.

'Where are we going, Mummy?' he asked, while they waited at the traffic lights by the railway station.

'We're going to get Toffee from Rachel's.'

'Yay! Then can we take him to the park? And see the other dogs?'

Zoe swung round in the front seat. 'This isn't a treat, Spencer. Mrs Barratt thought you should go home because you needed to calm down. And I'm very upset about you hitting Callum. He's your friend!'

Spencer's lip quivered. 'He's not any more.'

'What did he say? You can tell me.'

The lips flattened into a defiant clam.

Zoe sat back as the traffic moved off, and let out a despairing breath. Spencer and Leo had been such easy, undemanding children up until now; she wasn't sure she had the parenting skills to deal with real naughtiness.

Spencer began kicking the back of her seat, but Zoe just turned up the radio so she couldn't hear it.

\*     \*     \*

Megan was in the kennels office with Toffee when they arrived, in the middle of one of the two-minute training lessons she said she gave him throughout the day.

Zoe was pleased to see Toffee's fat tail start wagging at the sight of her: it was the first uncomplicated reaction she'd had all day. Megan looked nearly as pleased to see them too. But Megan was, Zoe thought, about as close to a cheerful yellow Labrador as a human being could get.

'Hey, guys!' said Megan. 'You're just in time. Watch this! Toffee? Toffee! OK, put him down, Spencer, would you? Toffee, sit!'

She raised her hand, which might or might not have contained a biscuit, and Toffee's bottom hit the deck obediently.

'Good boy!' Megan made a huge fuss of him, and slipped him the treat.

Zoe wondered how long it had taken Bill to teach Lulu to balance the biscuit on her nose and if the same trick was within reach of a Labrador.

'Has he been OK?' she asked, watched carefully as Spencer tumbled around with Toffee in the corner of the office.

'He's been as good as gold, like he always is. Freda and I would pop him in our pockets right now, wouldn't we, Freda?'

'Mm.' Freda was behind the desk, writing out the telephone messages for Rachel, but her eyes were following Spencer around the room. Toffee was scampering under the leaflet dispenser, which Spencer was spinning with jerky swipes of his hand, so the photocopied sheets of dog-training tips were spilling out.

'Do you want to take Toffee to see the dogs?' suggested Zoe, anxious to distract him before the spinner got knocked over. 'Be nice and quiet, Spencer. And don't poke at them.'

Freda opened her mouth, possibly to raise an objection, but Spencer had already charged off towards the double fire doors. Zoe started after him, but Megan was there first.

'I'll go with him,' she said. 'You stay here and have a cup of coffee. You look like you've had a bad day. Come here, Spencer. Let's put Toffee's lead on, get him used to it. No, not too tight. Hold it like this . . .'

Zoe watched as Megan gave Spencer firm instructions, the same way she talked to Toffee, then led the boy and the dog out of the office.

Once the fire doors had shut behind them, a sudden quiet fell on the office and Zoe's shoulders slumped.

'You're very early,' said Freda. 'Is everything all right?'

Zoe bit her lip. 'Yes, fine.'

'You could do with the coffee, though?'

She nodded. In her bag, she could feel her phone ringing. David, probably.

Zoe hesitated, then she remembered it was David's stupid girlfriend and his stupid mobile-phone-and-puppy bribes that were stoking up the problem. She grabbed the phone from her bag and answered it while she was still cross.

'What the hell's going on, Zoe? I've just been told my son's been kicked out of school!' David wasn't bothering with pleasantries. 'What's happened? They wouldn't tell me any more.'

Zoe glanced at Freda, who tactfully backed into the kitchen with the used coffee mugs. 'Sorry!' she mouthed, then turned to face the window.

'Stop over-reacting, David. He hasn't been kicked out – I've just brought him home for the afternoon. He won't tell me what the fight was about – he's very moody at the moment. I don't want to make him feel worse.'

'For God's sake, Zoe, he's too young to be in fights! He's seven! What next? Bunking off school to nick stuff? You've got custody because *you* claimed *you* were the best one to deal with all this.'

She stared out of the window into the orchard where Rachel was throwing balls for a couple of terriers. It was so peaceful, with the forest in the background and the rows of apple trees. Rachel threw the ball in a long, elegant motion; the dogs bounded eagerly after it, and dropped it at her feet for her to throw again. Easy. Neat.

'I am dealing with it,' she said tightly. 'But I don't think it helps, introducing him and Leo to—' She made herself say it. '— to Jennifer so soon.'

David let out an exasperated sigh. 'So soon? Why? We've been together for . . .' Now he stopped short.

'Go on,' said Zoe, masochistically. 'It can't be longer than I've already guessed. You've got the divorce now – admitting the truth can't change anything.'

'It doesn't matter how long we were seeing each other,' he blustered, and even though Zoe didn't feel a thing for him any more, something inside her wizened up. What a pushover, she thought. Everyone just runs rings around me.

'He's got to know sooner or later that we have our own lives,' he insisted. 'They've got to accept we're not getting back together.'

'But in the meantime I've got to pick up the pieces?'

Rachel was throwing two balls at a time now, much to the terriers' delight. For a moment, Zoe wished she had Rachel Fielding's life: cosmopolitan, sexy in an unusual, media sort of way, great legs, no ties. No one ran rings round Rachel; she did exactly what she wanted, and got what she wanted.

As soon as she thought it, Zoe wanted to wipe her traitorous brain clean.

'And *I'm* not seeing anyone,' she added, just to twist the knife – in whom, she wasn't sure. '*I'm* trying to put the boys first.'

'If you want to live like a nun that's up to you,' said David. 'Not my problem. But Spencer is.'

He sounded so sanctimonious, like he wouldn't kick off if she sent him the invoices for the child therapist.

Zoe rubbed her eyes. Getting bitchy wouldn't help.

'I'll find out what's been going on, and let you know what you can do,' she said, in the calm voice Mrs Kennedy had used to such amazing effect on Spencer. 'And in the meantime, maybe you could get a book out of the library about helping your child cope with divorce? And one for your girlfriend. Though preferably not Snow White.'

'Very funny,' snarled David, and hung up.

Freda poked her head around the door. 'Are you done, pet?' She proffered a cup of coffee. 'Put two sugars in. Thought you needed it.'

'Thanks.' Zoe sank onto a chair, barely feeling the heat of the mug cupped in her hands. The dogs were barking up a storm in the kennels, and she hoped Spencer wasn't playing up too. That was the last thing she needed: Megan deciding that Toffee and the Grahams were too much to handle.

'Does it get easier, Freda?' she asked. 'Parenting?'

'No,' said Freda. 'Our Lynne, bless her, was a terror. Motorcycles, boyfriends with tattoos, the lot. Then she moved to New Zealand, got married and we don't know the half of what she and her family are up to.' She smiled, wistfully. 'But you get into the habit of worrying. That's why Ted and I fostered dogs for Dorothy – gave us something else to worry about.'

'But small enough to put on your knee.'

'Yes! And unconditional with their love, too.'

Zoe sipped her coffee. Between her madhouse at home and the madhouse at work, the kennels were turning into the only place she felt relaxed – and that was with all the homeless dogs yapping away on the other side of the doors.

'But enjoy it while you can,' Freda added, unexpectedly.

'Because before you know it, they're off, and you're telling a Yorkshire terrier that her mummy loves her.'

Zoe looked at the old lady, and suddenly saw a melancholy in Freda she hadn't noticed before beneath the busy façade. She was about to ask more, when the doors burst open and Megan came in, with Toffee on the lead and Spencer trailing behind her, sulking and looking a lot like David when his team lost a home game.

'Spencer,' she began, with a warning tone, but Megan held up her hand. She didn't look as cheerful as normal, but there was a set to her jaw that suggested she was determined not to lose her temper either.

'Training!' she said brightly. 'That's what Spencer needs. He's going to teach Toffee a new trick, and Toffee's going to teach Spencer some patience.'

Neither Toffee nor Spencer looked particularly convinced, but Megan got out her training treats and caught Zoe's eye. 'You want to join in, Zoe? We're going to learn "Stay". And this might take some practice.'

If Spencer had decided to play up for attention, Leo had gone completely the other way, and was happy to be put to bed as soon as he'd had his bath.

'Am I a good boy?' he murmured as Zoe tucked him into his duvet, his eyes closing in the baby-powdery darkness.

'Yes, you're my good boy,' she replied, her heart aching. He was asleep by the time she pressed a quiet kiss on his forehead – or else he was pretending really well.

Zoe let Spencer stay up an extra ten minutes, 'because he was a big boy', but really so she could have a quiet moment to herself with him.

They sat cuddled up together on the sofa, listening to one of his story tapes while Toffee slept between them, curled on Zoe's lap, but with his paws on Leo's leg. Their breathing seemed to mingle in a soft puppy/child smell that Zoe loved. She tried to imprint Spencer's sleepy face on her mind, the way his still baby-soft hair curled around his ear, the nectarine sheen of his perfect skin. He wouldn't be curling up on her knee for much longer, but for now he was still her baby. It was impossible to imagine him lashing out in frustration, this docile angel in her arms.

She stroked his head, still warm from the bath. 'Spence, you'd tell me if you were unhappy, wouldn't you?'

He said nothing, and she wondered if he was asleep.

'You can tell me everything, because I love you,' she went on. 'I'll always love you. So will Daddy. It doesn't matter what happens, because you'll always be our most precious thing in the whole world.'

He didn't reply and she felt relieved she'd been let off explaining something she didn't totally understand herself, how she and David had loved each other so passionately once, and then almost immediately the babies had come along like a sign that it was perfect and meant to be. And then they'd found more and more to dislike about each other until he'd preferred to be at work – with Jennifer. She didn't understand, and she was the grown-up.

Her gaze fell on the photograph of her and David, and Spencer and Leo, on a model railway, up in the Lakes. The last family holiday they'd had. It seemed like it had happened to someone else now. A different life. Or rather, she had the same life, what was left of it – it was David who'd struck out and started again. It had taken all her strength to leave that photograph up there, instead of cutting David out of it, like a gangrenous foot.

Maybe I was wrong to leave it, she thought. Maybe that's why Spencer thinks Daddy will come back, so long as he's naughty enough.

Spencer was falling asleep, going by his heavy breathing. Zoe leaned forward to rest her lips on his head, drawing his drowsy smell into her lungs. It was the sweetest perfume she'd ever known. 'I love you, Spencer,' she whispered and squeezed her eyelids tight shut, to stop the fierce, loving tears falling on his hair.

## 21

It took Rachel several days to make the appointment at the surgery, but only five minutes for Dr Carthy to confirm that she was definitely five weeks pregnant.

'Congratulations,' he'd said, with a quick smile, and passed her a selection of leaflet-y reading matter, none of which Rachel could believe was even vaguely relevant to her.

And that was it, she thought, as she made her way back into the sunny waiting room, still recovering. It was official. She checked her diary obediently as Lauren made her appointments for a 'proper check-up appointment' the following week, and then drove back to Four Oaks in a daze.

I suppose I should tell George now, she thought.

Rachel and George had fallen into an unspoken but easy routine over the past few weeks – Saturday nights they ate at his house, where the food was excellent; Wednesdays, Rachel left Gem with Megan and took George out for dinner and a film in the out-of-town complex near Hartley, where the food was average but allowed George to make jokes about how she was missing the big city. Most days he called into the kennels, 'in passing', but it didn't bother Rachel too much on the days he didn't; George understood about leaving some space. It suited them both.

'You know I heard on the grapevine that George has bribed his locum to do his Wednesday night call-out so he can see you,' said Megan slyly, as Rachel arrived in the kitchen on

Saturday, ready to leave. 'Ooh, you look nice. I thought you were staying in?'

'We are.' Rachel pulled her hands through her hair. 'Just because George has formal and informal wellies doesn't mean *I* can't make an effort.'

She was wearing some expensive jeans she'd bought off the internet in a moment of reconnection weakness and one of Dot's swing jackets over a t-shirt. The jacket was handmade, with a gorgeous lavender satin lining – it didn't seem to have been worn at all, apart from a faint smell of Coco.

'I should get a move on.' Rachel whistled for Gem. Her stomach had been fluttering all day at the thought of how she was going to break the news. No amount of meetings had prepared her for this. There was no good angle.

Megan wasn't going to let her gossip go that easily. 'Freda reckons you're the first girlfriend he's brought to the pub, and you know how long she and Ted have been here. She reckons George has got that look about him when he's with you. She's talking about buying a hat!' Megan caught herself, seeing Rachel's expression, and added, ''Course I told her it's very early days yet.'

Rachel managed a bleak smile. 'Yup.'

'You going to be back late?' Megan enquired.

'I don't know. Gem! Come here now!'

Her tone was sharper than she meant it to be, and his ears flattened nervously against his head as he sidled towards her.

'Don't scare him,' said Megan. 'I know he's a farm dog by birth but he's not used to being shouted at.'

Gem slunk to her side, his eyes lowered, and Rachel suddenly felt utterly inadequate. She longed to be back on her own, in her own flat, in her old world. I'm better at being on my own, she thought, and immediately realised that that option would never be available to her again.

'I won't be late, Megan.' She slung her bag over her shoulder and grabbed the bottle of wine off the dresser. That was for George. He'd need it.

'You be as late as you want,' said Megan happily.

George pretended that he hadn't gone to much effort – he claimed to be just back from a lambing – but the kitchen of his house smelled delicious and there were yellow tulips in the jug on the table that Rachel knew hadn't come from his ramshackle garden.

He chatted away so easily that for the first twenty minutes Rachel was lulled into forgetting what she'd come to tell him, and it was only when he uncorked a bottle of wine that the new reality slapped her in the face again.

'Can I tempt you?' George showed her the bottle. 'I'm doing some venison so I've gone for a Shiraz, but if you prefer something different, just say.' He put it on the table next to her glass, and gestured towards a well-stocked wine rack. 'My cellar's at your disposal. I know you're something of an expert,' he added.

'I'll just have water, thanks,' said Rachel.

'Water? Are you all right?' George pretended to feel her forehead and her skin tingled at the touch of his hand. She knew he was conscious of the casual contact too; they were still at the shivery 'can I touch you?' stage where it wasn't a given.

Bit late for that, she thought.

'You don't have to pretend you don't drink,' he went on, cheerfully. 'Don't forget we've already got the embarrassing drunk face out of the way.'

'No, I'm not drinking. I can't . . . I'm . . .' Rachel held onto the back of the chair. This was as good an opening as any.

She looked down at Gem, who had curled himself in a ball in the basket by the Aga. He looked utterly relaxed, and she realised that he probably had been here before, with Dot. He was more at home than she was. He'd probably prefer to live with George.

Rachel felt the running away urge again, more strongly. How could this be *happening* to her?

'What? On antibiotics?' He stirred a pan of gravy on the hotplate. 'Something I should know?'

'George, I'm pregnant,' she blurted out. 'I know, it's irresponsible and stupid. But you don't have to do anything or say anything. I wanted to tell you, and if you don't want it to get out, then I'm fine. Everyone will think it's Oliver's, anyway. If that's what you'd prefer.'

Some dim part of Rachel's brain registered that none of that had come out the way she'd meant it to but it was too late.

George's hand froze but he calmly removed the pan from the heat, placing it on an iron trivet, and turned to face her. 'What do you mean by that? I don't have to do anything?'

'I mean, you don't have to offer to marry me or anything. I've decided that I'm going to have the baby though. It's not a great time, and I know this isn't what you'd have planned either, because it's certainly not how I'd have chosen to do things, but please don't try to talk me out of it. I can't explain and it's not rational, but I want to have it.' Rachel wasn't quite sure where these words were coming from; they certainly weren't the ones she'd rehearsed. 'Please,' she added.

George wiped his hand over his face and left it there, while he thought. When he removed it, his expression was incredulous. 'Let me just get this straight. You think I'm the sort of man who'd try to talk a woman into an abortion? Is that *honestly* what you think I'd do? I know we don't know each other very well, but I hope you'd think more of me than that.'

'I didn't . . .' Rachel began, and then realised she'd based her whole approach on what Oliver would have said. Not George.

She'd basically accused him of wanting to wriggle away from her and the baby.

He carried on staring at her. 'Anyway, aren't we meant to start off with, "Darling I have some wonderful news"? For someone who wants to have a baby so much you don't sound very happy about it yourself.'

'I am! And it is wonderful news. It's just that . . .' Rachel's insides prickled. This was so wrong. He wasn't ranting like Oliver, but he seemed distant, and her defences rose instinctively.

'Well, you're right. I don't really know much about you at all,' she said. 'I didn't want to assume. I didn't want you to think I'd planned it. Hijacked your sperm like some mad woman.'

'*Planned* it? How?' Now he looked baffled as well as offended. 'I mean, is that what some women do? You'll have to forgive me here, Rachel, I'm just a hick from the sticks.'

Gem whimpered at the sound of raised voices and curled his head tighter.

Rachel sank onto the chair and put her head in her hands. Of course he wouldn't think that. He didn't read *Grazia*, or know many IVF-crazed women, or listen to the agonisings of career-driven mistresses. George was a decent, old-fashioned bachelor. Not that that made him easier to deal with than the slippery married man she was used to.

Just because he'd said he wasn't really interested in a family didn't mean that he wouldn't insist on his paternal rights being respected. Maybe he would insist on marrying her. She hadn't thought about that. She hadn't thought about what *he* might want for his child. Or the mother of his child.

A chill swept over her stomach as the door clicked shut on her independence. A child she could take with her; but she couldn't take the child from a father who wanted to be involved.

'Sorry,' she said. 'This isn't coming out right.'

'No, it's not.' He raised the bottle to pour her a glass of wine.

'No, George,' Rachel reminded him. 'I'm not allowed to drink from now on.'

'Right.' He looked at her, then filled up his own glass, nearly to the brim. After taking a long swig he sat down opposite her at the head of the table and looked more like his old self. 'Well, congratulations,' he said. There was a moment when she thought he was going to get up to hug her, but her body language must have put him off, because he didn't.

Rachel stared longingly at the wine bottle. Just when you *really* needed a drink, she thought. 'Thanks.'

'How are you feeling?'

'Bit sick. Bit fat.' She pulled a face. 'I've never been pregnant before. Maybe you should tell me what I should expect.'

George laughed, rather tensely. 'That you should be ready to drop in nine weeks, and I'll be on hand with my rubber gloves?'

'Can I have a glass of water, please?' asked Rachel.

He poured her a glass of water from the big jug on the table and she drank it gratefully. The jug had ice in it, and chopped up lemons. Suddenly the effort he'd gone to without wanting to show it – the good plates, silver cutlery, the tulips he'd obviously bought – made her feel like crying. From promising date to this, with just one sentence.

They sat in silence for a few moments. Rachel listened to the pots bubbling on the stove and the whoosh of the Aga re-firing itself. Noises that would have made her feel warm inside last week; warm and excited about a new relationship with a man who could cook and liked wine.

'Look, it *is* my fault,' said George, rubbing his face again. 'I wasn't as, um, timely with the condom as I could have been. I did tell you I was out of practice.' He looked up at Rachel and she could see he was anxious.

Her heart melted.

'It's as much my fault,' she said. 'I shouldn't have been so pissed I didn't notice. I shouldn't have been so pissed we ended up in bed at all, but we did. What's done is done. I don't think my dad's going to come round and horsewhip you.'

'Have you told your parents?'

She shook her head wryly. 'No, I haven't told anyone, except you. My mum'll be driven mad by the chance of another grandchild on one hand, but by an irresponsible one-night-stand on the other. She had me down for the cat sanctuary, to go with Auntie Dot's dogs' home.' Rachel swallowed, trying to keep her voice light. 'Not the single parent with the baby daddy she barely knows.'

'Don't be flippant, this is serious,' said George. 'You can tell her you won't be on your own. I'll support the baby financially and . . . Well, with as much emotional support as you want me to offer.'

'It's a baby, George, not a tax inspection,' said Rachel. She couldn't work out whether she was niggled by his failure to sweep her into his arms and tell her everything would be OK – or whether, had he done that, she'd have been furious at the condescension.

'I know.' He chewed his lip. 'I know. Sorry, I'm just trying to get my head around it. I'm going to be a father. And I don't even know when *your* birthday is.'

'Maybe we should just get our passports out?' suggested Rachel. 'You've got nine months for me to guess your amusing middle names, anyway.'

'It's not funny.'

'I know.' Rachel shut her eyes. Joking was her way of dealing with it, but she didn't want George to get the wrong idea. That was the danger of only half-knowing someone.

'I'm only going to ask you this once,' said George, his voice low but gentle. 'But I am going to ask – you're really sure about having this baby?'

Rachel's eyes snapped open. 'Yes. I am.'

'It's just that . . .' George seemed to be struggling to find the right words. 'This isn't going to come out right.'

'It's just that what? Go on, say it.' Rachel stared at him. She could feel the force of a personality as stubborn as her own, and tumbled recklessly on, determined to push the worst out. 'We're not kids. We don't have a marriage to break up.'

'It's just that not so long ago you were putting up a pretty good argument for not wanting children, now or ever. Your white carpets, your holidays. Remember?' He looked at her, with his clear-eyed gaze. 'Don't tell me that's just vanished overnight. The independent woman with her own life – I totally understand where you were coming from. What I'm saying is that I'm not going to get on your case if you decide not to go ahead with it. It's your life.'

'What?' she countered, though she wasn't quite sure what she was countering. 'From the man who doesn't miss the stress of pleasing other people? The man who enjoys keeping his own hours and ignores the phone?'

He held up his hands. 'I'm just trying to work out what's going on. It's a big decision, and you're probably very hormonal right now.'

Rachel recoiled. *Hormonal*? Like being pregnant stopped your brain working? This man clearly hadn't had a woman in his life.

'I *know* it's a big decision,' she snapped. 'But I'm not the first woman to have a baby she wasn't planning! Or to change her mind about her bloody carpets once it's actually happening. Everything's changed, just in the last few weeks.'

She gestured towards Gem, snoring in the basket. 'I mean, look – white carpets are a thing of the past anyway. I don't think I'm ever going to be able to go back to the life I had.' She paused, recognising she meant it. 'And I don't want to. What I have now is real. It's *mine*.'

George said nothing, and she realised he didn't even know her well enough to understand what she meant.

'You do *not* have to be part of this,' Rachel hurried on. 'I didn't come here to insist that you, I don't know, "stood by me". I'm telling you because you have a right to know. And because . . .' Her voice caught in her throat.

George seemed like Mr Rural Reliability now, but there had been a time when she'd thought Oliver was reliable too. Reliable and loving – and look how that had turned out. Wasn't it better to start off on her own, and not be disappointed?

'You make it sound like you don't *want* me to be a part of this,' observed George.

'Well, what's changed in *your* life? Nothing. You've still got the long hours, the anti-social job. You can't even say you've met the right woman because you barely know me.'

'What's changed is that I might now be a father,' he said, simply. 'That changes everything.'

Rachel paused to let the lurch in her chest subside; it wasn't hormones, it was a sudden longing for a man who seemed decent and strong. What kind of a mother was she going to be, after all? She had no idea. But they couldn't pretend to have a bond they hadn't had time to forge yet, and she hadn't turned her back on her old life of lies to start a new life based on a different sort of deception, even if it was for the right reasons.

'So where does this leave us?' he asked.

'I don't know. I don't want you to do something you don't want to, just because you feel you should.' Rachel pressed the tip of her tongue against her front teeth until it hurt. 'In fact, it might be better if I just left. I've had a few days to think about this – it's only fair to give you the same.'

'Rachel, please . . .'

It felt odd, hearing him say her name. She pushed her chair back, aware that she was making it all worse. 'I'm going to go. I'm sorry about dinner, it smells lovely. Gem?'

George was standing now too. 'If that's what you want . . .' he began.

'It is.' It wasn't. What she wanted was for him to sweep her into his arms and tell her it was all going to be fine, that they were meant to be together and that Dot had fated the whole thing, but she was too adult to believe that, and so was he.

Gem got up reluctantly from the basket, teetering onto his long legs and looking between the two of them with sleepy eyes, as if to say, why are we leaving so soon?

'Come on,' she said, reaching out her hand to the collie.

'I'll call you,' said George. He shook his head. 'I wish I knew what the right thing to say is. I'm just . . .'

'I know,' said Rachel, unhappily. The evening felt spoiled now. Curdled, like milk left out thoughtlessly. 'Me too.'

'I'll see you out.' George followed her to the door, and as she left, he leaned forward to kiss her on the cheek, but Rachel didn't see it coming, and moved away to nudge Gem away from a hedgehog curled by the front step.

By the time she realised what she'd done, the kiss had withered in the air and George raised an awkward hand to wave goodbye.

Proper morning sickness set in a few days later, along with extreme exhaustion and a desire to throw up at the mere sight of the dogs' Butcher's Tripe Mix.

Poor Megan was still convinced it was her flu bug that was making Rachel turn green, and wanted to let her off all kennel duties until she felt better.

'Stay in bed,' she pleaded, when Rachel dragged herself into the kitchen at eight, unwoken by the usual cup of tea. 'Please! I feel bad enough already without making you do walking.'

'I'm fine. Honestly.' Rachel sorted through the post on the pine table. 'There's so much to do, I can't let you . . . Oooh.' She gripped the chair and sat down heavily as a wave of nausea swept through her. ''Scuse me. Did you have a bacon sandwich this morning?'

'About an hour ago.' Megan eyed her anxiously. 'You're sure you won't go back to bed? Freda will be here any minute and the sixth-former volunteers are in today.'

'I'm sure. I've got a lot I need to get through.'

'Ooh, with Open Day stuff?' Megan's face brightened. She was even more enthusiastic about the Open Day than Rachel and Natalie, and was convinced the pair of them were hotshot business geniuses to have come up with it. 'I had a brainwave – Freda can do a bacon sandwiches stall! We could sell them for two pounds, and then tell everyone they're free when you volunteer for dog walking!'

Rachel swallowed hard at the thought. 'That's a great idea, Megan. Do you want to stick it on the ideas board?'

As Megan happily scrawled it on the whiteboard by the door, Rachel sorted the junk from the post. It was mainly supermarket offers and feed catalogues, but Rachel spotted a couple of official-looking letters in there too, and her heart sank. Things were moving on the probate front; she'd sworn whatever it was she was supposed to swear to, and Gerald Flint had warned her that the inheritance tax bill would be on its way.

She took a deep breath and opened the brown envelope, then gasped when she saw what the tax liability was.

'Bad news?' asked Megan.

'Depends.' That was what Gerald had said when the final valuations had been submitted by the estate agent – 'There's good news and bad news, Rachel.' The good news was that she didn't have to pay any tax on the kennels because they were a business, and also that the estate agent had put an astonishing value on the land behind the house.

The bad news was, of course, that the tax Rachel would have to pay was truly enormous. Nearly two hundred thousand pounds, according to this invoice.

She closed her eyes, then opened them. The horrific amount was still there. Her heart sank as she read the details: she had to pay an instalment now, with the rest to follow within twelve months, and then the house, the field, the outbuildings that were apparently worth so much money, the silver hairbrushes, the Acker Bilk albums and the rest of Dot's life would be hers.

To pay the bill, she would need to sell the house. To sell the house, she would need to pay the bill. It was like Alice in Wonderland logic, and Rachel's brain wasn't up to it.

She stuffed the letter into her big desk diary on the table and turned as cheerfully as she could to Megan.

'So! I reckon some fresh air would be good for me! What needs walking? Slowly?'

The relentless routine of the kennels kept Rachel's mind off the sickness and the inheritance tax for the next few days, but she couldn't help noticing that George still hadn't rung, or dropped in, and that Natalie hadn't been up with Bertie since the day she'd given her the test.

Rachel missed Natalie's calm company at the kitchen table. She had a feeling the inheritance tax bill would be dispatched with a few pragmatic business suggestions, once Natalie had glanced at it. She looked out for Natalie's red jacket while she was walking the dogs, and did think about calling her, to say that Gerald Flint had told her that they could go ahead and arrange the Open Day for the kennels whenever she liked.

But her hand had frozen on the telephone, because Rachel knew she'd have to tell her about the baby. And Rachel didn't want to lie to Natalie.

It's still early days, she thought, throwing ball after ball for the Staffies in the orchard. According to the leaflets and the internet doom-mongers, you weren't meant to tell anyone for three months, in case something went wrong, and at her age all *sorts* of stuff could go wrong. Rachel had actually turned off the internet one night, she was so freaked out.

Val. She'd have to tell Val very soon too. That could wait a few weeks as well. Once she told Val, that would be it. The explanations, the worrying, the drama – it would all start. And if it went wrong . . .

There were some secrets she'd prefer to bottle up herself, than have them paraded around the family like a badge of tragedy. Poor Rachel. She was poor Rachel already.

Loneliness washed over her like a wave, and when she looked down at the eager little faces of the terriers, so easy to please, she felt like crying.

She let Megan have Wednesday evening off, since she was feeling so much better at night, and went to sit in the kennel office, where she could keep an ear out for the dogs and make herself look again at the letter from the Inland Revenue.

Rachel didn't admit to herself that she felt better with some canine company, and Radio Four burbling away in the background.

She pressed her palms against her eyes and forced herself to be practical. She could just about manage the first payment, by selling Dot's diamond necklace, all her own jewellery and cashing in every single investment she'd managed to make in her life. But the second part? What else could she sell? The house to pay for the kennels, or the kennels to pay for the house?

Rachel dug out her address book and called a university friend who worked in financial services, who talked her through various options, none of which filled her with much hope. Reading between the lines of what the estate agent had said about the survey, it would be easier to knock Four Oaks down and sell the land to developers than start modernising a property that had some fairly serious issues. And mortgages weren't that easy to come by, when you were an unemployed PR manager with a kennels that hadn't made a profit for seven years.

Gem snoozed at her feet, his muzzle occasionally twitching. Could she pimp him out to a TV company, she wondered? Could she pitch the whole 'I've been left a kennels I can't pay for' idea to Channel Four?

The kennel doorbell jangled, and when she went to answer it, George was standing there with a plastic dog carrier, looking as he always did when he had a delivery – efficient but cross with the world. Rachel felt a strange mixture of awkwardness and relief.

'Sorry to interrupt,' he said, 'but I've got something for you.'

'What is it?' Rachel tried to look normal. 'Is it some supper?'

'Not exactly. Unless you like sausage dogs.' He came in, and Rachel heard faint whimpering noises from the carrier. 'It's a dachshund.'

Gem's ears pricked up at the sound of his voice. He hadn't been asleep at all.

'Oh, right. Should I call Megan? It's her night off.' Rachel turned to the phone, but George waved her away.

'No need. I'm sure you can do the paperwork, that's all he needs. I've given him his shots up at the surgery, cleaned him up, but I wouldn't put him in with the others just yet. He's terrified, poor chap.' George's voice softened. 'He was obviously someone's pet, but one of the farmers up by Rosehill found him in his barn, all covered in scabs. They're hunting dogs but this one's probably never even seen a rat before, let alone tried to catch one.'

He peered through the mesh door of the carry case. 'I reckon they made a better job of nibbling him than he did of them.'

'I just don't understand how people can be so cruel.' Rachel pushed her fringe off her face and tried not to let George see the distress in her eyes. No wonder Dot gave up on make-up once she came here, she thought. She probably cried it all off.

'Are you crying?'

'No, I'm just hormonal.' She swiped at her eyes with the back of her hand, and made a note to ask Natalie where she could get a reliable eyelash dye. 'Is he OK to pick up?'

'Nope. He's very scared.' George put the carry case down on the floor next to the spare basket. 'Just let him come out of his own accord. Pretend you can't see him.'

'Do you want a coffee? Now you're here?' Rachel went through to the kitchen, taking care not to go too near the plastic case. 'I've only got decaff, I'm afraid.'

'Sounds fine. I didn't expect to find you in here.' George stepped through and leaned against the mini-fridge, keeping one eye on the office, where a wet nose was now sticking out of the case. 'Shouldn't you be sitting with your feet up reading *What Mum?*'

It was a tentative start, more like their old banter. 'No, *What Mum?* is all internet-based these days. And I've got paperwork to do.'

'You could be doing it in the comfort of your own home,' he pointed out.

'I don't want Megan to see it.' Rachel sighed. 'It's the inheritance tax thing. I've got the most enormous bill to pay.'

'How enormous? Queen Mother enormous?'

The kettle started to boil and Rachel spooned coffee into the mugs. 'Big enough to be a nightmare.'

'Don't take this the wrong way,' said George. 'But how? It's a nice house and everything, but, is there a gold mine in the back field?'

'Almost. There's more land than I thought, but Dot – or Dot's solicitors – applied for planning permission to turn one

of the old barns into accommodation for future kennel staff.'
She returned George's look of surprise. 'I know. She just never
got round to it. Anyway, land plus planning permission round
here is worth a fortune, apparently, which is great, only I'll
have to sell the house to pay the tax on it.'

'Get a mortgage. You'll be a homeowner.'

'Apparently it won't be that easy.' Rachel passed George a
mug. 'According to the survey, even the mice wear hard hats
in the cellar.'

George sipped his coffee and made a face.

'What?' said Rachel.

'Your coffee making. It's as terrible as the rest of your
cooking. Milk, please.' She passed the carton and he stirred
in some more.

The dachshund had crept out of the travel case, and was
sniffing timidly around the office. Rachel was shocked to see
how half-starved he was; the ribs of his tiny barrel chest nearly
poked through the dull coat that should have gleamed like a
chestnut. Gem remained at a distance, but alert, clearly in
charge, and slowly the smaller dog began to approach him, his
tail lowered in desperate submission. Her chest ached, but she
kept herself from reaching out, letting him find his own way.

'You could always get an investor,' suggested George. 'I
thought that was what this great Open Day plan was about,
raising some cash?'

Rachel shook her head. Suddenly the Open Day and its little
stalls and competitions seemed pretty pointless. 'It's a drop in
the ocean. Kennel sponsors will cover the daily running costs,
but it doesn't solve the bigger problem of where I'm going to
lay my hands on a hundred grand to keep the place.'

'Get an investor,' George repeated, so emphatically Rachel
looked more closely at his face. 'Someone who's already got a
vested interest.'

'You're offering?' she asked, only half-joking.

He nodded. 'Yes. I am.'

'A hundred grand?'

'I think you underestimate how much vets earn,' he said, pretending to be offended.

Rachel put down her coffee and looked him in the eye. 'No, I don't. I've seen your invoices. Thanks, but I'm not sure it'd be a good idea. I barely know you.'

'Bit late for that, isn't it?' said George. 'It's a sensible business proposition, from my point of view. Plus I spend so much unbilled time here anyway . . .'

'Is this about the baby?' Rachel could feel doors closing around her.

'Partly.' George didn't bother to lie. 'Look, we need to talk about that properly. Is that a terrible thing, wanting to help you?' He paused. 'I mean, it's in my interests in all sorts of ways. That you're here, and not stressed out. Isn't it better to put things on a business footing? Then you know where you are?'

'No.' Rachel got up and turned away, because she knew she sounded ungrateful, and churlish, but she couldn't help it. She'd been her own person for too long. This, on top of the baby, was just too much to get her head around. 'I can't let you do that. Sorry.'

'Don't turn away from me. I've been thinking about everything you said.' George turned her back round and left his hands resting lightly on her arms. 'I haven't done anything else, to be honest. I know I didn't react the way you wanted, and I'm sorry. Really.'

'It doesn't . . .' she began, but he stopped her.

'Of course it matters. You're right. I'm not going to pretend I know what to do, because I don't. I've been on my own for forty-odd years and yes, I'm a selfish old bachelor. But I'll do whatever you want.' He fixed her with his honest eyes. 'When you work out what that is, I mean. We're getting on all right so far, aren't we?'

She nodded, then pulled away to sit back down at the small table, stacked high with clean metal dog bowls. 'I don't mean to be so difficult,' she admitted. 'I'm just painfully aware that I'm making this up as I go along.'

George pulled out a chair and sat next to her. He was close, and Rachel felt comforted. 'Me too,' he said. 'But we're two intelligent, reasonable adults. And we can only do our best.'

It was a simple thing, but the way he said it made Rachel think of her dad. He'd never asked anything of her but her best try, and that had been a bigger spur than any amount of bribes or threats. Her mum – well, Val had operated on a complicated system of disappointment that had only resulted in Rachel moving to London where raging bosses were easy to deal with in comparison.

She took a few deep breaths, letting the delicate mood sink in, and George slid his hand across the table, to curl his fingers around hers.

He waited a minute or so, as if he was considering the right thing to say, and then spoke, very softly. 'It's no one's business,' he said, 'but when people ask about the baby, I'd like you to say it's mine. I mean, ours. I'll deal with any stupid questions.'

Rachel smiled quickly, then looked back down at their hands on the table, his chapped fingers rough against her pale skin.

She heard something move in the office, and turned her head. The dachshund was sniffing the water bowl in the corner, flinching as if it expected something to jump out. Gem kept well back, watching in silence, and then as Rachel held her breath, it began to lap at the bowl with a pink tongue, slowly at first, and then faster, as if it hadn't drunk properly in months.

## 22

Johnny snapped out of his black mood – or he seemed to – but in the days that followed his second sperm test Natalie could tell he wasn't back to his usual self. He lapsed into silences for no reason, and changed the television channel when anything to do with babies came on. She tried talking about their summer holiday, which they normally spent weeks deliberating over, covering the sofa with travel guides and magazine articles ripped out of the Sunday papers, but he just shrugged and looked evasive.

'It's a long way off yet,' he'd said, even though they usually booked by April. 'Let's see how it goes.'

Natalie had wanted to yell, see how what goes? But she hadn't, just in case he was thinking about fertility treatment. She hadn't told him yet about the letter from their NHS trust, putting them on a waiting list which could take 'up to a year' to get round to them. That was enough time to broach the subject again, she thought. Let him come to terms with needing it first.

The distance started as pauses where there would normally be silly jokes, but it spread quickly and silently. Johnny started going off to bed early, claiming he was worn out from school, but really, Natalie knew it was so he could pretend to be asleep by the time she slipped under the duvet.

One night, determined to show him how much she still wanted him, baby or not, she pulled off her t-shirt and curled around his solid body, sliding her hands under the pyjamas he never normally wore to warm his familiar chest and thigh with her soft naked skin. Johnny, half-sleepily, began to respond, rolling over to press his lips against her arching throat, but they both seemed to realise at the same moment how different it was, knowing what they both knew now, and the passion slid away.

He had rolled onto his back with a heartbreaking sigh, and they'd lain next to each other, not touching, pretending to be asleep.

Natalie wasn't sure how long she could bear it. There'd never been secrets in all the years they'd known each other, let alone thoughts that were too painful to share. It was as if they both knew the first person to speak would set off the miserable domino run of accusations and consequences, and neither of them could face the horrible thoughts forming like rainclouds in the back of their minds.

Next week, she kept telling herself. Next week, I'm going to *tell* him we need counselling for this. It's too big a conversation to manage on our own.

In fact, it was only through Bertie and his new role as an unwitting ventriloquist's dummy that they managed to start conversations at all.

'Are you ready for your social club?' Johnny demanded on Saturday morning. 'Bacon sandwich, eh? Bit of a stroll and a chat with your poodly girlfriend?'

Natalie knew he was talking to her really, not Bertie.

'I know we skipped last week,' he went on, glossing over the fact that he'd taken himself off for a three-hour drive, leaving Natalie to haul Bertie round the canal loop on her own. 'Don't want you to think we're neglecting your social life.' He looked up at Natalie. 'Bill rang yesterday, wanted to know if we were going up to the kennels to walk the homeless.' He paused. 'Said he missed us last week. We should probably go, before we get out of the habit.'

Was it only a fortnight since we got the results, she thought. It seemed so much longer.

'Well, do you want to go on your own with Bill?' She reached out a hand to stroke Bertie. He was sprawled along the sofa with his head on the arm and his ears dangling over the side. He shouldn't have been on the sofa, but then she shouldn't have been drinking caffeinated coffee either. What was the point? 'Eh, Bertie? Spend some quality time with your daddy?'

'Why?'

'Well.' Natalie shrugged. She knew it was childish but she had a sneaky feeling that Rachel hadn't been entirely frank with her. She just had an instinct that she was pregnant, and right now, Natalie didn't have enough energy to make her 'happy' face very convincing – and that would only make things worse for poor Johnny. 'Bertie sees enough of me during the week. He's pretty bored of my conversation.'

'Don't you want to come up to the kennels?' Johnny frowned. 'It was all you were talking about last week – this Open Day you and Rachel are organising. What happened to that? Is it all off?'

Natalie stirred her porridge. 'It's not off, but I've done what I can,' she said. 'I don't want Rachel to think I'm trying to take over.'

'I'm sure she doesn't think that. You're a marketing expert, Nat! I'm sure she's thrilled to be getting your help.' He sounded more like the Johnny she knew. 'Come on, get your coat. Bertie wants you to come, don't you?'

He crouched down and said in his Bertie voice, which for reasons they hadn't plumbed was a lugubrious Scouse, 'Hurry up, Nats. I'm gagging for me bacon sarnie.'

I should go, thought Natalie, watching him. He's going to have to go through far more mortifying things than me in the next few weeks. We should be putting on a united front here.

But still something held her back. 'Why don't you meet Bill and have a natter with him?' she said, brightly. 'I've got some stuff to do – I'll meet you up there and we can go for a pub lunch or something?'

Johnny gave her a funny look. 'Fine,' he said. 'Call me when you're on your way.'

As he left, with Bertie waddling behind him, Natalie wondered if this was how it would be from now on: doing things separately until slowly it didn't feel weird any more.

Zoe's patience was being tested to the very limits by the impossible task of hustling Spencer and Leo and their football kit and Toffee and some portable breakfast out into the car.

'I need a sheepdog, not a Labrador!' she groaned, as Leo darted back inside 'for an apple'. 'Spencer! Stop it!'

The plan was to take the boys to football, wear them out, and then go on to the dog walking with Toffee. Zoe told herself it was good for the boys to see what happened with the other dogs, and to see Megan training Toffee, but at the back of her mind she knew she was throwing Fate a challenge.

If Bill was there, and saw them, and met them, and realised how much a part of her Spencer and Leo were, then that was great. If he wasn't there . . . Well. It didn't matter. But she still put her lip-gloss in her back pocket, just in case.

She cast a warning glance at Spencer, who was kicking lichen off the front gate in a challenging way. He glared back and Zoe would have said something if her phone hadn't rung and saved him from an official warning.

It was Rachel. 'Zoe? You know that haircut you promised me? Any chance of getting it done today?'

Zoe thought about saying no, but heard herself agreeing, and went back inside for her scissor bag.

When she arrived at the Four Oaks kitchen two hours later, muddy and hoarse from cheering encouragement on the football pitch, Rachel practically had the towel wrapped round her neck in readiness. Her long fringe had grown right down into her eyes, and though it had a certain boho charm, Rachel's nervous habit of shaking it to one side had got even worse.

The kitchen was full of volunteers in waterproofs and Leo and Spencer made a beeline for the Aga, where Freda Shackley was serving up the bacon sandwiches.

'Zoe, you are a star and a half,' Rachel said, as Spencer squirted extra ketchup onto the bacon roll. He was ignoring the paper towel Freda was trying to wrap it in, to Zoe's panic. 'I'm really sorry to hassle you on your day off, but I just can't stand it a minute longer. It's driving me mad.'

Zoe's eyes flickered round the room, trying to keep track of her sons and puppy. Leo was rolling around under the table with Toffee, his face covered in ketchup too. Football hadn't tired them out as much as Zoe had hoped, even if for Leo it wasn't much more than a lot of running about and squealing.

There was no sign of Bill. Zoe tried not to feel disappointed.

'Sure,' she said. 'Spencer! You don't need any more tomato sauce on that.'

He gave her a dirty look and added an extra squeeze. Zoe lowered her eyebrows.

Rachel looked a bit queasy at the sight of his sticky face. 'Don't you feed them?'

'Constantly. It's like shovelling coal into a steam engine. It never stops. Listen, shall I get them out of your way? Where do you want to go?'

'The kennels office,' said Freda, a bit too quickly. 'Then you can keep an eye on the phones.'

'Great. Come on, kids.' Zoe hustled them out, wishing she could put leads on them the way she could with Toffee, who was, annoyingly, behaving as if butter wouldn't melt in his mouth in front of Megan, his adored teacher.

\*　　\*　　\*

Even if she didn't already know Rachel worked in PR, Zoe could tell from the rough shape of her haircut that she'd been going to a pretty good salon in London, and she tried not to feel intimidated as she sized up the thick layers of black hair.

Everything about Rachel was glossy, she thought. The nails, the hair, the clothes, the car. But that's what happens when you don't have kids. Plenty of spare cash to spend on hundred-quid hairdos. For a second Zoe felt a pang of envy, then remembered that even if she didn't have kids, there'd be no way she'd pay that much.

At Megan's suggestion, Spencer and Leo were trying to train Toffee to stay, now he'd more or less mastered "Sit", but he was having too much fun chasing them around the office to want to be quiet. They were making so much noise, especially Spencer, who was bossing Leo as much as Toffee.

Zoe could feel the tension radiating from Rachel as she combed and snipped. It wasn't just her hunched shoulders; Zoe's fingers were picking up a tautness in the hair itself, something she occasionally felt in the salon. You got a knack for it, tuning into the client's mood like a radio.

'Will you two keep it down?' she demanded, embarrassed. 'I'm sorry,' she added to Rachel. 'They're mad at weekends. I should be crate training them, not the puppy. Do they do small boy-size crates at Pets at Home?'

'Can I ask a personal question?' Rachel sounded tentative, not her normal confident self.

''Course. If it's about hair dye, there's no question that's too personal, believe me.'

'No.' Rachel paused, and dropped her voice. The boys were too far away and too absorbed in their own game to hear. 'Is it very hard, being a single mum? I mean, is it hard being everything to them, and still having your own life?'

Zoe wasn't expecting *that* sort of personal question. 'Well, it's not how I planned it, put it like that. Originally there were supposed to be two of us on duty.' She sighed, remembering the very early days when Spencer was a baby. David had been a good dad then. They'd been a good *team*. It wasn't the stress that wore her out now, so much as being on call twenty-four/ seven, primed for disaster. You were never primed for cuddles or funny moments, but the possibility of something going wrong haunted her.

She focused her attention back on Rachel's layers. 'Yes, it's hard. Why? Am I making it look like the worst job in the world?' She sized up a lock of hair, and spotted several silver hairs. Best not say anything. 'It's not all fighting and squabbling. They do have their moments.'

'No! I didn't mean it in a critical way. I think they're lovely boys!' Rachel didn't turn around. 'I meant, well, the rewards are worth all the hassle, aren't they? When you see them growing up, and loving you, and turning into their own people.'

'Absolutely. But it is hard.' For once, Zoe was glad there wasn't a mirror for her client to look into. She wasn't sure what her face was doing. 'It's like climbing a mountain, I guess. You don't know how exhausting it is until you reach the top and it's all wonderful. But it's knackering at the time. No question about that.'

'But they're yours.' Rachel's voice wobbled.

'They're mine,' agreed Zoe. She decided Rachel was probably having a bad case of PMT-related broodiness. She sometimes got it herself, even though there was no way in hell she could cope with another baby, even if one arrived by DHL. 'Well, mine, *and* their dad's. Which is where it gets more complicated. You don't want to get into that if you can help it.'

Rachel didn't reply, and Zoe wondered if she'd said the wrong thing. Rachel was old enough to be divorced herself, even if she didn't wear a ring. Oops. Tactless. Maybe she was considering doing one of those single-woman turkey baster things you read about.

She ran her fingers through the top of Rachel's hair, lifting it up and dropping it to see how it fell. Not a bad cut, Zoe, she thought. Well up to London standards.

'Tell you what,' she went on, trying to sound as if she'd been joking all along. 'You can have Spencer and Leo on a timeshare basis, like Toffee. I'll drop them off with you for a couple of hours a week. That should be enough to satisfy any mothering instincts.'

The phone rang on the desk and Spencer grabbed it before Rachel could move from her seat. 'Longhampton Police, Sergeant Fartipants,' he said.

'Or you could have them now?' Zoe suggested. 'Long as you want?'


Natalie felt bad as soon as Johnny and Bertie left to meet up with Bill.

She tried to distract herself by doing some housework, and arguing that she was giving Johnny some time with his best mate, but Natalie was too honest to ignore the truth – it was more to do with her avoiding Rachel, and she was ashamed of herself.

When Natalie's conscience got going, it didn't let up. What was the next step? Avoiding all pregnant women? Boycotting streets with Mothercares or primary schools? She and Rachel had really been getting on well before that – and it was rare for her to make new friends. If Rachel *was* pregnant by this married man she'd left behind, she'd need all the new friends she could get in Longhampton.

She stopped in the middle of the sitting room, and turned off the Dyson. Rachel had been honest with her, confessing that business with Oliver. She hadn't needed to do that. And how was she repaying her?

*But it was so unfair.*

Natalie swallowed hard. The unpleasant truth was that Rachel had seemed like another member of her no-baby, no-worries club. But now even forty-year-old single women were more likely to get pregnant than she was – who'd be next? Freda? But it wasn't Rachel's *fault.* It wasn't anyone's *fault.*

Natalie managed another five minutes' internal wrangling before she gave up, put on her coat and drove up to the kennels. Bill and Johnny were still out with the dogs when she arrived in the kitchen, but Freda and Megan offered her a bacon sandwich anyway.

'If you're looking for Rachel, she's having her hair cut in the office,' said Megan. 'Ooh, do you think Zoe would do something like that for the Open Day? Haircuts?'

'For the dogs, maybe,' suggested Natalie, unable to stop herself coming up with fundraising suggestions. 'Quick trims for the pets? You could do that, couldn't you?'

'I certainly could!' Megan reached for the marker pen and added it to the ideas board. It was full of suggestions from the volunteers, ranging from 'Quickest Recall Competition' to 'Apple Bobbing – Dog and Owner'. 'What do you reckon? Two quid a trim?'

'Yes, why not?' Natalie's fingers twitched to add 'longest ears' onto the competitions list. There had to be something Bertie could win.

'Have you come to talk about it with Rachel?' Freda asked. 'I must admit, I'm looking forward to this dog show idea. It's great to get people paying more attention to what we do up here. Get the little doggies into new homes. Ted and I have been talking about doing some kind of catering. I know we had a grill at the café, years ago.'

'You could always just adopt a dog, Freda,' said Megan.

'Oh, we're past that now.' Freda sighed. 'And we'd never find a dog like our Pippin. Did I tell you about . . .'

'I'll just go and find Rachel,' said Natalie quickly, and went through the back door to the kennel complex.

When Natalie put her head round the office door, she wondered if a new vanful of strays had been delivered, judging by the hysterical racket emanating from the place.

It turned out to be Leo and Spencer, who could both do creditable Labrador impressions, plus Toffee, careering round the filing cabinets. They were smeared with tomato sauce and laughing gleefully, while they sent leaflets and stray bits of paperwork flying.

Rachel was sitting in a chair in the middle of the room, with Zoe finishing off the last snips of a new haircut that grazed her eyebrows and hung shaggily around her face. She looked unfairly sexy, even without any make-up and her eyes rimmed with dark shadows. Zoe looked a bit stressed, but that was probably because she was sending furious glares in the direction of her sons, every few snips.

When Rachel saw Natalie standing in the doorway, her expression changed from a faraway anxiety to something more focused. A more focused sort of anxiety, in fact.

'Hi, Rachel. Hi, Zoe,' said Natalie. She smiled at them both, as naturally as she could manage.

Zoe seemed to tense up a bit too when she saw her, but Natalie put that down to being Bill's friend. It was always a bit weird, getting to know your new man's mates, wondering what was being reported back. She tried to make her smile extra-friendly.

'Don't suppose you know what time Johnny and Bill will be back?' Natalie asked Zoe. 'I've been working at home, thought I'd let Bertie and his dad have some quality time together,' she added. 'The plan is to have some lunch – do you want to join us? If you haven't already made plans?'

'Oh, I don't know.' Zoe shrugged. 'I haven't seen Bill today.'

'Oh.' Natalie wondered if she'd missed something.

'Actually, I should get a move on.' Zoe put her scissors in her bag. 'Spencer, can you be a big boy and get a broom? So you and Leo can help Mummy by sweeping up this lovely hair?'

Leo ran off at once, but Spencer stuck out his lip.

'Don't make me ask again,' warned Zoe, and he slunk off.

'I saw the ideas board in the kitchen,' said Natalie. 'Looks like there's been some brainstorming going on. Open Day is go, eh?'

'Yes, Open Day is definitely go. I've got the nod from the solicitor – apparently it counts as running the business, so I don't have to wait for the rest of probate before we set a date.' Rachel sounded a bit stiff.

'Brilliant!' Natalie moved out of the way as Leo returned with a brush twice the size of himself, followed by his reluctant brother. 'When are you thinking of having it?'

'Well, when does the weather start getting nice out here?'

'July?' suggested Zoe. 'We have three days of summer, usually, but not in a row. Careful, Leo, mind the table . . . Well, where are we now? Last weekend in March? I'd make it early May. Gives you a good month to get things arranged, and that lovely cherry tree at the top of your drive will be in blossom by then.'

'Will it?' Rachel looked surprised. 'I didn't even know there was one. Are you volunteering then?'

'Spencer!' roared Zoe. 'Thank *you*, could you put the hair in the bin? The *bin*. Yes, I guess it's the least we can do.' She rolled her eyes at Natalie. 'We're going to get out of your hair, if you'll pardon the pun. Better get these two home.'

'You're sure you won't hang around and see if Johnny and Bill get back? There's a great pub out near Rosehill that lets dogs in. And kids.'

Zoe seemed torn.

'Go on,' urged Natalie. She felt like making amends for her own negative mood in any way she could.

'If you ask Megan nicely, she'll give the boys some doggie drops for Toffee,' said Rachel. 'And she keeps a stash of headache tablets in the pantry too.'

'I'll see you later maybe,' said Zoe, and she ushered the boys out into the corridor where they clattered their way towards the kitchen.

'God, I feel like I've just gone deaf,' said Rachel, twisting a finger into one ear. 'Is it just me or has it gone very quiet?'

'No.' Natalie realised she hadn't really thought about what she was going to say. She felt as awkward as a teenager, and about as rational.

Rachel seemed to be grasping an imaginary nettle, and she did it with more grace than Natalie thought she'd have managed herself, had their situations been reversed.

'I'm really glad you've come over,' she said. 'I've got something I need to tell you. To get out of the way.'

Here we go, thought Natalie, and fixed her happy face as her stomach dropped with misery. 'OK.'

'I *am* pregnant.' Rachel didn't look thrilled, but her eyes searched Natalie's face and she could tell Rachel was trying hard to say the right thing. 'Nearly six weeks now. I haven't told anyone else because it's such early days, but I wanted you to know.'

'Congratulations.' Natalie tried to summon up her earlier reason, but inside she was kicking and screaming like a red-faced toddler. How could someone who hated their ex, who didn't even have a happy family to offer a baby, be luckier than her and Johnny? How could that be *fair*?

'Don't say "congratulations".' Rachel flinched. 'I'm not going to pretend it isn't a massive shock because it is. It's so random. That's not what you want to hear,' she added quickly. 'I'm sorry.'

'Well, no. Maybe it's better that it's random.' Tears of frustration were building up on her eyelids. 'Makes it less . . . personal.'

'Natalie, I weighed up how hard it would be to tell you, and how hurt you'd feel if you found out.' Rachel reached out and touched her sleeve. 'I really, *really* appreciate how kind you were when Kath turned up. It meant a lot to me. I wanted to be honest with you.'

Natalie acknowledged it with a brave nod. She could tell Rachel was tied up in knots, and she tried to be generous. 'Have you told him? The father, I mean?'

Rachel's face had begun to lighten, but now the faint lines around her forehead tensed again. 'Yes,' she said, and paused. 'It's not Oliver, though,' she added in a rush of honesty, 'it's George.'

'George – Fenwick?' Natalie frowned, and a whole new wave of unfairness broke over her head. 'Blimey, when did that happen? I didn't even realise you were . . .' She paused. 'Dating.'

'We're not, really,' said Rachel, unhappily. 'I mean, we're seeing each other now, but it was just the one night. I know that's all it takes, but that's what I mean by random.'

Natalie looked her in the eye, and bit her tongue before she said something really cruel.

She kept it to herself, since it didn't reflect well on her general humanity, but Natalie had a complicated system when it came to being happy for other pregnant women, based on how long they'd been trying, how hard they worked, how much they loved their husbands. Rachel's miserable split from a man who'd denied her a chance of a happy marriage was one thing, but to get pregnant totally by accident by a single man who'd barely even met her . . .

'That is complicated,' she said instead, and hated how much like her mother she sounded.

Rachel covered her mouth, and for a second, she looked exhausted. 'I know. Please don't tell anyone. I just wanted you to know. To be honest, half the time I can't believe it's happening to me, and the rest of the time I'm terrified.'

Natalie struggled between furious jealousy and sympathy for the woman sitting in front of her. Rachel was well on the way to being a friend, she reminded herself. Don't let your baby obsession spoil everything. It's already driving a wedge between you and Johnny.

Easy to say. Much harder to do.

For the moment, though, Natalie battened down her negativity, and managed to smile as if she meant it. 'Thanks for telling me,' she said. 'And thanks for telling me why.'

Rachel smiled back, though tears were running down her face. When Natalie went to hug her, she realised she was crying too.

# 23

When the baby was just in her own head, Rachel found it surprisingly easy to carry on as if nothing untoward was happening.

It wasn't an issue around the kennels, since Megan and Freda didn't know, and Natalie didn't want to talk about babies at all. It wasn't even completely impossible with George, who treated her more or less the same as he always had done when he called in on various pretexts – most of which even Megan could tell were made up.

They carried on with their twice-weekly dates, but the biggest difference there was that there were no kisses at the end of them. Somehow it seemed wrong now. The first night, as he'd walked her to her car, George had bent down as if he was going to kiss her, and without knowing why, Rachel had kissed him on the cheek. He'd looked at her, surprised, and that had been it.

I need us to be good friends now, thought Rachel as she drove back, not to set up more complications. But there was a heaviness in her stomach that she couldn't explain away.

George had come with her to the first proper check-up at the surgery too. She'd mentioned it casually, and he'd obviously taken more notice than she'd thought at the time, because he was waiting outside in the car park when she pulled up, parking her shiny new Range Rover next to his battered Land Rover.

'You're sure?' she'd asked, leaning out of the window. The waiting room would be full, but not with anyone she knew. People he'd know though.

'I'm sure,' he'd said. 'Want to make sure you concentrate.'

The check-up made it very real all of a sudden. She had a due date – December 20th – and an appointment for a first scan. And with that, Rachel knew she couldn't put it off any longer: she'd have to tell Val.

Rachel waited until Megan had taken the dogs out for the first lot of walking, and Freda was safely installed in the office, manning the enquiry desk.

Then she went right to the top of the house and dialled her parents' home number from the old telephone on the upstairs landing, and stared at herself in the mirror while it rang. Her mind was blank, apart from a nagging feeling that she should have asked George to check Gem's vaccinations along with those of the other dogs.

I used to be good at telephone calls, she thought. I used to spend all *day* on the phone.

Val answered just as she was about to hang up. 'Oh, Rachel,' she gasped. 'I thought it was going to be Amelia. Grace's poorly.'

'Should I get off the line?' asked Rachel.

'No.' Val didn't add, 'so long as you're quick', but the implication was there.

'Um, how are you?' Rachel remembered a colleague once telling her that the best way to frame bad news was to pitch an even worse story first, but she couldn't think of one, barring Dot's keeping a hundred-thousand-pound diamond necklace next to her piccalilli, and an emergency marriage licence in a shoebox. That might just distract too much.

'I'm fine, Rachel.' Pause. 'Are you all right? Are you lonely?'

'No, not at all!' She swallowed. 'Look, Mum, I've got some news – I'm having a baby.'

The pause on the other end of the phone stretched out so long that Rachel could hear the front door bang, and her dad come in with the paper. She wondered if her mother had passed out.

'They didn't have your magazine, Vally, so I got you some mints!' he called, and Rachel's throat squeezed at the years and years of gentle domesticity her parents had shared. That wasn't going to be her child's pattern, for good or bad.

Get a grip, she told herself. That's not the life you wanted either. You went to quite a bit of trouble not to have a life like Mum and Dad.

'Sorry, love,' said Val, faintly. 'Your father came in, I'm not sure I heard you properly. What did you say?'

'I said, I'm having a baby.' Rachel tried to make her voice lighter this time. So Val would know to be pleased.

'How?' Her mother sounded winded. Not angry or disapproving, but baffled, as if Rachel had told her she was growing a third leg.

'Oh, the usual way. Man meets girl. Stork finds house.'

'Rachel, don't be flippant. I thought you might have gone off and had whatever it is those single women have done. Artificial insemination or something.' Val sounded huffy. 'I mean, you don't have a boyfriend. Not that you've told me about,' she added.

'I have now. Sort of. And this wasn't planned but I've decided to go ahead and . . .' Rachel grimaced at her own reflection. These weren't words she'd ever thought would come out of her own mouth. 'Take the chance to be a mother.'

'Well, congratulations,' said Val. She sounded about as happy as the last three people who'd said that, thought Rachel.

The mouthpiece went muffled as if she'd covered it with her hand. Rachel could make out her mother saying, 'It's Rachel. She's having a baby . . . Yes, a baby. No, not the dog. *Her.* I don't . . .'

Then her dad came on. 'Hello, love. Congratulations! Is it right what I hear? That you're going to be a mum? Wonderful news!'

'Thanks, Dad.' Rachel's emotions churned again at her father's genuine warmth. 'Bit of a shock.'

'*You* were a bit of a shock. So was Amelia. All babies are. I'm very pleased for you, love. Are we going to meet the lucky dad?'

'Yes, well, that was what I was calling about.'

'I'll put you back onto your mother,' said Ken. 'She's gesturing.'

'Mum,' said Rachel, heavily, as the phone changed hands. 'I thought it would be nice if . . .'

'Who is the father, Rachel?' Val's voice trembled. Such soap-opera conversations weren't really in her repertoire.

'His name's George. He's a vet I've been seeing, he treats the dogs here at the kennels.'

'But you've only been *there* ten minutes!'

'I know. It's like I said, a bit of a surprise. But that's life, isn't it? Anyway, I was wondering if you and Dad would like to come and stay for the weekend. You can meet George properly, and see what's been going on here. You might like to have a look round the house and see what you'd like to have of Dot's.' She tried a joke. 'You don't *have* to take a dog home with you, but if you'd like one, there's a really lovely spaniel here that'd suit you.'

'You can't bring this George home to see us?'

'Mum, I can't leave Megan here on her own with all the dogs. It's not fair. And George is really busy with work – it's still lambing season.' Rachel tried not to think too hard about what 'bringing George home to meet the parents' would be like. They were two obstinate adults, not a pair of teenagers who'd been caught out. At least if they met in her own house, she'd be able to control the dynamics, and divert too many awkward questions.

'Well, if that's the only time you can fit us in, then I suppose that's the best time,' said Val, and then immediately corrected herself. 'I didn't mean that to sound critical, Rachel. It's just . . .' She struggled. 'I never know what to say to you. I never know whether you want me to be pleased or not.'

'What do you mean by that?' Rachel was thrown by the strange, sad tone in her mother's voice.

'I don't mean anything. Now, what dates are we talking about?' Val continued, sounding more like herself. 'I'll rearrange some of my hospital rota. Can we bring anything? Have you been to the doctor and had your check-up? I can ring Amelia if you want, and see what things she has left from Jack.'

Rachel leaned her head against the wooden banisters. Now it was really starting.

'To be honest, Mum, I'd rather you gave me some advice about running a fête,' she said. 'I'm holding an Open Day to raise some money for the dogs. Next month. Don't say anything. I know it's not like me.'

The pause on the other end was only just shorter than the baby pause.

'What a nice idea, Rachel,' said Val. 'Have you thought about what you'll do if it rains?'

Rachel let her mother furnish her with plentiful advice about the importance of keeping a good float on every stall. Maybe it was her way of making everything normal again.

Downstairs, the kitchen was deserted, apart from Gem, who lay waiting for her at the threshold. Megan's jacket was thrown over her favourite chair, nearest the Aga, suggesting that she'd arrived back from her walk, but there was no sign of her or Freda, who normally took it as a signal to start elevenses.

'Are they both in the kennels?' she asked, as Gem followed her through to the office.

Sure enough, Freda and Megan were both in the kennel office; Freda was at Rachel's laptop, while Megan leaned over her from behind, trying to help her understand what was going on.

'We've had some emails,' Megan explained. 'About adopting some dogs!'

Natalie and Rachel's new website had started to gain momentum, after Rachel had registered it with a couple of national dog rescue sites, and enquiries were trickling in at a rate of three or four a day. Rachel was trying to put up two special pages per day, and the final one had gone up the night before.

'Well, one dog,' Freda corrected her, and at once, both her and Megan's eyes turned guarded.

'Who?' Rachel put down the coffee mugs she was taking to rinse out and went to see. She scanned the screen over Megan's shoulder. 'Oh.'

Four emails in a row had the subject heading, Bertie the Basset Hound.

'Who's going to tell them?' asked Freda, as all eyes – Freda's, Megan's, Gem's – turned to Rachel.

Natalie was walking Bertie down by the Longhampton canal when her mobile rang in her jacket pocket.

She was in a bad mood already, because the waitress in the deli wouldn't let her in to order a takeaway coffee, and had deliberately failed to understand her 'cappuccino' mime through the glass. And Johnny, who normally took out the bins without fail, as part of his husbandly duties, had left them festering for two weeks in the garage – a smell cocktail that had proved too tempting for Bertie and his Nose of Doom.

She pulled out the phone crossly and answered it, expecting to hear Johnny apologising or Rachel asking how to make an Excel document.

'Hi, is that Natalie Hodges?'

'Natalie Hodge, yes,' she said automatically. Bertie was snuffling around in the undergrowth, on the trail of something disgusting, and she gave his lead a tug. He looked up at her, balefully, and she wagged a finger.

'My name's Maria Purcell, from Blue Sky Solutions – I'm sorry we haven't been in touch before now.' The woman's voice was brisk and professional, and Natalie had to concentrate. 'We've been moving offices, had some IT issues. But I'm calling to touch base and to run a few possibilities by you, if you've got a second? Is this a good time?'

Natalie stopped walking. She'd almost forgotten she'd registered with the recruitment agency – it was something the HR department had told her to do on the weird day that Selina had told her she was to be made redundant.

'Um, yes, it's fine,' she said. She tried to refocus her brain into a sharper gear, but it was hard when Bertie was leaning over in the gleeful about-to-roll-in-something motion, his ears already caked in something noxious.

'No,' she mouthed, giving him the hardest stare she could manage. He rolled anyway, closing his eyes in delight as he coated his neck in Fox No. 5, the rank stench of which *didn't* come out with tomato sauce, no matter what the internet said.

Natalie toyed briefly with the idea of hanging up, dragging him away and calling back, claiming they'd been disconnected. Instead she offered him a treat from the bag in her pocket and he was at her side like a shot.

'Are you still there?' Maria Purcell prompted her.

You need a job, she reminded herself. This is a six-month sabbatical, not a way of life.

'Yes, I am! Go ahead,' she said, marching Bertie swiftly away from temptation and down the towpath.

'I've actually got an amazing opportunity coming up in the next few weeks, something that I think you'll be glad you were made redundant for,' the recruitment lady went on. 'I'm going to email the details over to you now. Are you near your computer?'

'Not exactly,' said Natalie. 'I'm just walking my dog!'

'Oh.' There was a note of surprise, not entirely approving either.

Dog walking wasn't something that went on a CV, Natalie reminded herself. No one actually gardened on gardening leave.

'Well, maybe you could call me as soon as you get back. There's an element of time sensitivity with this. It's just that your experience matches perfectly with the client's requirements and I know you'll be thrilled when you see it. The salary is negotiable at the moment, but with your background . . .' She could almost hear the keys tapping on the agency's cut.

'Of course,' said Natalie, in her best office voice. 'I'll get back to you a.s.a.p.'


Natalie printed out the details as soon as she got back in, and once she'd shampooed Bertie, because the smell was unbearable within four walls, she spent the rest of the afternoon staring at the job description.

She'd only been off work for a few weeks, about the length of Johnny's summer holiday, and yet something about the wording of the job description made her want to turn her phone off, not ping her CV straight back to Maria.

'. . . *you will crave responsibility and empowerment* . . .'

'. . . *strong strategic vision and a stop-at-nothing attitude to make it happen* . . .'

'. . .*you must be someone with tenacity and resilience* . . .'

She looked at Bertie who was reclining on his spoiled-dog leather beanbag, chewing a disgusting pig's ear: his reward for enduring a pretty rigorous bath. 'Look at this.' She waggled the paper. 'Do they want a brand manager or a gladiator?'

He regarded her with his tragic eyes, and Natalie dug out her phone and took a photograph of him, to remind herself that that was how mournful he looked when he was warm, damp, eating a pig's ear, and had her full attention.

There were too many photos of Bertie already on her phone.

She turned back to her CV on the laptop. The job was to lead a marketing team for a small organic chocolate brand that had just been bought out by a major food manufacturer. They wanted someone with big corporate experience, but with a delicate touch – something she had, from the organics launches she'd worked on in her last job. On paper, it was perfect, and it was only thirty miles away, outside Birmingham.

'How bad would it be,' she went on, 'to tell Maria Purcell that I don't want to take this chance of a lifetime because I'm trying for a baby? It's better than going for it, then bailing out on maternity leave, right, Bertie? More honest?'

She paused, and looked down at Bertie, now rolled onto his back, offering her a view of his speckled ermine tummy. He was a different dog to the creature she'd taken in a few weeks ago. He hadn't been cowed, like some of the dogs, but there'd been a sadness about him, as if he was trying extra hard to make them love him so they wouldn't leave. Now when he rolled over, he closed his eyes, knowing a tickle was seconds away.

How had they lived properly without him?

Johnny's reaction wasn't quite what she'd expected.

Or rather, Natalie couldn't quite put her finger on what his reaction was. He seemed keen in some respects – typically proud that she was obviously qualified for what was a pretty high-level job opening, and typically rude about the management jargonese – but at the same time, she got the feeling he was holding something back.

They were lounging on the sofa after dinner, one at each end with Bertie sprawled across the middle. It was a huge sofa they'd bought as a wedding present, big enough to lie on together to watch television, but not so big that Bill or any of their other single friends at the time would see it as a spare bed.

'So, do you think I should send them my CV?' she asked.

'Up to you, Nat.'

'I know, but should I?'

Johnny put the job description down. His face was deliberately blank. 'It's a great opportunity. You've always wanted to lead a marketing team on your own, it's a small team in a bigger player, you like chocolate. Sounds like you made it up yourself.'

'I know.' Natalie pulled her lip. 'But didn't we agree I'd take six months out, you know, to calm everything down for the baby?'

'Didn't we just discover it's not going to be so simple? And that I'm the one who should be taking time off to get fixed?'

'Don't say that. You know it's not like that.' She nudged his thigh with her socked toe. 'Anyway, Dr Carthy hasn't had the second tests back yet, you don't know what he's going to say.'

Johnny gazed at her, mutinously. 'I think we do.'

There was no talking to him in this mood, she thought. Overnight, he seemed to have gone from imagining everything would be OK, somehow, to imagining that it was all over.

'Well, maybe I should go for it,' said Natalie, trying to play devil's advocate with herself. 'If it's going to take a while for us to get into the NHS system, maybe I should build up some maternity-leave entitlement?' She paused. 'The salary's not on there, but she sort of hinted it was more than I was getting before.'

'It's up to you, Nat.'

'Will you stop saying that?' She nudged him again, but harder. 'Johnny, this is serious, we need to talk about this properly. This isn't my job, this is our future.'

'Well, what if you said no?' Johnny turned his attention to Bertie's ears, which Natalie drew the line at cleaning. They got properly waxy and disgusting. He wound a wet wipe round his index finger and began to probe inside the long velvety flaps as Bertie squirmed with pleasure. 'We could manage for a bit. We've got your redundancy money, and my salary. And we don't go out any more now we've got this big lump.'

'Yeah,' said Natalie without much enthusiasm. 'Weren't we talking about investing that, though?'

'It's a time investment, giving you a break,' said Johnny. 'Look, we can manage. When you're on maternity leave we'll have to budget, anyway. Didn't you want to have a year off, at least, with the baby? You used to talk about being a full-time mum till he was at school.'

'Well, I'm not sure about that now.' Much as she loved Bertie, the routine of being stuck inside with him – not allowed in cafés, or shops, or libraries, or anywhere apart from Pet World – had burst Natalie's full-time childcare bubble a bit. And she could leave Bertie alone for up to two hours.

'We just have to cut back,' he said. 'People do.'

'Johnny, I don't want us to have a cutting back life.' Natalie shut her eyes and saw her one chance at a dream job hovering before her eyes and then vanishing, never to be offered again. 'I've always worked, I don't want to stop working! And if we can't have kids then I want us to have the best kind of . . .' She stopped, realising what she'd said. 'If it's not going to be *easy* for us to have kids,' she corrected herself, 'then it makes sense for me to earn what I can so we can save up and go private. Jump some queues.'

'I know what you're saying,' said Johnny stiffly. 'Don't sugarcoat it. I need all the medical help I can get to make you pregnant, so you've got to get out there and earn the money to pay for it – because mine isn't enough. Do you think you could have put that any worse?'

She reached out for his hands, but he refused to take any notice, instead dropping the waxy wet wipe on the floor and starting on the other ear. 'I didn't mean it like that. I just meant, I want us to be as happy as we can be.'

'And we're not now.' His voice was flat. 'And if we're not now . . .'

Natalie didn't reply immediately because she wasn't sure what she could say that wouldn't make it worse. She'd never had to tread on eggshells with Johnny before. It had always been him telling *her* it wasn't as bad as she thought.

'This isn't about money.' Natalie tried to look into his face, but his head was down. 'This is about me, and you, and what we actually want . . . Johnny, look at me. We really need to talk about this. How much do you want a baby? Because the conversations are going to get a lot harder than this.'

'I don't know what I want.' He stared into the garden that neither of them really knew how to look after. It was the garden that everyone else in their drive filled with trampolines and they'd filled with a ridiculously huge barbecue.

She took a deep breath and asked the question that had been hovering on her lips for weeks. The first domino in the line.

'Are you happy?' she asked, and slowly, to her horror, he shook his head.

Natalie bit her lip. She knew he wasn't. She wasn't – and it was her broodiness that had dragged them into this.

They sat in silence for a while, and then Johnny said, 'Have you really thought about what going back to work will mean?'

'Of course,' she began, but he interrupted.

'It's so obvious I can't believe you haven't said it.' Without speaking, he pointed downwards at Bertie's drowsy head.

'What's going to happen to him if you go back to work?' he half-whispered. 'I can't take him to school. We can't leave him here. He'll have to go back to the rescue. Soon, before he bonds any more with us.'

She looked up and met his eyes. They were full of tears, and she wasn't sure they were all for Bertie. Natalie knew Johnny was avoiding the real issue, but suddenly she wasn't sure any of it could be separated so easily. Bertie *was* their family now.

His houndy smell, the hairs she was constantly sweeping up, the snoring on their bed at night seemed to have been part of their house for ever. How could they send him back to the kennels now, believing that he'd let another family down? That he wasn't loveable? Just when his naughtiness had calmed down into low level mischief.

Natalie put her hand up to her mouth and tried to make herself think like the business professional she'd been – that she still was. But her heart was breaking, not least because she now found it impossible to separate sad-eyed Bertie and her equally sad-eyed husband.

'Nat,' Johnny began, 'I've been thinking, and . . .'

The front doorbell rang, and immediately Bertie sprang from his slumber, threw his head back and howled.

'What?' Natalie said, over the howling.

'It doesn't matter.' Johnny swung his legs off the sofa, but Natalie caught his arm.

'It does. That can wait. What were you going to say?'

Johnny shook his head. Bertie was sniffing the air now, as if he could identify the visitor through brick walls and the front door.

If it was someone from school or a charity collector Johnny would be there all night. Johnny was a polite chatter, whereas Natalie wasn't.

'I'll get it,' said Natalie, and went through to the hall.

When she opened the door, to her surprise she saw Rachel standing there with Gem at her side.

'Hi.' Rachel swept the thick black fringe out of her eyes, to reveal a tense expression that set Natalie on edge. 'Can I pop in for a moment? Is this a bad time?'

Natalie shook her head, trying to make her face seem normal. She really hoped Rachel hadn't come round to confide something pregnancy-related to her. That would be . . . She pushed away the shudder.

'No,' she said. 'It's fine. Come on in.' She opened the door further. Bertie didn't rush out to sniff Gem as he normally would. Instead he lurked behind Natalie's legs, like a shy toddler.

'Don't be silly, Bertie,' said Natalie, slightly embarrassed. 'It's Rachel. Sorry, Rachel.'

She stepped back to let her in, and Rachel and Gem went through to the kitchen, where Johnny was standing by the kettle, now beginning to boil.

'Have a seat,' said Natalie, getting out the biscuit tin. Bertie slunk into his kitchen beanbag and regarded Gem with suspicious eyes. 'So! Is it about the Open Day?'

Rachel sank onto a chair and looked between the pair of them. She put her elbows on the table and cupped her chin in her hands.

'I won't beat about the bush,' she said. 'I've had an enquiry from the website, about Bertie. Well, several, actually.' She tried a sad smile. 'He's a very popular dog – I put his profile on the internet two nights ago, and he's had more responses than any of the others.'

Natalie couldn't speak. Her hands gripped the biscuit tin.

'I've been in touch with everyone who's emailed,' Rachel went on. 'I wanted to check they were genuine before I told you, and I managed to weed out a couple of them with some Basset hound horror stories. I told them about him drooling on your laptop, and the food pinching.' Her eyes turned sad. 'But there's a couple with two other rescue Bassets who are pretty serious about adopting him. Big fields, company all day, plenty to sniff.'

'Sounds perfect,' said Johnny, in a hollow voice.

'I know. Anyway, they're going to come along to the dog show and meet him. I put them off until then, to be honest, so you'd have time to think about it.'

'Oh,' said Natalie, and her voice choked. She couldn't bear to look at him in his basket; she knew he was looking their way and listening. The eyes would be unbearable.

'I know you two love Bertie, but I couldn't say no.' Rachel looked wretched. 'I mean, if you're going to be going back to work, he'll be on his own.' She paused. 'You are going to go back to work, aren't you?'

Natalie bit her lip, wondering what the best thing to say was, just as Johnny blurted out, 'We don't know yet.'

She swung her head to look at him.

'Well, we don't, do we?' he repeated.

Rachel looked between the two of them, embarrassed. 'Sorry, did I get it wrong? I thought you were on sabbatical, Natalie. Has that changed?' She added a hopeful flick of her eyebrows, and Natalie knew what she meant: was she pregnant?

'I don't know,' said Natalie. 'Everything seems to be changing right now.'

The kettle finally finished boiling and Johnny made some tea, which filled the awkward silence.

'Milk? Sugar? Biscuit?' he asked, and Rachel murmured in reply.

So that's why the English are so addicted to tea-making, thought Natalie, bleakly. It fills in the need for hard answers. There was so much going on in her head that she couldn't work out which was most important: a baby, this job, Johnny,

Bertie, peace of mind, her career – which was supposed to take priority?

Could she go back to a twelve-hour day, where she'd have to work at full stretch for the first year to establish herself, knowing that she'd have to take time off to go through fertility treatment? Did she have the right to delay their fertility treatment for the sake of her career, knowing it would only get harder? What would that do to Johnny in the meantime?

Natalie couldn't stop herself: she turned her head and saw Bertie gazing at her from his basket. Her heart melted at the simple trust in his eyes and she felt torn between her responsibilities.

It's about making him happy, she reminded herself. These new owners are going to love him just as much as we are. I shouldn't give up my career for the sake of a dog I've only had for a few weeks.

But as she turned back to Rachel, a little voice in the back of Natalie's head muttered that it wasn't just Bertie she was getting upset about. It was something much bigger even than that.

# 24

Rachel knew she should have been making a pregnancy calendar, as recommended by the enthusiastic young midwife, but instead she found herself marking off the time by dogs rehomed, and new dogs brought in. It took her mind off all the things that could possibly be going wrong inside her, according to the internet, and also made her feel she was doing something useful with her time.

Between the day she called Val and the date they'd fixed for the 'meet the parents' dinner, she and Megan rehomed two of the Staffies, Treacle the chocolate Labrador, and Oskar the abandoned dachshund George had brought in.

In fact the little dachshund got the best home of the lot. He was too nervous to be put in a run with the other dogs so Rachel let him live in a big open crate by the office desk, where he'd always have company. The first time he saw Freda stomp in wearing her short red wellies, he'd scuttled in terror under a chair, but something in her voice obviously instinctively calmed him. By the time Freda tied on her scarf at the end of her shift, ready to drag Ted away from the café, Oskar had moved his hiding place to beneath her desk, where he observed her with his beady eyes, twinkling out from under his bushy eyebrows.

'Freda,' said Rachel. 'You know I don't make these sort of saddo dog comments very often, but I think I see a match here.'

'Oh, I don't know . . .' Freda began, but Rachel sensed a sort of glow around her face when she looked at Oskar's grizzly beard. And she could see Oskar glowing too. As if they already knew each other.

'Won't you think about fostering him, at least?' she went on, filled with a sudden need to put them together. 'He's his own man, like Pippin was, but he's happy to nap with you, and he'll keep you safe from all sorts. I think you'd make a lovely trio, you, Oskar and Ted. Ted can get some fresh air instead of slaving over a hot grill all day.'

'You tell Ted that.' Freda watched as Oskar sniffed her leg. His scabs were starting to clear up, thanks to the ointment Megan was diligently applying twice a day. 'Ted reckons if he retires, that'll be it. He'll just turn up his toes and leave some poor dog without a daddy. Not me, mind you,' she added. 'The poor dog. Doesn't want it to end up somewhere like this.'

Megan patted Freda's arm. 'George thinks Oskar's about ten already, and I reckon you've all got at least another five years in you. In fact, you know what George said to me? He said I should be running special retirement matching – one golden oldie with another.'

She nodded as Freda looked delightedly outraged. 'He said that? He called me a golden oldie? The cheek of him!'

'But, will you?' Rachel realised she was holding her breath just watching Oskar and Freda check each other out, seeing the smile form on Freda's face, and the confidence grow in Oskar. Suddenly she knew exactly why Dot had given up everything to do this. Matching one lonely person with one lonely dog was like creating your own happy ending out of real sadness.

'I'll speak to Ted,' said Freda, but Rachel knew from the motherly smile that she'd be telling her husband, not asking his opinion.

Megan cast a quick look in Rachel's direction and raised her thumbs under the desk, mouthing, 'Yay!' Rachel grinned back. It was a good feeling. It was the best thing she'd done for a long time.

'How about a cup of tea?' said Freda. 'I make it exactly tea time.'

Rachel checked her watch; it was three-thirty, although Freda worked on snack hours. 'Listen, you'll have to excuse me. My parents are coming tonight to stay this weekend, and I've promised to cook dinner.'

'But I thought we were going to go through the list of people to call about the sponsorship?'

Rachel and Natalie had tentatively fixed a date for the Open Day – a Saturday, in three weeks' time.

'Can we talk about that tomorrow?' said Rachel. 'You have no idea how long it's going to take me to make supper and then clean up the kitchen so that my mum can't *tell* how long it took me.'

'Special dinner, is it?' asked Freda.

'Um, yes. I'm inviting George over.'

Megan and Freda exchanged a quick glance.

'Meet the parents, is it?' Freda folded her arms across her bosom, and lifted Oskar up into her lap. 'I see! Shall I get a hat picked out?'

'No, no. It's not . . . it's not like that. Mum wants to see me, and the house, and I thought it would be good to show her round,' Rachel said hurriedly. 'And George is, you know, well, I mean, we are seeing each other. And . . .'

'I'll go out,' said Megan, decisively.

Ken and Val's estate car pulled up outside Four Oaks at seven on the dot, and Rachel rushed them through to the sitting room with big glasses of gin and tonic, leaving their bags in the hall.

She was irritated with George. He was late. He'd promised to be there as early as he could, but his mobile had been going straight to voicemail for nearly an hour. She'd had to squirt air freshener around the downstairs hall to mask the smell of dogs and burned toast from her first attempt at paté corners, and hadn't had enough time to make up the spare beds.

Luckily Val was more than happy to wander around the sitting room, picking things up and putting them down again with a murmur, and Ken seemed happy to browse through Dot's collection of old records, stacked in the drawing room, ready to go to whatever sale room Rachel could find to take them.

At ten to eight, Rachel was about to give up on the roast chicken that now looked more like crispy duck, and actually had the takeaway leaflet open by the phone when George appeared with a casserole under one arm, and a bottle of wine in the other hand.

'About time,' she hissed, letting him in and hustling him through to the kitchen.

'Good evening, George,' he replied. 'How lovely to see you! Is that the main course? Oh, you angel. I've burned the one I made.'

He hadn't had time to brush his hair after washing it, but he was wearing a new blue shirt, open at the neck, and his dark green cords. Privately, Rachel thought he looked like the archetypal Colin Firth-ish confirmed bachelor, but wasn't sure if the tieless, tousled look would play that well with Val. Amelia's husband, Paul, wore a suit to take the kids swimming.

'Let me get you a drink.' She followed him into the kitchen, where he put the tray straight into the oven, removing her hopeless attempt at a roast. 'You'll need one, my mum's already asking me where the cleaning materials are.'

'Calm down.' George put his hands on her arms. 'They're only people. And if need be, I have some animal relaxant in the car.'

Rachel gave him her best cynical raised eyebrow.

*    *    *

Even with two large gins on board, the conversation didn't exactly flow as Rachel had hoped. If anything, it made the gap between her and Ken's valiant attempts and Val and George's silences more noticeable. Neither she nor George were drinking. Rachel wished there was something pregnant women were allowed to knock back.

'So,' Ken made another desperate bid to fill the sound of clinking cutlery, 'lovely casserole, Rachel. Have you been on one of those posh cooking courses?'

Rachel tried not to catch George's eye, but he was nowhere near sniggering. His earlier good mood had vanished, though he'd remained very polite in the face of some inane questions from her mother, and now the line between his eyebrows had deepened. He kept checking his phone, to the point where she felt like grabbing it off him.

It's me, she thought, masochistically. He's looking at my mother and thinking, bollocks, how can I get out of this.

'No, I cannot tell a lie,' she said brightly. 'George made it. Game casserole – local pheasants, aren't they?'

'George cooked this? Valerie? Did you hear that?'

Ken was really trying, Rachel thought. She hammed along with him. 'See, Dad? A man who can cook. Not as rare as you'd think.'

Ken raised his glass a little. 'We should have a toast to the chef.'

'Mum,' prompted Rachel. 'Toast to the chef.' She raised her glass of elderflower water, and George acknowledged it with a half-smile.

'Very nice,' said Val. 'Unusual flavours.'

Rachel noticed she had picked out all the fragments of bone, and the carrots, and anything she didn't like the look of, making prissy piles at the side of her plate like an archaeologist.

'Well, I've had plenty of practice,' said George. 'You can't eat baked beans every night when you're a bachelor.'

There was a pause where Val's response should have been, but she said nothing, and instead directed a look across the table at Rachel.

Rachel wondered what on earth that was supposed to mean, and when her mother was going to launch the grandchild missile. So far, they'd avoided the matter completely, but it was hanging over the table, not so much like a giant elephant as a giant baby.

George suddenly shoved his chair back and pulled his phone out of his pocket, making Rachel jump.

'I'll have to get this,' said George. He was already rolling up his sleeves. 'My locum vet's covering my on-call tonight, but he did warn me that there might be a problem with a horse we're treating up in Hartley. Darren!'

His voice faded away as he went into the hall, but Rachel could tell by the brisk instructions that something was up. Or else he'd got one of the other vets to ring after eighty minutes to release him.

'He's very busy,' she explained, half-wishing she'd arranged the same thing with Megan and a 'stray dog'. 'It's a big practice.'

'Does he work most nights?' asked Ken, to fill in the silence.

Rachel nodded.

'So when do you see him?' Val asked.

'Couple of times a week. During the day. Actually, it suits us,' she said. 'I like to have my space, and so does he.'

'A couple of times a week?' echoed Val incredulously.

When you put it like that, Rachel thought, it did sound a bit . . . odd.

'Will he give you some extra nights when the baby arrives?' Val enquired.

'Mum! Of course.'

'I'm just saying. When you're not in a conventional relationship it's all the more important that these things are properly stated.'

'Yes,' said Rachel heavily. 'When the baby is born then George will either move in here, or I'll move in with him. But we haven't talked about that yet.'

'Why not?'

'Because I'm only seven weeks pregnant, Mum!' hissed Rachel. 'A lot can still go wrong! And there's no point in . . .'

'Ah, George!' Ken saved Rachel from saying any more. 'Everything OK?'

''Fraid not.' George was already pulling on his thick jacket. 'The hunter's taken a turn for the worse and I'm not sure Darren can really handle it on his own. I'm going to have to go up there and help him out. I'm sorry to run off but every minute's critical.'

By now Rachel was used to the sudden sea change in George's manner when there was an emergency with an animal but she could see her mother's face freeze.

'Good luck.' Ken got up and held out a hand. George shook it quickly. 'We'll see you again, I'm sure, before we go?'

'Yes. Probably.' George looked around for his keys, grabbed them, pressed a quick kiss on Rachel's cheek and headed for the door. 'Rachel's got some ice cream for pudding, can't go far wrong there. Bye!' He raised his broad hand and was gone.

They listened to the front door slam, and a stillness descended.

'Seems like a good chap,' said Ken. 'Can't turn down a man who can cook, eh? Is there any more of that casserole?'

'I'm glad you like him, Dad,' said Rachel, dishing out a second helping. 'Mum? You've been very quiet.'

Val put her fork down, and pursed her lips.

'Go on,' said Rachel. 'Whatever it is you're thinking, say it.'

'How well do you know him, really?' her mother asked.

'Enough! He's not married, he's not known locally for strange behaviour and he's kind to dumb animals. You should hear the girls at the rescue talking about him. And they're incredibly picky.'

She wanted to add, I thought I knew Oliver Wrigley for ten years and it turned out I'd barely scraped the bloody surface.

Her mother wasn't buying it. 'Rachel, I've read about men like that, in the *Mail.* What sort of man hasn't had a girlfriend in years? What sort of man doesn't want to settle down?'

'Valerie . . .' Ken turned to Rachel. 'She's very tired, love, it's been a long drive.'

'No, Dad, don't make excuses.' Rachel glared at her mother. At least it was getting it out of the way. 'I'll tell you what sort of man – a man who gets up at five to go lambing and doesn't get to bed until it's all done! And I'm sure he could be saying the same about me – but he isn't. I'm not exactly twenty-one myself.'

'Don't start on that, Rachel,' said Val. 'I've worried about you for years on that front.'

'So why aren't you happy now? What is it you want?' Rachel wasn't sure if it was the hormones or the stress of organising the fair, but all her emotions were prickling away just under her skin like tiny hot ants. 'I'm pregnant, I know who the father is, he's not married or unemployed or . . . or . . . weird.' She got up, and walked over to the Aga, so she could hang onto the rail. 'So he hasn't had a serious girlfriend. So what? Would you rather I'd got knocked up by some married man?'

Val flinched. 'You're going to have to stop all this drama queen business when you're a mother,' she pointed out. 'It won't all be about you then, you know.'

Rachel looked at her dad for help. 'Dad?'

'I think he seems like a nice chap, Rachel,' said Ken. 'I like him.'

'Have you asked anyone around here why he hasn't had a woman in his life?' Val hissed. 'Don't you think it's odd?'

'If you're hinting that he might be gay, Mum, I think the evidence to the contrary is staring you right in the face,' snapped Rachel. 'He didn't come after me with his AI kit, you know.'

'Maybe he just wants a housekeeper!'

'He's going a very complicated way around getting one – and one that can burn a boiled egg at that,' said Ken, in a jovial tone that only made Rachel and Val frown at him. He raised his hands. 'Sorry!'

'Why can't you be happy for me, Mum?' asked Rachel. 'It's done!'

'I'm not getting at you, love.' Val looked anguished. 'I just . . . Look at poor Dot! I couldn't bear it if that happened to you! It's bad enough that I let my own sister end up having her heart broken by a man who wouldn't commit himself. I said the wrong thing then, and—'

Rachel interrupted her. 'Oh, no. Dot did pretty well as far as I can see, Mum. Did you ever see her wardrobe? Or her jewellery box? She had a bloody good time, with a man who gave her diamonds, and *she* called off the wedding!'

'Wedding?' Val's eyes rounded.

'Yes, wedding.' Rachel couldn't believe that for the first time ever, she knew something about her family that her mother didn't. 'They were going to get married, and she called it off. I found a note from him, and the diamond necklace he was giving her as a wedding present. So don't blame poor Felix for being a weirdo bachelor, when it was Dot who decided she didn't fancy being married.'

Rachel was on a roll now, and missed the danger signals Ken was trying to telegraph. 'Maybe she was as selfish as everyone made out! Maybe she just didn't fancy being the same as everyone else. There's nothing wrong with being different.'

'What have you found?' demanded Val. She stood up, and for the first time in her life, Rachel saw her mother was really upset. Her shoulders were shaking under her best silk blouse. 'What have you read?'

'A note. A note from Felix. Why?'

'Vally,' said Ken. 'Don't start this. I've told you a million times, it had nothing to do with you, love.'

'It isn't always to do with you, Mum,' agreed Rachel. 'People are perfectly capable of screwing things up without your help.'

Valerie stared at her across the table, her mouth pinched at the corners. 'You're just like her, Rachel,' she said. 'You look just like her, and you sound just like her. I don't want you to end up like her, lonely and sad.'

'So why are you being so bloody mean now?' Rachel couldn't stop herself.

Val opened her mouth to say something, but a silent sob came out instead. She marched swiftly out of the kitchen, throwing her napkin down on the chair as she left.

'What did I say?' The fight seeped out of Rachel and she leaned wearily against the oven. She was getting tired all the time now. 'Dad, I know it's not how she imagined it would be but come on.'

'She's had a drink,' said Ken. 'And it's upsetting for her, this Dot business. You've got to remember, she blamed herself for most of it.'

'If someone would just tell me what that Dot business is, then maybe I could be more sensitive to it?'

Ken looked at her, then looked at the door. Then he patted the chair next to his and jerked his head towards it. Rachel went over and sat down.

'There's something you ought to know,' said Ken, very quietly. 'About Felix, and Dot. Your mother doesn't know, and I'm not sure she needs to.'

Rachel wondered how on earth her dad could know if her mum didn't, and prayed, hard, that it wasn't something to do with her.

'I don't know how to put this,' said Ken. 'And it was a very long time ago, but there was a good reason Dot didn't marry Felix.' He coughed, and paused, as if he was trying to get it all in an order he could understand. 'Felix and Dot – we didn't see much of them. Dot liked London, liked her life down there. Your mother never really understood that.' He looked at her, with a twinkle in his eye. 'Maybe you do, though.'

Rachel nodded.

'We heard a lot about Felix, mind – how good-looking he was, and what a nice house he had, how his family owned this, that and the other. I think Dot might have been a bit ashamed of us, being just simple Lancashire folk.' Ken went into his Northern self-parody voice. 'That was how your mother saw it, anyway. The only time Dot brought him home was Amelia's christening. They arrived in his lovely white Jag, looking like a pair of film stars. I think your mum was a bit put out by that, it being her day, so to speak, and you'd been playing up, so after the tea, she took you and Amelia home, and we stayed on at the hotel for a drink – me, Dot and Felix and some friends.' Ken looked nostalgic. 'I'll say this for Dot, she was laugh-a-minute in her day, and Felix had put some cash behind the bar, as a christening gift.'

'Bet Mum didn't like that either,' said Rachel. It was building up into quite a list.

He gave her an 'I won't disagree' look. 'Well, the afternoon wore on, and everyone had a few too many, shall we say. Towards the end, as we were all leaving, there was a bit of friendly hugging ...' Ken turned bright red. 'There's no nice way of putting this, Rachel, but when I went to spend a penny Felix made it clear enough that he'd be happy to take things a bit further than hugging. With me. Soon as I told him it wasn't on the cards, so to speak, he sobered up sharpish. Said he hadn't meant anything by it, but I could tell.'

'Dad!' breathed Rachel. She tried to picture her grey-haired dad back in his early thirties – he'd been a good-looking, football-playing pie-and-pint bloke. Not the sort of man who'd known much about that sort of thing; *women* probably rarely made passes at him.

'Don't get me wrong, I'm not saying I've got a problem with men like that.' He shot a quick glance towards the door, in case Val had reappeared. 'Each to his own, as they say. And he was mortified, poor sod. But I had to tell Dot. I thought she had a right to know, what with them going steady. I didn't want to see her getting hurt.'

'What did she say?' How plain-speaking Ken had engineered that conversation was beyond Rachel's imagination, but she loved her dad for doing what he thought was right, even though he probably wanted to wipe the whole incident from his brain.

Ken let out a sad breath. 'She said she'd known, deep down. There'd been something about him that she couldn't quite get to. She put it down to him being, you know, a bit posh. Buttoned-up. In fact, when she tackled him about it he admitted that he'd had these flings, with men, since he was at school – couldn't quite give them up. Even with Dot.'

'So what happened?'

'Well, you know what happened.' Ken looked uncomfortable. 'She told me he turned up with one of those emergency marriage licences and said she had to decide. If she could put up with him having the odd dalliance, he'd give her a lovely home, whatever she wanted. They could have had a very nice life. Felix did love her, you know. And she loved him.'

Rachel nodded. 'This note I found, it's so sad. It sounds like his heart is really breaking. But she said no? Did you ask her why?'

'Dot came up to see me one day, didn't tell your mother. We went out for lunch – her in big sunglasses like a film star

– and she told me she didn't want a marriage with secrets.' Rachel could see from Ken's wistful face that a little of Dot's London glamour had rubbed off on him that day. 'She didn't want to know who he'd been with, or what was going on, but she didn't want to *know* that she didn't know. If you get my meaning. She said she envied me and your mother, because we had a very boring marriage with no secrets whatsoever.' He smiled. 'I mean, she put it a bit more nicely than that. But that's what she meant.'

Rachel looked round the kitchen. Gem lay in a basket by the door, in the room where Dot had nursed discarded puppies and brought in starving strays, caring for them until she could put them back with an owner who'd love them. A simple match.

'Did Felix buy her this house then?'

'I suppose he did. I know he gave her an allowance until he died – she spent it on the dogs, not herself. But we didn't see much of Dot after that. I don't think she liked to be reminded, you know, of what had happened.' He gave her a long-suffering look. 'Your mother, of course, blames herself.'

Rachel rolled her eyes. Only Val could transpose the blame for Dot's decision not to marry a bisexual man onto some imagined fault of her own. 'Why?'

'Oh, something she said to Dot at the christening. She's never told me what it was. Says it's too embarrassing.' Ken balked at the contrast. 'Probably something about Dot's hat.'

'So why didn't you just tell her the truth?'

He raised his hands. 'Because I promised Dot I wouldn't. I know.' He deflected Rachel's accusing gaze. 'She made me swear I'd never tell a soul. For Felix, and for herself. She was quite proud, you know. I think she'd rather people thought she'd been selfish than know why she'd broken it off. And it wasn't up to me to tell.'

Nice one, Dot, thought Rachel, marvelling at the drama queen persona emerging from the placid dog-loving disguise. Plant a secret at the heart of my parents' nice transparent marriage, why don't you? But she didn't say it out loud.

'You could tell Mum now?' she suggested. 'Just so she doesn't spend the next thirty years wondering if Dot hid something in this house for me to find?'

'What? Tell her I kept it from her for over thirty years that her sister's boyfriend tried to grope me, and that I stopped Dot getting married? Do me a favour, love.' He paused, and looked at her meaningfully. 'Actually . . .'

'Oh, no,' said Rachel. 'No. Not you as well.'

Dad wanted her to tell Val. And so did Dot. *That* was the secret she'd left in the house for Rachel to find and share with Val, not with anyone else – the real reason for her lifelong spinsterhood, and the reason she hadn't spoken to her sister for the rest of her life.

Dot and Val. About as bad as each other, thought Rachel with exasperation.

'Please,' he said quietly. 'You can pretend you found something in a drawer. Some note she left for you, maybe?'

'But . . .' Rachel stuck her hands in her hair, 'Mum and I don't have those sorts of conversations, Dad. She only ever calls me to tell me to do stuff.'

'She's worried she's losing touch with you, Rachel,' he said. 'I know your mother's a bossy boots, but she means well, and she misses you. This baby – she won't say but she's over the moon inside. If she nags, it's only because she worries about you.'

'She doesn't need to worry,' Rachel protested. 'I'm a big girl! I'm nearly forty!'

Ken's eyes looked straight into hers, clear with fatherly adoration, and Rachel felt her chest tighten. 'You might be nearly forty, but you'll always be our little girl, Rachel. Our first little girl.'

If only he knew how little I felt now, she thought. How much I wish I could just bury my head in his chest and have all this go away.

Val's Clarks sandals clomped along the tiles outside the kitchen, and Gem's head sprang up from his sleeping position. Before Ken and Rachel could exchange glances, Val was back in the kitchen, pink lipstick refreshed, eyes bright with tears and fresh wipes.

'What are you two gabbing about?' she asked, in an upbeat voice that was meant to telegraph a total change of subject. 'And do you think George will be dropping back in for a cup of coffee after he's dealt with his horse?'

'I'll text him,' said Rachel, hearing her own voice mirror her mother's. 'You never know. Ice cream, Dad?'

'Lovely!' Ken smacked his knees, his usual sign that the tricky emotional stuff was over. He seemed relieved. 'Where's the loo in this place, Rachel? Excuse me, ladies.'

'Now then, I was looking at the wallpaper on the stairs.' Val launched into a helpful stream of advice about redecorating as Rachel picked Dot's china pudding bowls out of the crockery cupboard, but though she smiled, Rachel wasn't listening.

Instead, she was trying to imagine what it must have felt like, to hear the man you'd let inside your head, whom you thought you knew, tell you that he'd been someone different all the time. She probed her own heart. What if Oliver hadn't told her about Kath, for all those years? What if she'd discovered *that*?

In fact, Kath *had* known. She'd chosen to live with that bitter knowledge that Oliver loved someone else, in exchange for security, and a family. Wouldn't that erode your spirit, like battery acid?

It wasn't quite the same, she decided. What Felix had asked Dot to keep secret meant changing everything – including who *she* was. Someone who hadn't known her lover well enough to pick up on those secret needs. No wonder the shock of it had washed Dot up here, devastated and directionless. And she'd been younger than Rachel was now.

Maybe you never really knew people. Rachel laid Dot's silver spoons mechanically on the table. Mum wouldn't guess that Dad could have pulled a bloke, if he'd wanted to. Dad never knew his little girl had been some man's mistress for longer than Amelia had been married. Maybe Mum was right: George *could* be a closet bigamist for all she knew.

A shiver ran over her, not about George so much as for herself, and the future that she hadn't a clue about, with the baby she still couldn't quite believe would be here by Christmas. Dot had been right about this house being full of secrets. Four Oaks, if Felix had paid for it, was an enormous secret in itself. Maybe it would be better to sell it, and make the fresh start Dot should have made, instead of tying herself in knots trying to keep Dot's mad displacement passion going?

Val laid a hand over hers and Rachel looked down at it.

Her mother was smiling contritely. They were alike in that respect. Always sorry at once for their outbursts.

'Lots to think about, darling?' said Val.

Rachel nodded. She felt too tired to argue. 'Lots,' she said. And she managed a watery smile.

## 25

Rachel wasn't looking forward to finding 'a quiet moment' to talk to Val about Dot's painful family secret, but luckily, she didn't have to, thanks to the most frenetic Saturday the kennels had had in months.

The doorbell started ringing just after she'd finished making breakfast, when the first wave of dog walkers arrived, encouraged by the bright morning, and spring air. It didn't stop, and soon the kitchen was full of volunteers, all chatting and scoffing bacon sandwiches, which Val insisted on making, leading to some pointed jostling at the Aga with Freda, Queen of the Grill Pan.

To dispel the simmering tension, Rachel suggested that Ken and Val take Gem for a walk and when they'd gone, she started dealing with the queue of people waiting in the rescue office. Natalie's website had brought in a new batch of would-be rehomers wanting to meet the dogs and, while she and Megan chatted and discussed home checks, a heartbroken family turned up with their three terriers, in tears because their new council landlord refused to allow pets. Megan had only just calmed them down, when George arrived with a Yorkshire terrier that someone had abandoned outside the surgery.

He said he couldn't stay, despite Rachel's pleas.

'I'm only flying past on my way to a call-out.' He checked his watch, tension deepening the line between his eyebrows. 'I should really have sent Darren down with this one.'

'Can't you stay ten minutes? Mum and Dad'll be back soon.'

George pulled a face, and Rachel wished he had just a smattering of Oliver's people skills.

'My sister's had some crisis and they're going to have to leave earlier than they thought,' she went on, reluctant to tell him the truth – that she wanted to prove that he *did* put her before work. 'I know my mum would like to say goodbye.'

'You know I can't.' George looked tetchy. 'Rachel, there's a sick dog waiting for me. I can't tell the owners, sorry Tucker copped it, but I was making small talk about car restoration with my girlfriend's parents.'

'Well, if you put it like that, you'd better sod off now.' Rachel knew she was being unreasonable but something about the previous night had set her nerves twitching. She and George were just too used to being their own people to play happy families at such short notice. Maybe they'd never be able to.

He opened his mouth to say something, and then clearly thought better of it. A short silence opened up between them, and Rachel felt a twinge of regret that she didn't feel she could press him on it, in case it was something she didn't want to hear.

George didn't back down. 'Tell them I'm very sorry not to have seen them before they left,' he said courteously. 'But I'm sure I'll see them again. At your Open Day perhaps?'

'They're going to be in Mallorca.' Rachel paused, before adding, 'With Amelia and the children.'

'Oh.' He looked sympathetic for a second. 'Lovely. Anyway, I'll give you a ring. Are you doing anything tonight?'

'I'll see how I feel,' Rachel replied, before she could stop herself.

He flashed her an unreadable look, nodded at Megan, who had returned from checking in the new arrival, and left.

'What was that all about? He's a grumpy so-and-so.' Megan

handed Rachel a cardboard kennel tag, to go on the door of the Yorkie's new run. 'Can you write a good heart-rending message for Mitzi, please?'

'Mitzi?' Rachel sat down at the desk and got her marker pen out. She had to blink back tears and she wasn't sure why.

'All Yorkies are called Mitzi, it's the law. OK, how about: "I loved my humans, who fed me treats – but didn't clean my teeth! Then my teeth started hurting, and when they found out how much it was going to cost, they just dumped me at . . ."' Megan stopped. 'Sorry, is that too sad? Rachel, don't cry.'

Rachel wiped her streaming eyes with the back of her hand. 'It's not that, it's my stupid hormones.' She looked up from the desk, and decided that Megan needed to know. It was rude not to warn her about the horrendous mood swings if nothing else. 'You have to keep this quiet, but I'm pregnant. I'm having a baby.'

'I know what pregnant means.' Megan's eyes widened. 'Is it . . .'

'It's George's. Yes, it's a bit of a surprise.'

'That's *lovely* news.' Megan clasped her hands together, and looked as if she really meant it. 'That's so *great* for you, and for George!'

Rachel raised an eyebrow. 'It's early days. In every way.'

'You know, that totally restores my faith in whirlwind romance, and chances coming just when you'd given up,' said Megan. 'I mean,' she added, apologetically, 'for *George*. We'd all given up for George.'

'Yeah, right,' said Rachel, with a wry smile, and turned her attention back to making Mitzi's story good enough to bounce her straight into a new home.

In the end, Natalie sent in her CV to the dream chocolate job, but when she wasn't called in for an interview ('we had a fiercely competitive selection process') she wasn't as disappointed as she'd thought she'd be. In fact, a tiny part of her was relieved the decision had been made for her – for now, at least.

Maria Purcell from the recruitment agency wasn't overly concerned, although she did ring while Natalie was out with the dog to suggest that she come into the offices 'for a follow-up meeting, to assess our strategy going forward'.

'That's a great idea,' Natalie had said, with one eye on Bertie's slobbery jaws. 'Um, I'm about to go on holiday for a fortnight, so maybe we should liaise when we get back?'

She knew, even as she said it, that Maria's eyes would be narrowing with suspicion, but she didn't care: she needed more time to work out what she wanted to do. Johnny was no help; in fact, he'd refused to offer any advice about anything – keeping Bertie, her going back to work, going on the IVF waiting list. It was all up to her, apparently. She was the only one who deserved to make decisions.

Johnny's sudden and horribly uncharacteristic slump into apathy had started when he'd decided on the morning of the appointment that he didn't want to go for the fertility consultation at the hospital, and no amount of pleading could persuade him otherwise.

'What more do I need to know?' he'd whined. 'My sperm's rubbish. Face it. I'm trying to.' And then his expression had turned stony and he'd refused to discuss it further, storming off to school with a face that had probably scared his first three classes into total silence. Natalie had stared at the door for five minutes after he'd gone and then she'd lain on the sofa and cried until Bertie scrambled up next to her, and licked the tears off her face.

With Johnny refusing to discuss treatments or even consultations, there didn't seem much point carrying on with her 'baby sabbatical' plan. It seemed so indulgent now. So, she reckoned sadly, she might as well call Maria Purcell back and get her career back in gear.

She kept her voice professionally breezy until the call was over, and then hung up with a sigh. Bertie had bounced up onto the park bench next to her, ignoring her attempts to remove him, and was now burying his head in her bag, in search of KitKats.

Natalie leaned back and gazed across the canal, where a swan was escorting a flotilla of dusty cygnets towards a lock she'd never known was there until she'd started walking Bertie along the towpath.

I'm going to miss this, she thought, with a pang. It wasn't like being on holiday any more – it was like having a different sort of life.

Walking Bertie had opened her eyes to the town she thought she knew back to front. Their strolls had taken her past elegant Georgian villas, houses with faded adverts for bakeries and coachbuilders still in the brickwork, pretty bridges over abandoned railway lines, a hidden church hall, and a community of nice old people who'd almost become familiar faces as she and Bertie had passed them, day after day. Natalie wondered how she'd ever found time to think properly before she had an hour to march around the footpaths, letting her mind turn over the problems as her feet followed the yellow footpath arrows.

Bertie's head emerged, triumphantly, from her bag; he'd found the sock Johnny had hidden in there, to 'train' his tracking abilities, back in the early days when they both believed Bertie could be persuaded into advanced canine skills.

'That's two weeks old, Bertie,' she pointed out, removing it from his mouth, and felt a tug of sadness, remembering how she and Johnny had held hands as they strolled through the park, and watched their dog potter on ahead of them. A family.

Bertie gazed up at her with eyes that melted her heart, every time. He was trying so hard, and she was going to have to give him back too. Life was bloody unfair sometimes.

Back in the main square, Rachel was having another meeting with Gerald Flint at the solicitor's office, in which he was 'tidying up' the loose ends from the probate process. It seemed to have taken for ever to Rachel, but Gerald seemed pleased about how quickly everything had progressed.

He was even more impressed about how promptly she'd sent off the cheque for the first bit of the inheritance tax to get probate moving, but then he hadn't had Val nagging him about divvying up the contents of the house to deserving relatives and redoing the bathroom decor.

'It was lucky you had some savings to fall back on,' he said, when she glossed over how she'd raised the money. 'We tend to advise clients to make arrangements, so their benefactors aren't embarrassed. But that was Dorothy, I suppose. Every penny spent on the dogs.'

'Mm,' said Rachel.

Dot *had* left arrangements, albeit – typically, Rachel now realised – complicated, secret ones that required day trips to London jewellers. In addition to the necklace, Rachel had also sold a ring she'd bought for her thirtieth birthday, a flashy 'I don't care that I'm not married' sapphire she'd bought in a fit of self-pity, and some tiny diamond studs Oliver had given her. They were the only jewellery he'd ever given her, in fact, and so they'd been harder to give up, but Rachel wanted to disguise Dot's necklace among her own pieces, in case any questions were asked. One unfaithful lover's gift was as good as the next, after all.

'We can try to negotiate with the Inland Revenue about a timeline for the rest of your liability,' Gerald went on, 'but it might help to discuss what your plans are. Do you want to sell the house, or maybe some of the land? If you're intending to stay.' He paused. 'I don't mean to rush you into anything, but these processes can take a while. You could be looking at a good year or so, given the state of the current market.'

A year? I'll have a newborn baby by then, thought Rachel. That put things in a different light, all of a sudden. If she wanted to make a fresh start somewhere else, she'd have to decide fast, so she wouldn't be trying to juggle estate agents, movers and midwives all at the same time.

Still, no more agonising over Heals or Liberty for Christmas decorations this year, she thought.

'I don't know if it helps – and this is off the record,' said Gerald, hesitantly. 'But the agent who valued the land, nice chap, handles a lot of the larger estates locally, did ask me if I thought you were planning on selling. He has a client on his who'd be interested in buying the whole place outright. He's looking for a big family house, with outbuildings for studios, and a bit of land for privacy. Cash buyer, I should think. Worth bearing in mind, maybe? That house needs a fair bit doing to it, going by the survey, and to be honest, why take on the stress if you don't need to?'

'That's quite a tempting option.' Even the idea of arranging decorators made her exhausted right now. 'Maybe I should take his card?'

'It's good to have options,' said Gerald, searching out the agent's details. 'You could parcel off some land, but given that you don't have any connections here, I'd be inclined to sell the lot and start again with a tidy sum in your back pocket.'

Rachel toyed with the mental image of a lovely cottage somewhere, mortgage-free, and money in the bank to tide her over for a while. In all honesty, she couldn't make up her mind what she wanted – some mornings she woke desperate for her old life, some nights she went to bed buoyant with happiness at the thought of one more dog and one more new owner neatly matched up. It was impossible to work out which reaction was real and which was hormones, when even the sound of birdsong could reduce her to tears.

'I need some time to think,' she said. 'I've been run off my feet arranging our Open Day. Well,' she added, in the spirit of honesty, 'I've had a lot of help. It's been one pile of admin after another, but hopefully it should kickstart the kennel business for Megan. Then if I do decide to sell, it's a going concern.'

'Ah, yes!' Gerald's face lit up. 'The Open Day! Our secretary had a letter from ... is it Natalie, your new sponsorship director?'

Rachel nodded. 'Natalie's our new kennel director, full stop.'

She wasn't sure she'd be half as far on with the Open Day without Natalie's feverish intervention. She'd breezed through the insurance admin, and the permissions, and sent off for all the details about registering as a charity 'if it made life easier'. Rachel wasn't sure how it could, but Natalie seemed to relish the challenge. 'Can we count on Flint & Sunderland to sponsor a kennel? Or a dog bowl with your name on it, for a year's tinned tripe?'

'Ha! Seems appropriate for a firm of solicitors. Yes, I should think we'll be in touch about that. Only right, since I've had so many happy years with my two.'

Gerald always seemed to come to life when she got him onto the topic of dogs, Rachel thought. The stuffed shirt turned quite avuncular. The more she got to know about the dog world of Longhampton the more it seemed like a canine version of the Masons. Everyone knew everyone.

'And I got my letter from Megan too,' he went on. 'Or should I say, Molly and Spry got their letter from Gem!'

'Right,' said Rachel, less confidently. She hadn't had a chance to check over Megan's letters, but she'd noticed there was a paw-print stamp on the office desk, which made her suspect the worst.

While she and Natalie were sorting out the sponsorship/ kennel promotion, Megan had offered to get in touch with the various rehomers who'd taken on Four Oaks dogs over the years, inviting them to support the day. All their details were on handwritten files in the office, usually with photos and Christmas cards clipped to them.

'I always said, if Dot Mossop could have matched up people the way she matched up dogs and humans, we'd all have been queuing up the road.' He beamed. 'We'll be there – this Saturday, is it?'

Rachel flinched. Four days off, and there was still an enormous amount to do. 'Yes,' she said bravely. 'Shall I put you down for the Waggiest Tail competition?'

'Absolutely.' Gerald paused for maximum comic effect. 'And you can put the dogs down too!'

'Not literally, I hope,' joked Rachel.

Gerald looked confused, then guffawed. 'No! Very good! No, certainly not!'

Oh, my God, thought Rachel. Now I'm even doing dog jokes. The end is nigh.

Zoe's contribution to the Open Day planning was to find a local celebrity judge for the various competitions. She secured the services of the Lady Mayoress, while she was safely trapped under the colour heat lamp: Mrs Haileybury was delighted to help, even though she was 'more of a cat person'.

Zoe was beginning to think that she could easily become more of a cat person, too. After a long, long day at work, in which two staff were off sick and she was too soft to say no to their clients, Toffee had decided to shred her one good pair of shoes, and Leo had started scratching his head with a depressingly familiar concentration that she'd seen before, during the Great Nit Plague of last summer. Spencer's stroppy mood hadn't let up, and she was finding it harder and harder to keep her cool.

She knew she should have started making Leo and Toffee's fancy-dress costume earlier than the night before, but that was just the kind of week it had been. And like a guided missile, Spencer chose the half-hour before bath and bed to deliver his latest bombshell.

'Daddy says we're going on a summer camp for our holidays, in America.'

Zoe looked up from the leftover hen night bunny ears she was adjusting for Toffee to wear in his fancy-dress role as a rabbit. It wasn't the most genius idea she'd ever had, but funds were tight. Leo didn't mind putting on the cute paisley waistcoat he'd worn for her sister's wedding to go as a conjuror, and Toffee's costume had to be chew-proof, pee-proof and ideally Leo-proof.

'Mummy?' he said again, in case she hadn't heard. 'Daddy's taking us to Florida for our holidays.'

'Really?' she said evenly.

'Yes. It's a special one for kids and dads.' Spencer announced it in the same smug voice that David had probably used to tell him. 'It's got log flumes and a special area for skateboards, and you can eat barbecue every night.'

'When did he tell you this?' Zoe concentrated on stitching the elastic onto the headband. Florida. *Florida*! Either David was so gripped by the credit crunch that he couldn't pay child support, or he wasn't.

Or Jennifer was underwriting the holiday in an attempt to make her sons love her. She blanched.

'Last weekend. When we saw him.'

'Well, summer holidays are still a few months away, Spencer. Daddy needs to discuss it with me.' She tried to seem positive. 'We were going to go to Cornwall, weren't we? That'll be fun, won't it? Toffee's going to *love* the beach. He can't go on the plane, can he?'

Spencer tossed his head. 'Toffee can stay here with you. We're going to Florida with Daddy. Cornwall's *rubbish* compared to America. I'm not going. I *refuse*.'

Something in Spencer's tone startled Leo, who glanced up fearfully from his Dr Who figurines. He began collecting the plastic Daleks and Cybermen, putting them in a safe pile behind the big Tardis. It was from a different play set and looked ominous next to the figures.

Zoe forced herself to breathe slowly. For a seven-year-old, Spencer had developed a scarily teenage attitude all of a sudden. She knew he was trying to provoke her into calling David to sort it out, and bringing them together even if it was just to tell him off, but that didn't make his rudeness any easier to ignore. Spencer seemed to have an unerring knack of hitting her right where she felt sorest.

Much like David and his outrageous expensive holiday bribes.

'Spencer,' she said, 'I make the decisions in this house. Daddy should have discussed this with me before he told you – it might not fit in with our plans.'

He looked at her fiercely. 'Me and Leo are going to Florida and you can't stop us.'

'I can.' Don't get into a fight with your own son, Zoe told herself.

'You can't. I'll run away. I've got my bag.'

'Don't be silly.' She shot a quick look at Leo, who had now pulled out the bottom of his t-shirt like an apron, and was hiding his Daleks in there, curling his arm around them. 'Spencer, why don't you show me how you're going to lead Toffee around the ring tomorrow?' She tried her best to smile. 'What are you going to wear? Your special football top?'

'If you loved us, you'd take us to Florida too,' shouted Spencer, his face red with fury. He glared at Zoe as if he was about to run off, then suddenly he marched over to the sofa where Toffee was sleeping, shoved the startled dog onto the floor and ran upstairs.

'Spencer!' Zoe was across the room in a flash. Toffee wasn't the small puppy he'd been when he'd arrived, and he landed with a thump on one of the big floor cushions the boys lounged on to watch television. He didn't seem to be hurt, but he was confused and upset. Zoe picked him up to soothe him, and felt his heart banging hard against his ribcage. So was hers.

Leo began to grizzle anxiously. 'Why is Spencer shouting? Why did he hurt Toffee?'

'He hasn't hurt Toffee, darling,' said Zoe, reaching out to hold Leo with her spare arm. She pulled him in towards her. 'Look, he's fine, aren't you, Toffee?'

Toffee wriggled as Leo tried to stroke his black nose and Zoe struggled to keep her cool. What was she supposed to do first? Discipline Spencer? Run Toffee up to the vet's? Convince poor worried Leo that World War Three wasn't breaking out in their house? It was too much to deal with on her own. The pressure of being Mum and Dad and everything else crushed her for a second, but she pushed it away for later.

'Leo, why don't you put Toffee in his basket for two minutes, while I go upstairs and talk to Spencer?' she said, trying to guesstimate how long she could leave the two of them alone. 'Don't let him chew anything and if he starts whining, call me.'

She ran upstairs two at a time and yanked at the bedroom door, but Spencer was holding it shut.

'Spencer, I am so disappointed with you.' Zoe said, through the door. 'You could have really hurt Toffee!'

'Don't care.'

'I don't think I can let you lead Toffee in the dog show tomorrow,' she said, determined to punish him for the way he'd hurt the little dog. 'He's going to be very scared of you, if you won't apologise. I'll have to let Leo do it instead.'

'Don't care.'

'Fine,' said Zoe, and leaned her forehead against the door, pleased that Spencer couldn't see how beaten she felt.

She didn't know what else to say. This was going to go on for the next ten years. She closed her eyes and imagined how nice it would be to have that time in her day that had been dog walking with Bill again – not for any romance, just for the reassurance that there were some things she could still get right.

'Muuuuuum!' Leo's voice floated up the stairs, and Zoe pushed herself away from the door and went to deal with the next set of crises.

# 26

As soon as Bertie got a whiff of bacon sandwiches he was almost impossible to keep on his lead, and nearly dragged Natalie across the car park towards the house. She didn't like to think what he would do when Freda's bacon grill got going.

'Johnny! Johnny, you're going to have to take him for a walk, wear him out a bit!' she gasped, trying to keep hold of the extendable lead. 'Just don't let him roll in anything. I want him to be nice and clean for as long as possible.'

Although they'd bathed Bertie first thing that morning, all ready for meeting his new full-time parents, a sneaky part of Natalie hoped he would roll in something so disgusting they'd be put off by his filth, and decide to go for something smaller and more hygenic.

'Do you think he knows?' Johnny gazed at Bertie forlornly. 'Can he tell?'

'No,' said Natalie, more to cheer Johnny up than because she believed it. 'Course he can't.'

'Do you remember the first few times we walked up here with him, he got all whimpery and thought we were bringing him back?' Johnny looked nearly as miserable as the Basset hound. 'And now he's fine?

'Johnny, let's not go through this again,' said Natalie. 'Please. Go on, give him a good long trot. You'll both feel better for it.'

'Are you going to come with us?' He didn't say, 'for our last walk,' but it hung in the air.

Natalie tried to sound more determined than she felt. 'I can't. There's loads to do – I've got to make sure the sponsorship packs are all finished, and there's enough leaflets and stuff.' She tried not to look at Bertie, and his beautiful velvet ears that she could arrange on his face like eye masks. 'Just give him a quick once around the orchard and then down that bridlepath towards the woods. Don't go down the hill to the park – he'll just get over-excited.'

'OK,' said Johnny, and clicked his tongue at Bertie. When that didn't work, he rattled the bag of treats in his pocket, and Bertie trotted obediently after him, his white tail arched like a question mark above his long back.

Natalie watched until they were out of sight, and then sighed, and headed for Rachel's HQ – the house kitchen.

It was even more of a hive of activity than normal. All dogs had been banned, for a start, and several sad pairs of eyes peered forlornly through the baby gate to the annexe, including Gem. Freda was making a massive catering pot of tea and bacon sandwiches for everyone, while Rachel, in jeans and a black t-shirt and some incredible vintage jacket, issued instructions to the volunteers. Natalie recognised Ted, Freda's husband, as well as the regular sixth-formers from the school, and Lauren from the surgery.

Bill was standing by the counter, going through a first-aid kit so old Natalie half-expected to see leeches coming out of it.

'Morning!' she said, and Rachel whipped round. Her dark eyes were ringed with shadows and she looked as if she'd been up all night.

'Brilliant. You're here. We're just missing Zoe now.'

Natalie caught Bill's eye, and he turned a faint shade of pink. She wondered what was going on there; he hadn't mentioned seeing Zoe for a while, after talking about her more than she'd ever heard him talk about a girlfriend, and she'd been too distracted by her own problems to ask. Natalie made a mental note to get him on his own and see if there was anything she could do. After all, it was partly her fault that they'd had that awkward moment with the dogs.

'What can I do?' she asked.

Rachel looked harassed. 'I don't know. Everything? I was up until two this morning, washing bloody dogs and sweeping out the kennels. I can't remember what my own middle name is.'

'Let me see.' Natalie stepped forward, took the clipboard out of Rachel's hand and started moving everyone around like planes on a runway. At least it would stop her thinking about Bertie.

At eleven, the sun came out, and by midday, people began arriving, despite Rachel's panic that it would just be the ten of them eating their way through a metric ton of bacon.

Natalie did her best to calm her down, but she sensed something jittery about Rachel from the moment she arrived.

'Are you feeling all right?' she asked, when they were on their own, checking the kennels. So the dogs wouldn't be distressed by too many visitors, the plan was for Megan and Rachel to take turns showing potential local donors around in shifts, and serious cleaning had been done to make the runs sponsor-worthy.

'I'm just . . . under pressure,' said Rachel. She hesitated, and Natalie knew she didn't want to bring her pregnancy into it.

'Are you still feeling sick?' she asked bravely. 'You must be coming up to three months now, aren't you?'

Rachel looked grateful, and Natalie felt a bittersweet sadness that she'd gained a friend, but one who'd never understand how hard it was to be around her.

'Sick? I don't have time to be sick. I'm panicking I haven't done enough here,' Rachel said. 'I don't have Dot's touch with the dogs, if it all kicks off. I'm not a businesswoman like you, and I worry my sums are wrong. I don't know what I'm doing half the time. It's like a weird dream, where the dogs'll start talking, and then I'll wake up back in London.'

Natalie touched her arm reassuringly. As usual Rachel looked cool in her jeans but she could see the t-shirt was pulled over the unfastened top button.

'You're not on your own. It's going to be a huge success,' she said. 'I have my reputation as a marketing manager staked on this.'

Rachel's eyes clouded.

'You've done your best,' Natalie went on. 'Just wait until five-thirty, when we're back in here, counting the takings, eh?'

She seemed to pull herself together at that. 'Yes,' she said, with a crooked smile. 'Five-thirty, drinks all round. Apart from me, obviously.'

Natalie stood by the gate to the orchard, welcoming visitors in, handing them the short leaflet about the kennels and the rescue, and soon there was a healthy stream of dogs and their owners, some of whom actually recognised her from her daily rounds with Bertie.

The orchard looked gorgeous, with most of the trees covered in foamy blossom, and underneath them was a modest selection of stalls – a cake stall, a raffle, a table with all Dot's leaflets about dog care, now updated by Rachel, some doggie stuff donated by the pet store, face painting and mini grooming (dogs only) run by the students, and a table with cups on for the Fun Dog Show.

According to the entry forms Megan had pinned to the trees, there would be classes for Waggiest Tail, Dog Most Like Owner, Fancy Dress Pairs, Handsomest Dog, Prettiest Bitch, Guess the Weight of the Dog, and Best Friends.

Bertie could win at least three of those classes, Natalie thought, and pencilled in his name next to Waggiest Tail, Handsomest

Dog and Best Friends. She paused over Dog Most Like Owner and decided to risk it, if only to force a smile out of Johnny. There was no sign of him and Bertie, but Natalie assumed he'd taken off on a long walk, if it was going to be a farewell one.

She took out her mobile to check if he'd rung, but there was nothing. As she was dialling his number to see where he'd got to, Megan waved at her from over by Freda's catering table, and Natalie knew at once from the two people standing by her side what she wanted her for.

They looked like nice people. That was even worse.

She took a deep breath and went across to say hello, plastering her happy face over the new aching in her chest.

'Natalie! There's someone here I'd like you to meet?' Megan smiled as she pointed to the couple who shook her hand eagerly. 'This is Adam, and this is Paula. This is Natalie, who's been the most amazing foster mum to Bertie for the last few months.'

'Oh, he's been very easy,' said Natalie. 'He's such a lovely, lovely dog.'

'He's a cuddle bug,' agreed Megan. 'We can't understand how anyone could have thrown him out!'

'He is naughty, though,' Natalie added, before she could stop herself. 'He's worked out how to open our fridge. And he howls like you wouldn't believe. And he'd sleep in bed with you if he could.'

'Nat!' Megan gave her a sideways look. 'Don't put them off!'

'Well, we're used to Bassets,' said Adam. He rolled his eyes. 'We know all about the fox poo and the deafness and the hairs everywhere.'

'We've got two others,' his wife explained. 'Wouldn't have any other kind of dog now! They're such characters.'

'But good for you, fostering,' Adam went on. 'I couldn't do that. Our house would be full of rescue dogs in a month! I wouldn't be able to hand them over to the new owners!'

'Natalie and Johnny are very special people,' said Megan quickly. 'I think they'd keep him, given half a chance.'

'We would,' said Natalie. 'Like a shot. Um, Bertie's with my husband at the moment – I sent them off for a quick walk and they've been gone ages. Shall I ring them?'

'Please!' said Paula. She looked genuinely excited. 'We can't wait to meet him.'

Natalie's heart sank as she imagined Bertie in the back of their car, driving off to his new life, leaving his empty basket behind in their kitchen.

'We'll just mill around here,' said Megan. 'Come and find us when you track them down?'

'I won't be long,' said Natalie, and slipped off into the crowd, where they wouldn't see the pain on her face.

'You might have to hold these on, Leo. Toffee, sit! Sit, please!'

Zoe was trying to make Toffee's rabbit ears stay on his head when she heard a familiar voice behind her.

'That is the best rabbit and magician I have *ever* seen!'

She turned round awkwardly, since she was crouching on her heels at Toffee height. Bill was standing behind her, with Lulu on a smart new silver lead. She looked freshly clipped, as if she was going to Crufts even if the rest of them were slumming it.

'You know what you need, don't you?' he went on, smiling down at Leo, who gazed in awe at the very tall man above him. 'You need . . . this!'

He whisked a white handkerchief out of his back pocket and handed it very solemnly to Leo.

'Say thank you,' prompted Zoe.

'Thank you,' said Leo, obediently.

'Muuum,' whined Spencer. 'I want an ice cream.'

'Not now, Spencer,' she said in a firm Toffee-training tone. 'Leo's about to go and do his competition. We'll get ice cream when we're all ready.'

'Give me the money and I'll go on my own.'

'No.' Zoe glared at him, then glanced up at Bill. The last thing she wanted was for Spencer to throw a wobbler now. 'Just wait.'

'How are you?' Bill asked. 'Lulu and I have missed your company at lunchtime.'

'Oh, I've been rushed off my feet. Bit of nice weather and everyone wants their highlights doing.' Maybe it was the spring sunshine filtering through the blossom, but Zoe felt as if the air around them was suddenly warmer. She'd forgotten how much she liked just standing next to Bill. His easy company made her feel younger and less frazzled.

The megaphone crackled and Megan's voice boomed out over the orchard. 'Would all entrants for the Fancy Dress Pairs please make their way over here? Cheers!'

Zoe began to lead Leo by the hand, but he shook her off. 'I want to go on my own,' he announced. 'I'm a big boy.'

'No, you're not, you're just a baby,' snotted Spencer, and Zoe gave him her hardest, scariest stare, to which he responded by shoving his tongue under his lower lip.

Don't rise to it, she told herself. Ignore the bad, reward the good.

'Go on, Leo.' Zoe gave him a little push. 'We'll be watching you from right here! Good luck!'

She and Bill watched as Leo wove his way across to Megan, who welcomed him and Toffee with open arms and a little round of applause.

'I think he's a shoo-in,' said Bill, nudging her, and little sparks of electricity shot down her arm where his shirt touched her bare skin.

She glanced down and saw Spencer staring sulkily around the field, then asked Bill how things were going with his plan to get the patients dog walking to health. They chatted away easily, and then clapped heartily when Leo and Toffee took first prize from the Lady Mayoress against a boxer who'd come as a Dalmatian, two clowns and Superman.

'Ice creams all round, I reckon,' said Bill.

'Yes, ice creams! What kind do you want, Spencer?' Zoe turned round when he didn't answer. 'Spencer?'

He wasn't behind her any more.

Oh, for God's sake, she thought, crossly. He's wandered off.

It was another of Spencer's new range of irritating tricks to wind her up: drifting away in supermarkets or shops to do his own thing, leaving her breathless with panic. It was irritating because it worked every single time, and every single time, when she found him, he did his 'Muuuum, I was only reading the magazines/looking at the dog/picking my nose' whine.

'Problem?' asked Bill as Leo came bounding across to them, with Toffee in hot pursuit, minus his bunny-girl ears.

'Spencer. He's gone to get his own ice cream, I think.' She grimaced apologetically. 'Sorry, he's going through an arsey phase.'

Bill looked around the orchard. 'Get used to it. I understand it lasts about fifteen to eighty years with average males. Do you want me to stay here in case he gets back?'

'Would you?' Zoe was relieved at the casual way Bill offered. 'I won't be long. Here, take Toffee's lead. Can I get you anything?'

'Chocolate and a flake.' Bill winked at Leo, who was looking askance as Toffee sniffed around Lulu. 'Don't worry, Leo, they're old friends.'

'Come on, you.' Zoe picked Leo up. Baby or not, she wanted to get back before Spencer reappeared and started giving Bill the worst possible impression of her family.

Natalie tried Johnny's mobile, but he didn't answer, and then she found herself distracted by two charming ladies from the bakery by the town hall, who were awfully keen to sponsor a kennel, so long as it was just used for German shepherd dogs.

By the time she'd shown them round, and explained about the random selection box of dogs the rescue cared for, there was still no sign of Bertie and Johnny, and she walked down to the bottom of the orchard to get better reception. Before she could dial she spotted Johnny coming up from the footpath, and waved to get his attention.

As he came nearer, she realised he was on his own. No Bertie. Her heart sank and she rushed over.

'What's the matter?'

Johnny's face was red, and beads of sweat stood out on his forehead. 'I've lost him.' He bent over, his hands on his knees, panting.

'What?'

'I've lost Bertie. I let him off the lead, just for a second, to have a pee in that thickety bit at the end of the orchard, and he must have smelled something because he . . . vanished.' Natalie could tell he was panicking. 'One moment he was there, the next all I could see was his tail, and then nothing! He must have smelled a hare, or something.'

Natalie felt sick. Bertie looked like a couch potato but when he decided to move, there was no way of keeping up with him. He could vanish in the woods in seconds.

'Did you call for him?'

'Did I call for him? Of course I bloody called for him.' Johnny looked despairingly at her. 'But come on, Nat – you know what his recall's like. Zero, unless you can make the noise of a roast chicken.'

'That's not funny. What were you thinking? I never ever let him off where I can't see him.' Natalie grabbed her head. 'How big is that wood? It's massive.' Collingdale Wood stretched all the way back from Four Oaks towards Rosehill, with the big dual carriageway on one side. But there was a wall, Natalie reasoned, and fields on the other side – he'd have to run a long way to get onto a main road.

But the wood itself was huge. A horrible thought suddenly struck her. 'It's got traps in it, hasn't it? And rabbit holes. Jesus, Jon, what if he's gone down a hole and got stuck? Or put his nose near a rabbit trap?' Her voice cracked and she had to cover her mouth. She knew she was over-reacting but the combination of the past few months' tension and fear for unsuspecting, curious Bertie was unbearable.

Johnny put his hands on her arms. 'Look, don't panic. We'll find him.'

'Don't tell Megan. She's with the couple who want to adopt him. They're looking for us now! Oh God; what if he's hurt? How will we find him?'

'Natalie.' Johnny shook her gently. 'This is Bertie. He'll probably run around the wood for half an hour, get covered in deer shit, and then head back to the kennel for a bacon sandwich.'

'Maybe we should look there.' Natalie started walking, then stopped. 'Johnny . . .'

She was about to say, please let's keep him. Please don't let him go.

He stopped, his face red. 'What? We're wasting time.'

'Nothing,' she said and carried on.


When Spencer had been gone for half an hour, and Zoe had done four laps of the orchard with Leo and Toffee in tow, her annoyance started to take on a sharper edge of panic.

'Are you *sure* you don't know where he might have gone?' she asked Leo, for the tenth time. There were so many people and dogs milling around now that it was hard to see if Spencer was just lurking behind a tree. 'He didn't say anything about wanting to go into town, did he? He hasn't walked down there on his own?'

Leo bit his lip and wouldn't look at her. Zoe dropped down next to him, wrapping Toffee's lead around her wrist so he couldn't escape.

'Tell me, Leelee,' she soothed. 'I won't be cross.'

'Spencer said last night he was going to see Daddy but I thought he meant next week. Not now.' Leo started to go red. 'I didn't think he meant now. How will he find Daddy? Daddy isn't here! And he took the bag with Toffee's things in it.'

Oh shit, thought Zoe. She straightened up and tried not to let Leo see how rattled she was. Spencer could have gone out of the gate, through the garden and down to the town, or he could have headed across the open fields.

He was too smart to get into anyone's car, she told herself. But if he was planning to go all the way to David's?

'I think we need to start looking a bit harder for him,' she said. 'Naughty Spencer – he's going to make poor Toffee miss his special class!'

'Naughty Spencer,' agreed Leo, and grabbed hold of her hand as if he was scared she was going to leave too.

'Let's see.' Zoe searched the crowd for Megan's blonde plaits, and spotted her over by the leaflet stand, cooing over a fierce black Scottish terrier that looked like a giant Hitler moustache. 'Why don't we find Megan and show her your lovely costume?'

She marched over so quickly Toffee and Leo could barely keep up, and arrived just as Megan was rapidly withdrawing her hand from the dog. 'Megan, can you mind Leo for five minutes?'

'What's up?' Megan shook her fingers and put on a brave smile.

Zoe dropped her voice. 'Spencer's vanished. I've got to tell Rachel so she can make an announcement or something but I don't want Leo to get worried. Can you distract him?'

'Oh no!' Megan's eyes rounded. 'Course! But he'll turn up, Zoe – he can't have gone far. Do you want me to send one of the hounds after him? They'll pick up his scent! Might be quite interesting to see how quickly they find him.'

'No! He'll be terrified! It's my own fault. I was talking to Bill and he was pestering me and I told him he'd have to wait and to stop being a pain! Because I wanted to talk to Bill!' Zoe gulped. 'I'm a terrible mum. I put my own stupid crushes before . . .'

Megan grabbed her arm. 'Zoe, that's ridiculous – you're allowed to have friends, for God's sake. Is this going to happen every time you meet some new bloke? It's boundaries again. Spencer's got to know you love him, but you can't put up with him flouncing about for attention. You wouldn't let Toffee howl or pee for attention, would you?'

Zoe shook her head miserably.

'Well, then. Find him, and tell him, really calmly. Now then, Leo Graham!' she said, changing her voice. 'I hear there's a Guess the Weight of the Dog competition going on, and I need a dog expert! Can you help me?'

She led Leo away towards the enormous St Bernard sitting patiently next to Natalie's sponsorship table, and Zoe made a beeline for Rachel and her microphone, her heart threatening to force its way up her throat.


Bertie wasn't in the kennels.

He wasn't by the bacon sandwich stall either, or anywhere in the house.

Natalie was frantic, and she could tell Johnny was just as upset, even if he was trying to do his usual calm-in-a-crisis teacher thing. He kept telling her to stop panicking, but he was chewing his hangnails and frowning when he thought she wasn't looking.

'The best thing we can do is to go back down to the woods,' he said, leading her along the side track so Megan wouldn't spot them without Bertie. 'It's the last place he saw me, and he might be able to smell us.'

Natalie didn't want to tell him that the guides she'd read warned that once Bassets got their noses down, they didn't look up until the scent went dead, by which time they were miles away. 'But what if he's lost?'

'He's not lost, he's just off for a run, in broad daylight, a couple of miles from his own house!' Johnny said, putting an arm around her as they stumbled over the molehills. 'Come on, Nat, he doesn't *know* his new parents are here. Stop thinking he's packed his little knapsack and run away.'

As soon as Johnny said it, Natalie couldn't help imagining Bertie's bewildered face as they handed him over, and she let out a racking sob.

'Natalie, I love him too, but he's a *dog* . . .'

'It's not just Bertie.' The dog was just the final straw at the end of a long chain of miserable what-ifs. 'It's *everything*!'

'What everything?' asked Johnny.

She stared at him, unable to believe he was still pretending not to know. 'Everything we're not talking about! My job, our baby, your sperm tests. Everything! There's all this going on, but you're making me make the decisions, and I can't stand it any more.' She waved her hands around frantically. 'Do we keep Bertie? Do I go back to work? Do we sign up for IVF? And you're like, "It's up to you, Nat." It feels like last month I knew everything there was to know about you, and now . . . Now you're like a stranger who won't tell me what's going on in his head! You lie there next to me every night, but it's like you're miles away.'

'Don't.' Johnny started to turn his head away, but Natalie wouldn't let him.

'You've got to snap out of this, Johnny. Otherwise we might as well not bother!' Natalie wasn't sure where it came from, but she realised she meant it.

That jerked a reaction out of him. 'What?' he demanded.

'I mean . . .' Natalie stared at her husband, seeing him for the first time as a grown man, not the gangling sixth-former he still was in her mind's eye. This was the man she'd promised to spend the rest of her life with – the silent, troubled man, not the hopeful teen who thought everything would work out. He'd gone for ever, after the first sperm test. Natalie wasn't sure she knew this new Johnny.

'I mean, I don't know what you want any more,' she said.

'You don't know what I want.'

'No.' She shook her head, feeling that they were standing at a junction, where one careless word could send them hurtling down the wrong path, with no way back.

This is the worst possible time to be discussing this, she thought, her nerves jangling – Bertie could be getting away, lying hurt somewhere, but if we let this conversation go bad, or if I stop him now he's finally talking, it could end everything. Adrenalin was surging through her so hard her fingers were twitching.

Johnny stared out towards the wood, and then turned back to her. His face was grim, and scared. 'All I've ever wanted is *you*,' he said. 'You and a family. I thought it would just happen, like us getting married, us getting jobs. I've been so lucky. And now I can't give you a baby, I'm bloody petrified about what happens next. That's why I don't want to talk about it, all right?'

'What did you think I was going to say?' Natalie demanded.

'That you wanted out,' he said simply. 'To find someone better. Someone richer. Someone who can let you stay off work for ever, looking after his dog and having babies and being the one thing that makes him rush home every night. Instead . . .' He took a gulp of air. 'Instead, I'm just an inarticulate sod with inadequate sperm, who can't even tell you how shit he feels. I know you're too kind to leave so I was thinking that . . .' Johnny blinked. 'That maybe I should be the one to set you free to find someone else.'

'What?' Now Natalie was stunned. 'Have you gone mad? Is that what you've been thinking?'

He nodded, unable to speak.

'Don't be so bloody stupid!' Natalie flung her arms round Johnny's sturdy neck and stretched onto her toes to look him right in the face. Just the idea of what he'd been working out in his head, shuffling out into the cold like a penguin sacrificing itself for the rest of the nest, made her want to cry. 'You're all I've ever wanted – and if we don't have babies, we don't have babies, Johnny. I'm not going to leave you, and everything we've got, because of something we *don't* have. That's ridiculous.'

'It's too much to ask,' he mumbled. 'I can't let you make that sacrifice for the rest of your life. For me.'

Natalie stared fiercely at him. Her toes ached from standing on them, but she didn't care. 'It's not a sacrifice. It's what I want. And if you'd asked me, I'd have told you that. Why didn't you ask?'

'It's hard.' Johnny's face twisted with shame. 'It's just so hard to talk about. For a man.'

'Johnny, no one has everything. We have a *lot*. And I tell you something else,' she went on, barely knowing where the words were coming from, 'I'm taking the rest of that sabbatical. I'm going to find out everything I possibly can about low sperm count problems and we're going to get help. And we're not giving Bertie back either.'

'But what about your job?' Johnny looked confused but relieved.

'We'll work something out.' Natalie felt her whole self lift up as Johnny suddenly put his arms around her and hugged her tightly to him. 'Now, I don't want to sound panicky,' she added into his ear, as he kissed her hair and neck. 'But we've still got to find our dog.'

He let go at once, his face serious. 'Right. He might have found his way out by now.'

They set off at an urgent trot towards the wood, Johnny calling Bill on his mobile as they went. The main track split into two paths, down each side of the trees, and as they approached it, Johnny pointed towards the left.

'You head down that path and I'll carry on along the main track. You've got his whistle, haven't you?'

Natalie nodded, although Bertie hadn't responded to it ever. Her spirits sank as she strode across the rutted ground, sweeping the undergrowth for signs of a white tail or brown ears. Branches scratched at her arms and legs, but she barely noticed.

'Bertie! Bertie!' she yelled in between blasts of the whistle. She could hear Johnny yelling on the other side, through the pine trees, and horrible images crowded into her mind.

Just let him be safe, she thought, as tears coursed down her face. If Bertie's safe, then things will be OK. Johnny and I will be OK, if he just comes back.

It felt as if she'd been walking and yelling for hours when suddenly she saw a flash of white and brown in a clearing, and something clicked inside her.

'Johnny! Over here!' she screamed, crashing through the undergrowth. If that was Bertie he wasn't moving, and as she got closer, Natalie's relief curdled into horror; there was a sticky red trail of gore plastered over the snowy whiteness of his throat and muzzle.

# 27

Natalie didn't know how she scrambled so fast across the bushes, but she couldn't get to her dog fast enough.

As she got closer, she realised that he wasn't on his own.

Bertie was lying down next to a boy, who was sobbing miserably – big chest-aching sobs that shook his small frame. His bare arms and legs were covered in scratches, and he cradled Bertie's big head on his lap for comfort. The blood all over Bertie's mouth and nose didn't seem to have come from any bite on the child's body, and the way he was hugging the dog didn't suggest Bertie had attacked him.

Oh, my God, thought Natalie. He must have put his nose in a trap and broken it! She couldn't imagine what sort of agony the poor creature must be in.

The Basset was lying quite still, but when he saw Natalie, his tail gave a faint wag. It wasn't his usual sofa-thumping strength, and she wished passionately that she could have the pain instead of him.

Natalie fell to her knees next to Bertie and the little boy. She couldn't help it; her instinct was to comfort the dog first, pressing her head close to his, and reaching out for the boy at the same time. He threw himself into her side, clinging on tight with both arms. He seemed familiar – Natalie racked her brains as to where she'd seen him before. At the kennels?

'Is he OK? Are you OK?' Natalie choked back her tears. Bertie! What had happened? What had this poor kid seen? 'It's all right, it's all right. Shh . . .'

Johnny charged breathlessly through the undergrowth, and a few seconds later Bill came running over, with Lulu following, bouncing over the branches like a fluffy deer.

When the boy saw Bill, he started crying even harder.

'It's OK, Spencer,' said Bill, kneeling down next to him. Gently, he moved Natalie aside, ostensibly so he could examine the boy, but really so Johnny could examine Bertie without Natalie seeing. 'No need for the waterworks, chap. Are you hurt? Or just a bit scratched up?'

Johnny was leaning over the dog now, trying to shield him from Natalie's view. 'Don't look, Nat,' he said. 'Look after Spencer.'

'I want to see!' she sobbed. 'What's wrong with him, Johnny? Should I call the vet?' She pulled out her mobile with shaking hands. 'He's down there now . . . Oh God, I don't have George's number.'

'What happened to Bertie, Spencer?' asked Bill, in the calm doctor voice. 'Did you see?'

'He chased me.' Spencer hiccupped so hard he could barely breathe. 'And then I fell over. And then he tried to get in my bag, and he . . . he . . .'

'Natalie,' Johnny began, in a serious voice. 'You need to see this.'

'And then he ate my sandwich!' Spencer dissolved into tears, looked up tragically at Bill, and then vomited copiously all over him.

Johnny held up two large bacon sandwich wrappers, both smeared with the tomato sauce that was now coating Bertie's white bib. 'You're going to have to teach Bertie better table manners if we're going to keep him, Nat,' he said gently. 'But ten out of ten for his acting.'

Zoe's mobile rang just after Megan had asked everyone there to look for a seven-year-old in a white 'Ben 10' t-shirt.

'Are you missing a son?' Bill asked.

Zoe could have fallen to her knees with relief. He gave her directions and she hurtled down the path to the woods, where she met Bill, Johnny, Natalie and Spencer coming out, with Lulu and a sheepish Bertie in tow.

Natalie and Johnny looked drained, and Bill was covered in vomit, all over his new shirt and jeans and suede trainers. Spencer, on the other hand, had one small splash of puke on his t-shirt.

'Oh, my God, what happened?' she cried.

'Spencer. We think you've eaten something you shouldn't have, don't we?' Bill turned his head sideways to check Spencer's expression, and Zoe couldn't help thinking that he was even more amazing, covered in sick. 'Some berries, did we think they were? And you were a bit upset too.'

Spencer nodded unhappily.

'But we're going to get you back to the surgery and checked out,' Bill went on, apparently unconcerned about the state of his clothes. 'With the special vomit tester.'

Spencer's face picked up a bit at that.

'What did you eat?' Zoe asked anxiously. 'Didn't I tell you we don't eat things off the ground, Spencer?' She was trying not to cry, but the sheer relief of finding him safe was making it very hard. 'I was so worried!'

She held out her arms, and he ran into them, shoving his head under her arm with puppyish malcoordination. When they'd hugged enough for Zoe to regain control of her face, she held him a little way from her, so he could see how worried she'd been. 'Where were you going, Spencer? What were you doing in the woods?

His lip wobbled, then wobbled harder. 'He ate my bacon sandwich! Both of them, and I had none to take with me!'

Natalie crouched down and put her arm round Zoe's heaving shoulders.

'We think what happened was that Spencer had *very sensibly* decided that if he was going to run away, he'd need some supplies.' Natalie's voice was matter-of-fact, like Bill's. 'So he'd got two bacon sandwiches from Freda, and put them in his bag, but we know someone else who likes bacon sandwiches and going for a wander around, don't we?' She glared at Bertie. 'Someone who thinks it's OK to put his head in other people's bags and have a rootle? He must have wandered around the orchard, found Spencer and followed the scent of bacon.'

Bertie said nothing, but Zoe could see the traces of tomato ketchup on his jaws and the faintly guilty air.

'Anyway, we'll leave you to it. We need to get back to Rachel.' Natalie exchanged a meaningful glance with Johnny. 'We need to talk to her and Megan about something.'

'Thanks,' said Zoe. 'I owe you two an ice cream. And you,' she added to Bill, trying not to notice the mess her son had made of his shirt. By the way Natalie and Johnny were staring at him, even they seemed shocked that he wasn't making more of a fuss about it.

'Can we get an ice cream?' asked Spencer hopefully.

Zoe steeled herself. She knew she had to face the troubles her baby boy was struggling with, even if she wasn't sure how to fix them. She wanted him to know she was trying. 'Won't be a moment, I just need to have a quick word . . .'

'Sure,' said Bill, embarrassed. He waved the lead at the black poodle. 'Lulu! Lulu, come here!'

'Spencer, look at me.' Zoe lifted his chin up, so he could see her face, and how upset she was. 'What's all this about? Why were you running away?'

Now it was just them, his bravado fell apart. 'I don't know what I did.' He buried his face in her shoulder and she could barely make out the words.

'When?'

'What I did that Daddy doesn't want to live with me and Leo. Why he only wants to see us at the weekends.' He lifted his streaky face up, and she could tell he'd been wrestling adult logic as best he could. 'Callum from school says Jennifer's going to be our new mummy. And you're going to find a new daddy, and then you'll only want us at the weekends and where will me and Leo go?'

Zoe's heart broke. 'No,' she said. 'No, no, no, no, no. That's never *ever* going to happen.'

'Why can't we be a proper family?' His mouth turned upside down, like a cartoon dog.

'We are a proper family.' Zoe pulled Spencer onto her knee, and hugged him hard. 'Me and you and Leo and Toffee. And then Daddy and . . .' she made herself say it, for his sake, 'Jennifer. Families are people who love you! And we all love you.'

'Are you going to get us a new daddy?' He looked at her with his clear eyes, and Zoe felt the terrifying mother love pulling them together like magnets. Spencer would always be able to look right into her head.

She remembered something her mum had once told her, when Spencer was very little – that she should be careful what she said in front of him, because kids stored up remarks like a tape recorder.

'You've only got one daddy, and that's Daddy,' she said. 'But one day, I might meet someone special, and he might want to come and live with us. But he would have to love you just as much as he loved me, because you and me and Leo and Toffee, we're a team, aren't we?' She squeezed him again. 'Aren't we?'

Spencer nodded.

'And you'll always be my special big boy. And Leo's best friend. And now Toffee's best friend too.'

She looked over Spencer's head and saw that Bill was still hovering by the tree, pretending to train Lulu with some biscuit or other. While they'd been talking he'd wiped some of the sick off his shirt with grass, but Zoe felt bad for his nice shoes, the ones he'd probably only got so he could ask her opinion about them.

He'll never get the smell of sick out of the suede now, she thought. You never knew sick-removal tips until you had kids.

Bill let Lulu jump for the treat, then smiled, tentatively, raising his eyebrows as if to say, 'All OK?'

What kind of man let your son puke all over him, and then hung around to escort him back to the surgery? The sort that probably wasn't going to mess you and your family around, even if they didn't have much track record by way of childcare.

'How's your tummy?' she asked Spencer. 'Shall we go with Bill to the surgery and get you checked out?'

'I'm hungry,' said Spencer. 'Can we get some ice cream? Why does his dog look like a sheep? Why is it so fuzzy? Bill says Lulu is a friend of Toffee's and that you go out walking the dogs on Saturday when me and Leo are at football. Is that right? Can we come too? Actually, can I have another sandwich?'

Zoe stood up, and Bill immediately came over.

'I think he's recovered,' said Zoe. 'Enough to want a replacement bacon roll, anyway.'

'Do you want a lift back?' enquired Bill, and as Spencer nodded, he bent down and swung him onto his shoulders – a brave move, Zoe thought, given Spencer's nervous stomach. Spencer let out a quick squeal of delight, and grabbed hold of Bill's curly hair.

'I'd like a sandwich too,' said Bill. 'And a bath.'

'I'll wash your clothes,' said Zoe. 'I'm so sorry, it's the least I can do.'

Bill glanced at her, and Zoe was pleased Spencer was too busy shouting at Lulu to see the mischievous look that passed between them.

'You can't keep dropping things off at the surgery,' he said. 'Flowers are one thing, but a shirt? People will talk.'

'Good,' said Zoe, and kept her eyes firmly forward as they headed back towards the orchard.

If being rushed off her feet meant the day was going well, Rachel reckoned that her blistered heels made it a raging success.

There was a lot of interest in Four Oaks' official boarding facilities, but it was the rescue that everyone wanted to see. Megan had arranged short visits, so as not to over-excite the dogs, and they'd been taking it in turns to show people round, explaining how it worked, and tugging shamelessly at the heartstrings.

Much to Rachel's relief, the dogs had been great – they were getting short walks around the orchard with the volunteers, proudly sporting 'I need a home' leads – and the little tags on the kennels were almost worn out with reading.

Natalie had vanished unexpectedly, and Rachel had to handle most of the sponsorship-pushing herself. Despite her worries that she didn't have Natalie's knack, it had gone really well, and she'd found herself answering all sorts of doggie questions she'd normally have palmed off onto Megan. They'd run out of sponsorship forms by two o'clock, and Rachel had dashed into the office to print out some more, so great was the demand. By half three, ten out of the fifteen rescue runs were spoken for, and they'd had promises of supplies, transport, newspapers, foster homes, homecheckers – it was overwhelming.

The only fly in Rachel's ointment was that George hadn't appeared. He'd sent Darren, the graduate vet so newly qualified he looked about twelve, to act as the emergency services, and though Darren had come equipped with a donation cheque from Fenwick Armstrong Associates, Rachel wasn't impressed. She wanted his time, not his money.

It would have been nice, she thought crossly, if George had been there to back them up. He wasn't to know how much hung on today – but then maybe that was the point. She had to make a decision to go or stay based on real life, not on best behaviour.

'He's probably on call,' said Megan, reading her mind as they finished showing out a team from the council, who were 'more than satisfied with the new arrangements'. 'I'm sure he'll get here as soon as he can.' She let Yoshi, one of the newest Jack Russells, out and popped a lead on her. 'Now I've got Freda matched up with Oskar, my next target's George and one of these lads. Easy to pop in a Barbour pocket, don't you think?' She lifted the little white terrier up to demonstrate, and it licked her ear eagerly.

'George says he doesn't have time for a dog.'

'Yeah, right. 'Course he does. That's just what he used to say to Dot when she tried to set him up with untrained dogs. He got into the habit of saying no.' Megan put Yoshi down and looked at Rachel. 'If he's going to have a baby, he can have a dog, right? You can look after another.'

Rachel twisted up the corner of her mouth. There was something plain-speaking about Megan that she felt inordinately grateful for, when everyone else was tiptoeing around her hormonal outbreaks.

'Doesn't that break our own rule about rehoming dogs to pregnant women?'

'Gem'll keep any new dog in line.' She hesitated. 'Don't take this the wrong way, but the thing you've got to remember about George is that he's been his own boss for so long, and you get into habits when you're on your own. Dot used to say that to me. You suit yourself, because it's easier. He's a great guy and you're a great couple, but he's going to need house-breaking.'

Rachel sighed and put a hand on her tiny bump, which she hoped the jeans weren't making too obvious. 'I don't have time to house-break a man. I need a fully trained one. Now.'

'Good job you're trained yourself,' said Megan. 'Listen, I need to scoot, I've got something really cool to arrange. Are you going to be outside in about quarter of an hour?'

'I can be.'

Megan beamed with delight. 'Coolio. Can I borrow Gem?'

Gem was sitting in the office basket, his head on his paws, waiting for the next instruction. As Megan spoke, his ears pricked and he leaped to his feet and followed her out.

Rachel checked her clipboard and wandered over to the fire doors, to look in on the dogs. She didn't have any tours booked in for twenty minutes, the runs looked clean and the phone wasn't ringing.

God, I am exhausted, she thought suddenly. How am I going to cope when I'm properly staggering around with a bump? And then a baby? Why can't someone come and look after me, as well as the bloody stray dogs?

'Cup of tea,' she said aloud to dispel the rising panic.

'How kind of you to ask!' said a familiar voice. 'Milk, no sugar.'

Rachel spun round so fast she nearly lost her balance.

Standing behind her, looking utterly incongruous in his grey suit and handmade shoes next to the sacks of kibble, was Oliver.

'What the hell are you doing here?' she demanded.

It wasn't the opening gambit in any of the monologues she'd rehearsed with Gem, but it was the one that sprang to her lips first.

To his credit, Oliver didn't flinch. 'I've come to rescue you. This *is* a rescue shelter?'

Rachel's treacherous heart thumped hard in her chest as longing flooded over her. Oliver in a suit. His jaw clean-shaven and his hair freshly cut by some Chelsea stylist. His dark eyes contrite and hopeful in his handsome face and his hand – she swallowed – he was stretching out his hand to her, and the wedding ring that had mocked her for years had gone from his finger.

He's a total rat, she reminded herself. He cheated on boring Kath, he cheated on you, he's having a midlife crisis and *he never really loved you.*

'What if I don't need rescuing?' she managed, forcing herself to stay cool.

Oliver dropped his hand. 'Then maybe you can rescue me,' he said smoothly. 'I've come to apologise.'

'Go on then.'

He looked slightly surprised by her attitude, but carried on, 'I've been incredibly stupid. I can't explain what happened to me these last few months, but I'm over it now. You brought me to my senses and I'm so sorry for everything.'

'Is *Tara* aware of that?'

He raised an eyebrow, then realised she knew everything. 'She's . . . not in the picture any more.'

There was a short silence, but Oliver stepped in to fill it, like the skilful presenter he was. 'I know I can't ask you to forget what happened, but I hope one day you'll be able to forgive me.'

'And Kath?'

'Kath's not in it for forgiveness. She's getting my house, my children and half my business, so if anything she ought to be sending you some flowers as a thank you.'

'I can't just pretend nothing happened, Oliver.' Rachel leaned against the table. Her legs had gone weak. 'I've been through the worst time of my life. I lost everything! My home, my job, the love of my life—'

Damn, she thought, as soon as she said it. He'll love that. I shouldn't have given him that.

'I know,' he said, 'and that's why I've come. I want to put things right again. I've had to sell the agency – solicitor's advice, don't ask – and I want to set up again, on my own. I only want the best team around me, and so I wondered – can I offer you a job?'

Rachel stared at him, astonished by his chutzpah. He was appealing to her professional pride. As if that mattered more to her than her broken heart.

'You're the best PR I know,' he went on, 'regardless of your other qualities. I can double your salary straight away, and make you a director.' Oliver took a step closer and Rachel could smell his expensive cologne. Her head began to spin. 'But what I really want, what I can't even hope for, is that maybe you might consider coming back to me as well. Not as my office wife, but as . . . well, as my home wife too.' He gazed into her eyes, and Rachel's resistance slipped even further. 'I know I've behaved appallingly, but it was the wake-up call I needed, Rachel. And now I'm free, Kath's off my case – we can make a proper new start together.'

'I . . .' Rachel didn't know what to say. Too many things were racing across her mind, not all of them as honest as she'd have liked.

Already the weight of responsibility was lifting off her weary shoulders as his familiar magic snaked around her, and into her resistance, like smoke. Oliver would look after her, he was old-fashioned like that. Kath had never worked in all the years they'd been married. And the baby . . . Maybe it *was* Oliver's. She hadn't had any tests done or anything – there was an outside chance *his* condom could have failed, not George's.

George would probably be relieved, argued the sneaky voice. He didn't want his bachelor life screwed up by an accidental baby and a woman he didn't really know. It was kinder all round to leave now. Neater for everyone.

'I want you to come back,' said Oliver, as if he could hear the sneaky voice. He took a step closer and put his hands on her arms. It was a soft, romantic gesture, not a cheap grab; Rachel knew he knew her too well. And he played the trump card he'd held back for years, the one he only brought out at absolute catastrophe points. 'I love you, Rachel.'

Rachel wanted to scream about how much he'd hurt her, but she was too spellbound to speak. Oliver always knew how to charm her, and now he was clearly pulling out all the stops. Because he *wanted* her. She couldn't deny how flattering it was.

'Do you have any idea what you did to me?' she began, but from the look on Oliver's face, she knew he saw it as a prelude to a 'yes'.

The fire doors to the kennel office banged suddenly.

'Rachel! I'm really sorry I'm late, I've been at a calving bloodbath up at . . . Oh.'

She stepped back from Oliver as if an electric shock had gone through her.

George was standing at the door with a dark expression creasing his honest face. He nearly filled it with his burly frame, especially with his working jacket on, still stained with mud and other noxious substances.

*He's so much taller than Oliver,* though Rachel, distractedly. *Or rather, Oliver's so much smaller than George.*

'Sorry to interrupt,' he went on stiffly. 'Megan wants you to come outside. She's got something she needs you for.'

Rachel glanced at Oliver, who was managing to look as if he was the one at home in the office, not George.

'Oliver, this is George Fenwick, our vet. George, this is Oliver Wrigley. My . . .' The second the words left her lips, Rachel knew she'd made a horrible mistake and now George's wounded eyes confirmed it.

'Her old flame,' added Oliver, with a confident smile. 'Lovely to meet you.'

George didn't bother to reply. 'Our vet,' he repeated. 'Right. Well, *your vet* is happy to hear things are going so well here, so I'll be off. I'll leave that ear ointment with Darren.'

He nodded, and left, before Rachel could stop him.

'Are all country men as terse as that?' asked Oliver, amused. 'No wonder you get so much done – no time wasted on idle chit-chat round here.' He reached out for her again, this time bypassing her arms and going straight for her waist, pulling her close enough to kiss. As he touched her t-shirt, and felt the extra few inches underneath, his smile increased. 'Now where were we? I see rural life agrees with you too . . .'

His hands squeezed her stomach and Rachel suddenly felt like she was betraying not only George but the baby as well. 'There's something else,' she said, forcing out the words before she could think. 'I'm pregnant.'

Oliver took it in his stride. 'OK. That's unexpected. When were you planning on telling me that?'

'I don't know.' Rachel knew she was wading into dangerous waters now. He knew far more about children than she did. Dates, times, development. He had three, after all. She pulled away. 'Oliver, I can't get my head around it all.'

'I understand.' His voice was soothing. 'But you're not on your own now. Say the word, and we can be out of here. I've got solicitors who can tidy up any deals in forty-eight hours. Leave everything to the dogs if you want.'

It was a smart touch. That would balance the emotional guilt scales, she thought.

'I need to be outside. Megan's got some display going on,' she said, playing for time. 'Come on and meet our rescue pups, they're lovely.'

'I didn't think you were a dog person,' he said, gingerly picking his way through the kennels to the orchard door. The remaining Jack Russells growled as he went past, and Rachel had to shush them.

'No, I didn't think I was either. But you change, don't you?'
She blinked as they stepped into the bright May sunshine,
and saw Megan at the far end of the orchard, with a huge
crowd of dogs and owners behind her.

When she saw Rachel, she raised the megaphone to her lips
and started talking. Her Aussie accent sounded even stronger,
wobbled through the amplification.

'Thank you all for coming this afternoon to support our
rescue operation! This is the most important part of today's
events – the Grand Reunion! But first, I'd like to introduce
you to our president, Rachel Fielding, who is the niece of our
founder and an old friend of many of you, Dorothy Mossop.
Rachel?'

She beckoned her over, and self-consciously Rachel walked
across the space Megan had cleared.

'What is this?' she hissed.

Megan winked and raised the loud hailer. 'These are just
some of the friends who Dot put together over the years, and
they wanted to come and say thanks for their second chances.
Without Dot's love and commitment, most of these dogs
would have been put to sleep at the pound, or left to starve
on the streets. So please can I have a round of applause for
Gerald Flint, with Spry and Molly . . .'

*Oh, God*, thought Rachel, shrieking inside. I don't have time
for this. I don't have time to look at *dogs* when I should be in
an office, with Oliver, working out what to do with the rest of
my life! Her nails dug into her palms as she clenched her fists
tight.

But Megan was looking at her expectantly, and she forced a
smile onto her face, and watched as first Gerald walked past,
looking weekend casual in beige slacks and a Cotton Traders
polo shirt, proudly leading two beautiful blue-roan spaniels.
He smiled as he passed her, and she could see how the dogs
changed his whole manner.

'Bridget Armstrong and Muffin! Jim and Lesley Horrocks, with Richard and Judy! Gavin and Kaden Laine, and Marley!' A grey-haired lady and a tubby Labrador were followed by an old couple with two bouncy crossbreeds, and a young man with a small boy and a collie cross.

Rachel's hands began to unclench as she took in the happy smiles directed at her. The people kept on coming, like a walk past of veterans. Old dogs, young dogs, three-legged dogs, each one led by an owner beaming with pride.

As she was watching, one old lady with a Maltese terrier dropped out of line and approached her.

'Here you go,' said the old lady. She pressed a twenty-pound note and a sponsorship form into Rachel's hand.

'What's this for?'

'I can't give you a lot,' she said, 'but it's to buy pig's ears. I had my Kipper from Dot, and he was the best friend I ever had. Sweet as you like. Never a bark out of line, even when he was right at the end.'

'Thank you,' said Rachel, moved.

'What Dot did . . .' The old lady blinked behind her bifocals. 'It's marvellous. Not for the dogs, but for folk like me. We were the lucky ones. They got homes and a nice bed, but we got someone to listen and to keep us company. You can't put a price on that. It's like Dot knew just what we were missing.' Then she clicked her tongue at the dog and moved off.

'Lovely,' said Oliver, in a deep, sincere tone straight off a coffee advert. 'It's really very touching the way people feel about their animals. You must let me make a donation.'

Rachel wasn't listening. She was thinking about Dot, and Felix, and the strangers that would have lurked in the shadows of their marriage, just as she'd lurked between Oliver and Kath for so many years. Dot could have had everything she wanted, so long as she didn't ask for all of Felix. Instead she'd gone for a companion she could trust, uncomplicated Gem, and the other cautious, broken animals who'd washed up here, hoping for a second chance to show their capacity for loyalty. And what was Oliver offering her now? All of himself? But for how long? At least Felix had been honest with Dot. She knew Oliver wouldn't be.

And what was *she* offering – all of herself, apart from the secret growing inside her? And the other secret, that part of her that wished it had turned out differently with the big gruff vet.

'No,' said Rachel aloud.

There couldn't be any secrets anymore.

'Oh, you must,' said Oliver, slipping his arm round her with the old, easy confidence. 'I can write it off as a charity donation. I'm all for rescuing waifs and strays.'

She turned to him, shrugging off the arm, and looked him in the eye. In her new boots she was slightly taller than he was, but she felt like a bigger person altogether. Taller, stronger, confident. Finally.

'No,' said Rachel. 'I'm sorry. I wasn't talking about the dogs. I was meaning me. I won't come back. I don't need rescuing by anyone, thanks.'

## 28

It was nearly six before the final visitors left, and nearly eleven at night before Rachel had another moment to herself.

Oliver left almost at once, after sheepishly asking her for the flat keys. Now he was selling the business, he needed them. Rachel could tell when she flung them into his hand that he was relieved. Maybe he'd anticipated some unseemly West London squatting. Maybe Kath had goaded him into action. Maybe he just wanted his horrible jeans back. She didn't want to think how big a part the keys had played in his return, or how she might have played the cards better, to help with the looming tax bill; she just wanted him to leave her new life.

The atmosphere in Four Oaks was like the last stages of a feel-good musical, with much bonhomie and loud music. Megan, Johnny and Natalie had done the evening feed-and-clean routine accompanied by Radio One, instead of the usual soothing tones of Radio Four, and Freda had made everyone sit down while she and Ted cooked them a full English breakfast for tea.

Rachel was so shattered she'd nearly fallen asleep in her fried egg, and Freda had sent her to lie down for a couple of hours. Despite the constant churning going on in her head, she fell sound asleep until eight and when she came downstairs again, they were all still in the kitchen. Johnny had counted up the takings from the various stalls, and Natalie had presented her with a neat pile of sponsorship forms.

'It's all going to work out,' said Natalie. She seemed intoxicated with cheerfulness. 'I've been on the internet, and downloaded all the forms you need to register the rescue as a proper charity, so you can claim tax relief and stuff. We've talked about it,' she glanced around the table, 'and I'm happy to act as a trustee, and so's Johnny.'

'That's a great idea,' said Rachel. 'Um, thanks.'

The scales tipped further in favour of staying. If Natalie was happy to help with the paperwork . . .

'You know we're keeping Bertie?' Natalie went on, nodding towards the dozing Basset curled around Gem in the improbably small basket.

'You are?'

'We are. We had to persuade those nice people who'd come all the way to see him to take one of the Jack Russells instead,' said Johnny. 'I fear for them, I really do, but Megan said it would be OK.'

'But what about your job?'

Natalie grinned, and Rachel realised she and Johnny were holding hands under the table. 'I'm having a life-laundry moment. So you can count on me for extra volunteer work up here.'

'We should make a move,' said Johnny, pushing his chair back. 'Ted, Freda? Can we give you a lift?'

'Much obliged,' said Ted, and Rachel noticed that Natalie and Freda had their heads together as they left the kitchen.

She was too tired even to be curious. I'll find out soon enough, she thought, stacking up the plates to go in the dishwasher.

'Go back to bed,' said Megan. 'I'll finish up here. You looked bushed. No offence.'

'None taken. I know I look like the living dead.' Rachel put her hands on her aching back. It had been a long, long day, and she hadn't done half of what Megan had. 'I haven't said thanks,' she added.

'What for?'

'For all you did today. That little walk past – it made me cry.'

'I think it made everyone cry,' said Megan. 'That was kind of the point. You should have seen the change buckets by the gate.' Her expression changed. 'But seriously, you did the work. If you hadn't decided to kickstart the rehoming and do all this . . .' She smiled, and her whole face lit up with genuine friendship. 'For a non-dog person, you've done all right, eh?'

Rachel blinked, because she suddenly felt quite emotional. 'I'll just go and check on the mutts,' she said. 'Then I'll turn in.'

She let herself into the kennel office, trying not to disturb the snoozing dogs, and sat in Dot's battered leather library chair. It was peaceful, apart from the muffled radio and the occasional doggie grumble, but Rachel sat with her head in her hands, nearly deafened by the voices in her head.

What to do? Stay? Go? Sell?

Today had shown her just how much her world had shifted – she didn't want to go back to London, to Oliver, to her old life. Dot hadn't left her the kennels to bail out on her dream. She'd left it to Rachel so she could feel she was making a real difference, somewhere.

But it was still a commitment, just when she didn't need extra pressure. She hadn't even worked out where to find the money to pay off the rest of the inheritance tax, or the money to pay to fix the various problems with the house itself. The boarding kennels might make a decent turnover, but she still had to get them up and running.

Maybe I should sell up, lock, stock, and barrel to that client who wanted the country retreat, she thought. It'd be cleaner. I could give some money to a different dog charity, help find Megan a new job . . .

There was a knock on the door. George put his head round. 'Sorry it's late. Can I have a word?' He sounded stiff but determined, as if he'd been sent to the headteacher's office to apologise.

''Course.' Rachel sat up and pulled her hair about. She wished she didn't always look so shattered when she saw him. Their relationship was so back to front that he might never get to see her looking fabulous. She caught herself. What relationship was that?

'I came to say sorry about before,' he said, without preamble. 'That was the serious long-term ex, I take it?'

'Yes,' said Rachel. 'Oliver. And I want to say sorry too. It wasn't that I didn't want to call you my boyfriend,' she went on, feeling she had most to apologise about. 'I just didn't know whether . . .' It was so stupid. 'I didn't know whether you'd be happy about being my . . . whether you think of yourself as my boyfriend or not. We're both a bit too old to be at this stage, don't you think?'

George squeezed his chin, though his eyes were still flinty. 'Yeah. When you put it like that, I'd rather be introduced as your vet than your baby daddy, or whatever they call it now.'

'I've heard worse.'

She waited for him to say he was happy to be introduced as her boyfriend, but he didn't. Instead he pulled at the sleeve of his good jumper and blew his cheeks out thoughtfully.

'Do you want to sit down?' suggested Rachel. 'You're making me feel like I'm interviewing you for a job.'

George pulled out the chair where prospective new dog owners sat, but didn't cross one leg over his knee as he usually did. He folded his arms and looked at her, and Rachel couldn't meet his searching gaze.

'I've got something for you,' he said, and pulled a cheque out of his back pocket. He unfolded it, and chucked it into her in-tray.

'Oh, I've had this already,' Rachel began. 'Darren gave it to me – very generous. We'll get a special plaque for the Fenwick kennel . . .'

'It's a different cheque,' said George, without unfolding his arms.

Rachel didn't look up as she reached out and picked it off a stack of sponsorship forms. It was a personal cheque, on the account of George R. W. Fenwick, for one hundred thousand pounds.

'I can't take this!' she said automatically.

'You can.'

'I can't.'

'You can. Stop being so bloody stubborn.'

'I can't . . .' she started, and suddenly remembered something Megan had said – how Dot had 'got into the habit of saying no' to things. She was just the same, guarding her privacy, in case anyone discovered her secret life with Oliver, or intruded on her bachelor life, where she did what she wanted. But really it was because being alone was easier. It was a masochistic form of selfishness, dressed up as independence, and it was fiendishly hard to break.

She looked up from the cheque to George's broad, windswept face, pink where the day's sun had caught him out, and told herself that she was mad to say no. Mad, and selfish.

Her instinct was to turn George's offer down because she didn't want anyone to have control over her life, but it was too late for that now. The tiny dictator inside her was already controlling her moods, her appetite, even her balance. And if anyone was going to be let into her life, then who better than a man like George? Who'd be able to wrangle this baby just like he wrangled calves and dogs – and Rachel herself. She felt hot at the thought of him, the way he knew exactly how she worked.

'I . . .' she began.

He raised his hand before she could go any further.

'I've got something to say and I'd be grateful if you'd hear the whole lot out at once. I'm not very experienced at big emotional discussions. I need a good run-up.'

Rachel inclined her head. 'I'd noticed.'

George flicked a dark look across the table, then pulled his spine straight. 'I want you to take that cheque. Not just for yourself, but because Dot's kennels deserve it. And I want you to take it even if you decide to go back to London with Lover Boy. I'm not stupid. I could see this afternoon that there's still something there between you, and if you want to call it a support payment for the baby, then call it that. I can . . .' He paused. 'I can see why it might be better that way. As you keep reminding me, we don't really know each other that well, and maybe a clean break before it gets messy's the best thing.'

Rachel's heart dropped to the pit of her stomach.

'Is that what you want?' She searched his face neurotically. Was he trying to palm her off on Oliver? Was that it? Didn't he want the complications she'd brought?

Maybe someone had filled him in on her murky cheating past. That would be exactly the sort of behaviour he'd despise. Didn't your sins always find you out? she thought bitterly.

'Is it what *you* want?' he countered.

God, we're crap at this, thought Rachel, gazing at him through swimming vision.

'OK, well, I'll tell you what I want,' he went on when she didn't reply. 'While I'm making a fool of myself. I want you to take that cheque, let me invest in the kennels – as a serious partner – and try to work out a way this sad old bachelor can be part of your life. Properly. Hard as that might be for both of us.'

He raised his eyes to hers, and Rachel saw they were bluer than Gem's, and just as frank. 'You've got to realise that meeting a woman like you was something I'd assumed would never happen to me, not now, not here. Not just because you're beautiful, and smart, and bloody . . . unusual . . . but because my life is just so cramped. It's been full of stress and responsibility, building up that practice, and what time I had at the end of the day – I wanted that space for myself.' He gave a self-deprecating half-laugh. 'I was even too selfish for a dog, for God's sake. Dot used to tell me off for that. But then I met you and I suddenly realised how small it was. How small *I'd* got.'

George's voice dropped and Rachel instinctively reached her hand out across the table. He was taking a real risk, she thought, given that he believed she was about to bail out with Oliver.

'I'm not going to spin you a load of horse shit about Fate and true love and what have you,' he went on. 'We're both a bit long in the tooth to fall for that, and I know that it's going to be a steep learning curve. But I feel as if we've got a connection that I've never felt with anyone else. Ever.' He looked at her, simply. 'When I'm with you, I feel like I'm at home. Even in your home. And I could talk to you for ever, and never get bored.'

'I know,' said Rachel. 'I feel exactly the same. And this isn't even my home.'

'It is. It's always been.'

He tightened his grip on her hand and she slid the other one across the table too so that they were clinging together like a pair of shipwrecks, not close enough to kiss, but close enough to stare into each other's faces with passionate intensity.

Rachel's whole body tingled at the touch of George's capable hands, but she glowed at the same time, as if there was a lightbulb at her core, radiating a Ready Brek warmth. It was a security she'd never felt with Oliver, a security that started in the proud, bewildered expression in his eyes. It was going to be an unimaginable journey, but they were doing it together, because they wanted to.

They sat gazing at each other for whole minutes, neither one wanting to break the moment by saying the wrong thing.

Rachel sensed that George was nudging her to speak. It was her turn, after all.

'I'm not getting back with Oliver,' she said. 'And there's nothing between us. That was a goodbye, nothing more. I couldn't go back to my old life either. It was empty. I was empty.'

These weren't feelings rehearsed in the orchard with Gem; something totally fresh was flowing through Rachel, feelings she'd never found words for before.

'My job that everyone thinks was so glamorous was basically just telling white lies for people. Selling ideas and internet stuff, nothing you could actually touch. Being here, seeing how the dogs put up with so much abuse, and then change with a little bit of love, and some attention – it's changed me too.'

She ran her thumb along the hollow between his thumb and forefinger, feeling the texture of his skin. They still had so much to learn about each other, but he wasn't a stranger. 'Watching you with the dogs, how you care for them without denting their dignity – it's wonderful. I wanted someone to care for me like that.'

George said nothing but he moved his own thumb against hers, in silent agreement.

'You're an amazing man,' she went on, feeling herself getting carried away by the moment and a cocktail of pregnancy hormones. 'If I'm acting defensive, it's because I can't believe I had to wait all these years and come to the middle of nowhere to find someone so handsome and kind and good at cooking and sex and funny conversation – and for him to be available. It's too good to be true. I'm even cool with the grumpiness and the red socks – they just mean you're not a figment of my imagination.'

Rachel paused now, her turn to wonder if she'd said too much. 'So if you can put up with a total novice, I'd love you to invest in the kennels. And if you can put up with someone who's never even shared a bathroom . . .' she hesitated, 'I'd love you to try to be with me. And Gem.'

'So you're staying?' he asked, without looking up.

'Yes. I'm staying.' Her mouth curved into a slow smile and she leaned forward across the desk, tilting her head so she could brush her lips against George's mouth. He didn't move at first, and his shaggy blonde hair tickled against her cheekbone as she lifted herself partly onto the chair, for a better, more forceful angle.

Rachel got a brief flash of how ironic it was that she'd come so far from Chiswick to be snogging over a desk again, when George's lips parted, and he kissed her back with a ferocity that took her by surprise. He slid his hand up into her hair, cupping her jaw and then tracing the line of her throat until her whole body ached to be pressed against him.

This was Dot's real legacy, she thought. Not the kennels or the house, or any money. It was her second chance, and she wasn't going to look back.

# Epilogue

Val waved away Rachel's attempt to pay for the coffees, and for once Rachel decided it was better to let her have her own way.

She had, after all, struggled with nearly all Val's suggestions about prams, maternity clothes, baby extras, hospital bags – her mother had only been in Four Oaks four hours and already Rachel felt as if she'd signed up for a childcare seminar.

But it was worth it, she reminded herself. Building bridges with her mother was top of her list now, along with everything else that was going on at the kennels, starting with the redecoration and working downwards. It saved reading the stacks of baby manuals, for a start. Val was like a sort of talking book version of Zita West, Miriam Stoppard and Mumsnet, in slacks.

'This is nice,' said Val, looking round the pretty blue-and-white interior of the café. It was barely recognisable as Ted and Freda's family greasy spoon, apart from the stained glass deco sign over the door. 'Is it normal to have so many dogs inside, though?'

'It is in this café, Mum,' said Rachel.

'It can't be hygienic. There must be some regulations ...' Val gazed around the airy, freshly repainted room. A row of mini kennels by the door housed a selection of terriers and a Labrador, while two spaniels sat patiently beneath the table next to them, attached to handbag hooks.

'If there were, then Natalie would know all about them.' Rachel sipped her decaff latte and smiled over at the counter, where Natalie stood in her crisp white apron, making the most perfect cappuccinos in Longhampton. Pride of place in the café went to Bertie, whose basket in the window attracted toddlers from all over the town.

Children weren't really encouraged in Natalie's café. She pretended it was for their own safety, because of all the dogs, but Rachel knew, as a regular, that the doggie customers secretly preferred it that way. If – *when* – Natalie and Johnny had their own baby, Rachel was pretty sure Nat would just open a second branch, for yummy mummies.

'Well, it's doing good business, I must say,' said Val. 'Not everyone must care about hairs.'

'Plenty don't, Mum. She's a smart cookie, Natalie. Would you believe this was a greasy spoon two months ago? When Nat puts her mind to it, she certainly doesn't waste any time.'

'She owns it?' Val looked impressed and swivelled in her chair to look more closely. 'Natalie from the kennel? Oh yes!' She waved.

'Our charity manager, if you don't mind, Mum. Bought it with her redundancy money. Painted it with our volunteers. You should see the money she's taking on the mobile coffee machine in the park.' Rachel shifted in her chair to allow her neat bump more room. 'She does a special cap-pooch-ino with ten per cent to Four Oaks Rescue Kennels.'

'Very enterprising.' Val smiled, and Rachel felt a genuine, womanly companionship that had never troubled her relationship with her mother before. Pregnancy was doing odd things to her. She'd even written Amelia a thank-you note for the mountains of baby clothes she'd turfed out of her loft, with a photo of the dog she was now sponsoring for Grace and Jack. It was a collie, called Dot.

While the mood between them was warm, Rachel made herself broach the last remaining thing on her emotional to-do list.

'Mum, there's something I've been meaning to tell you.' Rachel hesitated, before framing the white lie as best she could. She didn't want to wrap one secret in another, but she could see her dad's problem. He didn't deserve the backlash, just for protecting Dot's pride. 'I found something while I was clearing out the cupboards . . .'

As she told her mother about Dot's one big love, and Felix's confession and proposal, Val's eyes filled with tears. Rachel left out the unfortunate encounter between Felix and her dad, and tried to make the rest sound positive – her years of unconditional love from the dogs, and the respect she'd been held in locally – but she knew her mother was crying for something else: the children Dot might have once dreamed of having, her nieces and nephews to shower love on. That, for Val, was Dot's sacrifice, not so much Felix, or the life she could have lived.

'I'm sorry.' Val dabbed her eyes as Rachel finished. 'Oh, poor Dot. What a thing to live with all those years. I had no idea. Oh, I'm glad you told me. I always blamed myself.'

'Why?' Rachel held her breath. Was this the terrible thing she wouldn't tell Dad? She wondered whether she should declare a parental secret amnesty and see what else came out.

Or maybe not.

'I thought I'd cursed Dot. At Amelia's christening.' Val stirred her cappuccino until the froth began to vanish.

That was pretty good, thought Rachel. Even for Mum's masochistic passive aggression. A whole curse. 'Do you want to tell me?'

Val looked up. 'I suppose I can now, now you're having a baby.' She sounded pleased, as if it had just occurred to her, then her expression turned guilty again. 'You won't remember, because you were just little, but it was very hot that day. I'd bought myself a new outfit, because Dorothy was gracing us with her presence, with this new man we'd heard so much about . . .'

'The dress with the big flowers, like Gran's bathroom wallpaper?' Rachel pointed at her. 'And the hat like a UFO?'

'It was very expensive, that outfit,' said Val, hurt. 'And very fashionable. But obviously next to *Dot* I looked like some fat old housewife.' She sighed. 'And I *was* a fat old housewife, and she looked ten years younger, and everyone fawned over her, all, "Oooh, Dorothy, tell us about London", even though it was my day. I mean, Amelia's day. Our family day! And then you were sick because of the sweets she'd brought for you, and you wiped your hands on my dress, and I had to take you home early.'

'I don't remember that,' said Rachel, thinking, 'Dad obviously doesn't either' at the same time.

Val pursed her lips and sighed. 'I went into the bar of the hotel, where everyone was listening to Dot and Felix holding forth about the Rolling Stones and some nightclub they'd been at, and I tried to say goodbye to everyone. No one paid me a blind bit of notice, and then Dorothy pipes up, "Off to the nursery then, Mummy?" like it was some sort of punishment.'

Val's face darkened, and Rachel could see the clouds of contradiction battling in her face. She'd never seen her mother so conflicted before. She'd never seen her so emotional, full stop. She wanted to tell her that Dot's flippant comment was the sort of painful joke she'd often made herself, to hide her awkwardness around happy mums, but Val was lost in her memory.

'And the thing was . . .' Val twisted her mouth, 'right at that moment, it *did* feel like a punishment. I loved you two, more than anything in the world, but it was hard work, two of you under three. I never had more than two hours' sleep. I smelled of vomit for years. *I* wanted to be in that bar, in that skinny trouser suit, with my own money! I'd have *loved* it. And so I said something I shouldn't have.' She bit her lip as if she was trying, too late, to stop it coming out.

'What did you say?' Rachel breathed.

'I looked right at her and said, "You'll never know what love really is, Dorothy, until you have children. And you'll never have children, because you're just too selfish."' She gazed contritely at Rachel. 'My own sister. I said that, and I meant it, but only for that one second. I could have bitten my tongue out the next.'

'I'm sure she didn't . . .'

'And then Felix broke it off with her, and she never married, and she spent the rest of her life taking in strays, and cutting herself off from us.'

Rachel pushed a paper hanky towards her mother. 'Mum, do you have any idea how many Yummy Mummies have told me that I'd never understand real love 'til I had kids? And do you know what I said to them?'

'Don't tell me, Rachel. You know I don't like salty language.'

'I just said *nothing*, and told myself they'd had a bad day with their whiny, screamy brats and were jealous of my nice life. I only hated them temporarily.' She hesitated for a moment, then added, since it was the time for getting things into the open, 'It didn't help that you more or less said the same thing to me for years.'

'I didn't!'

'You did, Mum.' Rachel widened her eyes. 'Every time you called me and told me how blissfully happy Amelia was with her two, and then immediately asked if I'd met anyone. If I was thinking of settling down. If I'd thought about getting my eggs frozen.'

'I didn't mean to.' Val dabbed at her runny mascara. 'And if I did, I was so scared that you'd end up like Dot. On your own and lonely. I couldn't bear to see my beautiful little girl on her own surrounded by mangy dogs instead of a family that loved her. Though now I know *why* poor Dot broke it off with Felix, I suppose it's understandable . . .'

'Mum, I don't think Dot was lonely really. I'm not just saying that to make you feel better.' Rachel finished off the last few muffin crumbs with her finger. 'And I haven't been your little girl for *years*.'

Val slapped her hand away from the plate. 'You're always my little girl. And you didn't make it easy for me, Rachel,' she went on. 'I never knew whether to talk to you, or not talk to you, or what. And that reminded me of Dot, as well.'

'I'm sorry.' Rachel knew in her heart what Val meant. But that had been a different life. That was in the past. She slipped her hand into her mother's and squeezed. Val squeezed back, her thick gold wedding ring pressing into Rachel's finger.

There was a knock on the window. George was standing outside, his Land Rover parked on a double yellow, and his sleeves rolled up. He still wore a padded gilet and checked shirt, despite the August heat.

'He's come to pick us up,' explained Rachel. 'I said three o'clock – there's no more shopping to be had here, I'm afraid.' She waved back at him and made a 'C' for coffee shape with her hand. He shook his head and tapped his watch, a pretend stern look on his face.

Val nodded at Rachel's hand, where a pretty old sapphire ring glinted in the light. 'Is there an announcement in the offing?'

'That's Dot's,' said Rachel. 'Before you get any ideas. George and I like to do things backwards. If we get married, it'll be after this one does.' She patted her stomach happily. 'There's no rush.'

'Well, I'm glad he's making time for you.'

'Mum,' said Rachel seriously. 'He's doing a lot more than that.'

'All your father and I want is to know that you're happy.' Val lifted an eyebrow as she began gathering her bags together. 'And that's something you're going to understand soon enough.'

Their eyes met, and Rachel felt the years of mutual suspicion begin to crumble away. For the first time, she saw something of herself in Val – she wasn't just her father's daughter, or Dot's strong-featured niece, she was stubborn like Val too.

Maybe she'd be the same mother hen type, thought Rachel. Maybe motherhood would bring out the cleaning gene. She'd found herself echoing Val's caustic thoughts on expensive travel systems for babies. It could be all downhill from there.

God help us, she thought, as the waitress cleared away their plates. If someone had told her last year that she'd be bonding with her mother over the most economical pram, prior to being swept off home by a country vet, she'd have had their blood tested for narcotics.

'Thank you,' Val was mouthing through the glass at George. 'Come on, Rachel. There's a parking warden on the other side of the street and you know they've got cameras these days. Do you need a hand?'

'No. I don't. I'm still trying to pretend this is a big lunch, not a baby, Mum.'

Rachel's bump was definitely hiding a whopping country-side baby. With another four months to go, she still wondered if it might be twins. Amelia had sent her two whole suitcases of maternity outfits, but so far Rachel was clinging to her one good pair of jeans and George's t-shirts. It was her high-heeled boots that she really missed but George had given her a pair of Hunter wellies ('like Kate Moss has, I understand from the man in Countrywide') as a present, and she rarely took them off.

Gem sprang up from under the table where he'd been waiting patiently, and wagged his tail, ready for the off, wherever that was going to be.

'Aren't you coming with us?' Val's face adopted a familiar concerned expression. 'Oh, you're *not* going to walk back up that hill, are you?'

Rachel glanced down at Gem, and felt a tug of wordless communication, the same tug she felt every morning when she woke to see him lying by her bed, and each night, when he lay down with a contented sigh.

'He needs to stretch his legs,' she said. 'And so do I. I'll see you up there.'

'I'll tell George to put the kettle on.' Val gave her a quick kiss on the cheek, and Rachel didn't brush her away. Instead she kissed her back, then clipped the lead onto Gem's collar.

'Come on, you,' she said, waving at Natalie and Bertie as she left the café.

With the café bell jangling behind her, Rachel and Gem strolled slowly down the high street towards the park, where the path curved around the lawns and then led up the path towards the hill. Rachel nodded at the other dog walkers as they passed, and Gem sniffed them politely in greeting. Familiar faces, familiar dogs. The routine of it made her feel as rooted and as joyful as the late summer roses still blooming in the ornamental beds.

Then, once they were safely onto the quiet footpath, Rachel unclipped Gem's lead, and let him herd her gently and silently home.

# An Interview with Lucy Dillon

## What inspired you to write LOST DOGS AND LONELY HEARTS?

Getting a dog of my own! I never realised, until I started walking Violet, our Basset hound, that there's a Secret World of Dog Walkers: you meet so many different kinds of people on the same paths, at the same times, day in, day out. It's like being in a club. I don't know anyone's names, but the dogs usually introduce themselves. Violet's very fond of spaniels, but sometimes the bigger dogs look at her, as if to say, where have your legs gone?

As a writer, always looking for new ideas and characters, I found it fascinating to watch how owners interact with their dogs. My imagination rambles all over the place – why Scottish terriers? Why 'his and hers' dogs? Why so many? When I finished *The Ballroom Class*, Longhampton's municipal parks and canal paths were still very vivid in my mind, so it was very easy to create another community of different people who are brought together by a shared interest, and have their ideas of love and loyalty challenged by family members who can't actually talk back. Just as people can express emotions they can't articulate through dancing, sometimes we use our pets as a way of communicating our real feelings. You only have to see British stiff upper lips wobbling at Battersea Dogs' Home appeals to know we're a nation of softies.

## Tell us about Violet! How did you come to adopt her?

Violet adopted us, more like! My husband and I wanted to get a dog, and went to meet some Basset hound puppies as part of our endless research mission. We were cooing over the pups when Violet strolled in, took one look at me, and arranged herself on my lap, all five stones of her. That was it – I was utterly smitten by her huge brown eyes and lovely ginger eyebrows. Violet's story melted my heart too: her breeders wanted to find a new home for her, because her first owner had became ill and had to give her up. She and I were a similar age in dog years, and I was, apparently, the first person she'd snuggled up to since she came back – we had an immediate bond, and from then on, I knew we had to be together!

## Is she the inspiration for Bertie? And is she as naughty as him?

Violet isn't naughty, but her amazing nose does get her into trouble – she once sniffed out a bag of sausages I'd left in my handbag, removed it very delicately, and was in the process of carrying the bag back to her basket to enjoy the contents in comfort when I caught her, red-pawed. Every shopping bag is a tempting carnival of smells to her. She also loves rolling in anything disgusting – not very ladylike – and reverts to her ancient tracking instincts if she smells a hare. That's when I learned how fast Bassets can move when they want to!

**There's been a lot of bad press about pedigree dogs. Why did you decide to get a pedigree rather than a crossbreed?**

My husband grew up with a Basset hound, and for him, no other breed was ever going to do. I'd never had a dog before, so I leaned more towards giving any rescue dog a second chance, and Violet was a perfect compromise. I certainly don't think a dog needs a pedigree to be a fantastic, loving companion, but if you're looking for specific characteristics (poodles don't shed, so are good for allergy sufferers, for example), then a pedigree with known family history will give you a good idea of what to expect. Recent press coverage of pedigree breeding has highlighted some dubious practices in some quarters, but the breeders I've met are passionate about their dogs, health check them regularly, breed very carefully and are horrified by anyone who doesn't put health and fitness first. All dogs have potential problems – pedigrees can have hereditary issues, whereas you don't always know what genetic problems a crossbreed has until they pop up. But chances are the dog will pick you anyway, and take the matter out of your hands!

**If one of your readers was thinking of getting a dog, how would you suggest they went about looking for one, and preparing for its arrival?**

Think very hard about how much space you have at home, how much time you have for walks, and how much mess you're happy to put up with – those are all far more important considerations than how cute the dog is. Visit some rescue shelters or local breeders for guidance. If you've fallen for a particular breed, contact the breed rescue who can put you in touch with adult dogs looking for new homes; never buy a puppy from a pet shop, or from a small ad, unless you can visit the house to check it out. Then buy a vacuum cleaner with a dog hair attachment and prepare to use it.

**You must have come across some sad stories when researching this novel . . .**

Too many – I can't urge people enough to support their local rescue, who have to deal with some terrible cases of animal neglect. I won't go into the stomach-turning conditions that puppy-farm bitches live in, but put it like this: centres that rescue them advise that they're rehomed with a 'normal' dog, just to teach them how to live inside, and not be terrified of a human voice. More generally depressing is the casual way in which owners discard healthy, loving animals, just because they can't be bothered any more, or neglect them by over-feeding and not walking them enough – that's animal cruelty too.

**Some people don't have the time and/or space for a dog. But several characters in LOST DOGS AND LONELY HEARTS, like Freda and Ted, enjoy volunteer walking. Is this possible in real life?**

Absolutely – rescues always need volunteers to get their dogs out in the fresh air. It's good for the dogs' mental *and* physical well-being, and with most local rescues run on a tight budget, time is as valuable a donation as money. It's a great solution for full-time workers who'd love a dog but can't fit it into their lives, and what better way to get some exercise at the weekend?

**How did having Violet change your life?**

We had to trade our Golf GTi for an estate car, so her crate would fit in the back. That was the only painful part! She's fitted into our lives more easily than I'd expected, and she actually organises me: she gets me up on time instead of letting me hit the snooze button, she makes sure I exercise in all weathers, and she saves me putting on the heating in autumn. One Basset on the lap is all the warmth anyone needs. We also now have a live-in excuse for odd smells, and my mother-in-law's collie, Morris, has a bossy new friend.

**What lessons have you learnt, as a dog owner?**

I've become much more patient – rather like Natalie in the book, I've realised that there are some dogs who don't want to learn new tricks, and you just have to live with it! I've also stopped being so flaky because Violet has a routine that I need to stick to, since she can't help herself to supper or pop out for a walk. I think it's great preparation for parenthood too – stinky nappies, early mornings and the "naughty step" hold no fear for me now.

**And finally, do you think of plots for your novels when you are out walking Violet?**

Whenever I get writer's block, I take Violet out for a walk and I nearly always come back with at least one new idea. I don't know whether it's the fresh air, or the blood pumping to my brain, or just seeing things more slowly when you're pottering along with a dog, but walking is great for untangling problems. I'm always trying to devise fresh routes for Violet's nose, and that turns up some surprising old houses or ancient footpaths, which are great for the imagination. I must confess to Rachel's habit of rehearsing important conversations too – but only when we're up on the Malvern Ridge and no one can hear me! (I hope.)

# QUIZ: Who would Dot match you up with?

1. Your ideal exercise routine is . . .
   a. A hot and sweaty workout, followed by a nap
   b. A game of football with your mates
   c. A long hike through the countryside
   d. A yoga session

2. Housework is . . .
   a. Something you only do when your mum's coming round
   b. A weekly tidy-up everyone has to join in with
   c. A long-running battle – but a messy house is a happy house!
   d. Something you secretly enjoy, even if everyone thinks your colour-coded dusters are weird

3. Your dog-training ambitions stretch to . . .
   a. Getting the dog off the sofa on command
   b. Good basic manners: come, stay, fetch, down, paw, etc.
   c. Full outdoor skills: retrieving, agility, sniffing out socks
   d. Impressive indoor party tricks like playing dead and looking sarcastic on command

4. The car parked outside your house is . . .
   a. A sporty hatchback
   b. A people carrier
   c. A 4x4
   d. A convertible

5. Out on the dog walking circuit, you can be spotted by your . . .
   a. Classic mackintosh
   b. Bright red jacket
   c. Green wellies
   d. Statement hat

## Mostly As
### A greyhound
Most people don't think of greyhounds as pets but retired racers make sensitive homebodies. They're gentle, biddable and not too hairy. Because they get rid of their energy in bursts, greyhounds are happy with two half-hour trots, followed by some mellow sofa time – so they're ideal for older owners, or those who can't spend hours on the other end of a lead. They're extraordinarily elegant, yet functional – the Porsches of the dog world.

## Mostly Bs
### A Staffordshire Bull Terrier
If any breed deserves the 'no bad dogs, just bad owners' defence, it's the much-maligned Staffie. Staffies are loyal and loving, but they make up a sizeable proportion of the rescue population, often because of backyard breeders and careless owners who under-estimate their exercise needs. But harness their natural exuberance with calm, firm leadership and lots of walks, and you'll find Staffies make wonderful family companions.

## Mostly Cs
### A springer spaniel
If your car's always muddy from outdoor activities and you don't mind pawprints everywhere, then let a springer spaniel bounce into your life and lick you into submission. You can't beat a springer for friendly charm or boundless enthusiasm – he'll run all day, follow every command, yet still have energy for mischief. The long spaniel coat needs combing to prevent knots but those gorgeous feathery ears and paws are worth the effort.

## Mostly Ds
### A poodle
Their coats might be fluffy, but their brains certainly aren't; independent-spirited poodles are quick learners with a secret tough streak – they were originally bred to be water-retrieving gundogs. Even maintenance grooming is a labour of love, but poodles don't shed, making them great for allergy sufferers, and they come in three different sizes, from the perky little toy to the magnificent standard. If you're a stylish dog owner looking for a real meeting of minds, a poodle is perfect.

# Five good reasons to get a rescue dog

*The bond that grows between a rescued animal and the people who give it a second chance for love is really special. Don't overlook the oldies, either!*

**They're house-trained:** Puppies are adorable but housebreaking them is torture for you and your carpets. Older dogs, on the other hand, are usually clean in the house, and barring a few accidents while they settle in, should take little or no reminding of where the facilities are.

**What you see is what you get:** Cute puppies turn into unexpectedly huge and demanding dogs within a matter of months – which often leads to them being dumped at a rescue centre. Adopting a fully-grown adult means you can plan for exercise needs, feeding needs, and how he'll fit into your family life.

**Not all rescue dogs are 'rejects':** Marriages break down, owners die, circumstances change, and model pets can find themselves looking for new people through no fault of their own. Dogs that are turned in for being 'too boisterous' or 'rough' are often just in the wrong home; with the right amount of exercise and mental stimulation, they can be transformed into happy companions.

**You're getting a support network:** Rescue shelters don't want to rehome a dog twice! Not only will they guide you through choosing the right dog for you, they'll be on hand to offer advice and support afterwards – and with the experience of dealing with so many dogs, there won't be many questions they can't answer.

**Not all rescue dogs are Heinz 57:** If you've got your heart set on a particular kind of dog, it's simple to track one down, either by searching internet rescue sites, or by contacting the national breed rescue. Responsible breeders will always take back puppies if the owners can no longer look after them, and will make sure they're going to a good new home, second time round!

# If you're buying a puppy

*Puppies don't make good presents, as Zoe found out. But finding your canine companion the responsible way is just a matter of a few simple rules . . .*

**Don't support puppy farming:** Never buy a puppy from a pet shop, from someone who wants to meet you in a car park, from anyone who has more than two or (max) three breeds, or from a small ad that has appeared many times in the same paper. Most likely they're puppy-farmed, from exploited, exhausted mothers, bred in appalling conditions. It's heartbreaking to see a sick, scared puppy, but by buying it, you're giving the puppy farmer money to carry on a disgusting trade. Report it to the council, the RSPCA and the police, and find a puppy from a reliable source.

**Contact the breed club:** Doing some research into your chosen breed is essential, and most clubs will point out the pitfalls as well as the joys of owning their particular dog. They'll often know when litters are planned – don't expect any around Christmas, as most breeders avoid it, to protect against gift-wrapped pups – and can put you in touch with local owners.

**Always ask to see the mother:** Good breeders will be proud to show you their dogs, especially the mum. She should be friendly, healthy, and not aggressive. Ask for the sire's details but don't be surprised if he isn't there on site as well – rather than mate their pets over and over to produce puppies, responsible breeders will often travel miles to find the best sire. The owners should have thoroughly health-tested both parents beforehand, hip-scoring if appropriate, and won't want the puppies to leave before they're 8 weeks old.

**Watch the litter together:** Don't go for the bossiest pup or feel sorry for the weakling – watch them and see which one responds best to you. The pup's eyes and nose should be clear and clean; check the ears are clean too; they should move around well, and be free from diarrhoea. Check that they've been wormed, and had their first vaccinations.

## Some useful websites

RSPCA: www.rspca.org.uk
Dogs Trust: www.dogstrust.org.uk
The Blue Cross: www.bluecross.org.uk
Dogpages Rescue Sites: www.dogpages.org.uk
Retired Greyhound Trust: www.retiredgreyhounds.co.uk
Battersea Dogs and Cats home: www.battersea.org.uk
Many Tears Animal Rescue: www.freewebs.com/manytearsrescue
The Kennel Club: www.thekennelclub.org.uk

*The new book from Lucy Dillon*

Gina Bellamy is starting again,
after a few years she'd rather forget.
But the belongings she's treasured for so
long don't seem to fit who she is now.

So Gina makes a resolution. She'll keep just
a hundred special items — the rest can go.

But that means coming to terms with
her past and learning to embrace the future,
whatever it might bring . . .

As heart wrenching and inspirational
as *One Day* or *Me Before You*,

# *a* hundred pieces of *me*

is a story about what it means to finally
live life to the full.

In paperback and eBook February 2014
Available for pre-order now

HODDER